LOVERS &
COHORTS

also by Herbert Gold

novels
Birth of a Hero
The Prospect Before Us
The Man Who Was Not With It
The Optimist
Therefore Be Bold
Salt
Fathers
The Great American Jackpot
Swiftie the Magician
Waiting for Cordelia
Slave Trade
He/She
Family
True Love
Mister White Eyes
A Girl of Forty

short stories and essays
Love and Like
The Age of Happy Problems
The Magic Will
A Walk on the West Side—California on the Brink

memoir
My Last Two Thousand Years

reportage
Biafra, Goodbye

HERBERT GOLD

Twenty-Seven Stories

LOVERS & COHORTS

DONALD I. FINE, INC.
New York

Library of Congress Catalogue Card Number: 85-82496

ISBN: 0-917657-75-6

Manufactured in the United States of America
10 9 8 7 6 5 4 3 2 1

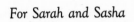

For Sarah and Sasha

Contents

Introduction

What gathering these forty years of stories teaches me is that time is shaped like an accordion. The stories might teach someone else that I'll never learn. Another way of saying it is that my passions as a teller of tales have remained: love, family, Jews, Bohemia, wanderlust, and the meaning of life. What I think about these complications is not yet complete, but especially when I find the meaning of life, I'll be sure to let you know. I've asked my children to listen very closely to my last words in case they are something more significant than "Turn off the light when you leave." I'm hoping they will be "Now let me tell you the story about . . ."

The other discovery I've made is that, indeed, I've been writing stories since I was a child and publishing them for forty years. Recently, I recall, a letter of acceptance (bluish typewriter ribbon, pale blue stationery) came from an editor of *Harper's Bazaar* (bluish fountain pen ink, the signature skyblue with insight) in response to a story I had mailed her from my college dorm. I noticed that I had grown so tall I could peer over New York skyscrapers as I obeyed her summons and marched down Madison Avenue to meet her. The foamy soles favored by college boys of that period did not account for my sudden altitude. That was yesterday, and the editor was kind. Now I am Collecting My Stories, though not the one she was so kind about.

This process of collection is deeply astonishing, since I am still a Young Writer and will probably remain so when my great-grandchildren are gathered dutifully about my running shoes to ask what it's like to be the oldest young writer in the retirement home. It is a vocation to be a Young Writer, perhaps a metabolic flaw, a genetic fault. My father, who died in his nineties, had a similar problem about age until near the end. My mother, still vigorous in her late eighties, wonders why her friends are getting old.

The stories reflect several generations of asking related questions. They are not autobiographical (well, some of them are), but they are journeys into the worlds of If and wanderings through the midnight maze: Why am I here? How can I go on? Who are those others? Who are those *attractive* others? Why can't the blessed moments be made permanent except by recollection, by re-creation? How can the painful times be redeemed?

And then, when the pen appears in the hand:

Can I take this awful or marvelous thought or occasion and make it bearable, funny, *interesting*? Can I find the words and rhythms to perform the act of communication? Will some sturdy soul out there be willing to listen?

I learned early in adolescence the important truth that no one commits suicide in the middle of writing the suicide letter. A story saves my life.

The story is also, unlike a dream, which is a private gratification, supposed to save another person's—the reader's—life. I'd be disappointed if anyone took time out to kill himself in the middle of reading one of my stories. I would feel I had done something wrong or, the same thing, not done something right.

Of personal satisfaction in digging these stories out of boxes and corners is reenacting their archeology and biology. I began with some idea, some itch and impulse, some image or phrase or conversation or person, some memory, a fanatic metabolic concentration, and thought to satisfy the impulse by a clean act of soiling paper. This was like play, and it made me happy. When I finished, there was a definite internal easing until the next story began.

It didn't always continue to work that way. Some stories refuse to end; they don't go to bed, neat and secure after hard play, like good little children or even like happy honeymooners, sure that tonight is all there needs to be. Most of my novels have begun with a story that refused to quit. "The Smallest Part," included here, caused my novel *He/She.* "Cohorts" incited *Family.* Often the novels turn out to be stories that go on going on even after they have been published, when I find myself asking: What happened before? What happened afterward? What caused this? Where are these people now?

I awake scribbling, I sleep dreaming, and the story continues, sometimes when I'd rather be doing something other than taking orders from a fiction.

As Nabokov said about Gogol: He builds the firm foundations for his novels after he finishes them. I have told myself a work is completed, and then it turns out to have another shape entirely, like a perfectly satisfactory child who insists on becoming an adult. The story, which I labored to see well made and shapely, turns out to be one clear moment during a mysterious clamoring history.

Some of these stories have appeared in previous collections, *Love & Like, The Magic Will,* and *A Walk on the West Side,* and in these magazines: *Harper's,* the *Atlantic, Playboy, Penthouse, Hudson Review, Midstream, Esquire, Ms., Playgirl, Tri-Quarterly,* and the *New Yorker,* to which I express my gratitude. Some of them have appeared in no magazine at all, for which I also express feeling.

TI-MOUNE

Monique first came to me one morning when I lay upstairs, sweating with blackwater fever, in our house on a road just outside Port-au-Prince. She already knew my wife. I heard her downstairs asking, in French, "And Monsieur, how is he today?" She spoke with the somberness and concern of a little girl grown used to illness, trouble, and sorrow. Because I was not really very sick, it seemed to me another of the incongruities of life in Haiti that Monique should have enough sympathy to be able to squander some on the visiting Americans in their splendid house, with its refrigerator and running water, next door to her family's clay-and-straw *caille*. "May I go upstairs, madame?"

A moment later, she was at my open door, curtsying, smiling with many teeth but shyly all the same, and asking, "Comment va Monsieur?"

"Better, Monique. Tell me, how old are you?"

"Eleven. You will certainly be well soon, monsieur. This is the fifth day already."

"Thank you, Monique."

I sat up, and she walked over and took my hand, then curtsied again and went out. That afternoon, I felt a click in my head, as if I had suddenly switched off the disease, and half an hour later I was strong enough to sit on the gallery. I felt grateful to Monique.

Skinny from rapid growth, although not tall for her age, knob-kneed, barefooted, and venturesome, with enormous, watchful black eyes and with her kinky hair tied up in little ribbons, Monique was the leader of the neighborhood children, who included her brother and two sisters and my two daughters—Ann, six, and Judy, four. She led them all by her imagination, which was both gay and grave, by her weight of years, and by the authority of gentleness and self-respect, which the children all sensed in her. Her dresses, faded to pastels by sun and soap, were always neat. Every button and every thread-made loop were in place. Once, I saw her with her mother in the ravine below our house, where the Rivière Froide sang past. She was standing knee-deep in the stream, soaping clothes, rinsing them, spreading them on rocks to dry, and then splashing them with water again and again to keep them from stiffening. Her mother, shaded by a tattered parasol, sat on a rock and directed her.

Monique's perfect skin was of a deep chocolate, but mixed blood declared itself in her straight nose and narrow lips. Sometimes a shiny black Oldsmobile would park briefly in front of her family's hut, and a lighter-skinned man with bags of English mints would go inside. Monique was apparently the poor cousin of some family of money and station. She would share her bag of candy with the neighborhood children.

After I recovered, Monique, sometimes accompanied by her brother and sisters, came often to greet my wife and me and to ask permission to take our daughters out into the yard to play. She would teach them French and Creole songs, patiently making them repeat the words after her, and then she would grasp their hands and whirl them in a dance, as they all sang:

> Rond, rond, les écolières
> Sans rire et sans parler

Celle qui rit la première
Sortira du rang
Un! deux! trois!

I remember particularly one dance she did with Ann. I was watching from the gallery, and I tried not to let them see me, as I was afraid
I might disturb Monique's gravity, which was deepest when she led
a younger child in a dance. This dance, like the others, was a modifica-
tion of a French children's dance, one of many introduced by the
colonists and passed down by their former slaves, who in freedom had
made the dances and the songs their own. Monique bowed; our
daughter bowed. Monique curtsied; our daughter curtsied. Then they
joined hands, singing and dancing in a circle:

Ba-teau, ba-teau-teau
Mon bateau s'est défoncé
À la rue Saint-Honoré

Monique would also ask our children riddles and tell them some
of the Ti-Malice stories, which are folk stories, something like Br'er
Rabbit stories or fairy tales, and known to all Haitian children.

When there was special cooking or baking being done at our house,
Monique would help peel the vegetables or beat the cake batter.
When she licked the spoon the first time, it was for a taste she had
never known before. And when she bestowed her sedate approval on
a cake, it seemed almost an act of piety. "*Merci, madame. Il est très bon,
ce gâteau.*"

Frequently, she took lunch with us. Meals were so irregular at her
home that it was never necessary to ask her mother's permission. (Her
father, if there was one around, never appeared.) After lunch, she
would insist on wiping the table and sweeping the floor. In a land
where domestics receive as little as eight dollars a month, we had
servants underfoot, but Monique *wanted* to do some of the
housework. Once, while wielding a broom taller than she was, she
sang in Creole probably the saddest child's song there is, the only one
I know that tells of a boy about to commit suicide:

I need corossol tea with sugar,
Biscuits and some fruit.
My stomach hurts me.
I am not a glutton, Maman,
I am only hungry.

She never sang this song with our daughters.

Often she would stay all day, and in the evening, when she said good night to my wife and me, she at first shook our hands. Before long, however, she was reaching up and leaning forward to kiss our cheeks. She did this with such smiling grace that our embarrassment was only momentary. One evening as she left us, my wife called after her, "Bonsoir, ti-moune." Monique smiled and ran across the way to her hut, where the oil wicks were already lit, and the charcoal smoke of her mother's stove sent up a screen between our evening and theirs.

Ti-moune, derived from the French *petit monde,* is a Creole word that means "little one." It is also a word that has to do with a custom, now gradually passing in Haiti, under which a peasant family sells or gives its unwanted children—the children it cannot feed—to a more prosperous landed or town-dwelling family. The *ti-moune* works as a servant without wages, beginning at the age of five or sometimes even earlier. The word, partly because it is ambiguous, is not thought of as being uncomplimentary, and anyway, there was no doubt that my wife was using it affectionately. Monique understood.

Sometimes when Monique came to visit us, she would take our children into a nearby woods and teach them the Creole names of plants and trees. One afternoon, Judy received some painful ant bites while digging in a banana grove outside our house, and Monique ran into the woods and returned with an armful of leaves. She insisted on putting these into our bathtub and then putting Judy in with them. Trained to use drugs out of tubes and bottles, my wife and I felt foolish swishing a mess of oozing leaves about a bathtub, but when Judy emerged, the irritation had disappeared.

Monique, usually the most modest of children, said, "I know the leaves, myself," and wriggled with pride.

During the mango season, when the trees are so rich and heavy that even the poorest Haitian can fill his stomach, Monique showed Ann how to knock the mangoes down with rocks and then how to peel the luscious fruit neatly. One day about noon, having eaten a giant Madame Francis mango and a sweetsop, Ann came home to say to my wife and me, "I already had my lunch. I had lunch with Monique."

We later thanked Monique for her hospitality. Her pleasure betrayed itself in her shy smile and in the twisting of her handkerchief.

One afternoon, Monique made a rag doll from an old dress while Ann watched. When it was finished, she offered it to our daughter. Caught by surprise and delight, Ann took it and in return gave her a magnificent plastic doll with swiveling eyes of china blue—the gift of an aunt when we left the States. Monique brought this doll to my wife and asked if Ann would miss it. "Sometimes a child wants her own doll back," she commented solemnly. My wife assured her that Ann had made an excellent trade.

I had come to Haiti on a State Department fellowship for a year's study of Haitian culture, and now the time was almost up. We began getting ready to leave. Ann told the news to Monique, but without emotion, for she did not believe we could really leave this fine place. Monique came to my wife and me for confirmation. We said yes, but we hoped to be back someday. "Ça me fait de la peine," she said in her sedate, grown-up way. "It grieves me, monsieur and madame."

The next evening, as my wife and I were having our after-supper coffee on the gallery, Monique's mother walked over to the foot of the stairway. Strangely, it was the first time that we had seen her at close range. Her skin was quite light, and she had what Haitians call bons cheveux—straight hair. It was a reddish color. Her appearance surprised us. She could almost have passed for white. I had somehow never doubted that she would have Monique's chocolate color, and glimpsing her from a distance through a banana grove or down in the ravine, I had even seen her as dark. She had a thin face, tensed by poverty and anger against poverty, with none of the patient resignation of the peasants.

My wife asked her to have coffee with us, saying that we were pleased to meet her at last. She thanked us and said that she would come up to speak with us but that she wouldn't take coffee.

When she joined us on the gallery, we insisted that she sit down, and she reluctantly did, perching on the edge of her chair. We insisted also that she have some coffee, and at last she consented. She was an extraordinary Haitian, having to be urged to accept a cup of coffee.

We made talk with her. It was odd, of course, that Monique should have spent so much time in our house without our meeting her mother, but we had long ago accepted this aloofness. Perhaps the formal Haitian rules of politesse, under which she would have called on us long before, had been thrown awry by the presence of a grand house, full of foreigners, in a settlement where a roof of tin instead of straw is the great sign of coming up in the world.

Neighborly gossip came hard to her. Her stiff perch on the edge of the chair seemed to say that only important business could have brought her to us. She smiled the fixed smile of convention; she obviously was uneasy among us—"Americans! *Blancs!*"—although, tanned as we were then, we were hardly more *blanc* than she. When she had finished her coffee, she put down the cup and then sat up very stiffly again. By this time, we were as uncomfortable as she was.

"I see that you like my Monique," she said. "Thank you very much." The tone was chilling—a mixture of fierceness and unction.

"She is a fine child," my wife said. "You must be proud of her."

"Her French is excellent, is it not? I forbid Creole in the house."

"Yes. She's very sweet, madame," my wife said.

"She is in perfect health. Strong. A willing worker." Monique's mother folded her arms as if challenging us to disagree.

My wife and I both understood. I gave a little start of surprise; my wife began to pour more coffee, stalling for time while we figured out how to respond. The woman did not touch her coffee.

"Monique will never again have such an opportunity to go to America," she said, her voice softening. "I have considered and I think you will not mistreat her—yes? Therefore, I do not even ask a *cadeau*, a gift, for my other children."

I tried to explain how impossible the suggestion was. There were no *ti-mounes* in the United States, I said. She was not our child; she had her own mother and her brother and sisters; we could not accept the responsibility of taking her from her family and country, even if the laws permitted it. It was out of the question.

She smiled faintly, as if she had already foreseen these difficulties, and then she shrugged them off. "No, no, that is nothing," she assured us. "Monique is very happy."

"What? You have said something to her?" I asked.

"I have already told her, monsieur. She has heard that there is ice on the earth in your country, but she knows you will give her warm clothes. I am confident also."

"You have really told her already?" my wife asked.

"Yes, madame."

We were astonished and miserable. Could the child's sweetness have been motivated all this time by the hope of a voyage and the sight of snow, and adoption by us? No, it was unthinkable; she could not have been pretending all these months. I remembered her worried frown—two creases between the eyes, and the corners of her mouth pulled down—when Judy whimpered over the ant bites.

"How could you say a thing like that without first asking us?" my wife demanded. "How could you do it to Monique? How could you, madame?"

"I thought you liked her."

"We do, we do—but we can't take her with us," my wife said. "We can't adopt her, either. She wouldn't be happy. Anyway, we're not rich—"

The woman looked scornfully at us, and then around at the furniture of the gallery, the entire house. How, an American not rich? Such foolishness. She smiled again, stiffly.

Her obvious conviction—that only our selfishness kept her from getting what she wanted for Monique—angered me. "It is completely impossible!" I said. "It is not done, madame."

"But she can wash, clean, cook, run errands. She can sew a little already. She is very strong. She has good character—"

"I know that, madame. She's a lovely child. It's not the point," I said.

"She will not complain, no matter what you tell her to do. She is good. I will miss her. You cannot refuse now." She paused, fixing me righteously with her eyes, and then went on, "You will never have to beat her for laxness, monsieur. She has even learned some English from your children. If you have a telephone, she will answer it for you."

"America is not Haiti," I said.

"This is not permitted in the United States," my wife said.

"Ah!" Monique's mother abruptly stood up, as if really hearing us for the first time, and stared down at my wife and me. I got to my feet. She put her hands caressingly, almost coquettishly, to her straight reddish hair. "Ah!" she said again, smiling and bowing, and the resemblance to our lovely, shy little Monique made my heart turn. "Ah," she said. "I see. You Americans are all like that. Because she is black."

And she went swiftly down the stairs, and was gone.

Monique, of course, said nothing. During the few days that remained, she came to play with our children, as always. She helped with the packing, quickly learning how to fold clothes neatly.

On the last day, when the house was cluttered with trunks and crates and we were waiting for the moving truck, she came inside to wait with us. The only difference in her appearance was that she had new ribbons in her hair and wore shoes. Our children, excited about leaving, hardly had time for her. She stood quietly at one side of the room.

She accepted the little gifts we had for her and her brothers and sisters but did not look at them. She put them outside the front door and returned to stand beside us. She watched the truck come and go, then walked outside with us and watched us climb into a friend's automobile. At the last moment, Ann remembered her, and called out, "Bye-bye, Monique."

Leaning out of the car, I lifted Monique to embrace her. My wife held her for a moment. Ann said, "Come on, Mommy."

Monique's shy smile and brilliant eyes were as for any other day, but instead of saying "*Bonsoir, monsieur, bonsoir, madame,*" she said only "*Adieu,*" and stood smiling and waving to us until we were far down the road on our way back to America.

SUSANNA
AT THE BEACH

1

First came the girl. Then one fat man idly floated beside a friend
in the water, lolling on his back, spitting, his great trunk rolling in
the pleasure of himself. He liked to watch the girl while taking his
pleasure.

Finally there were the people on shore. These September loiterers,
with thin hocks and thick, with waddling rumps in dank wool or
tendoned ones in Hawaiian shorts, with itching faces in devotion to
sun or a suave glistening under the equivocation of lotion, all of them
squinted and winked and finally moved toward her. They strolled,
they turned on their heels, or they merely leaned. They came limping
over the hot sand like the good wizards in a story.

The girl over whom the old men watched was diving from the end
of a breakwater into the oily, brackish, waste-ridden substance of
Lake Erie at Cleveland, Ohio. Her arms, deeply tanned, worked

firmly; and heated from within, she scrambled up the rocks in haste after her discipline. She had fled all the billboard schemes of the life of a pretty girl. Lips soft and half-parted, she had come to perfect her diving in a worn black cotton bathing suit which was already too small after her summer's growth. They were simple exercises, but she wanted them to be perfect. She had an idea of how they should be.

The old men, shaking off the sand flies which had multiplied among the refuse so late in the season, looked jealously to the thin cloth which held this girl and to the water which sheathed her. The girl measured the angle of her imagination against the remembered sting of an imperfect arc. Clean! she had prayed, but her worried brow was reporting: No, another flop. The black cloth gleamed in the wet. The droplets of water peeled down her body like broken beads as she climbed to try it again. The smile at the corners of her mouth was a promise to herself: Well! This time, then. Even in the brief instant of her stretching, a crescent-shaped slope at one shoulder flashed dry in the sunlight.

This time she went in straight and slender with the will of perfection.

It was a Tuesday afternoon, and a day of rare Indian summer heat. Still, only the most faithful had returned to the beach: the athletic grandfathers, white-haired and withered, with an eye for the weather; a student with his American history textbook and the glaze of sun in his face meeting the doze of exposure to knowledge; the kids pretending to fish and the dead shad belly-up at the washline of water on the sand; the occasional amorous ones, asking riddles, fondling each other slyly, their pockets a-jingle with desire and streetcar fare; women from the industrial flats nearby, sitting in housedress to recall, complain, worry, and take a sleepy hour's leisure together. Mostly, however, beneath the roar and thump of road construction on the slope above them, almost in the shadow of the Terminal Tower to the east, there were the old men: the salesman sunning himself with neck reaching out and pants rolled above the knee so that by evening he can look "just like Miami Beach, better even"; the flat-thighed wanderer in a straw hat and red woolen trunks with a white canvas belt, his sinewy breasts hanging—he sat in a patch of seaweed to observe the diver and stroke the sand from between his toes; another, the big-bellied swimmer, now paddling and spewing water, shaggily emerged onto the pier in order to get nearer to the girl. His friend accompanied him. Hairy-chested loungers, old-time beaux, their bodies both wasted and swollen, they joined the rest of the men along the breakwater. They watched the girl still diving, still climbing; her deep breathing pressed the erect buds of her adolescence against sleek black cloth, she rocked once on her toes, and then off she sprang.

This girl used herself hard, used her lightness hard; and each man there, turning to her from the beach or the pier, thought it a pity. A waste—her sufficiency unto herself silenced and saddened them and made their arms hang tensely forward. Challenged, they turned up the cards of their own sorts of sufficiencies.

The fat swimmer, swirls of hair on his belly and back, was now switching himself with a green branch as he talked business with his friend. They both studied the girl, and their discussion grew lyrical. They talked business and public affairs. He was saying: "You're John-cue Smith, let's put it, you want to get married—"

"I know! Got the taxes to pay, the down payments, the terms—"

"Yes, that's what I mean, to get ahead in life. The installments."

"I got the cost of living these days, Freddy."

"You got the government."

"Yes, Freddy, I got the taxes, yes—"

"The essentials of life."

"Yes, yes, all of that, yes"—and they both shook their heads mournfully and let their mouths fall open while the tips of the girl's feet, propelled by her dive, wriggled above water as she swam.

"Like to bite off a piece of that one, eh Freddy?"

"I saw it first, me, you want to say I didn't?"

A policeman on horseback on the beach looked for purse-snatching, nuisance-making, or drunkenness. Overhead, a pontooned airplane swooped low and up. The traffic rushed past the stillness of sun and beach and water, while, out on the lake, a single leaning sailboat, a visitor from the Clifton Club, kept its distance.

Two women, equipped for conversation with quart bottles of cherry pop, their dresses pulled over their knees and their stockings rolled down to their ankles, agreed on questions of mortality, bereavement, and the pleasures of a city beach. They sat on a log stripped by water and shaded their eyes first toward the industrial flats from which they had emerged, then over the lake and into the horizon and beyond. "My mama she die when she eighty-four," said the tanned younger one. "Just like baby, like new kid, she need milk to drink."

"Yah," sighed her friend, a fat and weary woman with concentric rings of flesh about her eyes. "Look that American girlie on the board, what she think? She hurt herself like that."

"She not able my mother care for herself or nothing."

"I know, dear."

"She die like so—sssst—after long life. She work hard."

"I *know*, dear."

"It ain't right, is it?" She nodded once, decisively, and said, "My father he still strong and smoke big cigar I buy for him. He sleep with woman and give her money and everything. Ain't nice old man like that. He make eye at every young girl—"

"Bad young girlie," said the plump woman to the sand, the water, and the figure now climbing back onto the rocks.

The tanned one pulled at her dress and said, "That's why, here in this country, many people go off on roof for fall down. My children all go away to Detroit and I give money to my papa."

"No justice on earth, darling," said the sad plump one.

2

The girl, the fine diver, went off the rocks again, measuring only with a frown the interior demands of her lonely stunt, absent from the beach on the parapets of ambition. She had scraped the cotton suit on a rock. The small split showed an edge of white breast, the first hard growth of the departure from girlhood. Some of the idlers had gathered in silence on the breakwater to watch her. "You want to tell me no, Freddy? I'm telling *you* no," the fat swimmer insisted. She did not see them; she had nothing to say to them; her regard was absorbed by the patch of black water and the rules of her skill.

Back on the beach, another immature and pretty girl sat with her feet drawn under her on the sands. No one, not even Freddy, the fat swimmer's friend, gave more than a glance to this one, whose tanned plumpness in stylish knee-length shorts promised an eventual stylish willingness while her profile remained strict, suburban, and pure. Her mother, shriveled to creamed skin rather than casual flesh, squatted like the image of her age by her side, but this was not the reason the free-ranging eyes of the beach passed over the daughter so lightly. The men sensed that she feared to lie on grass because of disease, dirt, and small animals, that she shuddered at the thought of diving into the tricky, steaming, polluted waters, that despite her prettiness, she had put herself apart from the play of caprice, open-mouthed laughter, and the risks of pleasure. "Look at the girl on the pier, the one that's diving again," this cute creature said.

"She's headed for earache, that's for sure," her mother commented with satisfaction. "Maybe she doesn't read the paper and how the water's unsafe. Dangerous for bathing. Full of organisms."

"I'm getting hungry, Mother"—wrinkling her junior-miss nose and hugging herself as her favorite starlet did.

"I *said* we'd stop at the Howard Johnson's."

Meanwhile, the diver scrambled over the rocks, up onto the pier, took three or four mincing, dancing steps, and bent her knees for her renewed essay at a controlled style. Her wide temples glowed pinker and pinker with the blood under her skin and the impact of water. Her innocence—an innocence of lessons—was informed by the heat and by the pressure of her blood which brought her climbing, diving, repeating this gesture again and again past the heaped-up rock. Had she seen them and gone on, it would have spoken for an angry and stubborn pride; but her way was the way of habit, of grace, and of a passionate ignorance, a deep communion with belly-smash on the shore of Lake Erie at Cleveland.

The plump lady from the flats was disturbed. "My doctor say: Playsuit! no stockings! Like that you have no more colds for winter-time. You have upper repertory affection, Dr. Sczymanski say. Neighbor she look at playsuit, close mouth, she say: Shame! What can I do, darling?"

"That American girl, *she* have no shame," remarked the tanned woman whose father smoked big cigars. "Everybody is look at her legs"—and they both fell into a musing silence, and looked.

The beach was silent while a skin of complicity tightened like the dry sun about them all. Gradually these visitors to the September sands moved toward the breakwater, each one marvelously hushed because, if they said nothing, it could be presumed to be their habit and their devotion, an abandon to mutism in the heat, a pious thing superior to their daily selves; and thus, if the rip in the girl's suit grew longer, it was not their place to warn her of it. Let each creature hunger for itself alone—Freddy poked his pal to mean this—and thus send only appetite in the pursuit of others. The veiny old men moved fastest.

Within a few moments the beach was almost deserted except for the couple busily twisting and tickling in their well-worn place. The girl sat up with a jerk, spreading sand in an abrupt movement of her thighs, while her friend grinned, saying, "I'm not connerdicting you." He pulled her down again.

3

The tear in the diver's suit widened; the gash in this black second skin showed, to the fat man, the whiteness of belly, and then, to Freddy's bemusement, the flexing folds of flesh. Just once Freddy saw her fingers feel for the rip, but her body's intelligence calculated on nothing but the demands of perfection, and the thought of care for that clothing which was outside desire did not move further than the impatient, rummaging hand. She did not glance at herself. Turned to her idea, fixed on some inner certainty, she closed the split with her fingers, then forgot it, then let go.

She dived and climbed without liability to the give of cloth or the alteration of her world which Freddy and the big-bellied swimmer brought. She scrambled up dripping, let her eyes roam absently over the tense strollers gathering on the rocks, and dived once more. The pale wetness of her flesh opened to them like a wound under the suit while the girl, if she thought of her body at all, thought only of her skill and of her rehearsals for its sake. She was secure (small splash and ripple) in the exercise of method. She was an expert.

"You trying to tell me no, Freddy?" Behind the fat swimmer and his friend, past the city beach on this September afternoon, the machinery of road construction throbbed and the insect hiss of an afternoon breeze occupied the trees on the slope leading up to the highway past the tables, the shelters, and the park restroom. Because his mouth was dry, the fat man pointed to the girl and whispered, "Lookit." He squeezed the muscles of his friend's arm, thumb and forefinger twanging, and then they both moved forward again. The heat and the effort brought shiny tears to his eyes and a dampness to his forehead. The thickness of his body in swimming trunks, sagging at the middle and the rear, bulging beneath, looked enormous in the sunlight and the intimacy of one leg's motion against the other.

Repetitious, formal, and oblivious, the girl's ambition seemed madness or a mad joke to the watchers. It pleased the fat man; it was a delight to him. He opened his mouth, like a swimmer, and put his tongue sideways to breathe more easily. Freddy—as to him—he could hardly believe it. He wanted to float up an inner tube and go out someplace to think about it.

When she climbed over the rocks once again, the rip widened almost audibly, and still she did not see that her suit was ready to hang in tatters. No one warned her—as we do not warn a madman that he is talking nonsense—but they sighed when she extended her arms for the dive. The fat man sighed. All of them leaned together now, men and women, sharing the girl and sharing each other, waiting for their world's confirmation against the challenge she brought it, an assurance of which they were in need before the return to autumn and the years rapid upon them. A whiteness of breast flashed out, its pink sprouting from the girl's body like a delicate thing nurtured in the dark. But the day was bright and the shadows short. Looking at this tender and abstracted girl, the old Polish woman shivered at her own memories of paleness, or resiliency, of pink colors. The fat man, too, partook of their communion, frowning darkly, the green branch switching at his flanks, his knees slightly bent. He pinched his friend instead of himself. Now, her hair flat on her head and the flush of pleasure high on her cheeks after the repeated slap of her forehead against water, the girl was diving in a diminished rhythm, worn-out but blind to risk, finished but unable to stop. The moment when her breast and belly slipped by the surface was the fat man's favorite.

The diver, that object for the vindictive imaginations of old men and old women, seemed to pause to acknowledge their study of her, but saw nothing, saw nothing again, and went on. The fat man's eyelids had dropped. He was moved. As she climbed, dripping and critical, bewitched by mastery of her body, feeling, if the presence of the others had come through to her at all, only a reward of praise earned through the long summer, the fat man released his friend's arm to break the silence at last with a shrill whoop. Then the old Polish woman screamed, "You're nekked, girlie! *Nekked!*"

The fat man, his friend, the salesman, the student, many of them were now yelling their cheers at her. Poised for her dive, she must suddenly have seen them and seen herself in their sight. Her look was one of incredulity. Her eyes turned from herself to their shouting, gaping, heavy-tongued mouths and back to the loose cloth dangling from straps. She did not speak. She turned her face from them. Its stern and peaceful determination hardly altered. Then suddenly the extended arms flashed down; she ran, she did not dive, she jumped and rolled into the oily water. Despite this folding upon herself, their eyes searched out a glimpse of sunlit flesh, white and pink and tender. While the crowd applauded, the student shouted, "She wants to drown herself," and leaped into the water.

"I'll get her! Me too! Me!"

The young man reached for her hair and only touched it before she wrenched free. She doubled under, holding herself, and then she was swimming. The crowd was roaring. Four, five, six of the men had pushed to the edge of the breakwater. The girl kicked forward and swam with short, quick, sure strokes, straight out into the lake, while a cluster of young men and old, their smiles strict in pursuit, tumbled down the rocks to be first to catch her. The fat man, paddling furiously, was ahead of Freddy. The righteousness of a mob's laughter urged them to be swift, but the girl was very strong, very skillful, gifted, and encumbered by nothing but her single thought.

WHAT'S BECOME OF YOUR CREATURE?

A girl. A gay, pretty, and sullen girl, with full marks for both sweetness and cruelty. When he looked in her desk for cigarettes, there was a silken pile of panties folded like flowers in the drawer, perfumed like flowers, dizzying him with the joy of springtime. When she put on a pair of them, suddenly filling out the tiny petals of cloth in two paired buds, it was as if the sun had forced a flower into delicate Easter bloom. Oh, he needed her, loved her, and so for honor to them both, let us tell the truth, as straight as the truth comes.

He taught one class at Western Reserve University just at the geological beginnings of the Allegheny Mountains in the city of Cleveland, Ohio—an abrupt slope after industrial plains. He told poetry students where Keats got his ideas (out of his head) and where Hart Crane got his (straight from his noodle). And why. And what therefore happened in the abstract line, "That is all we know on

29

earth, and all we need to know." He, Frank Curtiss, about thirty, making a living one way and another, was very inspiring on the subject of eternal beauty and truth, urns, Popocatépetl, Sunday Morning Apples, et cetera; also very unhappily married.

Until Lenka, having registered late, entered both his class and his life with all those aforementioned desperately particular flowertime devotions. She seemed to have been bleached by centuries of the fierce cold Finnish sun—transparent skin showing blue veins on her forehead and pink capillaries on her cheeks, thick wisps of hair so blond it was almost white, the bluest eyes with a brush of darkened lash above them and a savant use of crayon at the outer corners. She had a pouting mouth; she lazily and insolently strolled to her seat, putting on black shell glasses to examine *him*; she opened a frayed, thickly used spiral notebook. She turned out to be twenty-two years old and addicted to occasional efforts at gathering a bachelor's degree by evening classes.

During the first few meetings of the class, nothing much happened to Frank besides an exaggerated exaltation of commentary on:

> But with the inundation of the eyes
> What rocky heart to water will not wear?

Shakespeare was right: His heart dashed like water under her eyes. But he still had rocks in his head. Lenka stared at him, at a transparent, fidgety, too brilliantly nervous Mr. Curtiss, looked right through him with those enormous pale eyes, with that lipsticked mouth doing a lot of thinking about Frank Curtiss as he dissolved into foam and spray, with her vaguely pedantic heavy horn glasses being put on three or four times an hour. She bent her head to touch pencil to notebook, and smiled.

This did Frank Curtiss both harm and good at home. Good because it quickened his pulse, challenged his habitual faith that spring really must follow the dismal Cleveland winter under smoky, purple-gray, fouled industrial skies (at last the salted slush rustles into sewers, March scours the blue of heaven, sun tempts the folded leaves and forces open the bulbs in the gardens of the monkey house near University Circle); giving strength, it did him good in his private winter at home; and harm because it diminished his ability for loyal compromise in the hopeless bickerings, failures, discontents, silent starings over breakfast with his wife. Perhaps that was really harm and perhaps not.

Once Lenka smiled at him, for him, it seemed, for the first time. He had hurried through a late March snowfall, swinging briefcase, wearing his old paratroop boots, dressed for the weather; there was a crust of white like a monk's cowl on his head. He brushed it off; light crash of snow to floor; meltings on his neck; wet hair flung back with impatient hand; Lenka smiled. He saw small white front teeth, very close, one of them just slightly wedged forward. "What's become of your creature," Frank asked, "in the transparent swirls/Where her heart plunged her?"

"I left the book at home," complained a serious lady getting extra credit for her teaching certificate.

"Look on with Miss Kuwaila, please. *Jostled by the hurrying current* . . . This is about a trout. Now why does the trout, a mere fish—?" But he was confused, inspired, dizzied by the beauty of Lenka's wedged-forward tooth, and so said, "Let me give you the sound of the original. *Que devient votre créature dans les orages transparents où son coeur la précipita?*"

The schoolteacher who had forgotten her book raised her hand as if she knew the answer. Turned out that she only wanted to declare that the lines lost a great deal in translation, so why bother? Jostled by the hurrying current, *gravier où balbutie la barque*, her heart had plunged her to a compelling chauvinism about English language stuff, Americano-type sublimities.

Again Miss Kuwaila smiled! Lenka could be delighted!

By regulation, of course, such a class included conference time. Lenka wrote poetry and also what she called—until he taught her better—"poetic prose." He forgave her:

> Love's wild beast, truth in the sword,
> Self-stabbing couple whom we isolate . . .

And so on; ouch. Enough of that much-tamed beast, the stainless steel sword which needs frequent sharpening, that repetitious, myopic couple. Better she should dance, and in fact, she danced. She made her living by teaching modern dance to the children of Shaker

Heights; training accounted partly for the angle of her chin which meant pride to Frank Curtiss (his wife was abysmally discouraged, querulous); dancing and endowment accounted for the fine curve of calf into knee, then tuck and dip, then high and healthy sweep of behind. Don't forget ankle—slim it was. Don't forget high-arched foot. Now take mind off leg. She wore honest blouses, top button undone, second about to be, but she was really reluctant at this moment to show him her poetry, though Frank asked most sincerely (secretly relieved; he was spoiled by much art, and even Lascivia, the midnight angel of sweet lust herself, would have suffered if she wrote verse-to-comb-the-libido-by or breathless doggerel or random-focused Eliotic pretension). Lenka liked dancing, however, she liked jazz, she liked jazz people in Cleveland and hung around. "When I was sixteen, I had long hair, I pulled it back and they thought I was older. I sat in on my first after-hours session when I was—no, fifteen, I think— hair in a bun, dime-store earrings, very cool."

In music she liked Lennie Tristano, Thelonious Monk, Miles Davis, and of course the Bird. Since Frank was ignorant in the matter, he only blinked to indicate piety. She went as far out toward the commercial as admitting that she could listen to Kai Winding, pass the time anyway, also Bartók, Dessau, Carl Orff. No, she would never be caught writing Eliot's last-gasp-of-Western-culture harangue or boyish Auden's plaint for Demo-Christian politics. Dylan Thomas was the great menace to a postwar adolescent who had gone to after-hours sessions with her copy of James Truslow Adams under her arm, revised 1948, new Questions for Study.

After the class, about ten o'clock in the evening, Frank hurried straight home in the hope that some miracle had been worked in his absence, his wife had come to love him. Not this time. Another time? Hope had been his habit (flute music, dawn-rising, confidence that orange juice would always taste good); now duplicity also became his habit—he took coffee with Lenka before class in the early evening. They parted; they came to class separately and he called her Miss Kuwaila, though it was Lenka as they huddled warming over their coffee. She did not use his name.

After the first accidental meeting and invitation, they avoided meeting by design. They just went to the same little shop up the hill in Little Italy by accident at the same time, muttered greetings, sat down—soon stopped muttering. Slightly past the university zone, the privacy of this place cost them a brisk walk. Frank began gradually to feel that he was not a stick, a pruned twig, a failed romantic adolescent: he could be a successful romantic adolescent, meaning something to someone besides himself. He bounced on the balls of his feet as he swung back down the hill. Once an oddly exciting, disturbing event took place: She met him for coffee, they separated as usual, but she did not come to class. That was on a Tuesday. On Thursday he demanded, "What happened?"

"Oh, you know . . . Something came up."

She cocked her head, quizzical. *Say more, claim rights,* she seemed to be challenging him.

Jealousy meant private, most secret reassurance: He felt a quick and unhabitual liveliness despite his wife. A roller-coaster thrill of dread and rising release; prickly sweat breaking out along his newly shaved jaw. *Felt!* He was jealous of the something which came up, but first she had met him anyway in Little Italy—invaded he was by rapid hurt and stubborn hope, by these things yearning toward a prideful chin, an awkward-graceful dancer's walk, her small, fresh-lipped mouth. He asked her to meet him for lunch the next day.

"Why not?" she asked. She opened her eyes very wide, stared briefly at the hat on the rack at the next booth, saw no reason why not. "Yes," she said.

Since they had always met at night, her daytime fragrance and colors astonished him, delighted—the rich blue within her pale skin, the lemon shadings of her hair, she smelled different—cologne rather than the lightly astringent perfume to which she had accustomed him. Lord knows he did not need novelty; it merely pitched him higher. With an effort he stopped fiddling, put his pen back in his pocket.

She told him first about her friends, local musicians, dancers, oddball types, and then cautiously, without the habit of confiding— subtle tribute to him—about her own life. She had made her way from a farm near Elyria, leaving her parents firmly behind; she had made her own life, her own living, since she was seventeen; she was, she supposed, "a permanent student—very treacherous—interested in too many things."

He smiled tolerantly. The jitters let up. "You're rather young to worry about it. Why should you feel out of place in school? You're just at the age when the mob graduates."

"I feel older, Frank," she said.

It was the first time she had used his name. Like a spill of warm honey on his tongue—*Lenka,* he wanted to say. It was the first certainty that her little stirrings under the table as they drank coffee, her brusque, bumping, bumping motions against him when they walked, were absolutely not accident. Gravity brought them colliding together, brushing, touching away. After class he told her he was keeping that book for her—please come along. He had an office and a key to the building, which was dark, almost empty at this hour. They entered, they went down the hall without lighting, he shut the door to his office, he still did not need light. April. Night birds sleepily twittering in the tree at the window. He turned, she turned, they kissed.

His heart thumped like a fish on a drum. Even through the coats they both were wearing she could feel his heart. She laughed, low and thrilled; she was perfectly at ease, his teacher now; she put her hand over his heart on the coat as if to catch the fish and squeeze it in her fingers. "You're *frightened!*" she said, and more gently: "Don't be."

"I never kissed," he said, "anyone else . . . I mean since I was married."

She put her face up to his, pressing her hand against his heart through the coat. Again her mouth asked his to search it while she held up his heart, calmed it.

"But you know," she said.

It is not as if they let their clothes fall and made love then and there, with muffled cries, on the dusty floor of an overheated college office at night, hastily plucking at each other, anguished, grappling, tender, thrusting, greedy. No. She was not that sort of girl. She insisted that first they go for a walk outside in the spring evening. The thumping fish of his heart was eased.

From fresh air, from deep breathing of budded April trees and crisp, thickly tended grass, out of silent strolling by Lenka's side at night, he felt eased and content. Now they did not need to speak. They returned to his office. She was *that* kind of girl, intelligent and purposeful. The building was deserted, and anyway, the watchman, who liked to sit on his stool and contemplate his arthritis, never bothered faculty members working late. But after locking the door, Lenka also leaned a chair against the knob in case some joker came along with a pass key. She wanted no interrupting fantasies for that first time. Playful, delighted, breathless, but thinking hard.

Frank Curtiss found his late return home that night surprisingly uncomplicated. His wife assumed that he had merely taken a couple of drinks. No marks showed, no teeth, bruise, or joy interrupted his wife's dulled recognition of him. In fact, his controlled elation, his satisfaction and triumph, brought the unpredicted bonus of an immediate easing of his trouble at home. Thanks to Lenka, his wife did not grate his own edginess; she too climbed off the razor blade on which they had been sitting in slashed togetherness. His own rebirth seemed to provide a fresh resource for both of them. Since he was able to put up with her, his wife let up on him for a time. Success to the successful, he thought, ease to the easeful!

It turned out that unsheepish Lenka, that creature of brave yielding beauty, also had her troubles. Frank was not accustomed to the calm and cool varieties of wildness. At twenty she had been sent to Europe to have her baby—"a public man" was all she would say about the father; Frank found the remark cryptic, unyielding. She had refused an abortion, but in Europe she had sickened, the baby had been taken from her dead—"I saw it, he looked alive, I didn't believe the doctor, I screamed and screamed and they put me to sleep again"— and now she could never have a child. This, she understood herself, had something to do with the intensity of dance study, poetry study, art chasing of several sorts.

Cunning and pity filled Frank's heart. Once more he suffered that wild thumping, as if the heart might crunch his ribs. This time Lenka did not notice; she was telling the truth about how it was before she knew him, and so his heart's labor could not now concern her. "I'll miss it more later," she remarked. "I always wanted a child. I try not to think about it. At least I won't let myself take dogs, cats, parakeets, you know. I'll make it work for me. I do dance calisthenics when I feel bad." Then she folded her hands, fell silent, fluttered her thick pale lashes, was a girl again.

In Frank's heart cunning and pity. Pity for this troubled lovely creature who looked so pure and innocent, who surely was. Cunning because he need never worry about pregnancy. (This had bothered him. He suffered the usual fears of retribution.) "Lenka dearest," he said.

"That's all right. No need to feel anything. Want to see how I can stand with my foot higher than my head?"

They were in her room. Confused by confession, he too had talked about trouble in love. He got up to cross the lamplit space for a cigarette; then it was that he opened her drawer as she watched, in unconscious confirmation of intimacy, and saw the sheaves of tiny folded panties; no cigarettes in that drawer; naked, he stared across the room again, and caught her eyes on him, and the pity and the cunning and the pride at his ease and at her watching his recently slimmed middle (surprise! he was just strolling naked here) and her own curled loving body partway under the sheets, all these matters were brought together; her eyes shut, her teeth showed as he rapidly returned to her; perhaps she smiled because she remembered his timid and boyish heart's pounding of a few weeks before; now he brazenly strolled, sprang flopping, laughing across the bed. They cleaved together.

Their meetings became more purposeful, deeper in pleasure and trouble. Once he waited fifteen minutes in the corner of the park which, by May, was their property forever. He was worried; time problems of married men. Then he heard her sandals slapping the pavement, she was running, he saw her, *running*; she stopped abashed before him, blushing, murmuring, "I was afraid you wouldn't wait." He took her in his arms in the fading afternoon light, he kissed away the little beads of perspiration on her upper lip. They stood kissing, leaning, making passionate walking steps against each other, that vain effort to disappear into each other's bodies. He smelled her sweetness and heat and wanted to sink his arm into her back, stroking the curve, the yearning and folding into him.

But he saw his watch as he kissed her. "Later," he said. "Stay home. I'll come by your place."

"Oh, promise, Frank."

"Of course. Don't worry. I'll manage."

It was not so easy. When he got home, he found his wife worn and jittery, their child had an upset stomach: "Four times this afternoon," his wife said. But it was the heat, four wasn't too terribly many, she had given him paregoric and Kaopectate already. No, what was on her mind was a telephone call, an anonymous warning: "Do you want to know where to find your husband at this minute?" Nothing more; just that and click.

"Students," Frank said, his heart sinking. "You deal with crackpots at a city institution, especially evening classes. Happens to everybody. Remember when Mel Bargin had that siege of letters?"

She was convinced, or worn-out, or didn't care. Anyway, he was home in time for supper. They ate the silent meal of too many quarrels and the abandonment of hope. Frank knew he would have to wait until she fell asleep before he took his habitual long walk.

She slept; he walked. Lenka lived on the bottom floor of a converted mansion. He peeked through the window. She had set up an easel and had been working in charcoal, a lamp was on, but she lay breathing gently across the bed, fully dressed, even shoes, the garter belt showed under the sprawled, slipped skirt. He tapped at the window. It was after midnight and the street deserted. She got up blinking, pouting, peered out to him; and oh then her beautiful smile on her beautiful pout and she opened the window.

Later he warned her of spies, his enemies or hers, most likely hers. She frowned, turned tense and worried—that was why he had waited to tell her. She admitted that she was the sort of girl who might have vengeful suitors lurking about. Covertly thrilled, forbidding this excitement, Frank rolled over and faced the window: Could someone have peeked at them under the drawn shade? She sighed. "Maybe it's my fault," she suggested, "breaking all the rules."

"Oh, no!" And he thought: It's I who break the rules, crawling through a window for love like a burglar, and I hold on to my son and hope for my wife when it's hopeless.

"I guess both of us," she admitted softly, fairly.

But now they would have to be very careful. Frank could not be seen with her; they met in the park, in far corners of the city, or, most of the time, simply in her room. They sketched each other; they smoked, read, told each other stories; they made love. Frank found

himself wanting to talk about his son, but bit his tongue. Self-con-
scious, self-judging. "Don't be frightened," she said more than once.
Although almost ten years older than Lenka, he came to think of her
as wise and anciently mysterious within the desperate yearning gift of
herself, the will to be his of her open and lovely body. She had the
patience of confident love.

Despite the secret isolation of their life together, the close confine-
ment to odd places, then to her room, then, toward the end of the
spring, in a rising pitch of indulgence and claim, to her bed, he had
never considered his rivals. She had no right to be jealous of his wife;
he had no right to think of Lenka away from him with others. The
telephone call to his wife brought the others to mind. He asked
questions; she was reticent, unspecific. A few words about her mother
and father, the farm, a brother who worked it; vagueness about her
friends—he knew none of them—though sometimes a knock would
come at the door and they would lie still, listening to the repeated
knock, the slow steps away, the outer door slamming. He was marvelously flattered by her refusal to answer the telephone. Their time
together was simply theirs. Though girlishly hurt that he would go no
place with her, she understood. She proposed a back-room jazz session on the West Side where he could not possibly meet anyone who
knew him. He was too cautious. He tried to complete his knowledge
of her by looking up her records under camouflage of his faculty
credentials. Greedily he studied her previous addresses, the maiden
name of her mother, full of K's, the solemn statement she had made
on her first application. Her IQ score was extraordinarily high; this
reassured him because he wondered if she had simply cast a spell over
him—to some questions she merely answered with a stare. No, she
was a human girl creature, not a witch. She had lazy grades, brilliant
sometimes, sometimes mediocre. She was careful about picking up
graduation credits. He felt silly when he handed her folder back to
the secretary. "Hm, hm, yes indeed. Very interesting. Thank you."

There is a time in every man's life when he can do anything. It was this
time in the life of Frank Curtiss. Despair with his wife had given up
to deep gratification with a beautiful girl; he even did better at home;
matters cooled and calmed; his work went well; he hardly needed
sleep and did not suffer his usual rose fever during the spring he knew
Lenka. No sniffles, no pink eyes. Expanded breathing, sharp sight. Of

the occasional headache of fatigue and excess he was cured by the touch of her hand, her welcome when he came smiling, showing teeth, through her window. Slipping through, welcomed, he made love to her with the heavily settled industrial window grit still on his hands until it mingled with the secretions of love and summer—paste, caresses, perfume. Later he wrung his hands in soap, hot water, soap again, then cold water, in a gesture like expiation, rinsing away her smells, but soon became aware that this was not guilt—he found the scrubbing and splashing very fine to his summery blood. He did not think of the future; he merely lived and believed himself in love, in a kind of love, surprised by love's surprises, acquiescing.

Since he adored his son, whom we leave absent from this history, he could not imagine dissolving his home; but he thought: *I'll wait, I'll see. In the meantime, I'll ride.* Things were going too well to be interrupted by dreams of perfection. There is no perfection, anyway, in an imperfect world (philosophy of adultery); the unhappy husband has the right to save himself (more philosophy for adulterers); life on earth means a quest for the absolute, compromise, violation, tribute, delight in apples, worms, indigestion, purest love, gossip, peeking apes, donkeys, creeps, squares (still more philosophy, poetry, grand hysteria); *enough!* thought Frank Curtiss. He had a son, Lenka could give him no child, and anyway, he *had* a son. One last time, curled against him, Lenka murmured their password: "Don't be frightened, darling."

He began to laugh in the easy sprawl of his body, remembering the foolish creature he had recently been. "Frightened?" he asked, remembering mightily. Once weak and strict, now he floated down the river, agile, hale, and strong. Or so Frank Curtiss seemed to Frank Curtiss. And he laughed, prospering, holding her away and cupping her gratified breasts which had changed, just as his body had, during the past months. "But I'm not frightened anymore," he said.

He stopped laughing and very seriously, solemnly, thanked her for saving his life.

"I make you happy, don't I?" she asked. She had the sort of pale and delicate skin which flames at the first touch of a man's beard. With her downcast eyes, it gave her a perpetually astonished blush as they said good-bye. "Don't I make you happy, Frank? Oh, I do!"

She did; the god of judgment had become an angel of mercy—had

sent unmerited joy. No, he decided, everyone deserves to be able to
carry a tune, find that wanton flush on a girl's cheeks, recall sweet love
for a moment in the morning before going about the work of the day.
"Oh, I do love making you happy"—she couldn't say it enough. He
promised that it was the final truth and she should know it. Flowers,
rebirth, ripening gourds, purity of delight.

It was therefore a considerable surprise to go home later and find
a new lock on the door, a note from his wife warning him not to try
to enter, and his clothes thrown into hampers on the porch. It
shocked him that she had not even bothered to put out a suitcase for
his use. In this numbed state he telephoned her from the gas station
at the corner. It turned out that she had prepared rather carefully.
She had both keys to their car in her possession and advised him to
take a taxi someplace, away. She suggested that he use the opportunity to spend a whole night with Lenka Kuwaila and see how he liked
it. She remarked that she did not care to speak with him at all and
that further discussions could be held through the intermediary of
her lawyer. She gave him the lawyer's name and told him to look up
the number himself. She paused before saying good-bye and added,
"I waited until you finished final exams and you won't have to face
so many people over the summer. I thought that was pretty consider-
ate of me." She had also left about five dollars in their joint checking
account.

He spent the night in confusion at a friend's house. For the first
time he felt exhausted by his secret lovemaking with Lenka; he had
left her with her smell still on his hands and come back to this news;
there was an ache in his loins and a triangle of lead in his belly. It
turned out that his wife had exact information about his connection
with Lenka, dates and times and other, terribly intimate details.
When her lawyer confronted him, he dully submitted, denied nothing, agreed to everything. Greater than the shock of his wife's action
was his shock about the letters she had received. Lenka had simply
recounted everything in tormenting detail, with obscene precision.
He felt a lingering tenderness for his wife because of the jealousy she
must have suffered, but whatever this secret suffering, it had now
congealed to a buzzing, busy hatred and cold vengefulness which
deprived him even of his sympathy for her. He was stripped bare.

Lenka left for New York without seeing him after his anguished telephone call to her: "Why? Why? Why did you have to do it that way, Lenka? Can't you see how it destroys everything between us, even the past?"

"I don't care about memories. What's over means nothing. Over. You didn't want to do more than crawl through my window a couple times a week—"

"But to write to her like that—what meant—how—"

"You cared more about a cold bitch than you cared for me. Just because you had a child."

She hung up on him.

He stood shrugging at the telephone. Women were hanging up on him all over the world. He was disconnected. Maybe it was really he, Frank Curtiss, they were hanging up on. He went on shrugging; it was a nervous twitch, a shaking-off-the-burdens tic.

Here we need not detail the prolonged anguish of a divorce when there is a child, when there has been a habit of suffering and also some distant memory of joy (this only increases bitterness and determination to hurt). He survived in a rapture of numbness, like a mouse in a paw. His wife tried to set rules about visiting their child; he raged and cursed her. But finally he saw her coolly from a distance, he saw her as impossible, for years she had been a stepwife to him. He was grateful to Lenka for the brutal surgery she had performed; the operation was bloody, but the patient survived. Things were arranged about his boy; he found a new job; he went to New York; a year passed. Where it went, he did not know, but now he considered himself a brilliantly wise twenty-two years old. He had been twenty-one when he married; the next years were poisoned by enough misery so that he wanted to leave them out; his year of liberation made him now twenty-two. This was mainly a joke, and he had a fresh sprout of gray hair in his thick cropped black thatch, but the world seemed to be on his side once more.

He was hungry, he ate, he had enough money to invite girls for dinner, he ate voraciously, explaining everything, enticing them on long walks through New York, exciting them with his tourist's freshness of joy in the great city. He found a girl to join him in biting into an apple, sucking the sweet juice of it at dawn, finally kissing in good friendship and turning on their sides to sleep. Life went on with the freshness of the busy mornings and the hesitating nightfalls of Manhattan. He found a good job writing coy letters for a chain of magazines, the sort that are printed to look as if they are typed: "You may have neglected to open our first bill. We know that you are a busy and successful man, but remember! The workman is worthy of his hire! And we here at *Daytime Magazine* consider our publication . . ." He had no automobile because of the responsibilities of parking, but could afford taxis (the workman was worthy of his hire). He felt free. He didn't even have a cold for two years after he separated from his wife; every change seemed to cure him of something. He threw away his bottle of aspirins. His married vision of himself as a heavy, shaggy, weary buffalo, head low and muzzle hurt, gave way to another image—he was lean; his posture was good; he was an agile bucko. When his former wife remarried, his last vestige of guilt disappeared. Free, free. He played badminton twice a week with a French girl who pronounced it "badd-ming-tonn." Free and agile. "I'd never have matured otherwise," he solemnly told his friend.

"You theenk too motch," she answered.

So finally he decided to telephone Lenka, though his little French friend advised him that this was as bad as thinking. Just curiosity about how she was making out, he promised himself. ("Don't be frightened, darling . . ." And how she had buttered toast for him, making coffee on a hotplate. And the smell of her perfume when she had run toward him in the park, breathless at being late. "I make you happy, don't I?")

But after he told her how long he had been in New York, she said that she was not interested in seeing him.

"I held a grudge, you can understand that," he said. "I still think you were very wrong, but I'm grateful anyway. It worked out for the best."

"And it's over," she said. She told him that she had an official friend, a drummer with a well-known advanced jazz combo. She named him with pride. Frank asked later and discovered that her friend was known as "the Unholy Wazuli"—a gifted wild man with two breakdowns and a conviction for possession of heroin in his curriculum vitae. He claimed to blow finer drum under the hooves of horse, but others disputed the argument.

Disturbed by her refusal to see him, faintly jealous of the Unholy Wazuli, Frank bothered the friend who knew her. "Why do you want to mess with her more? She must be crazy."

"I just want to talk with her—"

"To do what she did to you is plain nutty, pal."

"Yes, nutty, sure. But she cared for me." This is very important to all men, that a lovely girl cares, and especially an unhappily married man will forgive anything for love, even a good dose of nuttiness. The man unhappy in marriage may seem merely somber, but he is also crazy. Frank had believed that Lenka cared for him.

Now, however, Frank was enjoying nonconjugal bliss in New York, and although a certain sideways questioning look while buttering toast meant girl to him, and a certain springtime slap of sandals on the pavement made his breath catch hard, his life went on without much thought of Lenka. One spring day, now two years after he had first met her, he was strolling through Washington Square when he saw a girl walking ahead and he thought first of toast, and then, recognizing the tilt of her walk, yes, this time it really was Lenka. He had an hour before dinner. Without considering it further, he ran up to her, first closely studying her because he did not trust himself to see anything but her eyes when her eyes met his. She was still very pretty, but she showed early aging, a new fleshiness at her upper arms and a slight thickening of the legs, and when he said, "Hello, Lenka," and she turned, he saw the fine lines about her pale eyes.

"Well, hello, Frank."

She waited coolly to see if he were merely greeting her. Before he lost himself in her, the thought came that she was paying the price for her ancient fragility, which had given her an almost adolescent grace; now she bore some unhealthy weight; she looked ten years older already. "You want to have some coffee?"

"Well, you know. No, man, no."

"What then?"

She smiled, showing her fine teeth, and consciously imitated someone else: "If I could have my druthers, I'd druther have a drink."

"Sure, let's go." And he hurried her by the arm. He was shocked because one of her front teeth was missing, and it gave the smile a wild blackness, again breaking the seamless dancer's grace which he remembered.

They talked; she recited as if he were an elocution teacher and she were doing her lesson. She was still with her Unholy Wazuli. He had cut a great record, more than one, but you know, people put him down. Hard to get the gig when people put you down. The nut on his habit was more dollars a day now. He couldn't make it by himself *no* way. It's no ball, a habit—people on the outside don't dig one bit —it's something to do—*you* know.

He did not know. Very squarely he asked. "Tell me what's bothering you, Lenka."

"A nut of more a day."

"Explain."

"Well, you know . . ." Her man wanted her to work to support his habit.

"What kind of work?"

She shrugged. "Well, you know, man."

He was deeply shocked. "Don't! Please don't!" he gasped, shouted. He drew back from his own excitement, ashamed at how it might look, and tried to be smart, a man of the world, her way, and at the same time trying to make her feel his way about it. He said, "Lenka, promise. You probably think I'm still mad at you—"

"You want to put me down, man."

"I don't anymore, Lenka. It's over now, past."

She smiled, showing the black place in her teeth. It was what she had said. What's over is over. What happens last night is dead.

"Okay. But I still care about you, Lenka. Promise you won't do that? God! To buy heroin!"

"It's usually why girls do it," she said. "I know lots of girls, that's how they join up—"

"Promise!"

"That's how they get in the Life."

"Promise you won't!"

She only shrugged and thanked him for the drink. He asked if she would like to meet him again soon. She smiled thinly and said, well, her friend was jealous. He remarked that this jealousy did not seem to go with the work he had in mind for her. "Well," she said, "you know."

Manhattan is very large, but sometimes far galaxies engage, interlock. Frank was not certain how it happened: He found himself with friends in the jazz world. The hipster bit, as they said, was very big that year. He knew his way around. The Wazuli was a famous character, "a crazy big talent, impossible," Larry Arnold, an editor of *Down Beat,* told him. They also knew about Lenka, though all they said was "Cute. Unholy's chick." Was she with him, Frank wondered, confiding, under his conditions? Larry explained, "It ain't the old days, mon. America has really changed in this here regard—you dig like Riesman, Kinsey, Fromm, those cats? A girl can't just patrol, just sell the basic product. Sex and air are but I mean *free,* mon. It's the specialties pays off now. When you're tired of air, you want to be gassed."

Frank was thinking: She called it the Life.

"She's just an unusually stacked chick is all I meant," Larry said out of pity for his friend's troubled frown. He took the black line between the eyes for jealousy, when everyone but a hipster knows that jealousy is a butt in the stomach and bile in the cheeks. "Besides, I got no news of her—just the Wazuli's chick is all I hear, and he's banned from Manhattan clubs. Tried to play the Embers stoned out of his head. Park Department, Hon. Robert Moses-san, Commissioner-san, picked him up for stepping on the grass. Joke. Yok yok. Whyncha laugh with me, Mr. Shelley?"

Frank fought down his imagination of her cool pale dancer's beauty being used in that way, the Finnish farm girl from Ohio with the IQ of 155 . . . He wondered if she had taken to horse herself. Someone who seemed to notice better than most said that there was no space in her teeth. She must have had money to get it fixed. She had seemed to lack vanity about it (and he recalled the confident disorder of her closet in Cleveland, the smell of her perfume and the bending body, dressing with her back to the mirror on the door).

Another year passed. Frank rarely thought of Lenka, though she was a part of his blood, his suspicions, and his tenderness with girls, and when he found himself liking a girl, he found himself reminded of Lenka's ways—tilted chin, curve of back, lazy easy dancer's walk. He now found one whom he liked very much and he was about to try marriage again, with hope. Settled in New York, his telephone number was in the book. And Lenka looked it up and called.

She asked if he would meet her. It was important. He agreed and named places, but to each she said, "No, not there. I don't make that scene." Finally she said, "Home all afternoon."

He was embarrassed. "Look, I'd rather meet you someplace else. How about under the Washington Square arch?"

"Well, Christ Almighty," she said. Paused. "Well, all right."

They met. She gave him a wan smile. She was not wearing lipstick; he had forgotten how her paleness needed the blatant red of lipstick, except when she tanned in June. But the tooth had been expertly replaced, and apart from a peculiar stiffness of her face, the cautious-ness of fatigue, she was a girl to make men turn around, shake their heads, and ask themselves if maybe. They strolled; she talked vaguely of having broken with the Wazuli—"and all that scene, you know, man"—and trying to write.

"How are you making a living?"

"I said I *write,* man."

"You're publishing things? What?"

"I wrote that article on hypnotism, you know." (He did not know —how could he?) "You know I left it there at that magazine. I never read the magazine, so how should I know what they did with it?"

At last, more and more uneasy, wanting to call his girl, thinking they should set the date for soon, he demanded bluntly, "I didn't think you really wanted to see me. What's on your mind?"

"I got these letters from your wife," she said.

"What? My *wife?* You mean my former. You mean she *wrote* to you? Lately?"

"Yes, sure, didn't she tell you?"

This exasperated Frank. Since he went frequently to Cleveland to see his son, he had frequently to see his former wife and he hoped for level dealings with her after all this time. He didn't like the idea of pen-pal exchanges between Lenka and her, those two distant chums.

"I'm worried about her," Lenka was saying. "That's why I thought you should pick up on these letters, see. You should fall up and look them over, you think?"

Yes, he thought. They walked across to her apartment on Christopher Street, a hall smelling of cat and a lazy custodian, mailboxes unmarked and flapping open, the locks broken. Lenka lived on the top floor. "I like air," she said vaguely, "I don't mind the walk up." She liked air, but the windows were shut and there was a choke of attic heat, close, hot, unclean. She called the place her pad and she actually had one—a thin mattress on the floor, with a cotton spread covering it, fresh from the laundromat but unironed, and orangish foam-rubber fat peeking at one corner. He remembered once making love to her and the sudden shock of four paws, a jealous cat leaping onto his back. She still had cats, but different ones, a pair of kittens. He wondered if the Unholy Wazuli and the temporary visitors had minded the cats. Lenka was moving against him, putting her head against his chest, arms limp, not moving now.

Frank stepped away. "Those letters."

She went to a card table and looked through a pile of papers, old copies of the Times, Down Beat, Variety, a row of paperback books leaning against the wall. A split-spined copy of Zen Archery had a letter marking her place, but Frank would have recognized the handwriting. This was Lenka's hand—an unmailed letter.

She shrugged. "I guess I threw them away. I kept them around, but I was cleaning up . . ."

Of course, there were no letters: His former wife was as done with him as he was done with her. What possible advantage could Lenka gain in making a fool of him like this?

She may have invented a foolish lie, but she recognized the glare of contempt on his face, and in her life of now a quarter of a century, she had learned only one way to answer the judgment of men. She slid against him, on her face a mixture of coyness and dread, a flirtatious half-smile, a slinking, catlike, practiced leaning against him, and her eyes filled with tears as she shut them, tears balancing on the wetted lashes, slipping down her cheeks. "Frank," she said haltingly. "I stopped remembering for a long time, I don't know, things were difficult, I thought you were too angry . . . But I've been remembering . . . That's why . . . Forgive . . ."

He put his arms around her. He stretched, feeling her light hair against his chin, looking out over the small hot gray-and-brown room. There was a pile of 45-speed records, probably the Wazuli's legacy.

She laid her head against his chest and waited, but waited cunningly, her body rising and falling with exaggerated breath, fitting itself against his. He felt desire for her. Then he thought of the letters she had written to his wife, and the letters she had just now lied about, and suddenly, as he held her, she had turned her head up and wanted to be kissed, and his most vivid fantasy was this one: *She was unclean.* His uncurbed dread ran toward a muddle—deceit, illness, secret pity, slime, retribution. Not knowing what he feared, he thought only: Filth, cunning, running filth, blotches, sores. Because he could not bear her sorrows, he thought: *Deceit and cunning and disease!* Her lips came open, slightly wetted, and her breathing stirred imperatively on his face. She was rubbing up against him, trying to make him kiss her, because it was another trick, like writing to his wife, like telling him so many lies; yet as before in Cleveland, she really wanted someone, wanted him, wanted the good comfort of love; and she also wanted to be kissed because she had a disease to give him.

He pulled away before their mouths touched; her nails clawed along his arm, shredding skin; he fled, hearing her sobs at the open door as he careened down the infected stairs and onto the free air of the street.

This was already long past the end, of course. But logic does not apply when a needful man has received love—even false comfort, false love. One more time, with the permission of his new wife, Frank telephoned to find out—what? How she was. He received the crisp mechanical answer: "The number you have called is not a working number."

It would be useless to go to her apartment, but he went anyway, and then to the post office; but no place, no way, was he able to find a forwarding address. She was gone. Finally she had disappeared from his earth.

His wife, who was now pregnant, shrugged with a certain amount of satisfaction and relief. He kissed her, grateful because she had been easy on him about Lenka. "But she did me a favor, Frank!"—the sweet logic of the practical wife. "Otherwise you might still be in Cleveland. Rub my back, will you? No, just hold me."

On the side of life, he was stroking and comforting this dear person who carried his child; she laid her head against his shoulder with a worn, anxious smile; there were only a few more weeks to wait. But

as he touched his lips to her hair, lightly moved his lips on her
forehead, he could hear the angel on the other side of oblivion
questioning that other girl, who bore no mark or sign of him: "Lenka
Kuwaila, what about Frank Curtiss?"

And she rendered her verdict: "Well, you know . . ."

PARIS AND CLEVELAND ARE VOYAGES

—for all those who step the legend
of their youth into the noon.

1

Even before he noticed the girl, he had already taken to the easy habit of strolling into this paneled, chandeliered, and interior-decorated suburban library of a late afternoon in Cleveland. He liked to pry on the travel writers gasping over the places where he had spent his wander-years with Helen: Paris, Florence, other pleasant towns. Nothing is so mysterious as the description by a stranger of a well-loved old friend. Such dim-witted joy in these arty photographs! What smiles for him in the mislabeled half tint of the very street on which he had lived in Montparnasse! "A meal can be obtained on the Left Bank of Paris for three to five dollars. Wine not included." (When did Helen and Gran pay so much except under the obligation of a holiday or a visitor?) "The greedy life pulses on Saturday night in Naples. A good nylon dress is recommended." (Apparently the lady expected to be eaten by some greedy pulser, gobble-gobble, buttons, and all.)

51

Who was this girl approaching his table near the travel section? He recognized Elliot Paul in her pretty little hands. The poor child probably wanted to dream that the Rue de la Huchette would be the last time she saw Paris, too.

Today he would try the *Blue Guide to Italy* and maybe Paul Morand, a native wanderer, on Paris. With a luxurious sigh, he sat down near the girl. Dr. Granley Hattan allowed himself this smugness of nostalgia in his afternoon pleasures, the pleasures of loneliness at thirty when bohemian days are past and the kid makes too much noise to let him work at home and the thesis is published ("François Mauriac: A Double Regard") and his tenure and rank as assistant professor at Western Reserve University are assured and maybe he doesn't have anything better to do anyway.

"Excuse me," he said to the girl, just touching her purse to move it. Otherwise it would look as if they were together.

She did not answer. Could Elliot Paul's prose be so loud as to deafen her? Gran was suddenly aware of his crew-cut hair and the touch of useful premature gray in it and his whole lounging length of critical body. She moved the purse and moved so that the long red scarf still hanging from her shoulders—as if she had been so eager to get to the Rue de la Huchette that she could not undo her clothes—touched his knee as it fell.

That was a kind of answer to him, Granley Hattan decided. A nice rise and fall of breathing at her small, intent, leaning body. Without a word he picked up her scarf and put it on the table.

2

College girl in velvet slacks, red canvas shoes with white crepe soles, fine tweed coat thrown over these items, that red scarf undone but never taken off, carelessly cropped hair, crisp little ears, strong, small, pretty animal mug of a face, a bright girl with her own ideas (the studied sloppiness) and a moneyed father (the coat)—these were Gran's notes on her into the pages of the book he thought he was reading. She was flushed with Elliot Paul, actually copying out phrases! The leather notebook and the chewed pencil were a studious touch, and the brightness and pallor perhaps stood for impatience with that rich father of hers.

Gran congratulated himself for knowing her well. This was not the kind that sat in the front row to try for an A by showing its knees; this was the kind that learned all the forms of *être* and *avoir* and read *Le Livre de Mon Ami* as if Anatole France meant something. Maybe this one even wrote poetry.

But it was odd how the fact of seeing her for the first time in the suburb, off-campus, made her different. Her body had the alert charm of youth, the trust in that charm, and the baby fat gone. Looking about at the vaulted churchlike fakery of this suburban branch library, he thought of his graduate course, French 410. Didn't the lovers meet in churches for Stendhal? Of course, travel folders and annotated memoirs could never replace the door to the confessional.

"Oh, damn."

"Pardon?"

"Oh, damn," she whispered to him, insisting on it. "Can you lend me a pencil?"

He grinned and touched the scarf. You broke it on purpose, he wanted to say, but said instead: "Surely, but if you take notes on Paris, at least don't read Elliot Paul. That's for schoolteacher tourists."

"How do you know?" And she answered the question herself: "You've been there?"

He knew by the way she said *there* that the sea was steady and the winds favorable. "How about some coffee and I'll tell you all about it."

"Yes," she said simply, packing up.

They strolled out together. She was an inch or so shorter than Helen, not her willowy type at all, but nicely turned. Helen, his wife, had worn her hair long at this girl's age, clipped in a ponytail behind. He had taken Helen's prettiness as the normal thing, his right at the time; perhaps it was; yet now in this strange girl at the same age ten years later, he was astonished at so much unmarked beauty, unquarreled, unsuffered, pouting, and dusky only with resentment of parents. Yes, the freshness of her skin went nicely with the dark, disputing rings under her eyes. Helen had not had them; she was another sort, married young for other reasons—pure gaiety perhaps, so romantic, blind, easy, and fixed in her own family that she could not suspect how hard it is to live in family.

The librarian's hairy librarian face turned on them, but it meant nothing. They could be fellow students, neighbors—they probably were near neighbors, anyway. He still looked young enough to be a graduate student. Down the steps, he watched this girl again, thinking of his wife and of himself. He had hickeys on his nose then—the word was still hickeys?—and his pictures showed him too-smooth, untried. Surely he was better looking now at thirty, the youthful spring of his step chiming well with the fret of thought in his face; experienced laughter is best, less braying.

"What's your name?"

"Carol."

"I'm Gran Hattan."

"Carol Dent," she said. He liked the way she gave her first name alone, as if they were playmates. Apparently she did not know that he was Dr. Hattan, the new man in Romance Languages. As if to answer this thought, she added, "I've seen you on campus. I saw you here yesterday, but you didn't see me. I knew you spent two years in Paris, wasn't it?" She looked at him with her bright red lips damp and slightly parted: "It's my *dream*."

Gran laughed softly because it was such a childish thing to say and because it nevertheless told the truth about a bright and adventurous suburban coed. Her saying it like that, *dream*, sent an odd little shiver up his back; perhaps she meant it to. Helen and he must have said it the same way.

"Funny thing," he answered, "this beer place at the corner serves the best coffee in the neighborhood. You usually don't find that at bars. I had a Fulbright in '49—first year it was. We were the forty-niners with our meat cards and travel allowances and our leftover khakis to sell to the Arabs. We were some smart babies!"

"But that wasn't really so long ago, Gran."

3

This was only the first time that she reads his thoughts with such flashing amusement. I'm older than you, he had meant to say. Six years ago was another age; we all still had boots and field jackets.

O not that much older, dear, her smile with buds of teeth replied. Clothes are only clothes, something to sell to the Arabs for a silk-screen print or an album of Gregorian. Bop existed already; so did

Van Gogh and the uplift bra—even if we called bop "bebop" at
Shaker High.

But then the baby fat would suddenly reappear, softly enveloping
her understanding of him in the book-struck, dream-struck, mirror-
struck adolescent's pout: "I'm perishing for St.-Germain-des-Prés,
Gran. Is it true they've remodeled the Dôme? It's one tricky job
convincing Dad how Paris won't ruin me for life. Really, he's a pain
sometimes. Used to read books, but you'd never know it now with
the television." And she tossed her head, which made the scarf ends
twirl. He had been touching them with his hand again.

"Don't try to reform your father, it never works," he said. "Just
get your way out of him if you can, it's the most you can expect."

"You've escaped the father image, huh? Luck plus hard work at
independence, I'll bet. How old were you? I will, too, I escaped Mom's
domination in junior high already, and without turning dyke, either."

"Congratulations. Lucky men of this world."

"Don't tease me, Gran, this is serious to a girl." She smiled—
where had she learned that nose, that quirk of grin?—and sat very
still for an instant. Untroubled by her bold words, she now blushed
a new thought and leaned forward with her smile renewed and
whispered near his ear—she didn't have to, but she did—"I'd take
a beer, but wouldn't it be embarrassing if they asked for identification? I'd die—"

"Of mortification?"

She gave him the turning-away three-quarter view. "Of embarrassment. I wouldn't *ever* say mortified, Gran. You're not sardonic at all
today, you're only sarcastic."

He understood that she expected him to do better than coffee for
himself. Wine in a neighborhood bar would precipitate a bad case of
sarcasm at the eyes; he wanted to take himself seriously. Beer the same
at the mouth corners—too obedient to Carol. Oh, Lord, someone
had told her she looked like a dark Audrey Hepburn. He ordered and
reverently nursed a bourbon on the rocks. She tapped her ashes into
her saucer and watched him meditatively. Now not A. Hepburn, she
was Vivien Leigh with Phi Bete her junior year and Olivier and
anxiety yet to come. This silence, fine-eyed and brooding, was succeeded by the information that she had memorized more than half
of Le Cimetière Marin and read Valéry's letters about it in the original.

They talked. They measured each other coolly but with a satisfaction which they were proud to admit. It's not so often you can be honest about liking a person, as Carol pointed out. You've got to have an agreement about basic personality. The bar, carved, paneled, and stain-glassed like the library, seemed to both of them the right sort of Elizabethan pub to be designed by a Cornell architect.

Late one afternoon, the third time that, without spoken arrangement, they had met at the library, she put out her cigarette decisively just as he said, "Carol, whatever made you start about the Dôme? That's Montparnasse, by the way—"

"Tell me about your wife," she demanded. "What's she like? What time do you have to be home for dinner?"

"Such curiosity! Which are you interested in, what she's like or when I have to be home?"

"Oh!" Boldness is fine, rather exciting, her piping *oh* seemed to say; indiscretion, however, is too much, and sometimes sordid. She pouted and withdrew her hand. He had been touching her fingertips over the table. This time she had removed the scarf and the short tweed coat, and his heart was sharp and busy within him at the sight of her untried ripeness, her sharp, flesh-and-muscled, held-in, held-out body, the rich expanse of well-tended woman rising and falling beneath sweater and fitted skirt.

"Carol, you're an extraordinary girl," he said.

She was not answering. He needed punishment.

Could he tell her about Helen? That she was too thin to be worried about getting fat but she worried all the same. That she took care of their boy as if he were precious silver that had to be polished and wrapped and stored or it would tarnish to death. (Gran Hattan was dissatisfied already with his mama-calling six-year-old—a softness in him, a female dependency of spirit. Bud wasn't his vision of a son, who should be shrill, tough, and bruised by hard play.) And that Helen and he quarreled over buying better furniture than they could afford—dare he tell Carol that? No, it was more penance than he needed to pay in the exact economy of the first contest between married man and suburban girl.

"My wife's taller than you, blond," he said. "Wears her hair up behind. Our kid was born in Paris."

"Isn't that marvelous! Doesn't it mean he can never be President?"

"Yes, but we cross that bridge when we come to it. I'm thinking about a constitutional amendment—"

"Was she pretty?"

That *was*! Such elegance! The sly creature had struck hard. That *was* spoke for her acquiescence in the erotic sense which their meetings had for him. Girl of innocence and craft! he thought. Wasn't it true, as one of his friends argued, that any woman is always at least ten years older than every man?

"Yes, Helen is pretty," Gran said.

Having made her point, she did not need to listen. He found her back in Paris. "Born there—the American Hospital, I suppose?"

"No, the Hôpital Foch."

"Ah"—so pleased. She busied herself sleekly with other words after her triumphal *was*. "Paris, this best garden of the world . . ."

"Shakespeare, only he said it about France. But Gérard de Nerval —I think it was—said about Paris that she's the paradise of misery and the capital of hope." Combining and misquoting two writers in thirty seconds, impressing her with his epigram and his memory and his pronunciation of de Nerval's name, Gran was impressed himself by his eagerness to delight her, that is, to make himself pleasing. It takes a light and sure foot to gain ground in this slippery contest. Outside the leaded windows with their rich tinting—drinks ran a good twenty cents more in a bar of such chic—the autumn weather was heavy and one Heights bus after another roared home with late shoppers up the hill to the suburb.

"What's Cleveland the capital and the paradise of?" Carol demanded. "White Motors and Glidden paints, that's what. I used to think I couldn't bear it another week."

"And you had to bear it all by yourself, Carol?"

"Sh! Stop teasing. Of course, Gran, now I'm growing up, I'm patient to get what I want."

Paying and signaling without saying it that his wife really would expect him now, Granley Hattan asked himself if Carol meant to tell him that he was her patience and what she now wanted. You could never know for sure about this girl. She always refused to meet him on campus; she only once refused their late afternoon meetings at the library. He never said anything except "See you here tomorrow?"— too proud to come off his age and tell her about his desire, just the desire to see her, to watch her toss the scarf about her throat while he took his pleasure in her high brightness, that subtle and gaudy play of first youth against the elemental needs of love and knowledge and power over others. Was it really any better to come to desire power over things, over self?

Finally it was she who admitted, "Meeting you saved my life, Gran. I don't even fight with Dad anymore. I even forgive him for making me dorm at home and take my B.A. at Reserve."

"I like you, too, Carol."

"You mean something to me, Gran. I really mean it."

He took to carrying his wedding band in his pocket when he met her. Once she caught him slipping it off before touching her hand, and her freshet of laughter poured over him in a fine light shower.

He smiled.

She understood and did not judge him. Growing up to his needs as she felt sure of her own, she even liked him for it. He asked if she had ever seen the old Slavic settlement down in the Flats near the Cuyahoga River—onion-domed churches and clapboard houses with vines for their age and good places for the usual coffee together.

No, she did not know it. Was it nice? Picturesque? Could it interest even a traveled man like him?

Yes, they would walk there someday, soon, late this week, maybe. Even if he could not walk Paris with her, he could show her the first place where Cleveland was settled, those cobbled and winding streets where every other shop is a shoe-repair and each drugstore an *apteka*.

In the meantime, in no hurry for anything, all patience, Gran would talk with her about literature, the world, himself. He had long ago formed the habit of walking at night; past the image of himself as a poet (or so many poets), his long walks now enabled him to plan his classes in peace and get the regular exercise which preserved his leanness of belly and agility of step. Often Helen was asleep by the time he returned.

Carol Dent met him under a streetlamp three nights later. That it really happened made it almost as good as a novel. Of course, he had spoken of his custom. She laughed and caught his hand. "I've been looking for you over five blocks," she said. "Which way do you usually go?"

"Varies." He took her arm across the street—the long scarf draped over his guiding hand—and did not let her go, because she had added:

"I wanted to talk some more. Forgive me! Am I disturbing you? You know so many things I want to know. Dad doesn't know what to make of me lately, says I'm getting so *cooperative*"—and a little wry face.

Her frank pleasure flattered him, yet made him uneasy. If she worried about how he felt about her—if she saw him at all—wouldn't she need to be more cautious, reserved? Wasn't that the economy of the suburban girls? The investment of stay-away-closer, the capital gain of come-to-get-me-for-I-do-not-care? She dared to care; she dared to admit it. So sure of herself, she saw no risks at all. Dangerous, dangerous. How did she manage?

What if he were to show impatience with her? He knew she was a child; she knew he knew. Very dangerous.

Gran Hattan was confused by so much irregular honesty in a lovely and pretentious child. She had no investment, it seemed; she liked being with him; that was all. What was the status of his own increasing investment in her? Where then was his protection?

But these doubts were not scruples and scruples would be a poor shield against the pure delight of her presence. He could not turn away from this sweet brashness. It was a lucky prize; luck is part of the well-planned life. Even her bracelets made a soft jingling in the warm after-rain autumn evening. He would give her a little silver bracelet. Why not give freely? It was time to let down the guards.

This time, admitting nothing but easy companionship through wet autumn leaves, under wet autumn branches, while they touched and jumped away in the hazards of walking at night down a dark suburban street, the skittish brush of arm and arm, shoulder and shoulder, leg and sometimes leg under raincoat, served their long silences most garrulously. In full flood of desire, Gran labored against the tormented tenderness of his overwise blood. Electric it was! Her scheming innocence a blessing! They pulled away. They both liked scenery.

4

The day they walked in the Flats, far from the university and far from the suburb, he took the role of guide ("St. Aloysius it's for. Quite Byzantine, isn't it? Those towers like tumors, aren't they?") and shut up finally when she did not answer and then abruptly, without pretending anything at all, he put his arm hard around her waist and let his fingers spread and luxuriate. They did not break step. It was a harsh dry day of early winter, the sun flashing over slate roofs and hot icy blue through the blue air over the industrial valley just below them. Thin streams of crystalline smoke arose straight into the sky. For answer to him, she let her body's rhythm speak, hard-soft and soft-hard, her hip moving against his, her cropped head leaning for a moment against his shoulder. No, no, at the moment he seized her like that, her hand fluttered against the small of his back, then fell.

They walked in silence, looking for a place.

The thought of his wife came to Gran Hattan only with relish. Helen would not wonder why he was late. He had managed well. She was off with their one docile child to pay a visit to the wife of the chairman of the department (three pampered children and a fourth on the way). Nevertheless, something about the sunny winter day and the abrasive midcity air put him out of time again as they walked and looked, and his breathing, frozen and excited, was almost a retrospective pleasure—a pain of desire, a dry pang of memory. The frank taking of Carol's hand had been a similar shock. How could a married man of thirty go so silly over the knuckles of a college senior? Did his boredom with Helen and his job require exactly this revenge—a warm, small, submitting hand that squeezed and then lay at rest? Yes, it was a pleasure to admit it, his grand discontents of Cleveland could be assuaged by a child who wanted to know all about Paris. He had talked to her, then, about how Hart Crane was influenced by the Symbolists and when he first came to Cleveland he had looked up Crane's friends, an old man in a bookstore, a retired high school teacher, a fairy cook—

She did not blink, of course.

"A fairy cook who went to Akron with him. They even wrote a poem together. Now this guy is a fat, bald old codger in a businessman's restaurant on Prospect Avenue—wears perfume even in the kitchen . . ."

"Will you read Hart Crane to me?" she had asked. "I know it's not done anymore, but I bet you read beautifully."

Permit me voyage, love, into your hands . . . He had let go of her hand because he was confused. Even then he had rehearsed his vengeful fantasies. Helen had it coming! No right to worry, fret, take it out on spoiling the kid! He was still a young man. Exactly ten years older than Carol. At her twenty-five he would be the same man—thirty-five. At thirty, forty—caught up and identical. Every woman always ten years ahead of any man? They know what they want.

He would take her back to Paris (back, Rodin's bellying Balzac at the Carrefour Vavin!), get a fellowship, settle the couple of thousand he had on his wife and the boy. He had a novel in him, too, why not? What about all the great men who deserted their wives, and sometimes with the kids in double bunks? (But what about their one son? And what if the novel were no good? And with her parents or somewhere in a too-small-flat—that Helen who had taken the prix fixe with him on the Rue Hautefeuille when she wore her hair long and clipped behind until the sixth month of pregnancy and then had it cut for three hundred francs. What about it? Well, Helen was a great one for neatness.)

All the time he had been thinking these thoughts, just from taking and relinquishing Carol's hand, they had been walking; and now a few days past his memory they were walking again, this time his arm tight around her and the same thoughts; and now he had made a small progress, a triumph of the neatness required, a jolliness of relief just because Helen was safe and busy with Mrs. Professor Chairman Durand until the kid's bedtime.

The sun was white, descending. Then, at the horizon above the factories, it performed for them: Suddenly a winter rose and the dry clouds set afire! Away with Helen, a citation for Carol: *Let us walk through time with equal pride* . . . Harold Hart Crane of Crane Chocolates was a local boy, too, although it's more complicated when a poet likes girls.

"Gran?" They had found their way around the steel-gray Russian Orthodox church, back behind the winter-closed pikes of the garden, in the wind-shuttered shadow of the turrets and domes, here just above the industrial valley and the rubbled river and just below the ramps of commercial Cleveland's great bridges, the sun lacking warmth in December but lovely, lovely—"Gran? Gran?"

Now he kissed her; now they met and made vain walking steps against each other; hot and busy-fleshed, they moved under their coats. They played out of time deep within the body's deep hungers.

Jeez, we were necking each other standing up like kids, he remembered later.

5

Driving primly back to the proper Heights, they watched the road. A signal turned green, but a stalled car blocked them. Carol looked out the window, remarking, "Last days for Christmas shopping already. It wasn't even Thanksgiving when you met me."

"You met me, too. Does it seem so long that you have to remark about it? A month almost."

"What are you so chilly about all of a sudden?"

"Nothing, Carol, I'm sorry. I'm crowded. This kind of driving makes me irritable."

She waited while he honked and they were moving in the thick passage again, then said: "Gran, would you like to see me some evening?"

"Yes."

"When?"

"I don't know how I can."

This small creature, hot and crafty and surely untouched, had it all figured out. "Tell your wife you have a meeting, papers to grade, late work in the library." She wrinkled her nose and shrugged. "You're doing an essay on Hart Crane and the Symbolists for the *Romance Languages Quarterly*. Figure it out. Do I really have to tell you how, Gran?"

Could there be another girl like her?—this cool brashness, this hot certainty, this virginal purity of intention in a girl who had bit his lower lip unnecessarily, a too-hard, overambitious, biting first kiss for him, just because she had studied up by reading Van der Velde or other deep thinkers on how to win lovers to be crazy about a person and influence their passion. Although she probably planned all day to give him a broken lower lip as a souvenir, he liked and licked it and took the salty taste with pleasure. A cold sore or bumped it, he would tell Helen.

"Where?" she asked, still counting the Christmas shoppers.

It was flattering and yet disquieting to be so obviously nominated and so quickly used. How young she was! Their evening walks and their bar and their visit to the Flats had no resonance of the past for her—how could they? They were pure potentiality, a thrust into the future; the first time for new love may be eager and happy, but it is dominated by the desire to move on. Innocent buds of teeth experienced in biting! What for Carol Dent was the first deep waking —as much as she could yet awaken—was for Granley Hattan an aching reminder of the long early play of love in many towns. Satisfactions recalled, dissatisfactions recalled complacently, what difference? Carol, however, admitted no memory at all.

"Where?" she insisted.

He thought he knew a place, yes.

"When?"

He told her that he could figure that one out, too.

"Is your wife the suspicious type?"

Gran felt tolerant of this quick bright red-scarved creature's playing her wickedness with such sweet, keen, and joyous directness. He suggested that she need not bother herself with worries about his wife, who used to be an artist herself, sort of, and did some very good painting for a student and did not ever nag or bother him like many wives.

"Helen was that?" Carol asked, using the first name deliberately, her bright gaze winking toward him, fingerpads touching at the eyes with their new fawn-lines in black pencil at the corners.

6

Jitters, itchings, headaches, dizziness, faintness, all those boyish pimples and twitters had reawakened in Gran Hattan. Dark jealousies, light-headedness, angers and switchings of his voice mid-sentence, mid-word—Hattan's unexpected yea-saying to another for what he had set in motion for himself, for pure self-love, brought a pitching fleck of terror to his eye when he looked at her. Carol turned up her lips for smiling and lowered her eyes.

Had he really begun this himself? Were will and self-willing ever enough? Would not the will to love overthrow even irony? He woke once strangling with excitement at the thought, *Today, today* . . . And it only meant they had set an hour to stroll in the garden behind the old monkey house in Rockefeller Park. If the adventure could no longer end with ennui or any other French word, how could it ever be ended?

Was it possible at last that *this* was love?

All his dreading body asked a no, no, no, and the hurt of it did not grant him retreat. Pleasure is awful. Sweetness is dangerous, the bittersweet most threatening. He had forgotten what a girl is! Complication, trouble, divided gaze, and washing with strong soap to be sure his wife did not sniff out Carol's scent on his shoulders and hands —poor Helen.

It would help to arrange a sharp quarrel with Helen and lump all his discontentments in one ripe justificatory gesture. Funny, although he had planned for it, that the quarrel was unexpected when it came. As always, their neat little, clean little, precious little suburban flat exasperated him. Leaving the murmurous early evening of winter for the cold gleam of all those modern lamps—cones on pulleys, aluminum reflectors, three-way bulbs in many cute disguises—he felt like another bleached modern gimcrack among the foam-rubber furniture, the driftwood pinned against a fireplace blocked with red plywood, the Lautrec *affiche* (not Dufy at least!) and the *original* Matisse etching, drawn by the Hand itself (one of twenty-four in the series, then the zinc destroyed)—extravagant anniversary gifts from his loving wife, yrs., Helen.

She had moved her own paintings into the hall, first, and finally into the attic. He had not noticed until weeks later, but who looks at the frames in a hall? She had given him that large mouth of pain for days until he noticed, refusing to tell him the matter, and then refusing even to let him move the paintings back down (she had studied with Hans Hofmann and at the Léger school in Paris).

On the dark afternoons of late classes, Bud customarily stayed up to have dinner with him. Arriving home tired, Gran found Helen frowning and hot, the house overheated, the boy in bed with a mound of toys heaped about him.

"What's up?"

"There's a measles epidemic going around. I think he's getting it."

"Any spots?"

"No."

"Does he have a fever?"

"Not yet."

"Then what's the matter?"

"I don't know, he's been so irritable. I wanted to get him off his feet. Spock says the complications—"

"Daddy! Daddy!" the excited voice piped thinly. "Mommy says I'm sick! I had soft-boiled eggs! Come and play with me!"

Without saying anything more to Helen, Gran put the thermostat back at seventy degrees, peeled off his clothes to the tee shirt, splashed cold water on his face and neck—the windows were all in steam, the house was a hotbox—and went to sit like a doctor on the edge of Bud's bed. The kid babbled away at him about all the recent exciting events, thermometer inserted so queerly, intensified attentions, consultations by home medical guide and telephone. Gran felt his wrist and forehead. The eyes had a hot sparkle, but they were clear, and the pleasure and the grin (my own mouth, Gran thought) were nothing abnormal in an excited child. "I'm sick, Daddy, I'm gonna have quarantine!"

The kid was not sick, no matter how many goddamn measles freckled out in the neighborhood. Gran felt deeply convinced of his diagnosis: too much mothering, overdose of fret and fuss. It would give any child spots of red in the cheek and a suspicion of fever. "Member how I had a cold and drank ginger ale, Daddy? That was when it rained all day."

Yes, and July is when Mother is convinced that you have polio, darling.

And fall is the time of burning leaves and an acrid beauty to the industrial skies and Buddy has possible vitamin deficiency, Mother thinks.

And winter is the time of struggling over the thermostat and penicillin for head colds and one fidget after another.

They waited until the kid finally fell asleep. Helen would deserve what she would get. She could pull her mouth down and let it spread with reluctance to answer him, but this would not stop him. He knew her well! "You're going to make him a hypochondriac! We're raising a goddamn sissy! Wait till he's sick before you jump!"

"*You* don't have to take care of him. You don't care. Measles can affect the eyes—"

"But I tell you he doesn't have it yet."

"You wouldn't care if he did."

"You *want* him to be sick, you want to make him need you more—"

She looked at him full, her tired, pretty thirty-year-old face flaming: "Maybe you're right! I read those books, too, before I became a housewife. Dust, clean, cook, but don't touch your papers! What an existence! Maybe I need a husband in addition to a son—"

"*You* need? What about me?"

"Oh, what's the use, Gran? You'll never learn."

Of course, when there's learning to be done, it has to begin on both sides, and maybe it was time to admit the fact of Too-Late. You have to exchange needs; you have to have a will for it. Gran admitted (yes, why not?) that he had withdrawn the will. They defined their rancor to each other hopelessly, helplessly, rehearsing the old lines, with Helen strangely cold and adamant and Gran finally the one to break into tears of rage although, yes, he had predicted, planned, and even desired this quarrel. He was a moral man: The quarrel gave him rights while his rage kept its purity. It was best to hate Helen's tall grace. Young matron! Handsomest wife in the department! Tea, somebody?

"All right, Gran, I'm sorry, you're sorry, let's go to bed or something. I made your supper . . . I suppose you don't want it now . . ."

It was silly of him to show tears; it was not required, although it added to his rights to himself. He gave himself no added credit, however, because he was thinking of the way Helen used to be (a great walker with him in the market of the Rue Mouffetard) and that was fine but probably not so fine (who can remember for sure?) as Carol would be even at her age. And Carol's gaucheries meant nothing because Carol would learn to be smart and better than Helen and smartness isn't everything—look at Helen! It didn't help her to have a master's and to have thought seriously of a career in art history or advertising or maybe doing books for children. No, he granted that he deserved very little extra credit for those tears before Helen. Many times he felt worse but did not cry. Nevertheless, the tears produced their pain even in him, and he said what seemed to stand most for that pain: "You're ruining my son."

She turned away, large-mouthed and sick, shoulders drooping, the housedress damp under the arms. "My son, your son, *our* son. Oh, never mind, Gran. Stop it now. You'll wake the kid. I'm sorry you feel bad. Please, I'm sorry we're not good to each other anymore. Would you like something to eat?"

No matter, no matter. He had put down his deposit; she would pay. He went about switching off the lamps because the light hurt his smarting eyes, and then submitted to supper while Helen, her hands folded in her lap, sat silently watching him try to eat.

7

The obliging hotel near University Circle had a chic dark bar for first and an opulent stillness for later, mirrors with black hangings in festive mourning, music discreetly from nowhere. Gran assured Carol, only because she asked, that he had arranged things. Things had been arranged by him in the most fantastically simple way: He told Helen that he was going out and would be out late. They were numb to each other. Maybe she simply took it as an extension of his walking habit. No matter for Helen now.

Carol met him in the bar, dressed up in dancing clothes and her subdued excitement signaling to him in every rich movement—older, yes, womanly, walking toward him now, possessed and possessing by the slip of hips, that great eternal female clamor! She seemed to have revised even her inner self-portrait: from sweet gamine with scarf to sleek lady with pumps and hat. Courtly, calm, Gran rose to greet her, biding his pang of regret for the red sneakers and the scarf and the velvet slacks of their first meeting, and the volume of Verlaine with every line penciled into English, plus critical notes in the margin:

Et on donne à Lui

And one gives to Him (Capitalized, must be God???)

But of course, like any vital creature, she could not spend her brightest flashing in the reading of French poetry. And she could not display in a hotel bar the pert, small-wristed, small-footed, dancing-after-life gaiety which was uniquely hers and could perhaps be his. She looked at his finger with a turned-up smile. The ring was in his pocket. Please don't do your Vivien Leigh cheek at me, he wished to her. I want you just to be Carol tonight, the girl I met.

"Please," he said aloud.

"Please what?"

"Please stop smiling and say something."

"Isn't that up to you, Gran?" And in a low voice for her new clothes, hat, and heels: "I'm happy, that's all. I'm glad to be here."

Better.

"You know, Carol, I was afraid maybe you couldn't come."

"I said I would, didn't I?" She pouted and pulled her hand away. "Never *couldn't*—I just decided, that's all. Never a question of couldn't with me."

"You're beautiful. You're prettier than Vivien Leigh."

Or was it Audrey Hepburn that she was supposed to be prettier than? No, stop that.

"Smell me, I wore the Lanvin you gave me—"

"Later, Carol." And he was thinking, not of her perfume, but of the tricks and straps of a dressed-up woman, so much loveliness in so much machinery, the flesh breathing, slippery, scented warmly deep within the frills and the lace and the elastic.

"Mind wandering? Penny? You like me in a hat?" She glanced at the card on the table: TRY OUR MANHATTANS. THEY'RE MADE BY THEODORE. "I want one," she said. "I got all dressed up so they'll serve me and not—"

She blushed. They had the drink. Then they strolled to the elevator together and rose to the top floor.

Sometimes things are as they should be! Carol was very happy, showered, fragrant, pleased. Therefore Gran was happy. She learned with athletic ease and delight. Therefore Gran was content. She frisked and played and was loving in a way which seemed almost abstract in its lack of complication—perhaps only because new, perhaps only because mystified at the miracle of flesh within her rigorous embracing of novelty. Blessed by the hot immediacy of her small, pointy, unused, and eager body, Gran nevertheless wondered at this abstraction.

Well, therefore something left to explore, he decided later, drowsy and pleased and thinking: Painless? So simple? Well, surely some deeper reticence. Therefore lovely, therefore fine in health, therefore —O *Carol*! He put his lips near her cheek on the pillow.

"Gran?"

She would not let him dream of her even now stretched cooling at his side. She propped herself on one elbow. "Gran, I have to tell you something."

"What?"

"Listen, there's big news in my life, Gran."

He was shocked full awake at once, and with a watchful irony. "There is?"

"I'm going to Europe! That's it. I saved it to tell you now. I knew you'd be so happy for me. Paris! It's my graduation present."

"If you want to talk," he replied dryly, "then let's get up."

The moment of silent modesty while she bent and unfolded her things (he had not noticed how carefully she had thought to fold) and then dressed, this odd, shy, empty moment was over before she had finished straightening the seam in her stockings. "Gran, I'm so excited," she said. "I've been wanting to tell you for days, but I thought I'd save it for—" And incredibly, at *this* moment she flushed. "—Saved it for now," she said. Was it a blush because she had kept a secret from him? "Oh, I'll miss you so," she added, wriggling her toes into the shoes and turning her foot to look at the heel.

"That's all right, Carol, I can give you some addresses."

"Would you? Darling! Some good cheap restaurants? Some friends?"

He sat at the desk and took a sheet of hotel stationery and could not write. His hand was shaking. She watched him with a fixed, self-regarding smile, the eager complacency of the dedicated art and artist collector. He was part of the preparation for the voyage. Typhoid injections, smallpox, triple tetanus, and this. A hotel room for practice.

"Of course, the Left Bank has probably—the *rive gauche*—changed since your day."

"Practically nothing but a memory," he said. "That happened in history when Gide was still alive. 1950. You were at Shaker High."

Her desire to talk was unquenchable. She had guarded her secret for him, well, this was a tribute of a sort. She applied her lipstick before the closet mirror. "You're teasing, I know! I was a senior then. And you of all people *know* I'm not a baby anymore"—and then came to slip beside him on the short bench before the desk. They faced each other in the glass over a hotel print, "Hunters in the Snow near Erie," and spoke into their doubled, dusty images—this bright slim creature, this rumpled and tired young man:

"I wanted to tell you all now, Gran. Surprised? Daddy's giving me the trip for my marks in French, thanks to you, kind sir!"

He had drilled her privately on her irregular verbs, was that it?

"You're such an *incentive*, an *example*, Gran darling. Don't be sad. I'll write to you. If I were a man, I would want to be just like you, so tall and lean and sensitive. I'll never forget you for ages and ages."

Is this the note of admiration to strike as one rises from bed beside that incentive?

"Of course, I do have advantages as a girl. I suppose I'll meet somebody and get married in Paris—a young poet maybe, who knows? Do you think I'm pretty enough? Do you think it's silly to think so far in the future? Did you meet Helen in Paris?"

"Yes."

"Do you think I'm pretty enough?"

"Ravishing," he said. "No, I guess everyone thinks ahead. You're ravishing, plus cute as a button."

Pouting, she mittened at his hand and peered into his face in the glass. "That started out like such a compliment, Gran, that ravishing. But I don't *want* to be cute as a button. Isn't that a cliché? Mom was cute as a button, and cute as a button only married a lawyer."

"Don't worry, you'll be a success in Paris." Gran was beginning to be pleased with himself. He was amused now, in another way from the way he had thought to be amused, that was true; but pleased and amused all the same by this busy Carol. He felt wide-awake and somewhat drunk, as if it were the last quick walk home in the snow after a late party. She's not a monster, he thought, she's only the new bright suburban girl thrilled by her adventure. She'll come back from Paris and marry an editor, or maybe be one, and pluck out the clichés for pay. She loves life and art, that's all. It only seems monstrous.

"Carol, I'll tell you what I'm going to do. I'll give you some people to look up. Some great friends."

She was really ready with pencil and notebook from her purse, the same notebook which she had used in the library to copy from *The Last Time I Saw Paris*. This was too good! She had brought the notebook with her! With deliberate hesitation in response to her impatience (afraid he'd change his mind? an attack of prudence about gossip somehow finding its way from the Fourteenth Arrondissement to Cleveland Heights, Postal Zone 6?), he wrote from memory, *Philippe . . . Michel . . . Stanley . . .*

She watched, her lips spelling with him. Then: "Who's he? Who's he?" She listened, and at last she let go the words which put his despair upon him, gave him what he knew he deserved (but afterward aren't all animals sad?) and must finally have brought the weather change to his face in a way which communicated itself even to her:

"Philippe who? Stanley who? What does he do? They were all your friends back in 1950? You don't think they're too old now, do you?" She clapped her small hand to her mouth. She turned from the glass and twisted to him on the bench. "Oh! Gran, how can you *look* like that? Don't *take* an innocent question like that. I didn't mean that about you, old. I just meant they're probably busy, attached, married and settled already, *you* know. Don't take it like that, Gran. Don't you *stare*. They will probably all be just *marvelous* contacts."

He remembered his responsibility and stopped staring. When he finished the little list of contacts, he had satisfied her. The bar was closed already, so they could not have another drink. She linked her arm in his and told him not to be like ice. He drove her home carefully over the January slick. He had been generous with all he could give.

Then he went back to see if his son's irritability meant that he finally was coming down with something. There were infections in the neighborhood, but the resistance had to be low first for a fever to take hold.

No, he decided at his own door, there was another precious gift which Carol had taken from him. His responsibility to her and to this gift for her had gotten him over the moment near tears when he had so stared and stared. There is that matter of nostalgia for the past which, more and more, the hard and arty person will come to need.

LOVE AND LIKE

1

He got to Cleveland rather late, telephoned his wife from the termi-
nal, and asked if he could see their children early the next morning.
She seemed easy and friendly and said sure thing, of course, why not?
He sighed when they hung up and he stared at the telephone. Maybe
his absence really could work to level things between them.

Why not? as she said. They had loved each other for ten years, or,
rather, for a part of those ten years impossible now to calculate. He
remained sitting in the telephone booth. He was a young man with
a thin, almost boyish body and a large head, heavily muscled at the
jaw. On his face he wore the haunted, eaten look of a man whose
accomplice has betrayed him. Whether his accomplice was his former
wife or his conscience was not yet clear to him. Conscience was still
talking to his wife: We didn't make it, kid! And he was remembering
one of their last quarrels before they gave up, when he said, "We'll

try! We'll try!" And paining badly with those fragments of the past, he heard again her quiet reviving words: "We'll try, darling."

If they had finally made out, it would all have been remembered as the progress and process of love; with failure it could seem all bad; he was determined to hold in retrospect to a mixed verdict—some pretty, some unpretty, and nevertheless the long Sunday afternoon habit of lovemaking spoke for a true intimacy. The hardest, most essential responsibility to a dead marriage is to preserve the ripe strength it once had. Must have had, must have! So without love now, if that's the way it was, why couldn't they simply like each other for the rest of time? Not just for the sake of the children. For the sake of themselves and what they had become through their marriage.

All this was a resolution. Done.

Then he fished for another dime in his pocket and called Sally. Okay, it was late, but wasn't she glad to hear his voice? She laughed sleepily and asked him how he could doubt it. She was sleepy was all. She had been thinking of him. All right then, dreaming. He could come right up—would it take twenty minutes? For splashing some cold water and getting good and waked and dressed.

"Don't bother," he said, and even in the telephone booth, under the falsification of wires and electricity, the laughter brought her back to him with all her soft, warm, childlike sleepiness amid the fragrant bedclothes. Sally's face was devoted to laughter, especially the very blue, waiting-to-smile eyes—those eyes of a blue which could give him what a strong awakening on a morning in the country give, courage and appetite and great belief in the future. The morning he left, she had made breakfast for him, hotcakes with butter, sweet syrup, three kinds of jam—mostly he remembered the sweetness and much melted butter. With his mouth stuffed, he shook his finger to warn her that he had something to say as soon as he could swallow.

"What's the matter, darling?"

"Oh, it's good! It's so good, Sally!"

And the lashes fell over the brave summersky eyes. She was timid despite her laughter's deep abandon. "Then why do you have to leave Cleveland?" she had asked. The question cost her heavily. Without me? her paleness said. The unsmiling blue eyes were trying to force his reply: Then why don't we. . . ?

Unspoken questions were, as always, the ones he felt he had to answer and precisely could not. Therefore he had spoken in a tone of stubborn exasperation. "Because my wife lives here. Because it's too soon. Because I have to." He reached across the debris of eating to touch her more gently. If he could tell her, he would. "Now, with you here, Sally, it's all right. Right now. But I can't tell you about my wife and what she did to me. What she does! What she still does!" he cried out abruptly. His heart was pounding and the good of the breakfast was gone. "And the children—I still can't imagine any other life than being their father—"

She was looking at his hand on hers with a curious withdrawn attention.

He said quietly, "Maybe I just haven't found the way to love them without loving their mother. Maybe that's it and there is a way."

His wife made him need Sally; if only she could free him entirely for Sally! This way, entangling him in her wrath, she hardly let him know who Sally was. He had to find her in a long history in which she had no part, past a furious, gyring woman, after outrage and love gripping each other as do alloyed metals under heat and pressure. Let Sally make him pure—as he never was—let Sally make herself felt!

But her eyes were answering nothing, were asking him: And why can't we? He realized that she had not heard him at all. Everyone is sometimes made deaf by intentions. He might as well have been brutal: And I just don't know about you, either, dollface. Seems as how I met you someplace before.

Now he shrugged and felt the damp shirt moving on his back. Every time he said the word *wife* she should interrupt and say, "Former wife." Shaper to Shaper—*over*, he decided, ferociously willing it as if he were passing a message by radio and the battlefield made communication difficult: *Over!* He had just finished writing a technical manual on the care and operation of a new, improved long-range walkie-talkie. In Cleveland he had worked for General Electric on instructions for the installation of intercoms in language any mechanic could understand; in the identical off-white New York office to which he had arranged a transfer, under the same Armstrong Cork soundproofing, with thousands of little holes conking, stunning every whisper of distraction, he had labored with a Signal Corps semantics expert on further explanations of how to keep contact open under conditions of stress. "Limited contact under conditions of vital stress

. . ." He was making mass poetry for five-stripe sergeants who don't like the word *war*. It was a career for a careful explainer. But now over to Dan Shaper, please!

Deciding: Condition of stress not total chaos if receiver flashes emergency transistor filters out static toward coded meaning (see Fig. 3). Put into heart's English. Also see resources of regret, hope, and desire for possible decoding toward good conscience.

2

At seven-thirty the next morning he was running up the stairway toward his daughters. The buzzer had admitted him; the door to the upstairs flat was open.

"Paula, honey!"

"Hello, Daddy. Mommy and Cynthia are still sleeping. I knew you were coming. I got up and took my own breakfast. Wheaties and prunes and a pickle. Mommy says I can eat what's on the bottom shelf of the fridge and that's where the pickle was. Hello, Daddy."

Exactly what he wanted always, this time Paula was a six-year old lady sitting on the couch. First she rang the buzzer to let him in, then she returned shyly to her place to wait for him.

"And I knew you would be coming back today because I counted the days," she said. "You said thirty. You promised." She was quivering with excitement beneath the formality with which she had vain hopes of hiding herself. A month is even longer in a child's life than in her father's. He took her in his arms and she said, "I'm *glad*." Her eyelashes were wet when he kissed them.

"I'm glad to see you too, honeybear."

They whispered together gravely to keep from waking the rest of the house. He felt strong in his monthlong convalescence. He forgot that he had slept only the sleep of the recently divorced, that is, no sleep but that profitless, dream-jammed one of might-have-been and exhaustion. Paula gave him her news. Not only had she lost a tooth, but also the ragged edge of the new, grown-up one had begun to appear. He looked and saw. At her command he appreciated it with his finger, too. They were interrupted by another child, running scared and barefoot to join the celebration, four-year-old Cynthia.

Disappointed, Paula bravely permitted Cynthia to catch up with a minute of greeting.

Then he pulled them both onto the couch beside him, still bed-warm in their summer pajamas, and so were they three sitting when his wife came out. She had heard them, stayed a long time in the bathroom, and emerged only after satisfying herself that she was sweet and alert and nice to look at. He was very much aware also of how he looked to her with the two little ones wriggling close to him.

She smiled and said, "Hello, Dan." Her hair had been cut in a new fashion and fluffed out to make a soft frame for the delicate bones of her face. Her brow, finely marked by frown lines, seemed wider now, peacefully expectant. What happens to a young woman when she divorces? Aren't her eyes puffy in the morning anymore? Where does the blue lymph go? Is she no longer stringy and dismayed after the first glimpse of herself in the bathroom mirror? Not this one. Dark, slender, and cool, she was mobilized for love again.

Shaper was pleased by her greeting and—with only a twinge of self-judging jealousy—by her appearance. He put it down to his credit that she was not ruined for the hope of love. His moving out of town had done them both good. Sally last night had started the visit auspiciously. Paula was a marvel and Cynthia a wonder. And now his wife was the decent human being he had almost always believed in.

"Yes, thanks," he said, and they all four had breakfast together, just like a family. Since the first years of their marriage, his wife had barely eaten in the morning, drinking black coffee and nibbling at dry toast and then rushing to the scales, but today she took an extra piece of toast and covered it with butter in order to show him that she could now enjoy food. Well, let her have that pleasure, he thought with a fine, expansive sense of tolerance. They both watched the girls munching greedily, proving something to their parents.

Later, while the children played with their new toys, they sat together in the front room and talked, balancing coffee cups on their knees. "It's all right now," she said. "You did right to go away for a while. There were good things, weren't there, Dan?"

"I'm glad you remember."

"I do. I do." Her narrow face with its wide brow wore a complex expression—frowning, tender, at peace. They had shared and not shared. They had been satisfied, unsatisfied. She had wanted, they had both wanted another child; but (stiff white mouth and tense, silent staring out the window) she had needed a guarantee that this time it would be a boy. She had found a doctor in Miami with fantastic notions about special diets, the power of raisins and lima beans and times of the month—litmus paper, fever charts, count the days—and a husband to be applied as an agent when the alchemical and astrological signs say yes. Desperate woman! Yet a man can grow to accept a partial madness when it is the condition of the rational universe he desires. Desperate husband! (Aren't many people superstitious? When she has her son, what difference by what illusion she was comforted?) But one day he faces the obvious question: All right, there's a fifty-fifty chance, say. And if it's not a boy? Kachoo—sneezing with boredom and despair.

And if it's *not* a boy?

As always, his besetting flaw was the one of perverse hope and pride —the crazy patience of the man who needs love too much to take the necessary risk of losing it. When this danger is not challenged, love and like both are doomed. He had feared to compel his wife to follow his lead. He would not submit to being dragged along by her frantic jittering after happiness; she could not follow his bone-tired, patience-ended assertions of will; for them it had long been too late for all but knowledge, and perhaps in love it is always too late for that. The terrible guilt which he carried with him was a hope, not an understanding: Once she might have been made to want what you want, if you had pressed hard enough, and if you had said in time, No, not that way! Follow me and come to yourself!

The enduring of wrong amounts to an acquiescence in evil, a sin of active malignance which grew on the body of their marriage like a tumor and, like a tumor, sapped its strength to proliferate in this cruel organism, divorce. When the body is dead and all health irrelevant, only then will the cancer cease. In the meantime, every joy, every lively nerve, every vein of health must supply food for the fibrillar parasite. The dying creature curses its strong heart, its tuned body, because these prolong the agony. Each motive for happiness must be bled dry.

Shaper knew that he had not acted in time.

But finally he had said *no*.

NO!

Said no to lima beans and love by astrological suggestion—and maybe, kid, you're right about wanting to see Dr. Kasdan, he's supposed to be a good one—although he believed in that cure almost as little as he believed in the efficacy of lima beans to induce suckling boy babies instead of beautiful but incomplete girls.

A nightmare. Yet this was the intelligent, accomplished woman who could charm a stick into life. Seething and plausible. She took a cigarette from the box on the record cabinet, very sure of herself, very much the fresh young divorcée, and said, "Dan, I thought about you while you were away. We both lost . . ."

"Yes, despite everything we've lost a great deal."

"We lost *control*," she said firmly.

He felt rebuked, but it did not touch his reviving humor. Often she was bad, but sometimes she was steady and knew the way. She was right! He longed to regain this old sense of his wife's rightness. He needed it to go on from where he was.

"I don't blame you any more about that . . . that," she said. "It was wrong of me to be so . . . so . . ."

This time he did not make the mistake of supplying her words. Perhaps she was testing him.

"So angry, nervous with you," she said. "*Judgmental*"—one of those damn labels again, he thought, but nodded encouragingly. Warily she went on with a speech that seemed almost rehearsed. He did not expect her to grant him a confession, but he thought maybe she was making it in her own way at last and that this could finally release both of them: I was jealous, and not merely jealous, also morbid and criminal and made furious by fantasies, until you had to give me justice for them because you too demanded someone totally committed to you, because jealousy itself is an infidelity which takes a wife from her husband. . . . But she said instead (and who would she be if she used his words? her own were good enough): "I think I've learned something. We each learned, so it wasn't so bad. We probably couldn't have married anyone else, or anyone better, so why blame each other?"

"Right! We won't anymore!"

She frowned and did not hear him. He felt her effort not to slip down and down into the despair which had driven him away. It had poisoned him—all that cleverness turned to making him out a monster—and it had poisoned her. Rage, like jealousy, is a fire which burns out the future: she apparently knew it, and the softness in her eyes, even this willed, desperate kindness at the door to the furnace, restored her to him as he needed her to be restored. Then they could both go on to love again, not merely beyond hatred, but also strong in a practical, difficult friendship. Perhaps that was too much to ask, his version of her romanticism, but at least it was a principle worth striving for.

"We had some good reasons together," he said.

"What? Oh! Of course! I know, I remember, Dan. It wasn't just our psychological set, we really liked each other—"

He grinned wryly. "So it seemed at the time."

She did not admit a poor effort at humor in his enforced grip on the past. "That's the way you remember it and maybe that's partly how it was. I suppose. Anyway"—with great solemn effort for which he wanted to thank and thank and thank her—"whatever our motivations"—although he winced at the word—"we—yes—Dan—*we loved each other.*"

"Yes!"

And again she retreated. "But it was sick."

"Okay," he said.

And she folded her hands contentedly. "That's what I've learned."

Who's been teaching you now? he wanted to ask. He resisted successfully. He wanted her to understand about the passive faithlessness of the woman who expects her husband to be what he is not, what no man can be, who lies with him locked in her lonely dream of perfection, who sees her real marriage by the strange sunless radiance of a dream marriage which is unaltered by growth and event, by this particular day on earth or that one. Absolutist! Idealist! Romantic! These had been his epithets for her. And you can't make yourself into Eleanor of Aquitaine and me into a troubadour by nagging me for talking with a girl at a goddamn party! All right, so I didn't, didn't, *didn't* light your cigarette! So neither of our children was a boy!

He managed. He said nothing.

The admissions she had just made were an extravagant yielding. She felt loss, they meant; relief and giving up pain could help to teach her to praise life, and when she could bear the din of pleasure once more, she might even be grateful to him. Together they had exorcised childish ways—the lesson was nearly fatal; they had also learned and practiced love. Once free of each other, they could go on with this lifelong music.

But how stiff she still was!

Nevertheless, in her own way, calmly, gently, and much sweeter than his secretly unleashed judgment, with but a slight stiffness of the mouth, she went on. He was impressed by her rapid peacemaking, so soon after the tears and threats and furious thrashing. There was a deep, quiet note of loss despite the artificial speech. He listened: "It was inevitable. You were my mistake and I was yours. But neither of us is *bad,* and we could have married really bad people, real stinkers —so if we know it was inevitable . . . Dan," she concluded rapidly, with a flush, "I said things, did things. Now I'm sorry."

She was in misery. He wanted to comfort her. Then she straightened up with a strong glance of resolution and touched her hair. "I'm sorry," she said.

"I'm sorry, too, kid, for all I did wrong."

Apologies and pride and gratitude. Shaper felt a reviving flow of tenderness for her because she said *stinkers,* and maybe even thought stinkers, and not that cant of hers, *destructive personalities.* They sat very still, in a heated blush both of them, their shame almost a courting shyness, and they listened to their children splashing in the sink and laughing. An odd music for courting. The children were his laughter and hers; her body and his were met on the children as they had been entangled in each other. All this willed and anxious sweetness between them might finally give him Sally, give her whomever she wanted, and not merely send them raging after others. It could be the final creative act of their marriage—the two of them educated by their errors, not bound to them, freed for love and not greedily clutching at it. They would always have Paula and Cynthia together.

Once, on the day when their lawyers had first met, before this resilient stupor with which he shielded himself had settled in, he had cried out in this room, after they had both put the children to bed and he was facing her, ready to say good-bye, when he was at the door with all the unfinished business of their life meeting him in her huge, hot eyes: "We didn't make it, kid."

"We tried. We tried."

"We tried, honey."

And they had fallen into an adulterous passion, still unshaken in their will on divorce, the adultery made painfully sweet. He remembered it with shame, his eye suddenly prickling and aching, and saw himself again covering her with kisses, forcing her mouth open while her body bent backward, arched, received him. She had given herself without a word, moaning, and then he had fled like a thief.

Now he was merely quiet. The ache in his eye was an unheard sound, an unseen tremor of desire.

Still, they would always have the children together.

He felt the day's heat already sweeping in and looked about for the fan. In his reticence in this familiar and very unfamiliar house, his and not his, he obeyed the stricture she had once made in anger—don't touch anything, nothing is yours anymore! (Nothing but the children.) "Put your hands on me and I'll get an injunction," she had said the next day. It was her only reference to that strange, silent last lovemaking. "I'll slap a court order on you so fast it'll make you dizzy."

"Okay, kid, do you really think I want to touch you?" And that time his eye had not ached, not seemed invisibly swollen. It was the end. Almost comfortably he believed in playing out the rest of their career together without the danger of intimacy. Of course, he was wrong, but something of the comfort remained in his waiting, his planning, his cautious observance of the new rules of tact and courtesy. It was only the children he needed.

She had rearranged all the furniture, painted, covered, hid, and replaced, so that the house could begin anew. He recognized it as he recognized her, from a distance, from a long time, from a dream of voyages. She had planned it that way. Fastidiously he had been plucked out of her skin and the scars dusted over, so that she could say, *Who? Who?* She wanted him to notice how much he was not at home. How managerial and intelligent of her to begin briskly anew! With what a rush she had retreated from him!

He smiled at her. "You look very well, kid."

She turned and pressed her lips together tightly. In pain she had a large mouth—childbirth, bereavement—he had been there with her; anger was a small one which sent him away. By the resenting white line at the corners of her mouth, he recognized his wife, the one who had first wanted him for pride in what he did—others wanted him, he was not like the herd of college boys; then wanted him to do nothing that did not include her, that might make others covet him; and then when they were cozy in a common, including misery, rebuked and rebuked him for his failure to be her romantic ideal. O father she lost, O son I did not give her, how amply I was repaid for trying to replace you! What foolish pride that thought this abstract hungering of hers was desire for me! Impossible victories that I wanted!

Now thanks to that bloodless thin line and the stiff tremor of her response to his word for her, *kid,* he felt entirely at home. It was almost like the last years of their marriage again.

She reached for an envelope in her purse. "You forgot to pay my dental bill. It dates from before our settlement," she said with her marvelous cool telephone voice, "so of course, you are responsible. Dr. Jonas's secretary called me about it and I said you had probably forgot. I said I'd give it to you personally when you got back to town."

He took the paper, put it in his pocket, and called like a drowning man, "Paula! Cynthia! Let's go outside, would you like that?"

They came screaming with pleasure into the room and he believed that, yes, he could still keep his grip on the green feelings he had brought in from his month away.

3

He liked everyone, even his wife. Perhaps he loved no one but the children—he was so diminished by the belly-ripping, face-clawing final year of marriage—but he felt a reviving and undiscriminating benevolence toward the world. Plus desire for Sally, ah, that's important! It was recovery from an illness. When he returned to his hotel after leaving the children for their afternoon nap, his thoughts wheeled around to Sally, and they were embedded within a silly glow of sympathy for everyone, irrelevantly, from the desk clerk with sinus trouble to the Japanese at Hiroshima. Symptom of convalescence. "Key, please! Hot enough for you?"

He wanted to share this precarious perch on health. Sally had agreed to drive out to Chagrin Falls and go swimming with him. The first time he took a girl swimming was important to Shaper. It's a risk and rousing. You run the challenges of dirt, ants, and fatigue; he took chances on a cold noting of his skinny body in boxer trunks, the scatter of hair and the ropes of tendons and no strong rhythm of distraction. Enjoying the happy vanity of a lovely object, long used to triumphant waiting, Sally might have an eye for some tumbling beach athlete, not Dan Shaper with his glasses and his bony knees. Admire, admire me! her every movement had been saying to him for months. He had done it well. Was that a guarantee that she would love him?

No matter, he thought as he shaved in his hotel room; I don't want love now, I couldn't take it yet, what I need is just what Sally is giving me. Why worry about categories? He remembered that warning song: "Silkless silk and milkless milk! Love oh love oh loveless love. . . ."

Fully dressed, he lay on the bed, organizing himself to meet Sally, feet straight and toes up, watching the hand of the clock move down to two. These few minutes of rest were necessary, despite his driving heart, after a morning spent with his children, seeing in their faces the intermingling of his wife and himself, feeling her breath with his gesture when they talked, his forehead with her dark, thick-lashed eyes when they laughed. Their eyes when he rolled on the floor to play bus or airplane as they had during the easy evenings of their baby-hood (they remembered, they demanded it)—they wanted him to bathe them again, as he used to—and their mother's eyes, the tragic pouched eyes of the beauty unsuccessful in love. And then the solemn politeness all around when he turned them back to her.

One minute to two! Think of Sally—full-breasted and full-hipped, blond, frequently amused—how lucky to be all those things that his wife was not! And Sally had her own secret sources, too! He remembered the yearning of her response to his first, long-delayed kiss, when in the renewal of timidity, the return to boyishness brought on by the long illness of his marriage, he had quite simply been afraid. No, it took wisdom to be full and warm like that. Her hand on his back was deep art, her weight on his shoulder was Plato and . . . and . . . Sally, not Plato! No romantic ideal! She did it for herself and for him.

Lord, ten after two already. He must have dozed. He threw swim-shorts, towel, clean clothes into the blue Air France bag he usually carried for tennis. He took a taxi to Sally's apartment, where she was waiting for him at the entrance. She had no need to keep him waiting;

she didn't play that game anymore—she felt his need for her and forgot to protect herself. She said: "Darling! It's such a beautiful day for us!"

That was intelligence, wasn't it? Her own marriage had been a revolving door, in and out with practically no noise or loss of heat, but she probably knew more about it than he suspected. Surely she knew more than she would tell. And she had her own automobile, a blue Ford convertible, to which she just automatically handed him the keys—that too made her clever and deep. Like all American boys, he had dreamed of girls like her with their blond heads thrown back against the leather seats of cars like these. . . . That it was her automobile only gave the joke a turn. Once he got over the divorce, lawyers' fees, travel costs, the rest of it, he too would have the open car which his wife had always thought too dangerous, bad for a dry skin, impractical.

"Why didn't I think of picking you up at your hotel?" Sally asked.

"Never mind, just move over and sit close to me."

"Are you a one-arm driver?"

"Like to be."

"Then I'll put a knob on the wheel for you."

Wryly he submitted to his retreat toward college-boy pleasures— the blond, the convertible, the exaggerations of flesh in erotic gaming. Well, he would tolerate himself, he would come out of it. Let the submerged fantasies see the light, why not? Sally was there waiting, and more than merely *the blonde*. She was Sally. Her silent smiling said that she was with him part of the way at least.

And they teased and played while he drove under the hot August sun through a part of the city, a part of the suburbs, out to the private country lake he had chosen because neither of them had been there for years. They paid to enter. On a weekday like this, they had the short, clean beach almost to themselves. When they met on the beach after dressing, he submitted to a moment of shocked, almost unpleasant awe at her perfection of body under the blaze of sunlight. Beauty is pitiless. She turned under his brooding with a model's pouting half-smile, her eyes blank, self-regarding, retreated into vanity. This must have been an old girlish habit. He hated the thought of her searching him for flaws, as he was now doing to her; but he needed to be looked at with pride, too. The different male and female ways about bodies would protect him, no? And hadn't they already begun the long study of each other in the close and secret dark?

Different, different.

She was a marvel, and that they both knew it somehow widened the space closed by their first tentative lovemaking. A monument wants a pedestal.

Then she turned and ran, elbows pumping, toward the water. He caught her and they went in together. They laughed and spluttered, and she began swimming, and he caught her again. "Let's go out to the dock," she said. She swam poorly, splashing and puffing; he swam well and easily. Sally's wisdom! When he helped her up onto the outer dock, she was no longer a monument. She leaned on him, gasping a little and laughing. He kissed her shoulder with its gleaming, running beads of water. She nipped his hand with her bared teeth.

They lay a long while under the descending late-afternoon sun, stretching against each other, talking at intervals, listening to the few shrill voices back onshore. He spoke a little of his wife. He did not speak of the children. "Just smile," she said sleepily, her face close to the hot whitewashed boards. "I don't want you to worry about a thing."

He stopped worrying. He put his arm on her back and rubbed the strong articulations of her spine until his fingers ached. She smiled, saying, "More, more, more. Ah, that's nice."

She was very young, overproud of her body in the suburban way, just beginning to get past using it as a weapon instead of spending herself through the splendors of flesh. But she was learning, she was. Thank her for limitations. She was learning to spend herself freely, too. And with him.

At sunset they sat up to watch. She leaned on him to share the radiating warmth of her body. They approved of the sky. He missed not seeing the children this evening, but he needed Sally now; he would go to them again tomorrow. With a fine sense of no hurry, no hurry for anything, they waited until the sun was gone.

But the swim back to shore made them furious with hunger. She suggested buying Chinese food and eating it at her apartment. They drank a great deal of tea and nothing else. The sunburn began to show on her face and arms. She put a stack of records on the machine. They made love slowly, patiently. "Why are you smiling?" he asked her, and she replied: "Why are you smiling?" He explored a generous body with its slowly stirring languors and bold risings to the touch. She explored whatever he meant to her. "Why *are* you smiling, now tell me!" His hand had discovered, with the sense of regaining a fine lost memory, the crisp, crinkly, blond hairs of her secret places.

They gave up talking. They loved each other until they both felt as light and pure as driftwood, and then all tumbled together they slept.

4

Paula, who was six, said to her father, "Mommy says you don't love her anymore."

Her father, who was thirty-two, replied, "No, but I like her."

"But, but," said Cynthia, who was just four. "But can I go out and find Gary?"

"Why don't you stay with me for a little while?" her father asked. Dismayed by his querulousness, he repeated the remark in another voice. "Stay here with me. I have to go back soon. Anyway," he added, "it's almost bedtime."

"Okay," said Cynthia, resigned. She was a very small child, pouting and serious, with overbusy limbs. She paced back and forth on the long, low couch which her mother had bought partly because her father didn't want it.

"But *why* don't you love Mommy anymore?" Paula insisted. "You always told me you did."

"That was b-b-before." Her father stammered for an explanation, dulled by knowing that there could be no valid one for Paula. "I tried —we did—I wanted to. We just weren't happy together. You know how that is, Paula."

"No," she said flatly and firmly.

"We have to live separately. It's like when you and Cynthia are tired and quarrel. We put you in separate rooms until you feel better."

"When are you and Mommy going to feel better?"

"It's not exactly that way with grown-ups." The sly innocence of Paula's question brought his hand out to touch her pleadingly; he wiped away the smudge of dirt on her cheek. She always made herself up with a stroke of dust as soon as possible when her mother washed her face. Cynthia, humming to herself, was listening with a smudge of prying watchfulness across her eyes. With a premature false security, the two girls frowned for serious discussion. The children of the divorced are engaged too soon in love as a strategy. Shaper touched the two girls as if to make them child animals again. It was not right that a father should feel this hopeless pity, and this need to enlist his daughters in the harried legions of rationality: "Here's how it is with grown-ups—"

"You mean Mommy and you?"

"Yes. Yes. Now listen. We feel better living in separate places. We're going to stay like that. But we like each other, Paula, and we love you and Cynthia. We both do."

"But, but, but, but," Cynthia sang, carefully wiping her feet on the pillows. "But heigh-ho, the derry-oh, the farmer takes a wife."

"Cynthia," said her father, "you shouldn't. Take off your shoes if you're going to play on the couch. It wasn't made for children."

Cynthia looked at him silently and, scraping the fabric, slid down beside him. Paula pulled between his knees, fighting to get closer than her sister. She began to suck her thumb. Her father pressed his lips together, resisted the temptation to remove her thumb from her mouth, and instead lit a cigarette. He decided that perhaps his silence would oblige her to remove the thumb and speak. It did not. At last he said, "I want you to understand. Mommy wants you to understand, too. Even though I'm not going to be Mommy's husband anymore, I'll always be your father. I couldn't change that even if I wanted to, and besides, I would never want to. Don't you want always to be my daughters?"

Sucking busily, Paula said nothing.

Cynthia announced with a grin, "But I want a daddy who loves my mommy. I think maybe Uncle Carl, he loves Mommy—" The look on her father's face told her that he was not enjoying her joke. "But I *know* you're my daddy for real."

"I am. For real."

"Okay," she said, bored with the discussion.

Paula looked at her wet and slippery thumb, considered putting it back, had another idea. "Why doesn't Mommy say hardly anything to you no more?"

"Anymore," her father said. "I already explained. Because we don't get along—just like we don't let you and Cynthia talk to each other when you don't get along—"

"But we do anyway! But that's only for a few minutes! But it's not, not, *not* the same thing, Daddy!"

"No," he said, "you're right. It's really not."

"Then *when?*"

"When what?"

"When are you coming to sleep here again?"

"I told you, I already explained. Mommy and I—"

"When you went away, you said you'd come back to live here in a few days."

"Well, we thought maybe. I hoped. But it's worked out this way instead. Now listen to me, girls, it's not really so different. I see you very often. We go out together for milk shakes. We're just like before."

Silence from Cynthia. From Paula, coldly, suddenly with her mother's precise articulation: "It's not the same, and you know it."

"Okay, you're right, it's not." Her recognition of his hollow heartiness made him flush. She cut right through what he said. She remembered very well that he had been a part of the life of the house and she did not like her new sense of the house. He said, "I guess you're right, Paula, but that's how it is. That's all. We don't have to talk about it."

Silence. Then:

"So you really don't love Mommy anymore." But she was a child again. The moment when she spoke with her mother's voice had passed. "Daddy," she said.

He resolved to go through it patiently once more. "No," he said, "and she doesn't love me. But we like each other, and we love and like you, both together, and we always will. You understand that, Cynthia?"

"Okay," said Cynthia.

Paula was sucking her thumb again. Her mouth was pulled around, working and bothering, as if she were trying to pull the skin off. She might be learning to bite the nail.

From the back of the house her mother walked toward the living room where the two children and their father were talking. She said hello, picked up a book, and returned to the bedroom. This meant that she would like him to notice that his time was up. A brisk, dark young woman, she was freshly showered and very pretty, although too thin. She wore a housecoat, but a girdle under it, stockings, and high-heeled shoes. Obviously she wanted to get the girls to bed early because she was going out.

He began to say good-bye to his daughters. He reminded them that he would come to see them at noon tomorrow. Cynthia threw her arms around his neck, laughing, and demanded: "Bring me something, maybe a surprise!"

"If you like," he said. He had a sick, lonely weakness in his stomach of something not yet done, not possible.

"Do you like me, Daddy?"

"I like you and love you, Cynthia kid."

Paula was rubbing her face against his hand, the thumb still in her mouth. He lifted her to kiss her, saying, "And Paula too. Now good-bye until tomorrow."

As he started down the stairs, Paula stood with her swollen thumb dripping and shouted after him: "Oh, how I'm sick of those words love and like!"

5

The next day there were fresh flowers in a new vase on the coffee table. His wife was cool and abstracted and the familiar house could not have looked more strange to him if he had returned to find it filled with angry, overheated growth, like an abandoned greenhouse. Even without the flowers, the entire room spoke to him with faint whispers of disarray about how his wife (ah, no! *former* wife!) had been out late and importantly that evening. A wrinkle in the carpet informed on her. The piled pillows on the couch were his witness.

"The children are having lunch," she said. "Would you like something?"

"No thanks, kid, I had a late breakfast."

She hid a small yawn behind her hand. "Me too." The yawn was excessive. It was more than required. She was putting it on with a trowel. Well, still, this was very much better than the hysteria with which she had sent their marriage into darkness, like a couple trapped forever at an abandoned Luna Park in the spinning, jolting cars of the Bug. "Sit down, please," she said.

"Make myself at home?"

She smiled tolerantly. He wondered if she had any imagination for how it disturbed him to visit the place which had been his home, which in some way still was, which was so mysterious, like a room dreamed of and then found and then you're suddenly unsure of whether you really dreamed of it or only now think you did. Of course she understood; she had worked the house out for herself, and had a right to. When he looked up at her, she was still dressed in that social smile. Excessive!

"Some coffee?"

"No thanks, really. How do you think the children are taking things? My being away. Visiting. I was wondering if maybe I shouldn't see them too much when I'm in town. You can't make up for the normal daily—"

"Yes, overstimulating them."

"Too exciting," he said, giving up his thought by agreeing with her.

"They don't show it, of course. It's funny," she remarked, smiling patiently, as if it really were funny, while she explained the joke. "At their age they can't express it, they're too well behaved, they don't have the vocabulary for discussions. . . ."

He gave up listening. He was trying to place himself in this room. Sometimes they had pulled the shades and made love on the floor. He heard her despite the noise of memory. Her mania for psychology had always annoyed him. Jargonizing. And yet, and yet, once when she could not sleep he had held her in his arms on the couch while they quietly talked all night about her father and brother—she could talk English when she wanted to—and she spoke of love and violated need and loneliness. Then they had talked about each other and their own children and how different it would be. Then they had gone out on the porch to hold hands in the chill spring dawn and watch the lights go on in kitchens and bedrooms down the street. See, we didn't need that sleep, we've gained a night on everyone, he had said, and she had answered: Yes, yes, yes, we have something they don't have. I'll even make you a better breakfast!

"But," she was saying, "I'm afraid they will express what they're feeling about us now when they get to adolescence."

Another time, after a terrible quarrel—thinking that maybe with the guidance of their bodies, which wanted to give to each other . . .—more than hopeful, prayerful, they had spread a quilt on the floor just below where she was now sitting. They had helped each other down as if crippled, slowly, slowly, and then safe on the floor, had flung all their strength into the cruel struggle to possess, a lurching, grinding, grasping assault on tenderness, and her head thrown back and her mouth open so that he could not see her teeth, only a dark place and a pulsing groan issuing deeply from within it, and then fiercely she closed and bit his shoulder and the cry, *You did it —you did it—you did it.*

What?

Oh, love, love, love.

Would the rock be there the next day for rolling up the mountain?

He blinked and straightened his shoulders in the heavy, inert grip of sweated clothes. Now was now and his former wife was talking. Now was also then, but his former wife was speaking. It was now ten summers for them. She had something to tell him about their children.

"—with sibling rivalry," she was saying. "They're beginning the latency period."

"Oh, yes, yes." Didn't she remember how he disliked those words? What was she trying now? He went into the kitchen for a glass of water. The children made him rehearse what they would do together after lunch. The park and the swings and a milk shake. All the milk shakes they could drink.

When he returned, she was sitting calmly in her chair, hands folded together, with a subdued half-smile on her face. He recognized her analyzed smile, the one she reminded herself to slip into when she talked psychology. That little smile cost me a year's pay. Okay, go easy, he told himself, it's only a year's pay. A convertible plus gas and insurance. Awhile in Europe. It's a funny nice little darling of a smile, really—no joy, no teeth either, but it's still better than the screams, much easier on the neighbors and a good deal easier on me.

"Did you visit Pete and Ellen last night?" she asked.

It gave him a little malicious pleasure in his turn to let her know that he had not been lonely, that he had not even gone to see his best friends in Cleveland. "No, I had something else to do. I'll see them in a day or so. I called them."

They were both silent. All the maneuvering and rivaling warned him. He was doing nicely, but better get the kids out soon, get out quickly. If she felt his strength of distance, if she sensed Sally and stopped being nourished by whatever it was in the room, the flowers, whatever it was, things might go poorly again. He followed her eyes. Three novels by Evelyn Waugh, new in their jackets, were piled on an end table. A quick twitch of grin crossed his face. He had never liked Waugh, neither had she; ever since college they had taken literature passionately and together, even after she had begun her long crush on the bound volumes of the *Psychoanalytic Quarterly*. Now the little pile of Waugh was a roadmark meant to state: See, I've come under someone else's influence. I'm reading the books *he* recommends, doing the things *he* . . . It amused Shaper, but when he finally spoke, his voice was husky and he had to swallow and it still didn't clear. "I talked with Pete," he said. "I suppose I should go out there."

"Yes, if you're not too busy. Really, Dan, you don't have to be afraid about our friends. I wouldn't spite you for the world—"

"I'm not worried. They know me. I mean to see them, but you know how it is, things come up, I'm only here a few days."

With a thrill of satisfaction, he felt the balance swing over: I'm giving it to her now! She's getting it! This while he knew how much she pained only by how she goaded him—so rusted together are the ways of untying man and wife. And this all the while that his eye began to ache, that he asked himself a fleeing, trespassing question about how he could expect to hold his job while committed to this continuous deep marital work, that he suddenly saw a tiny receding Sally fretting and scowling and making up her eyes and mouth three times over because she was jealous of his quarrel with his wife. Sally's moods were reflected in heavy ways with her lipstick. His own lip was sore inside where he had bitten it—his wife's habit which he had borrowed. Divorce, divorce! he thought. Let us be divorced in the flesh as we are by law.

She was watching him shrewdly. She knew him. He could keep the bitten lip from her; there was no way she could palp it. It was a contest to hold secret the hurt eye with its invisible throbbing. And then Cynthia ran up and put her hands in his pockets to see if he had gum.

"Get out, Cynthia! Go wait for your daddy in the other room. Paula has enough sense. Can't you see I'm talking to him?"

Like successive waves of fever and chills, chills and fever, his tenderness for the children, who resembled both wife and him, gave way to hatred, cold disdain for this woman who forgot so much, who destroyed so much. And then a sharp new ache in his eye, flicking all the way up into his brain, no, just the sinuses, no, cruelly into the brain: Maybe I should just have given in. Maybe I should have taken it on her terms.

No, no! He wanted to turn off one whole side of his head. The eye had a furious life of its own. He warmed it, comforted it with his palm. Bent to it for an instant, he looked up again strictly. "You don't have to sit here if you're busy," he said.

"Oh, I don't mind, Dan. And besides, there really are some little things we have to straighten out."

"Well, thank God most of that is over." And he added meaningfully, "We don't have to quarrel anymore. We can concentrate on the children. We can be friends."

"Yes, of course, but turns out there are some other expenses—"

"Oh, please, no, kid."

"Yes."

"What do you mean?"

"Some other little things. It's complicated raising children under these circumstances, all alone—well, never mind. Let me see. Not just Dr. Jonas, but—"

"What? That again? I won't bother pointing out about that one bill, but as to any others, you know very well—"

"You know very well!"

"Please don't be sarcastic. Let me finish." But she was staring at him with her enormous eyes turning black—as with anger, as with love—the pupils dilating and thick, congested hate squirting like black arterial blood from a deep wound over the thin face. He struggled to be without memory. He thought again (how many times like this?) that if he could keep calm, keep easy, maybe she too would make the effort. He said in a low, forced, effortful voice, "You know very well that our agreement states that you meet all expenses out of the check I send you every month. There's no other way to do it, kid—"

"Don't call me kid! I never liked it! Your idea of an endearment!"

He went on stubbornly, quietly, "You know what my income is. I don't even . . . Well, I'm not complaining. But there's nothing more to discuss about money unless I fail to send you the check some month."

"Kid! Kid! You still want to call me kid, but if one of your children needs some special care, what's it to you—?"

"What's the matter?" he interrupted, frowning. "*What* special care?"

She mimicked him with ungainly, ferocious sarcasm. "It's not in the agreement."

"Are you going to tell me? Or is this all nonsense again?"

"I want to send Paula to the Bainbridge School."

"What for? We—*you* can't afford a private school like that. Anyway, what does she need it for?"

"A fatherless child!"

"Is that my fault? Did you want me? Did you *want* me?"—and he felt the harsh sting of self-pity like dust at his eyes and he shook it out angrily. "Didn't I fight to keep us together long after any other man would have run off or gone batty?"

She tapped her foot and did not answer. He had a suspicion that he could peel off her skin now and find a genuine, very satisfied smile, but with a forced calm—like his—she began patiently to explain. "I've discussed this with several people. The Bainbridge School—"

"I'll tell you just one thing: I don't have the money."

"—is oriented toward difficulties, special problems, broken homes—"

"Oriented, oriented!" He called out the word as if it were a verdict brought down upon her. He stood up, shaking. He had a throbbing frontal headache just behind his eyes. "Please let me get out of here, I've got to get out," he said. "Let me take the children and get out for a while. The little thing we should orient ourselves to is orienting ourselves toward not talking like this when they're watching."

And they both turned and admitted the presence of the two, very quiet, very thoughtful little girls. "We were just talking," Shaper said weakly.

Shrunken and bent, all the pleasant civilizing of their time of separation scraped away, his wife managed to wipe the children's faces for their walk. At the door she turned to him and said severely, "When you come back, please leave them downstairs to play for a few minutes. I want to talk with you alone."

Blackmail! In order to see the children, in order to keep her from trying to rip him out of their lives as she had ripped him bleeding out of hers, he had to find some way of settling into a decent habit with her. The headaches that were already a tradition of their arguments made him almost blind in his left eye. He counted on her not interfering with the children—at least for this her psychology supported him —but he suspected that she wanted to think of him as an ideal monster, and then she could reason that for their own good they should *relate, transfer, orient* to some other man. Her words! That damn vocabulary! Lousy blackmail! He tried to soothe his eye by cupping the palm of his hand over it.

Within the dynamics of her passion for the ideal, each failure between them had to be complete and each small difference total war. Once her husband was defined by her needs ("It happened to me when I was immature"), there was nothing he could do to become human again. Even yielding to her—that most human of acts— enraged her because it violated her idea about him. She hurt herself, and could not stop, and threw herself and the husband she once loved and anyone else in the way, including their children, under the clanking treads of the interlocking syllogisms by which she lived: Good and Evil are pure; the ideal exists only in heaven; my husband is here below with me, on earth; therefore he is evil. I must have perfection; I do not have perfection; then this is hell I live in and I am damned and I will destroy, destroy, destroy. . . . Still, someday, O someday I will find pure virtue in a man! He must exist because I can imagine him. I need him right now! I deserve him, I call him, I insist on him! I am pure, I have waited for him, this other creature has no value because see the way he shrivels, vanishes, like a bad idea! I will prove that he does not exist by making him recognize it himself.

And so silly, smart novels. And bouquets of roses in a cut glass vase. Well, if he knew how she was getting at him, he should be able to get out of the way. And he didn't have to display Sally, either.

6

Fortified by assent to whatever she needed in order to do away with him, he could turn his back on her judgment and go to another. He did not believe in magic; her eyes could no longer make love to him, make harm for him, uncover into life that which was only recently buried and down the dust came sifting fast. It was done. There were the children left, forever and ever the heirs. He would shower again and scrub hard.

But always there returned the tangled memories which dragged him off the straight road leading from life into the violent death of divorce and back into life again. Their children were not the only heirs, the only judges. It would be useful simply to hate her until he forgot her. It would be fine to despise her. But when he had almost succeeded (for example, in a sweet moment of fuel and money while having the oil checked in Sally's car), abruptly his greedy feeding on resentment came back to him, his joy and suspense before what she would do if she discovered that, for almost a year, there had been another girl. She needed the lesson; he had almost told her himself to let her know how he too might be lonely. . . . But recognized his cruelty. And remembered that the night before she found him out, she had risen to his grief and guilt to comfort him in what she took for a passing depression; there had been a miraculous access of tenderness and gratitude, and she had said, "We have the best little kids in the world, I know it, Dan. I'm sorry about the boy, I know it's foolish. Be patient with me. Care for me."

And then the next day the gossip came round and she had confronted him and he had thought: Let her learn, let her burn awhile. We've tried everything else.

Divorce time, wake up! It was time to move past his malice and her answering sweetness, past his yearning and her vindictiveness, past their other swinging meetings and partings, and years of it, common efforts, successes, bitter ultimate failure. While she talked, talked, talked, harassed him, practiced meanness, he could still find the silent regret far away—deep in her eyes—apology, helpless apology—and yet the two of them could not settle together into firm admission of it. Her regret and her ancient willingness to love were resin-soaked roots. She consumed them. She refused to look at them. So be it, she seemed to have decided, abandoning her will with relief, and threw the uncured wood on the fire; and the destruction of what she most needed to grow from gave a wild hissing edge to her sarcasm, "I do wish that you would please stop calling me *kid*. Customarily that's for the children of goats. I seem to recall that I have a name."

She still remembered something more than that from him. On her face—as the lover in the morning finds on his darling's face the marks of their excess together during the night—he saw the brand of her secret self-appraisal, secret wish that it might be otherwise. It was like that thickness and slight purpling of eyelids in the morning after the flesh has made fantastic avowals that moments do not die (even as the moment is dying), that what the intentions of lovers have brought together no God shall sunder (even as spirit and life notify us of matter and death). Who desires what they had now earned? She had wanted to want only him. To him she had cleaved for everything, rest, trust, energy, hope. "But I need a son, too," she had said. "Lots of women have sons. No one is perfect. I want *your* son, Dan, no one else's. Why can't I have the one thing I need?"

For everything, for too much.

As he recalled his chill judgment of her fever, the summer and the city spun crazily around him and he thought: It is as she says—all my fault, all! I was bored with her because I could not admit my need of her, because I feared that her weakness excluded me and she could do nothing for me. I took for boredom my dull despair of touching her without the qualification of a son, of receiving what a husband asks *without qualification,* so that I determined to need nothing at all from her and to build a life which did not depend on her.

"You're a monster," she had shrieked when he admitted that his strength to indulge her had come from a little student at the Institute of Music.

"It didn't make any difference then. You were thinking about your skin, your waistline, your father, your analyst, your fantasies about a son—you didn't really care what I—"

The war again. Go! He leapt from the transport. His parachute was tangled. Other bodies hurtled free, mouths open, teeth bared, roaring with effort. They relished the free tumble into space; for him it was death. "Monster!" He plummeted. Didn't he have the same rights as

others? No. He would be a sickness of gore on the earth below.
"Monster, monster!" And then it came back to him, first with a
belly-jerking violence, earth and life crashing up toward him as the
parachute caught, opened, and he gasped, and then he lazily swung
like a pendulum on a great clock: I am not a monster. Nor is she. But
I am not, either.

He went to Sally that evening with something which he knew was
not love, but she thought it was. Surely she was not really deceived;
his need of her was what she needed, and love an irrelevance. Nevertheless, she showed her doubt in ways that made it harder for him
—her anxious trick of brushing and rebrushing her eyelashes with
mascara, her rather heavy step into the kitchen, giving him a glimpse
of the thickened waist to come, the overbright, slightly foolish, false
glee of her smile, responding to uneasiness by an American piece of
advice, *Keep smiling!* She came back with coffee, a glare of teeth, blond
eyelashes on which he made out tiny beads of blacking.

He asked her to take off her makeup and she did. His chill calculation shocked him. He wondered if his wife had so shot his nerves that
all he could bear now would be a sweetly boring girl, worried only
about pleasing him and getting the shine off her nose with the right
shade of powder, a lover of musicals and of her beauty sleep—and of
pleasing him. She watched, frowning. He grew tender and regretful.
What could he ever do for her? She meant to be good to him. She
studied him silently, unreproaching, with the pallor of the blond girl
without makeup under bad light, and she suddenly seemed very
beautiful, the most lovely woman in creation. He switched off the
lamp and they moved toward each other in the dark.

When they lay down together, she said something which surprised
him. It was trivial and familiar, like the breathless delicacies of un-
dressing, and yet it was a trouble that she should cry out to him with
words that seemed merely taken from a popular song: "Oh put yourself close to me baby."

How he wished for her silence then!

Afterward he realized that the shock of vulgarity came not from her
words but from his considering and judging her without interruption.
He stroked her hair gently and felt sorry for her, for him. Someone

was using someone. Somebody was somebody's weapon. There, there. "Sally, darling, I'm not good these days," he said. "I used to be, I want to be, but I'm in trouble."

"You are, you are, don't worry, you are good."

"I'm in bad trouble. I'm afraid. Nothing's clear any more."

"It will be, don't worry. You just need time, Dan. You make *me* happy."

"Do I?"

She put her finger on his mouth, shh. She wanted to sleep. He dozed too, asking himself: Why don't I ever think of her until I have to? That first day and the swimming were an accident, the false health of fever. Not right, not right, though I take my breath from her hair.

Then he slept.

In the middle of the night he woke with a start, with a sense of flapping inconsequential interruption, as if a cat had jumped onto his back. He lay staring into the murmurous dark and fearful of the dream he could almost remember which had awakened him. Oh, yes, yes. Forget about it. He had been falling without a parachute for years and years. He did not crash to earth; he diminished. The starving man could not take food—even the thinnest broth was an agony to his constricted body.

The air conditioner threw its chill breeze into the room. Gradually, very slowly, reluctant to disturb the fine integrity of her sleep, he began to stretch against Sally for ease and new rest. She was warm, spreading, slightly curled as she lay. He pressed against the softly sleeping girl. He put his hand over her back and moved it down through slopes and valleys. She stirred and their mouths were breathing and feeding into each other. In a few minutes he heard a hoarse voice, his own, saying, "Oh come to me baby." She gathered him in.

7

The last day of the visit. Shaper wanted to store up memories of his children so that, like a camel, he could survive away from them through a season of drought. Yellow-eyed, lurching, he was still not a camel; he could not live for oases; he could not carry Paula and

Cynthia in a hump. Still, he had hope. Although it was already several days past the end for his wife and him, he believed that perhaps they could manage one more meeting for the sake of the children.

Sally gave him her automobile to drive out to the house. This time the mild luxury, moving through traffic in the sun with the top down, failed to reassure him. He found himself singing an old Louis Armstrong tune:

From milkless milk
And silkless silk
Love oh love oh loveless love

On an impulse he stopped at Peter's, found him home, and asked him to come along. "My wife and I will both be on good behavior with a third party present." And he looked away. "That's the way it is, Pete. Sorry."

The children were shy; they knew he was going. They had no practice in good-byes. For them he was already gone. Paula gave him a drawing of flowers and the sun to put on his wall—"where you live, Daddy." The sun was sticking out its tongue.

As the subdued and uneventful visit ended, it occurred to Shaper that Pete might find his insistence on having a witness somewhat melodramatic.

"Good-bye," he said to his wife.

"Good-bye," she said.

"I hope everything goes well."

"Have a good trip back."

They shook hands. Peter looked embarrassed. They went downstairs. Shaper glanced back from the driveway and at the same moment two things happened: The children came out to stand on the upstairs porch and his wife came running down the stairs. She paused, breathing shallowly, before Shaper and Peter near the door of the automobile. She put out her hand with a slip of paper in it. "I enrolled Paula at that school," she said softly. "I forgot to mention it. Here's the bill."

He drew back and tried to look merely puzzled. "You know I'm not supposed to . . . I can't pay these bills. We already decided about that."

She held to the low tone, but there was a stir and hiss in her voice. "Who decided? Who? Who decided?"

"Look"—and he was pleading although he knew this was the wrong way to move her. He had only found a steady right way when he was sick and needed her out of helplessness. It was the only way he could count on for sure. It was no way by which he could live. "Look, I sent a check for that dentist's bill, although you were wrong about the date. It came after our agreement. Now please try to understand, there's got to be a stop."

"A stop to what?"

"We have to start living the way things are. We have to adjust. You've said it yourself. Money shouldn't get in the way now. Our lawyers—" And he watched the pinched face and the black, swollen eyes replacing that bright young divorcée which was her pleasant role. He had hoped, but once more he misjudged her. Through those inky eyes, through the cloud of hate with which she blinded herself and poisoned him, she would not see what they had sometimes been for each other—she never saw that anymore; she would not see the neighbors, she would not see Peter, she would not see the children. "Kid! Listen to me, please!" And he had no words to force her to remember how they had held hands and strolled in parks, and tenderly made up many quarrels, and congratulated each other that the girls were a fine combination of the best in both of them.

A *stop*? Her lips were saying, working within, white and diminishing.

"Listen, please, *please*," he said, "you have to understand how things are with me now. I live in a room, don't you understand? One room. I'm not a college kid, I'm not used to it anymore. One furnished room, do you hear me? I save my money so I can fly in to see the children—"

"Then don't do it."

"What did you say, kid?" He leaned forward, trying to see her. "I'm sorry, I didn't understand."

"I said stay there. Get yourself a kitchenette. Don't bother coming in."

He held his breath. He was peering into a night and his eye was tired. It throbbed and he wanted to warm it with his palm. It seemed very important not to let her know about the ache in his eye. He straightened up and said, "Look at me. Look at us, kid." His eye wanted an eye to return its gaze.

"Just don't bother," she said, as if her mind were far away with household thoughts. "Stay away. I could spend the money. Who needs you here? Don't bother."

She drew closer to him with a little smile on her face.

"And I may as well give you one other bit of information. Why not? Since you're leaving again." She spoke this last phrase slowly, as if it were particularly important. He recognized the angry, wenchy smell which her body gave up when she could no longer hold on. She said: "Now I feel like a woman. I've found a man who knows how."

In the first moment of almost prudish shock, he felt his face being fixed in a skeletal grin. "That had to come. The list is complete. Okay. All right." But the grin spread uncontrollably, attacking his bones, dissolving the sockets of his eyes.

"It was no good with you. Your fault. It was never any good."

"All right," he said, "congratulations." He turned to Peter. "You hear? My wife was a virgin all along."

"Yes," she said, "that's about it. I told Carl, too, how I was never touched. Since you're going away again, you might as well have this to take with you. Nothing. Never anything, though I tried to make you believe . . ."

Their children were leaning over the railing to peer down on them. His hand flew toward his eye; he stopped it midway and put it down. He said: "All right, there's no point in discussing this either, is there? Our lawyers have it all settled now. We paid the lawyers to do this job for us."

"Lawyers!" And it was done. Something new had been released, and in public, in the summertime, with people coming out on their porches or peering through the screens to listen and saying *a shame* and smiling to themselves. "You want lawyers to raise our children?" she shouted. "That's your idea of a father?"

"All right, all right," he said in a low, hoarse voice. He held himself stiffly, shaking with fury and disappointment. "Can't you control it? All this nonsense. There are people. You're doing it on purpose, kid, don't you see?"

She screamed as if he had struck her. "Don't call me kid! Just get out of my life!"

"Okay, okay." He turned to climb into the car. Peter was already huddled miserably on the seat. As he moved behind the wheel, he felt an almost physical eruption, a brutal crack in his throat, and the word came out: "Fishwife!"

"Corrupt! Corrupt!" she was shrieking at him. "Get out of my driveway! Go! Corrupt! You never cared for me or your kids—*children*," and desperately she sobbed the correction. "Or anyone but yourself! Get out of my life!"

That was how, standing silently together on the porch, the children saw him last. He was being chased by their mother's rage.

At the corner he pulled over to the curb and asked Peter to drive. "I'm not in control," he said, shivering, and went on as if this were the total explanation. "It was what broke us up. I had to stop, I couldn't be run by her temper. Once I saw Paula watching me back down like a fool just because of that look she gets in her eyes—you saw it, Peter—when she can't be reached. When I saw my daughter judging me . . . It didn't even help to slap her, I tried that once or twice. . . ."

Peter turned and drove through the long park along East Boulevard. He was explaining, comforting, merely talking. "Well, she has to feel better about what she's doing. She's not the kind of woman who can take ambiguity. You have to be all good or all bad, and you're *it*, man. Once you could do no wrong; now . . . Well, women are like that. Don't think she's going to be nice for the sake of the past."

"What about the kids?"

"The past has got to be wiped out. Women have their feet on the ground—anyway, they call it the ground, sometimes it's our faces—and one thing she thinks she can do for the next man—whoever he is, I don't know if she's telling the truth," he added hurriedly, "is just wipe you out. That way she gets to be a girl again. She said it plain enough. For her you've got to be pure mistake, friend, and nothing else. Evil Dan the Bad Young Man."

"No kindness at all? That's how I'd like to be. Let me tell you something: When we first decided to separate, we both wept."

Peter shook his head. "She told Ellen *you* cried. She said you're maudlin. She said you held her hand until it ached. Make up your mind to take it. Women—" Did Peter believe what he was saying? No, he was tuckered out and embarrassed and his mouth was uttering for him the cynical clichés about women which men in club cars tell each other. It was what he thought Dan wanted to hear. He may even have believed it true at that moment, true because it sounded familiar, and with a deep breath of fatigue (he thought this was sympathy) he again spoke what he took to be comfort to his friend: "Women," he sighed.

"But doesn't she look all yellow, sick? Her skin that color and those enormous black eyes. Yellow, sick, and mean. She used to be so pretty. She still is. Oh, she hates me!"

They both fell silent. When Peter felt that he had done his duty, he asked to be dropped at home. He needed to get away. He loved his own wife; he felt as disconnected, tired, and jittery as if he had been casually unfaithful to her. Naturally he resented his old friend for bringing him to this possibility, and also—because his wife was surely his best friend—he resented Dan for eliciting his jovial male cynicisms. And within, too, he felt a thrill of pride: not for him this failure. This is the pleasure we are said to feel at funerals. And at a still deeper, more solemn place, because he was a good and kind man, he felt regret for his friend and also knew something of what was happening to him. This sense came up through the barriers as discomfort, as a desire to squirm: I can't take it, I want to do my duty by you, Dan; I want to get away. He had his own wife and children to play with on a fine, dry summer afternoon. Ellen had asked him to do some shopping.

8

I held her hand until it hurt her! And what a bore she was with her whining and her headaches and her suspicions! Suspicions!

Better. He used his old ritual for remembering himself into gratitude for freedom: her nagging, her picking at her face in the mirror, her stiff, jealous mouth with the white lines. Sure, finally he had given her cause for jealousy, why not? But first he had warned her that she was making him lonely when she stood before the mirror, plucking, squeezing, hating herself, dreaming of miraculous sources of happiness—her father fantastically restored to life, a baby boy instead of girls, an analyst who really understood and *said* something.

> With dreamless dreams
> And schemeless schemes
> Love oh love oh—

It was fine to be driving Sally's car with the top down. She was waiting for him, and she would be all health and dazzling smiles, unskilled in moping, untrained for meanness.

But don't you have to take a woman from strength, not weakness, if you are to give her anything important and receive anything worth taking?

And after his ten-year marriage, wasn't he too distant from Sally to bring her anything but that cheating desire, the need for comfort? He had loved his wife despite everything, he knew he had, they had been young and unmarked together, he insisted on remembering— and he did not love Sally. He made too much of the hot pity of bodies. He had thought to find love by loving, but instead, at length, filled with crazy pride, he had discovered sex. The solution was as ineffective as the discovery was unoriginal. Like his wife, he made too much of things.

When what he needed to save his life was simplicity, a bare white room and sleep, restoring sleep, how long could greater and greater complication soothe him?

Didn't that mean only trouble to come?

He parked Sally's automobile on the street before the massive, teeming apartment building—luxury circa 1928—in which she lived with her closets full of clothes, her mirrors, her pink-feathered slippers, and her music-to-dream-by. But if he couldn't allow himself Sally, that beautiful and perhaps silly girl—yes, he should say it out, maybe it's true—he might be unable to prevent doing what he had too often already considered. He had stood caught in the middle of his furnished room and thought it through. He had first been indulgent, then shocked by the persistence of the idea. Apparently it was one to reckon with.

He went up the long walk to the stuffy, overdecorated entrance, found her bell, and rang it. Could Sally stop his idea?

As he often did, he tried to think of what would happen to the children. That was a puzzler.

FROM PROUST
TO DADA

Once in Florence I came to know a man who was reputed, by himself and also by certain practitioners of minor literary history, to have been a beautiful boy whose long, slender fingers and lively eyes were much admired by Marcel Proust. When I met him, his most startling characteristic was his great accumulation of years, but he was healthy, that mummified health of extreme tenacity, and he was still quick as a boy across the dust and debris of Tuscany in the summer of 1950. He also claimed to have enjoyed the particular friendship of a great English poet, dead in World War I, and to have inspired some of the poet's most memorable (now forgotten) lines.

Two generations ago Roland Mardi had been renowned for his beauty, his accessibility, and his wealth; he still had the last two qualities. You can imagine what an odd survivor he seemed to American students, GI Bill tourists, prebeat beatniks in our twenties. It was a time of selling GI clothes to Arabs for travel money, of dodging the committees of experts who came over to judge our Fulbright serious-ness and reliability while we, veterans by vocation, strove for a heroic bohemian freedom. We had had enough of roll calls.

I met him at a concert of medieval music in a monastery courtyard in Fiesole. "You are—am I correct?—an American student, an artist, perhaps a poet?" he asked me at intermission, pointing his parchment fingers like a maestro.

Golly, he was so right.

"You are interested in Proust, in dada, in futurism?"

Yes, oh, yes again.

"You would honor me with your company—?"

Well, I would be happy to honor us both by taking coffee and ices with him at the sort of plush café which would have been a black-market hangout in Paris and which here was simply out of my reach. He had many interesting facts to impart on many interesting subjects. Draw a subject, he suggested, in English or in French—which did I prefer? Ah, he should have been able to see by looking at me how well I spoke French, but there is so much deceit abroad in the world today. . . .

He smiled, he had won his conquest, he had pale, washed-out, feverish eyes; we returned to our folding chairs in the little monastery garden. I had left my wife at our *pensione* that evening (headache, as I recall).

The music was sweet and tinny Italian baroque, played slowly, as if it were aspirant Rossini. The girls wore white gloves and were mostly accompanied by ladies in black veils. I was down from Paris for a few weeks to love Italy and the Italians.

After the last encore Roland Mardi settled us into the café and studied his nails and told me to order anything my little heart desired —chocolate, cookies, anything. With my famous perceptiveness in both English and French, I understood at once that he hated the smell of beer and wanted to do the talking for both of us. "*Un café,*" I said, and he translated proudly into Italian for the waiter. He then asked why I had been staring at him in the monastery garden.

Hard to say. Maybe gazing intently, with deep interest—but no impolite staring. Why? His mummified body. His lacquered nails. The touch of rouge on his lips. There were so many choices, but I said

something on the order of: "You look as if you knew Proust personally, the origins of dada and futurism, all the—complexities and
mysteries of several generations of literary genius, up to and . . . and
. . . and including today."

What intelligent perceptiveness in a young man! What ability to
follow clues!

And what the devil, I asked myself, was on my mind? Well, I was
just idling. Back in Paris I knew hardly anyone but other students,
French, Scandinavian, Dutch, and American jetsam. My wife and I
were expecting a child. I was busy asking myself what I had gotten
myself into, and resolving to be serious about life, and not entirely
certain this was the best way to be. We had taken this trip to Florence,
and fallen in with a nest of late-risers, and it was Paris all over again,
in a splendid setting of umber stone, summer heat, sun-reddened
dust. This was the time of the first fine flowering of the Vespa. The
Ponte Santa Trinità was still an Army engineer's improvisation, black
steel over the dynamited ruins, and the racket of reconstruction was
just beginning to distract Italy in its stunned and goofy rage of peace.
We visited new Fascist-atrocity trials and revived summer culture
programs. The dark-eyed Florentine women were learning to parade
once more in their white gloves, and they paraded in these white
gloves near the American Express. We stayed at the Pensione Ber-
chieli, where, it was said, E. M. Forster and D. H. Lawrence had slept.
No doubt that was before the invention of the riveting hammer.

Well, I wasn't bored. But I felt there must be many things more in
Europe than what I knew, and Roland Mardi, grandson of the foun-
der of a great bank, author of twenty-two privately printed books
given to libraries and his friends—he did not deprive the world of his
daily journals—and two published by publishers for the wide public,
a Frenchman pared to the bone, with electric, exposed nerves, the
insulating meat worn off by time and friction, provided a bit of variety
to the spice which was our lives. Generously he offered to the judgment of history his recollections of Dreyfus, Jarry, Daudet, Proust,
and surrealism. Generously he offered my wife a bottle of his own
clear nail polish, bottled to his specifications in Lyons. "Otherwise
they crack," he advised her. "When you're not a child anymore, and
you won't be a child forever, you must be careful to look pleasing for
your friend."

And his face of an ancient child cracked with a burst of laughter, a short high-pitched squeal—so pleased! so pleased!

And so we hung out together in Florence. He took my wife and me to museums and lectured us, mostly me, about the traditions of Italian painting and his part in them, the beauties of the Boboli Gardens and his previous views of them, Florence and how it had changed during the sadness. He had kept track of it.

"What did you do during the war?" I asked. This rude question was one of my hobbies. You were supposed to wait until the explanations came pattering out of their own accord.

"Ah, ah, that is a long story. You see, I was very old then, you see, and I . . ." And that delighted shrill squeal of laughter. "I'm much younger now, today, my friend! It was a dream; I think I was ill. Now I have found my youth again in this new world, and you with the confessions of my old age. Shame, shame on you, nasty boy."

He did not have a definite or clear story. The lack of story pleased me after all the I-was-an-anti-Fascists I had met. Despite his old man's babble about the past, he disdained working this one out. Obviously, though, the money didn't stop. And there had been faithful retainers in Antibes while he wrote in his journals and organized his notes and waited for Ike's famous small-boy grin to debark after D-Day.

"The nasty war set me back," he said, pouting. "I could get my journals printed, of course, but it was impossible to mail the cahiers to my friends in all the cultural centers—London, Roma, New York, Berlin, Petersburg, Calcutta—I had subscribers in all the cultural centers—oh, by the by, do you know Mrs. Cornfield in Charleston?"

"No, I've never been there."

"Oh, my dear boy, she's of the Mosaic creed—are you sure? She sponsored chamber music at the college there, you know, the girls' lycée in Carolina?"

He looked expectant. I shrugged. No light in my eyes. At first I thought he meant she was made of little tiles.

He looked sad. "My memory is going. She was one of my dearest ladies in the period of 1915 to 1917, Volume Seven. She married an American friend, lovely boy, he drove an ambulance for the Red Cross. I do remember, do I not, my friend?"

We strolled back and forth across the temporary bridge where the Ponte Santa Trinità had been. We pushed our way through the tourist crowds on the Ponte Vecchio, pricing leather items with the Florentine crest on them, bargaining for items to express love or friendship or a happy trip, and he offered to buy me . . . "Please, no rings or bracelets," I insisted.

My wife had a headache—fumes, crowd, a Vespa leaping a curb onto an old woman selling a hatful of black-market Chesterfields— and we walked her back to the hotel. Roland said, "God bless you, sleep well and soundly," and wanted to set out again on a wander through town. He was tireless and determined. He showed me Settignano, where "your sublime buffoon, Marco Twain, lived in the Villa Viviano. I remember him very well. Of course, I was too young to appreciate the full value of his vernacular. I was here with my uncle. I cared for nothing but the Goncourt brothers, but Twain was a sublime artist, just entering, I believe, the time of his despair. He wore a white suit and carried a white cane. He had curls like a boy. There were children exactly like that in the Tuileries, and I remember . . ."

His vitality was real. He crept back for a long nap before dinner, and to have his nails done by his man, and perhaps his long, thin blue hair washed and rinsed, but he appeared in public again for the evening as fresh, in fresh starch, as the boys he remembered in the Tuileries gardens. I admired his brave and stubborn curiosity. "What," he would ask, "what-what—" and sneeze from the dust and use his inhaler and pat his nostrils with his frail and blue-veined hand and proceed with his question: "What do you do with your time, you Fulbright students and your colleagues, artists, *bohèmes?*"

"Well, we walk a lot, we hike," I said.

"I too, sir," he said, raising a finger, "I walk a lot, I hike."

And sure enough, he joined us in our touring of Fiesole and Florence, up hill and down trattoria, from the hallowed walls along which Dante may have idled (*pourquoi pas?*) to the Ristorante da Bing-Crosby, a popular spaghettying spot of that period when the U. S. of A. was still a novel delight to this part of the world. He would disappear for his nap, but then he would reappear, as agile as a spider. I already said fresh as starch. He climbed without sweating. He tramped, albeit lightly, pared down by time, care, and traditional routines. He offered me a bath in his suite at the best hotel on the Arno. He uttered a happy little aria about the nozzles on the tub—

I would adore them if I could only find it in my heart to give them a chance.

My wife and I had this tiny room in a boardinghouse. She hid beneath an umbrella while I sponged myself in the sink, but still, I never took advantage of his invitations to bathe in his bathtub in the hotel blessed by many Michelin stars. One afternoon he pressed his suit a little more closely. I was enjoying a lecture on futurism and the exaggeration of the buttock in the time of Mussolini, Numero Uno, when he suddenly said, "Come to Corsica with me, I have a beautiful house."

"Oh, I really couldn't do that."

"Do, do. You could read and study. I could show you my note-books. They are judged to be of great interest."

"I really can't. We have to go back to Paris soon. My grant—the commission. And my wife should be near her doctor."

"She could go back to be near her doctor," he said happily.

"No, really, I must be with her. She is pregnant."

"Well," he said, "well, well." He grasped at straws. He cried out as if he had suddenly discovered the perfect compromise, "Well then, she could go with us!"

His way of saying *us,* making *she* another, a stranger to whom I felt obligations, seemed to get through my thick skull the message that something peculiar was going on. Until that moment I had been amused, entertained, and flattered by M. Mardi's attentions. Nothing was really real; this was Europe, wasn't it? Now conscience began to appear, and even a bit of panic. It was as if I were suddenly on the Public Square back in Cleveland. "No, we're heading for Paris this weekend," I said, having just decided.

"So soon," he said.

"We have to go home."

"Ah. Ah. Oh dear, it's four o'clock. I must go back to my hotel —a friend, a close friend . . ."

But sadness was bad for him and he determined to recover. He straightened his body, he stretched his fingers—a little easing trick of pulling one hand in the other—and he said, "Then I must offer a farewell party for you and all your colleagues. I insist!"

There was no necessity for him to insist. I accepted at once.

By this time, having been in Florence for nearly a month, I knew the great places, the gardens, statues, museums, and walks, and I also knew a dozen or so other would-bees—writers, painters, students, retired veterans and their ladies. I carried the happy word from café to furnished room: *Free meal!* The old boy was buying.

We met at the Ristorante da Bing-Crosby. Roland adored America, and the place reminded him of the America he loved—a private back room with antipasto, spaghetti, rogatini, scallopini, Broglio wine, and "apple pie"—little diced pieces of apple, sweetened and spilled on a spongy cake. It also reminded us of the America we had left behind —plenty of food provided by someone else. He grinned and tittered and toyed with his meal, overjoyed by our appetites. Our ladies, in ponytails or bobbed hair and the cotton dresses which they had made themselves, occasionally chattered politely with him; most of the men drank and laughed and spoke English, which he understood, but not at him so that he could hear. He smiled, trying to have fun, and waved his hands in front of his face to ward off the smoke.

At the end of the meal he ordered the table cleared—at least the waiters listened to him—and new cups of coffee were brought, together with plates of cookies which were put at either end of the table. Roland tapped on a glass with a small silver spoon. He tapped lightly, but now he was not asking for our attention; he demanded it. Gradually the flushed faces gave a moment to this distraction; the jokes fell away; a little calmed by food and wine, a little startled by second or third cups of coffee, we turned to him.

He said, "And now I will read from my journal, sight-translating, from the original French into English. I have noted and discussed Marcel Proust, Henri Bergson, and Jean Cocteau in my cahiers, and tonight I have the delightful opportunity to include among these immortals the young people of the English and the American languages. And now I shall read."

He coughed and patted his lips. He must have memorized this speech. Eyes rolled. Knees were nudged, legs kicked under the table; no interruption. I suppose he had spent nearly eighty years developing his vision of the dandy, living a birdlike aloofness, singing in the wilderness for himself and for a few other birds; I suppose there was the melancholia of the ancient dandy. But then his head was bent and he was translating the foolish words—old man's words: "I met some very nice young Americans. We talked about the *belle époque*. One particularly seemed interested and nice to me. . . ."

There must have been great sadness in his heart, but we in that steamy room were impatient with his arteries. Someone whispered, "Gaga, completely gaga."

I sent a shut-up look to the whisperer across the table.

The high-pitched voice trickled on: "One of them, the one who was particularly nice, has informed me of much of interest to me about the new generation. . . ."

The room was filled with smoke. Having finished our meal, we were impatient with sitting. This old-timey article with clear polish on his nails was a total drag. Someone else whispered; someone answered; many of us were talking. For a few moments M. Mardi went on reading from his recent *Mémoires Litéraires*. He really did know Proust, Cocteau, Ezra Pound, Ford Madox Ford, and now us. "I got a stomach ache," Sam Moon, the painter, said very loudly. "*Yeecch*, I ate too much. Why doesn't he pay the check so we can get out of here?"

Roland suddenly sat down at the head of the table and his fingers were twisting about the tiny silver coffee spoon in his fist. Tears ran down his face. "Oh, dear, what's the matter with him?" one of the girls asked.

"Did he hear me?" the painter asked. He hated to hurt someone's feelings.

"I don't think so," his girl friend said. "No, of course, he didn't, stupe."

The tears were running off his face and onto the open notebook. "Then what's the matter with him?"

I heard myself answering as if he were alone in the room with me and I was taking notice of him at last: "*Il est ému.*" And then again, stiffly translating for the others, my friends, as if this stranger had disappeared from our sight: "He was moved."

YOUNG MAN, OLD DAYS

For many springtimes it was Frank Curtis's custom to pay a visit to a man we'll call Justin in the Left Bank hotel Le Grand-Sèvres, where he has lived for twenty years. Justin and Frank were among the great buzzing hive suspended in Paris after the war by Fulbright Act, by GI Bill, by veterans' pension, by remittance, by other mysterious conveyances and supports, intending to transform themselves from fretful would-bees, living by their nerves, to fretful celebrities, living by the adula-tion of others. Oh, yes, and some of them wanted to do good work, had projects, had visions. They were painters, writers, musicians; a few filmmakers came later to the askew *chambres tout confort* of the Grand-Sèvres.

Justin wrote movie criticism, poems, stories; he became a great friend of Alice B. Toklas, who thought him pretty and one of the few geniuses of the season 1949–1950; he took tea with André Gide a few months before Gide died (Gide liked him, he reported), and received advances from publishers and charmed everyone by being a friendly puppy and by providing an energetic transit system for gossip. He scrambled for money, but he made out. He seemed to like everyone in the life of art. He knew his way around Pigalle and sometimes found special White Russian clubs and dawn exhibitions for friends or friends of friends. He was small, curly, compact, and fast. There were new geniuses for the season 1950–1951, but Justin kept his spirits up. He bore no grudge against Alice B. Toklas. He was sweet and traveled unarmed, like a medic—he had just missed the war and the GI Bill—amid the rivalries, boredoms, and battles to the death in the life of Art.

Their friendship was attenuated by diverging paths, as friendships usually are. At first they were near neighbors down the hall. He showed Frank the Buci market and Shakespeare & Company and told him to be welcome in Lutetia. He took him to the Café Sportif to cash his first check. Then, expecting a child, Frank and his wife moved out of the Grand-Sèvres. The child was born. They decided to return to Cleveland. Before they left, after a second year in Paris, his wife wept as they strolled the *quais* of the Seine—bicycles, Vespas, fishermen, lovers, it was not yet a roaring mini-superhighway—and she said, "We'll never come back, it's all over," and he said, "Of course we'll come back," and of course she was right, it really was all over, Cleveland was a way station to separate elsewheres; and when they came back to Paris, they came back separately and very much changed.

Frank lost track of Justin. He was briefly a professor of French, then (alimony and child support) an international advertising expert for American corporations. He spoke the language of Racine and Camus to consumers of Otis, Allis-Chalmers, and Massey-Ferguson in France, Lebanon, and Senegal. When he began returning to Paris each year on various tasks and meetings, he knew nothing of Justin and scarcely thought of him. That was another time. He had not been a close friend. Nice Justin, sure he remembered, he had been around the scene.

But then, when the child conceived in Room 5 was ten years old, he heard that Justin was still holding the fort in the Grand-Sèvres— without telephone, without job, still piecing himself out in the city of light, a young man writing. He felt a heavy flush of nostalgia. What persistence and bravery, what stubbornness. If Justin was alive and well in the Grand-Sèvres, then Mouludji and the Tabou, the Rose Rouge and Juliette Greco in her *bloo-djeans* were still alive, fresh, true, beautiful, and existential. Frank went to see him with a bad case of the sentimental dizzies.

The old hotel was unaltered. A slightly larger bulb serviced the *minuterie*, but there were still only eight seconds to get to the next landing before the light went out. He used six seconds per landing, round and round to the top. He knocked without warning at about one in the afternoon. Long silence, and then a sleepy whispering and a voice crying out: *"Qui est-ce?"*

He gave his name.

"Uh, uh, say, could you come back in about an hour?"

Clockwise downward to wait with *Le Monde* and a *café crème* at the little bar on the Rue des Saints-Pères. When Frank returned, Justin was washed, dressed, and alone. The room under the eaves was pretty much as he knew it, crazily slanting, sinking into history; many somebodies had slept there. Justin's hair was slicked down by water and Frank's congratulations were sincere: "You haven't changed!" This pleased him, and Frank doubled his pleasure, doubled his fun by inviting him to lunch.

"I haven't changed?"

"Not at all," Frank insisted, "honest," and it seemed true, though the angle of slant had steepened and it was uphill from the bed to the alcohol stove and he knew by faith and theory as he hung on, getting his sea legs on the streets of Bohemia, that other, invisible matters must have altered and rearranged themselves in these ten years. The crumbling plaster was overlaid with ancient horror-movie posters—Karloff, Lugosi, Fay Wray, Kong—and they tunneled him beneath the late forties and early fifties, when he had known Justin, to his childhood in Cleveland, fright and magic time at Loew's Granada on a Saturday afternoon. Between two features, while he bought candy for the next ordeal, ghouls and zombies strolled the aisles with fleas and bits of popcorn leaping in their fur. The discontinuity with his time in Paris was odder than the whips, screams, hypodermics, and monochrome werewolves stretched and glued to the walls.

"It's an interest I have," Justin said.

"I didn't know."

"Oh, I didn't tell anyone."

They went to lunch and Justin gave him the little news of the people who stayed on and on in Paris. "Karen gave up journalism and opened a dress shop on the Rue de Beaune . . . Ferd works in the surplus export of the CIA or something kinky like that . . . Archie can't get divorced—his Italian waif got so fat, you wouldn't believe it—"

(Which Italian waif? What Archie? Ferd who? But Karen, he remembered her—youngest girl ever to almost get a review in the *New Statesman*—and wait a sec, Archie, begins to come back, met the Princess Marguerite Caetani di Bassiano—now there's a name that sticks—and she was going to publish him in—)

"*Botteghe Oscure*," said Justin. "She took a story of Archie's, same issue as the first draft of *Under Milk Wood*. He does mutual funds for the Army—that waif really laid it into him and got disgusting."

Frank never did place the waif. He vaguely recalled that Archie liked thin girls who read Kafka.

In return he tried to give Justin word of the States, but Justin got back every two years without fail, no matter how busy he was, to see his mother, and so he kept caught up. He wasn't interested in Frank's daughter born in Paris, conceived in the Grand-Sèvres one floor below him, and only mildly in what had happened to him since, but the lunch was affable and easy and they strolled about during the afternoon (a bottle of La Slavia at the Old Navy) and it was good to see each other (teatime coffee at the Tournon).

Justin did a little reviewing—music, opera, dance. He did some dubbing of films and once, thanks to a friend, had been commissioned to write a treatment for a *nouvelle vague* movie. No credit to him on the final product, but they came across with the down payment. He did irregular duty as the voice of a very thin secondary star in Godard-Truffaut-Robbe-Grillet off-Boulogne movies, who was, however, seldom dubbed for the Anglo-American market. He wiggled on through.

"Say," he said, as if to prove how well he made out, "someone gave me a couple of tickets to the Ukrainian Folk Ballet at the Théâtre des Nations—they've been sold out for weeks . . ."

But Frank was busy. A dinner meeting with a disc jockey from the Luxembourg station, and then a couple of ladies, one for each.

"Every time Sartre makes up with the Party again, you can't buy a ticket to an Iron Curtain attraction for love or money. However, pal, if you happen to have both love and money *plus* friends in high places—"

It was a generous gesture. Surely, he had many friends who would jump at the chance to watch the Ukrainians jump. Though he meant to, Frank didn't get around to the Grand-Sèvres again that trip. They exchanged New Year's cards six months later.

As it happened, he could usually work Paris onto his route to talk to the sheikh or set up a meeting with the Rumanians (they always conferred real well but had to check with the Soviets and it was therefore zero time in Auld Bucharest). Each year when he visited Justin he bought the lunch, Justin bought the coffee, they moved the news around. His changelessness made Frank Curtis feel young. Justin was still doing what a very young man does; Justin and Frank were the same age; therefore . . . The syllogism stroked some atavism in Frank; well, vanity is the truer word, despite how ridiculous he knew it was and how he tried teasing himself while he also took the gain. He aimed to keep the truth in mind, anyway. Another friend in the hotel when he lived there had had five children by a Sarah Lawrence girl he met on the stairway when the *minuterie* caught them both in the dark. They lived in Rockland County; he produced for educational television. The lesbian of the second floor was married to a famous Norwegian diplomat, superbusy with UN rescue missions in emerging and submerging African states. A season of glory had visited one of the writers in the hotel. He was now suffering a reaction of public and critics—the most famous failure of our generation, ready to be done up as an example in *Life*—but his accountant had tucked away some of the money from the good years in safe and tax-free places so he could stop to gather himself together. He wasn't dead yet.

And Frank himself? Well, having fun and getting ready for his move. Keeping a good grip on the past was part of it. A bit of it was seeking and prying, rooting about as a rest from consolidating advertising accounts, but as long as he was young, he could still be allowed to make ready.

Justin didn't change, but sometimes he looked tired, plucked early and preserved in brine. Under the fluorescent tubes of the revised café on the corner Frank could read some of the cost of his perpetual youthifying in smudges and veins around the eyes. His mother died, he got the money, but he tarried on in the hotel. The only difference was that he didn't have to return to New Haven every two years for those boring visits when she would ask him, *Aren't you ever going to settle down?* and he would answer, *Yes, Mother, I've settled down.*

It was she who eventually settled down. The inheritance meant that he could have bought a small apartment on the Rue de Fleurus, say, but he saw no reason to move. People knew where he was and how to find him. The crazily slanted, winding stairway, the wood now white from being scrubbed with strong soap in times of prosperity, time of the Malraux cleanup of national monuments, made a comforting space between the Left Bank streets and his room. He had worn his paths through the days and nights of Paris. The gypsy boy had pitched his tent in one place longer than anyone. He liked being a young man, making out okay in the city of light, paradise of hope, capital of desire, home of the first *cinémathèque*.

In the original line from Valéry, that's the capital of hope and paradise of misery.

The last time Frank saw him, he was again just getting up, just about to get up—"What time is it, pal?" It was three in the afternoon, it was early spring and raining outside, and there was a heavy wintry chill in the room. He was getting over the usual winter bronchitis, he said. As usual, Frank invited him to lunch, but this time he said he couldn't manage it; he was waiting for someone. The cough was a habit (Gauloises bleus, bronchial inflammation); it tuckered him out. There was rain dripping down the eaves and the broken pipe. Someone was bringing him some soup. Rain, gray rain outside, and rain in the air inside. A corner of Bela Lugosi was peeling off the wall; the sword dipped in the river Jordan was coming unstuck. "There's this friend—he's terribly shy—he never goes out except in the middle of the afternoon, when he won't meet anybody . . . I suppose it's pathological, but how we treat it, we humor it. . . ."

Okay. Frank supposed they had come to the end of these visits anyway. They had never been close friends; even the yearly renewals among the horror posters were crowding it a bit.

"But wait a sec, he won't be here for twenty minutes or so. It's part of the pathology—he's usually late."

Wearing a flannel bathrobe over his underwear, he made coffee on the alcohol stove. He had acquired a cat. The concierge must have changed the rules. Frank said, "When I see a bottle of Nescafé in Paris, I still think it's a black-market item—"

"Unh," he said.

Frank told him that his elder daughter was about to enter college. He didn't argue the point. Frank told him he couldn't believe it. Justin neither confirmed nor denied this analysis of the situation. Frank told him once more that he looked unchanged.

That always got his attention. He glanced up from the Nescafé. "I'll dye my hair if I have to," he said. He took a level spoonful from the jar of Lait Guigoz. "I'll go to Switzerland for a face-lift."

Frank started to laugh, but he meant it, and knowing this was their farewell, Justin pointed to his head. "Look," he said. It was as if he had spilled ink on his scalp. "Experimenting. Actually, though, it darkens the scalp, ick, I'll have to do a hair-knitting on it. They call it 'virile' baldness when it starts receding in front. That's not necessarily a good word for it. This is a temporary measure."

"Oh, a small matter," Frank said soothingly. "Actually, you know, you really do look the same—amazing. I jog a little when I'm home, but I'm never home. You do calisthenics, Justin?"

True, he hadn't changed at all, and he looked worn-out.

"It's partly your physical type," Frank went on. "And your life. Even now, when you're tired, you haven't been well, it's more like a tired kid . . ."

"Actually," Justin said in a cold rage—it was as if he had heard another judgment, "actually, wake up, will you? Do you know how long it's been since you cooked your supper on one of these alcohol stoves?"

"A long time," Frank said, smiling. But he drew his Burberry close around him.

"I face the truth my own way—do you, pal? Do you know how I pass my time, Monsieur Rip Van Winkle? I pass my time making out with boys who weren't even born when you lived in this terrible place."

A DEATH ON
THE EAST SIDE

"What we like, my friend, is give away a lot of money so we can catch a little of the overflow for tax savings in line with—oh, well, the federal and state provisions." A boyish forty-nine-year-old man was winking at me. He was also engaged in instruction. "We find that money tends to stick in the nets, a little for everyone, nice like that. Not that you should bother your insides about it. You, sir, are beyond such distractions. You are an artist, head in the clouds, aren't you?"

I would have appreciated his ceasing the flirty winking, and at last, when I looked up from the oysters he was buying me at the Algonquin, he did. He was momentarily busy with his own littlenecks— lemon, sauce, salt, and wine—or perhaps he was just checking out his next move.

". . . the strength of oysters and the delicacy of clams," he was saying. "For spiritual sorts. The Baroness Blixen lived to nearly eighty

125

on oysters and champagne." He rolled the last clam to its reward. "Isak Dinesen," he said. "We wanted to give her a year to write her final memoirs, but she said she couldn't spare the time. She said she was dying, and she was. Pity."

Philip Grove had served as vice president of various networks, he had been poetically handsome in his youth, he was a delight in middle age (luxuriant gray hair, ironic smiles); he had enjoyed twenty-five years of faithful drinking and seventeen years of psychoanalysis, both of them continuing nicely when we met. Two wives and three marriages confused matters; he had married one of the girls twice, numbers one and three—the oil lady from Tulsa had leapfrogged the chanteuse from Copenhagen and Cleveland. He was now redivorced from this first/third wife and paying her double indemnity, suicide, revenge, menopause, got-the-midnight-horrors alimony. Her wells had run dry. She was a 3:00 A.M. telephoner and even incited their daughter, Carol, to make trouble. "That hurts a bit," he said. "A lot."

A frequent refuge for Philip in times of stress was to enter public service. Now he was director of one of America's greatest second-rate foundations. They couldn't compete with Ford, Rockefeller, or Guggenheim, and that's how I came in: to help set up a program for catching the artistic fish and eels that the bigger endowments let slip through their valves.

Lunches at the Century Club, dinner at the Four Seasons. He wanted to get a positive result in whatever he did—even instructing me in how to live. I was flattered. We were both recently divorced, both trying out as gray-flecked Manhattan boys again. He had read my novels and thoughtfully quoted from me in conversation with me. That man knew how to make joy at small expense. (The person writing this story is no longer the person telling it.) I loved breathing the happy air. "Well, sir," he said with the courtly manner of a slightly older man who is signing all the checks, "I was probably paid more for reading your books than you were for writing them."

Somehow this made me feel important, though there was surely an edge to the compliment.

And advice on how to give money to artists? Now, there was a dreamy, restful deal. So I just let my mind expand, a few folds at a time. I suggested a program of special vacations for novelists, story writers, and poets. The idea was to waste and live well for a few weeks, to refresh the spirit with excess. A large sum of money would be handed out with the provision that it be squandered in less than a month. I invoked some traditional models—Dionysius, Bacchus, and C. Wright Mills (Philip expected nothing less from me). How would we check against the possibility of practical distortions—prudent midcentury poets laying on station wagons, laundry equipment, convertible preferreds for the children's education? Well, we could always go for receipts from Bahamian hotels and chorus girls freaked out on diet pills. Naturally, I preferred the honor system. I preferred to go that way.

Philip said he loved the idea, just loved it. As this meant he seemed to like it pretty well, I was sure the foundations would accept it, since he made all the important decisions. It was a brilliant day in the history of philanthropy. I was responsible for a great leap forward from the single flower of Puritanism into the thousand flowers of affluence and ecstasy. "Hmm," said Philip, "a keen article there for Gratefully Yours, the Journal of Applied Philanthropy. 'Affluence and Ecstasy; Expanding the Frontiers of Exemption . . .' " I was a mandarin ideologue in my first J. Press suit. Gongs, zithers, wine, silks, and dancing girls for the contributors to the Hudson Review.

At the next regular meeting of the governing board my idea was rejected.

Ah, so. Another miscalculation. Another case of too much enthusiasm and trust on life's way. Again a deep brainstormer had misplaced his faith in the ability of others to understand innovations in quantum money dispersal. Well, no matter.

Our friendship survived this reverse. I expected a small check labeled "honorarium" for drafting the idea, typing it, too; but evidently the high-level decision was to pay me in lunches, dinners, oral quotation from my work, continuing instruction, and the companionship of Philip Grove. Well, some things are worth more than money, though perhaps a plate of oysters at the Algonquin is not one of them. I put away my mandarin dreams.

Nevertheless, taking a consistent pro-oyster position, one evening I accepted another session of charge-a-plate seafood. Philip wanted to explain. He was tender in his own heart, too. "I know what you think, I'm smart enough," he said, "but the fact is I really want to do

something good every time I get into these—oh, complexities. The
problem is making it happen. I don't mean gimmicks, I mean the
clout, the thrust, the—" He smiled winningly. "The gimmick. I really
hate it that you have reason not to respect me, pal. I *know* about
respect and self-respect. Those are two of my fields."

It occurred to me, and I should have thought of it sooner, that he
really wanted to commit fine acts, read beautiful words, think powerful thoughts, go to bed with sweet ladies.

"Ah-ah." He wagged a warning finger. "I have insights. I stay in
touch."

"Sorry," I said. "I really like you, Philip."

"Not really," he said, "but you'll learn. However, I've called this
little group together for another purpose." He hinted that he was
looking about and planning to leave public service once more. It was
not quite—well, take my delicious project, for example. A terrible
loss, a personal embarrassment. How the bureaucracy of endowment
misunderstands the creative temperament, both administrative and
laboring in those lonely rooms which Sherwood Anderson of Elyria,
Ohio, described so eloquently in his collected letters.

His large, dark, intense eyes bored into mine to see if I had caught
his thought on the wing even before he had filed it along with the
request for accrued vacation time.

Yes.

In my turn I hinted that I was nearing the end of the first draft of
a new novel. Ah. New phases for both of us. We both sighed. We
would digest all this news and return to it in the fullness of time.

We then settled down comfortably to discussing our mistreatment
at the hands of women. We did not exactly wallow in our miseries,
but we inoculated ourselves against cholesterol and useless fret by not
keeping the secret. Although I had entered real life again, chasing
limber ladies through the canyons and rushing gorges of Manhattan,
I still took pleasure in these restful evenings of commentary and
philosophy. Philip, ten years older, claimed to admire my energy, but
liked to go at things a little more slowly. Bring them to him by taxi,
for example, or by limo when one was available. The permanent
truths—friendship, accomplishment, good taste—were what interested him. His daughter, Carol (a "teenie," as he described her), had
let him down. "Patience and cunning," he said, "that's what a man

needs. But no exile, it's impossible, the whole world is Manhattan now."

"I suppose."

"What good are victories?" he asked me. "What good is the hunt?"

"Are you asking me a question? I feel you're making a statement."

"Well, take Carol for openers. She is bad news for some old man, pal. If not for her dad, for some other chap."

In quest of permanent truth, he left the foundation and went to work for a buccaneer millionaire who had reached the stage in his development where he needed to finance art movies. On the day he told me about his new job I confessed to him that he looked a bit like a leading man. He was tall, slender, handsome, with suave weariness worn like a halo. That's a neat style. In his youth he had played polo. In his youth, he confessed in turn, he had wanted to be an actor, but: "I had too much—oh, premature afterthought you can call it. The lines they gave actors in those days—couldn't say 'em." His eyes were dark, soft and tender as he explained why he chose not to be a star of stage and screen. Producer—well, that's all the difference in the world. Because I had begun to weary of his dramatic cynicism, I redoubled my efforts to express friendship. After all, he had been good to me. But I began to suspect he was wearing eye liner to accentuate that dark, soft, and tender gaze.

Oh, it couldn't be.

I denied it to myself. He wasn't that sort. I put it out of mind. I looked for the telltale smear.

In an agony of difficult friendship we exchanged gifts like shy romancers. He put me up for his club as if to tell me I should now consider myself middle-aged. I gave him a copy of *Shakespeare's Bawdy* as if to tell him he could still have boyish intellectual fun. He asked to meet girls. I asked to meet interesting people. He was bored with the girls I introduced him to, and looked wan and bored. I was bored with the social people he introduced me to, and once escaped a party on Long Island through the library window. I hitchhiked back to Manhattan, frantic and drunk. We didn't see each other for a week, but then had a laugh over it and he wanted to take me to Southampton again so I could repeat my famous vanishing act. The cream that made me vanish was oil of small talk. He thought he might sell it along with excursions to Europe on Icelandic Airlines.

Ever since the peculiar thought about his wearing eye liner, I tried to conduct our meetings along with the company of ladies. Foursomes strolling Greenwich Village, four on weekends to Westport, that was my new idea. The old male intimacy dimmed a bit in our new occupations. He was irritated by my increasing implication in the temptations of Manhattan, as if only he had kept our interludes of talk pure, free of money and sex and ambition, just two friends sharing a flight through middle space.

One night, over the final brandy, he asked, "What's it all about? We are paper men, air men, we float and glide over this abstract town. Who are we? We are what we are—nobodies."

"I wish you'd speak for yourself, Philip."

He gazed mournfully into my eyes. Maybe he didn't wear eye liner, after all. It would be a sin to suspect him wrongly. He had hard, clear bluish whites, he had a fixity of gaze. "I suppose I should only speak for myself," he said. "It's part of the disease—abstraction. I want to take everybody my own way, as if a crowd of paper figures could make one man of flesh and soul. I apologize. Nothing personal." He waited for me to reply. "My daughter is breaking my heart."

I had nothing to say. I was tired after the long evening—a divorced Wellesley girl and her best friend—and the abrupt moment of King Lear found me unprepared. We had been amusing the ladies and it left my philosophic skills a bit threadbare. After so much laughter, nudging, and tickling, here came Carol. I must have looked distracted.

"Take the service elevator out," he said. "It's faster after one. Wait, I'll show you."

I found other friends. Philip joined a Unitarian group. We were both in search. He thought up a TV special to promote, something about the revival of irrational religion. He asked me if I liked his working title for it: *The Now! Churches.* Rational and irrational, he said; but in quest of some sort of purity. Ninety minutes of stomping and glossolalia, plus Erich Fromm and maybe Norman O. Brown— what did I think?

"Terrific, Philip."

"Sensational," he said, "*and* educational."

Also, as a remedy for that after-five feeling, that void, that anomie, that angst, those midcentury whatchamacallits, he fell in love.

In fact, despite the slow and stately stride of maturity, Philip the Pure was in love with the whole chorus line in the revived version of *West Side Story*. He had a friend whose skinny wife was a featured player and he would stand in her dressing room and look at the girls —High School of Performing Arts, Actors Studio, Merce Cunningham, readers of Buber and Frantz Fanon and *Variety*—through a crack in her half-shut door. They undressed with miraculous calm. Naked but for their eyelashes, long-limbed, cute, oh, cute, they primped and jiggled and waited for the Big Chance near massed banks of hot white bare bulbs. Gradually he narrowed his devotion to just one, Sandy Grasset, and gradually she came to understand that he wanted her for his very own.

Okay, one Sunday morning after an ecumenical mass at a Now! church, she gave herself to Philip for his very own. A man deserves a Big Chance, too. But then it wasn't enough. He wanted to marry her, to keep and cherish her. "Will you be my widow?" he demanded, dropping to his knees and mumbling, "George Bernard Shaw, an early play, I have total recall."

"*Wha?*"

"I was quoting. Shouldn't joke at a time like this. Total visual, not oral. Marry me."

She laughed and laughed, though not at the touching whimsy he intended, and he coolly noted that one thin tape of eyelash was coming unstuck. But he only loved her the more for this single blemish on her perfection of greedy little showgirl.

"Naw," she said. "I have my career, and my afternoons I go to the New School." Her evenings, of course, belonged to the Theater. She also studied creative writing, mime (*meem*), and existential psychodrama for a time of crisis.

He stared, hair thick and white, body thumped and worked at the New York Athletic Club. "I need you," he said.

"I like you," she said. "Isn't it obvious, really clear?"

"I would hope it all means something."

"Does, *does*, sweetie. I wouldn't do . . . *that*"—and she made a pretty little moufie, as if to say dirty-dirty. "I wouldn't do that for just anybody. Not even to get a job I wouldn't. I don't have to, besides. I'm well known for not doing it unless—"

"Unless you really like a fellow?"

"Well, you could put it." She got the point a second later. "Okay, then, you be sarcastic and see if it encourages an I-thou relationship between us."

"I'm sorry," he cooed, miserable.

"Aw, come on," she said, wrapping him in her skinny arms.

But she dawdled about marrying him. He worked out a miracle plan: me. I should persuade her, me, with my inspired pleading of his case. *Who?* It was like filling out a recommendation for a foundation grant. It was not like that, but he had his peculiar notion that I could help and he arranged for me to meet her alone at her apartment one afternoon (all of us supposed to be there, Philip delayed, last-minute telephone call, a carefully orchestrated plan). By means of straight talk, full of depth charges there in the shadow of Lincoln Center, I was supposed to win him his third/fourth wife.

I felt a bit wooden and pasted together. I said, "Um, he really cares for you. He wants you badly. I think you would do well."

"Icky," she said. "He's not icky, but he is too old. Hey, how's about I make us some coffee?"

"You said yourself he's not icky," I said, "and with vitamin pills and the new statistics from the insurance companies, he's got many carefree years ahead of him. How long do you think you can dance, Sandy?"

"Three wives. Icky."

"But you're different. And it wasn't really three. And he's a boy at heart."

"Plus he toll me I remind him of his *daughter*! I wanna stay in show business."

"True, he'd like you to be a helpmeet, entertain, spend his money." I hoped she was listening. I'd hate to have to repeat that.

"Hey, he's really loaded?"

"Then you won't?"

She fixed me with her violet eyes in that starved, bony dancer's face. Cheekbones and eyes in the context of violet and good definition always make a fellow think profound. "How much—how much you *bet*?" she asked. First she grinned with elfin humor. Then a hilarious peel of jeering laughter as the implications began to deal with her. Blacch, another natural screamer, I thought. She looks so physical, so much body and dance, but she's like an actress, a nice suburban girl, a nice normal hysteric. Abruptly she stopped laughing. "Maybe I will," she said. "You think the kid, uh—"

"Carol."

"—'ll bug us a lot?"

"No."

"Cause I hate kids like that—the selfish age."

"No, the kid is grown up, nearly your age."

That was three-fifths of a faux pas, but she didn't seem to mind. She was twitching with thought, tongue working in corner of mouth, Kleenex at eye, knees jiggling. Perhaps she was just practicing her new role of charming hostess, for she said, "Ooh, ick, the coffee's boiling over. Philip has a Chemex, doesn't he?"

On their honeymoon in Paris he suffered a ruptured blood vessel in one eye and had to go to the American Hospital. Too much drinking or lovemaking, an expatriate doctor commented, but I never heard that one before. That was one for Neuilly. Personally I thought he got some dirt in it and rubbed. And that's one for Sheridan Square.

They came back and it took a long time before they invited me over to their new apartment (condominium, East Sixties, excellent view of the write-off). Of course, they were busy fixing it up, but other friends got invited two, three times. I was out, it seemed. I had been too close to the premarital examinations, but I still saw Philip occasionally for lunch. He was keeping in touch and I'd be patient. His eye was red for months afterward, as if he had just been crying. Well, let him adjust to conjugal life again. It took some pressure off me, too. Our friendship would find its natural level.

One of the matters we shared was a friend, Baron Clausen, a Danish money pirate with castles in Austria, ranchos in Mexico, and ambitions to keep his tax-exempt fingers in all available tax-free pies. His nineteen-year-old wife (he was sixty) distracted him for a few hours each day, but then there were the sleepless nights and days in Manhattan. He liked Philip for the reasons of Philip's charm and savvy; he liked to discuss himself with me. Philip telephoned me one day at an odd early hour to say, "Clausen—you've been talking to him."

"Of course, sometimes, when he lets me."

"Too much, pal. He's been spreading the gossip about you."

"Clausen? What gossip?"

Philip reminded me of an incident involving—oh, a silly trouble about a party and a wife and her husband. I was irritated with Philip for reminding me of it. I was infuriated with my smiling Danish enemy. As soon as he next proposed one of his damn smørrebrød-and-cigar lunches, I'd give him some honest American lip. Senseless malice: why should he do that to me? I was shaking with the bachelor's dammed-up anger. I fretted, I sulked. I wouldn't deign to reach Clausen.

He never telephoned.

In a few days it dawned on me. Somehow Philip must have made him angry with me, too. What had I said of him? That he was too old for his young bride? That he was hanging about the artists to drink their blood? Well, I might have speculated along those lines—who doesn't speculate?

I should have had an explanation with Clausen, but the whole thing was a nasty bore. Foolish and foolishness. I let it pass. I forgot it. I fell in love. I let them pass, both of them, Clausen and Philip, and moved into another of the many worlds of Manhattan.

Only gradually, reluctant to admit the loss of friendship, did I guess that Philip was getting rid of me this way. He spread gossip about me among our mutual acquaintances because, well, he needed a bit of a change and he was in the business of opinion and that's how he did things. No matter. Another day, he must have decided from long experience, if I need him, I'll just come with my offer. He'll jump. There's no fun and profit in remembering history, which is mostly a series of grudges. He had once assured me that to his certain knowledge, people operate almost entirely in the light of their present interests. "Not principles or paranoia, friend, but what seems to be in the cards right now. I've found this to be true. It's tough, but it's nice to have confidence in the future, where you get what you want by talking about what's happening this afternoon. Say, listen, it's better that way."

Wine, oysters, talk, and the dangled carrot. Also, a continual earnest labor at completing my education. Corrupt and corruption, I thought; no matter. I had other business in life. I felt like Dick

Whittington come to conquer the great city. Although Philip had the knack of making his business seem important, more important than anything anyone else wanted to do, I found new routes through skyscraper and across plaza, up subway and into conference room.

Sometimes the crazy orbits of Manhattan intersect or collide. We remained acquaintances, but the old clubby exchanges were finished. We would continue toward new careers, wives, hopes and troubles on divergent paths.

I had a friend, J. Willis, a longtime Village writer, with three stories and a poem to his credit after twenty years and four grants, who turned out to be dating Philip's daughter, Carol. There's a crossed path for you. Willis had presided over his self-contempt for so long that it had become a friend to him—a deadly enemy to the ladies he sucked dry. Carol was a pretty thing with long blond bangs that tickled her eyes as if she had no interest in where she was going. Willis took his exercise on such girls and thought he was a man. If I had been Philip with a daughter . . . but I was not Philip with that daughter.

Baron Clausen started a foundation, incidentally, and made Philip the president of it. Philip may have suspected me of wanting to push into the foundation business.

Sandy was an odder girl than she appeared—girl making out okay in Manhattan. Dancing seemed to have trained the upturned corners of her mouth, but there were also secret downturning depths. She had been supported for several years by Rico DiRico, the Jukebox King, who had known the joy of seeing his picture in *Life*, not in connection with his Wurlitzer musical activities, but because he was a friend of friends of folks with complex police and FBI records. Rico preserved his friendship with Sandy after her marriage, and also with Philip. It seemed a sporty connection for that elegant veteran of Washington conferences on the arts and network efforts to upgrade popular culture. (*From Shlock to Kitsch*, an autobiography by Philip Grove. That was his idea. Subtitle? "Through Darkest Camera with Grant and Program.") Philip didn't fear for reputation, since most of Rico's arrests had not resulted in convictions.

There is a reason, or a season, or at least a cause for everything, as Ecclesiastes almost says. Philip wanted to produce his first movie, based on a forgotten novel about the Depression. There were many curious elements in the equation. The book was written by a man, now rather elderly and a senior editor of *Reader's Digest,* who at one time had been an iron-willed literary Marxist ("The land is the people! The people is the land!" was the last paragraph and hiccup of the novel). The original story aimed to show (a) the American working and peasant classes oppressed by county banks and agents of Wall Street in jodhpurs, then (b) their gallant uprising at the iron will of the novelist; the movie script aimed to show the warmth and humanity of immigrant racketeers, who managed by means of tenderness and vigor to crash through staid class lines, thereby getting the grateful girl in the end. The suspense for her was terrific. She would have to wait ninety minutes, eighty if cut for drive-ins, to discover she was worth more to the hero than land, people, or his mama's hand-stuffed lasagna. Much more; a symbol of the transcendence of Norman O. Brown's polymorphous perverse eros over economic determinism; a really modern scam, actual, contemporary, today, existential, and, within the limits set by the concept of redeeming social importance, dirty.

Sandy played a small part, mostly leaning against a white piano in a speakeasy, looking fearful, as if the chandelier might fall. The financing came from Rico diRico, who may have been crooked but who was not necessarily clever. The film lost money, even with a syndicated sale to TV. The Bonnie & Clyde epoch was not yet upon us. But was it real coin-operated money? Probably the lonely toy money of drugs and gambling that sought warmth and companionship in the real world of tax losses.

Anyway, it made sense for Philip to keep good connections with DiRico. Perhaps he could count on cultural impetus in the future, too. I used to run into the three of them, Philip, Sandy, and DiRico, at those steamy steak palaces on Third Avenue where you also find popular priests, daytime game-show emcees, and out-of-town buyers working hard at their expense-account cholesterol. Once I sat with them through dessert (I was meeting an option holder from the Coast, who was late). Philip, I noticed, played with his food. He looked pale, and the broken vein in his eye had never quite mended, so that it always seemed as if he were recovering from a recent crying jag or had spent too much time with his accountant. He was hoping to do his second film, maybe this time with Sandy as the star. DiRico was considering it.

Then one morning I got a call from Philip's secretary. Mr. Grove wanted to see me at his office. As soon as possible. Very important. Of course, like all writers, I seek any possible opportunity to avoid work. I was showered, shaved, and in a cab within half an hour. Manhattan traffic jams being what they are, I needed a shower by the time I arrived and wished I had taken a subway, but my shave was still intact.

I carried it through an honor guard of new receptionists and secretaries, Itkin décor, wormwood paneling—the DiRico touch. Philip began right off: "What do you do with people, chap?"

"Who people? What people?"

"The public. My daughter."

That pretty girl with the regulation straight blond hair, wan little face, dropout credentials from Sarah Lawrence, and those eye-tickling bangs. She had left J. Willis, my Charles Street pal. She had been moving pretty fast.

"I want to tell somebody," he said, "and then I want to forget it. I'm going to tell you." It sounded like a threat. Before I could say, *Oh, no, you don't*, or *What about your analyst?*, he was on the way and all the way there: She had died of hepatitis in San Francisco.

He looked at me with his peculiar courteous attention. I was frozen with misery and confusion. He waited until he decided I was okay.

"She was taking Methedrine sulfate, I think they call it. Speed. Dio-metha-something, I don't know. Affected her mind—memory, reasoning power, she was a skinny thing, not the pretty girl you met. But it wasn't speed that killed her. It was a dirty needle."

"Philip, I'm sorry."

"She was always careless with her things. Her mother used to complain, but what could I do? I wasn't responsible—could I be? That woman really cut me off from her, so how could I?"

"Philip, where is she?"

He looked at me through his one red eye, his two eye-lined eyes. "Ah, she was buried out there yesterday. What's the good?" He shook his head. "I wanted someone to know. Pass it on. Communicate." I realized he was slightly drunk. "I suppose it's better," he said.

"What's better?"

"Hey, fella, let's go to P.J.'s. You can have a hamburger and I can have a freshener."

"No, I can't, Philip."

"Okay, a small salad. I need it. I need to sit with you—someone."

"Okay, Philip."

He smiled, stood up, shrugged his shoulders in that handsome, boyish, stylish way. "What did she have to live for? Her life was a mess. Man, I know about the problems with my oedipal hang-ups. I tried as much as I could, I worried about her, fella. But that rusty needle probably just saved a lot of trouble, agony, and expense."

The secretary came in and he waved her away. "Please, I'm taking an early lunch." He waited until she closed the door. He turned to get his coat and said to me, "Life—what is it? Let's not frighten ourselves with that question, but we got to ask it. China. India. It's time for some perspective. Carol. It's pathetic. But when you've had as much therapy as I have, eighteen years and a small fortune, one thing you learn is admit your secret feelings. Expense and worry and what good is it?"

I was out of that office in a few seconds. I noticed I was gone when the elevator door showed me lobby and street. It wasn't grief that made me flee, or not only grief.

But it wasn't as if I could shake him so easily. That conversation about Carol had gone past the end for him, too. After I left the office, he waited a few weeks and then summoned me about what he called a "reasonable" project—miscalled. "Let's just discuss," he said, "with no obligations on either side. I always find you have an interesting mind." Which meant: I'm sure you'll want to do what I want you to do. He hired me to work on a film script he was "developing." That means, speculating in. First he told me it was to be based on a story of mine, but it turned out to be based on a story by the network computer which told him what he could (a) get into the nabes and then (b) presell to television. Rico was putting up the front money and Sandy had a slightly smaller part—one scene where we would all presumably share the curve of her dancer's thighs through the magic communion of the cinema art. While I wrote, she became pregnant; no connection. "I'll be an instant grandfather," Philip announced

with his shyest smile that invited you to think whatever you liked
about his feelings.

However, he didn't look well. His skin had become blue and his
body slow and spectral. He should have seen a doctor. He said he was
on to what they were selling. His nose bled. He sweated at night and
Sandy slept in another room because he felt icky in bed. He refused
to go to his doctor. I suppose he knew what he was doing, and buying.

One afternoon we had a meeting about the script. He suddenly
closed his eyes as if thinking, as if sleeping. He lay at an odd angle,
like a stick in his chair, and I caught him before he fell. He quickly
came out of the faint, blinking and smiling, but his secretary called
the doctor and we got him to a little private hospital nearby, in the
East Sixties. No problem with the heart. Weakness, general weakness.
The doctor ran blood tests to confirm what he already suspected.

There was an abnormal increase of white blood cells originating in
a disease of the bone marrow. They gave him transfusions to increase
his strength for the time being, temporarily. They do that to provide
a breathing space. Leukemia.

Philip got the news early. He conned the doctor into telling him
everything. Calm and elegant, he heard him out and asked intelligent
questions and it seemed the doctor was flattered by the patient's
interest. He might live as little as six months. He might last from three
to five years. The suppressant drugs have variable results. When one
wears out, or starts to wear out the body—the side effects are often
very disagreeable—the doctors shift to another drug.

"And of course," Philip said, "by the time you finish rotating the
known drugs, they may have some new ones."

"Or a cure," said Dr. Berman.

"Or even a cure," Philip said, smiling and nodding. "Thank you
very much."

I suppose there is no normal routine for handling the friends and
relatives. Philip told me, his wife, Rico; he told the poodle and his
newborn son; he told the people with whom he did business and
cabdrivers and stopped just short of writing letters to the editor
stating that he had six months left to live. He set up a means for
sharing the experience, irony in him, horror in others. He seemed
pleased and proud. I wondered if he was taking mood drugs, and

perhaps he was, but the euphoria seemed genuine, rooted in the vain and frantic blood. He would call me in the middle of the night to discuss "our" script, and then his illness. He wanted to get the script finished and shot before he "went." He dwelled in an ecstasy of energy and goodwill, popping into the hospital for transfusions and then flying off to do rapid business with banks and studios and networks. It made story conferences difficult.

"I can't write that girl as man-eater," I would say. "She's sad, but she's not mean."

"Look," he replied gently, "let's cut the crap. I may have only six months left and I see her for what she is: a bitch-whore-destroyer."

The only-six-months argument won his way about character, style, money, whatever the day brought into his office. As some people are name-droppers, he would sit in Sardi's East and death-drop his own death to get one up on me. He was doing it all around, with agents, creditors, secretaries, and even his wife. Ever since these two events had come to complicate her time—the birth of her child, the announced death of her husband—she had grown quieter and the silliness had disappeared. She had discovered something outside herself. She was interested, frightened, appalled. It was all happening at once. I believe she even stopped seeing Rico, though that may have been his doing, a superstitious fear. She had the eye-liner look which seemed to run in Philip's family—his daughter, too—but it gave her a bit of staring style. He may have succeeded in instructing her to care for him. For sure Sandy was going through the miseries.

Philip's production staff accommodated his various television and film projects. He used to charm them into working long hours, bending to his will; now he bullied them.

"What are you complaining for?" he would ask a secretary who needed something, such as time off, which he didn't want to give her. "After all, you have your whole life ahead of you."

She blushed.

"So do I, of course."

He got his way. Midtown Manhattan knows how to be nervous and even how to suffer, but this was one boss, handsome Philip, that a secretary couldn't handle.

"What do you mean, you don't like the project. It's changing into, okay, so kitsch. Never mind, listen, now is the time to communicate

—gut level. There will come a day," he told me, "when this will be the last project I can close. I won't be able to come to the office." He smiled. "It'll be *me* closing. I'll turn into a vegetable," he said affably, "except it'll hurt a lot, fella."

I was learning to hate him.

"That's for openers and up front," he said.

And yet I couldn't pull out at this stage, could I? Just because he was slurring and jiving and bullying, and using his own death as a marketing and production tool, was that any reason to give him more trouble than usual?

The job became more complicated than most jobs. Rico and Sandy had me talking to doctors; Sandy because she was brokenhearted, Rico because he couldn't believe the happy-boy partner would really let him down at some point in their business together. Philip was piling ahead, grandiose and furious, with the energy of a pink-cheeked young producer despite his bluish skin and his death's-head eyes.

The doctor said, "Remission. Like a lot of them . . ." He added cautiously, "Mr. Grove—Philip—seemed almost disappointed when I told him his place on the curve may be rather late. It won't be another six-month deal. He might well have five years, and then what? We don't know any more."

Disappointed?

"You'll see that sometimes—disappointed."

It was a hard campaign to live up to. It was a whirlwind campaign, intended for a six-month promotion; Philip wasn't programmed for a five-year plan. Nobody could put up with his dying for five whole years ahead. Speaking as an associate, it would kill us all. Or at least give migraine headaches, anxious nightmares, Manhattan boredom assaults, creeping paralysis. "They're out to get us," one secretary kept muttering. She meant the leukocytes. We became experts on the disease, as if it were an un-American conspiracy, like communism or Swedish art films.

He was killing friendship by falsity.

Let me be fair: He was also killing enmity by creating an eerie contempt for his suffering. He made his own suffering unreal by using it as a public relations trick. He was trivializing his own and everyone else's feeling about the primary fact. He was barring his own recognition of death the friend, death the enemy.

Bravado: manipulating his own emotion.

Worse, a public relations bravado: manipulating the emotions of others and calling them his own.

Which?

Both. I wanted to say: China, India, what is life? Your daughter dies. You die. Everybody dies; big deal. Phony trouble. But where then is the real trouble?

I tried to see through the strategy of management to the terror beneath, but felt myself failing beneath my own spite. I began to have nightmares about the emptiness within myself that made me want to destroy this man, or to take relish in his self-destruction; no, not nightmares, black insomnias full of shooting dreams like meteors and murky under-earth movements. Because I found myself hating him and hating myself, I was tied to him by a pity suspiciously like self-pity. What in the past gave him such energy and resolution? How could the mask fit so seamlessly, and leave him so malignant and joyous? He was a mystery to me, and a fearful one.

I visited him whenever I could. I let him work his will upon me. Submissively I awaited new indignities. Confusion. To live with the confusion made the life of New York seem avid, arid, abstract, and horrible. We spent our workday lives in those radiant East Side glass tombs. It was as if I had some wasting disease.

I entered his office one lunch hour—the secretary was out—and found him crooning over a photograph of Carol. He was bowing and rocking and his face was broken. When he saw me, he brightened up immediately. "I didn't hear you come in!" he cried happily.

He had not heard me come in. It was the truth. I had found him alone, entirely alone with his grief and regret.

And it was double the pleasure, double the fun, when he realized that this scene had just come naturally, it was a happy accident, it gave the touch of life and truth to his act, it was sincere. He profited handsomely from his own incontestable sincerity. The incident was proof positive. The secretary had gone to lunch and left him un-protected. I had walked in with no appointment. Who could find a flaw in the deep feeling which I had discovered despite the deep feeler's intent to keep it absolutely mum?

During this same sincere period in his life, Philip was using the opportunity to "speak frankly"—to bad-mouth friends, to encourage

confidences and then to betray them, immune to reproach. He
stalked like the white death in our midst, swaddled in graveclothes,
clutching at our sleeves and murmuring, "Hey, I'm dying." We
wanted to shake him off like those midtown alcoholics who beg for
sympathy in the lounges. But he was not dying on time. The months
passed. His friends wanted to say to the sleeve-clutcher, "Aw, go
away, will you?"

One day I said to him, "Don't."

"Don't what?"

He was spreading silly rumors—oh, silliness—such as something,
well, on the order of being mean to my former wife. In fact, that was
it. Exactly. Mean to stepwife. Now, what a stupid story! Who would
ever do a thing like that? But that was what he said—mean (me?) to
that dark lady of my miserable twenties.

Of course, I'd have liked to be meaner than I was. As mean as I
managed to be, it barely saved my skin. But he tried to tell people I
wasn't nice. And you know what? They believed him. People are
funny about believing what they are told, especially when the delicious news is coming from someone as credible, as mortally ill as
Philip; and especially if there are some really nasty tidbits.

"Don't what?" he repeated with great, earnest concern.

"Don't voice your opinions as if you know. Don't tell people you
think I'm this and that and wait to have them pick up on it and then
tell me what they say and then tell them how I react—just don't,
Philip. Okay, gossip if you have to, but I'd rather you wouldn't."

"I have no time for small talk, buddy."

"That's not what I'm asking you."

"Wait. You cut the crap at a time like this." He put his hand on
my arm and squeezed it gently. He made my gaze meet his. He gave
me a long look from dark, sad, beautiful, almost girlish eyes. He
squinted them slightly and looked deep into mine. "You fail to appreciate how this changes a man's life," he said, retreating, hurt, leaving
me to meditate on his soft turning away of my irritation. He had
become a master of the pronoun this, word with a subject and predi-
cate, a dense clause of unspoken explanations and commands.

"Okay, Philip," I said, "I don't suppose I should try to educate
you."

"I just try to call the shots how they are," he said. "I've said and done things in the past, things I regret. Carol. Well, you know. Now, with what's left to me, *this*, I'm just trying to be as straight as I know how."

"Okay, Philip, you've explained."

"I want you to understand me, pal, you above all. I've opened up to you. You've seen the worst. I don't even mean I intended it that way, that's just how it worked out. You're someone I really trust and count on."

That's a hard one to answer if it's only the eve of battle, but when it's leukemia time on old Madison Avenue, this country boy from Cleveland, Ohio, found he was losing the argument.

"Thank you, fella," he said, "for understanding where I live."

At first it only seemed like giving him his way on script changes because of *this*, but now it was letting him get away with undoing the little world in which we all moved. Digs, jabs, pryings, and do everything he wanted. Finally one six o'clock after a long session of mixed work and philosophy, I yelled at him, "Goddammit, don't! I don't care! I don't care what's happening to you."

"You don't want to say that," he remarked serenely, coming back into his office to hear me out.

"You have no right!"

He pulled the drapes and stood staring into the swollen orange-gray light of the late-afternoon Manhattan sky. Then he turned back to me, huge and spectral in the altered glow of our glass section of the glass tomb.

"Let's discuss a moment," he said happily. "You've brought this up before. I know I've changed, even as to manner. I feel I have a special emergency built in, a sense of crisis, and it gives me an intensity, a certain clarity and directness—"

I walked out.

I didn't see him for several days. Everyone brings confusion for everyone else. He brought too much of it. He left messages for me, but I took off for East Hampton.

Then Sandy called and got through to me. Her voice gave a correct but incorrect message. "He's in the hospital," she said.

"A relapse? What's up?"

"He may die."

"So soon."

Again the confusion. He had crept close in my life, and lent me moments of power. What right had I to judge him?

"Pills," she said. "They pumped his stomach, but I'm not sure . . ."

He recovered. They gave him blood, they kept him in the hospital for a few days, and then they released him, as good and as bad as ever. He had only taken six or seven Seconals. He apologized to everyone individually, including me. It was just an impulse, he said, a silly one, to spare us all the trouble.

"I'm a little foolish and desperate," he said. "I'm sure I'm being a little, ah, extreme, but who is to say what is proper behavior at a time like this?"

"Philip."

"Please forgive me—please? For the sake of old friendship? You once had a good feeling about me. Will you hold on to it, friend? I know I've done some bad things. We were friends. Try to remember, okay? Please?"

Despite all this busy play, it was finally about to happen. Philip's body began its mortal closing down. The rhythm of trips to the hospital, ameliorations, remissions, transfusions, new techniques, interventions, failures, hopes, desperations was now a familiar matter. Accelerations did not change the pattern. Hope and despair provided a kind of vividness; then the vividness, like an amphetamine, wore out its host. Sandy became a stilled, sick child with a grin like the beginning of tears and a strangled voice reading the packaging of Philip's old habits: "Hiya, fella." She had learned other things from him, too. "I think he's a little better today. You're going in to see him, aren't you?" She uttered her grief and made his demands for him and slid through the day stricken by the smiling horrors.

Their son was invisible. He had disappeared almost as completely as Carol. Well, this was no time for a baby.

For every man there is a last trip to his office. Philip made that final visit, knowing it was final, and walked out without taking his briefcase. He left his appointment book open, three lunches scheduled for next week. He walked with the stiff gait of a sick man under tight control. He told his secretary he would be back after the weekend; she knew he would not be back. He had drawn into his diminished body. The writer would miss his oysters at the Algonquin; the agent would miss his scampi at Fontana di Trevi; the expense account had drawn to its end.

I wonder if many men in business put an exact close to the work by which they think to define themselves. Well, nothing is eternal, not even a great tax gimmick, not even a good East Side address. But Philip made no plans for his uncompleted projects. He left no provisions. He walked out. It was dead to him—the public relations, the TV series, the movie. Someone else could do it; someone else could not do it. He felt nothing for it. Rico might move someone in to try to hatch the eggs, but Philip ceased to fret about it. It was as dead as Carol, and about this retreat from work he was as dry and cold as, it seemed, he hoped to be about his own death. It was no longer what he used to call a plus factor in the daily round.

I came to see him. He was propped in a hospital bed with a lever sticking like a key out of his back. No, there was a thin mattress behind his back, and then the crank. His eyes were burning out of the bluish skin. "They shave me," he said. "I can still shave myself, but this way I have strength left over to waste." He grinned. "I got to figure out what to do with the strength left over from not having to shave myself."

"How are you feeling, Philip?"

"How do you feel when you know the end is near?"

"I don't know," I said.

"You will someday, I trust, fella." As if to soften the malice, he quickly added, "I try to get Sandy to take the towels home from this place. You know what it's costing my estate?"

"I can imagine."

"Oh, boy. Imagine on through."

A nurse was standing in the doorway. "It's time," she said.

"A treat or a treatment?"

"Mr. Grove, it's time now."

He grinned at me and said, "You mind waiting? I'd like to talk to someone when I get back."

"What are they going to do to you?"

"Stick needles. In the veins, that's okay. In the bone to get at the marrow, that hurts. Would you wait? Do you mind waiting?"

The attendants wheeled him out. I waited. He didn't go far. There was an adjacent laboratory. I could hear a distant creaking through the walls, Philip howling with pain, and then abruptly nothing. I was soaked in my clothes when he returned. He looked stunned and goofy. His pajama top was unbuttoned. His chest was covered with unhealed needle marks—deep scars and lesions. He was panting, but quiet. He tried to button one button of his pajamas, but his hand fell away, exhausted. I thought maybe he wanted to sleep.

"No, don't go."

I waited.

He said, "What do you do when you *know?*"

I couldn't answer yet.

"They keep making experiments, I think. Pieces of marrow they drag out. I don't heal anymore either—the skin—not that it matters. All for sweet research. I'm happy to stop healing."

I had nothing to say.

"Relax and enjoy it, I guess," he said.

The nurse came in with two pills. She held them to his mouth, a glass of water in her other hand. She was a black woman with good country looks, a prim, intelligent face, an opulent, intelligent body in the rustling uniform. He shook his head to the pills and took them in his hand. "My friend'll give me the water," he said. I took the glass. His hand closed tightly over the pills. "Stay and talk . . ." He meant me. "No, you can go, Nurse. Thank you."

I had nothing to say, but I said it: "That must be painful."

"I'm sorry if it bothers you, pal. I found these tears in a test tube. The doctor gave me the sample, and I sprinkle them everywhere. It's convenient. Too bad I didn't have them when Carol died." He closed his eyes. "You're right," he said at last, "relax and enjoy it."

"I didn't say it. You said it."

"I thought you said it."

"*You* said it."

"Am I getting confused? Now, there's a nasty."

He was stretching and wiggling, and the sweat kept starting on his upper lip. He wiped it with his sleeve. I stifled my panic. "Can't they give you something for the pain?"

"Yes, of course, they did."

"Why are you suffering so?"

He opened his fist. The pills were soggy and crumbled. "I didn't want to get dopey. I wanted to talk to you first, before I take them."

"Take them!" I said.

He shrugged and put them in his mouth. I held the glass to his lips. He drank.

Yes, I wanted to turn away. It's not so easy! I wanted to take all the opportunities he gave me to trim the recognition of decay and death with disgust at a performance. I assured myself that his refusal to complain of pain, to confess his mortal fear, was just another matter of style; he knew it would capture me; it was the unspoken in art, the hidden dream of time in a melody, an esthetic trick like his other tricks. But no, his discretion was real, I think—the foundation of style and comeliness within all his cunning chic. He tried not to frighten me with his body so that he could teach me something with his soul. His selfishness may have been very deep, as his style was most pervasive. But his intention was also to make me learn from him. I could complain and strike back. I couldn't follow my itch to flee. I couldn't be honest and impulsive that way. I couldn't simply walk out on him. How nice it would be to withdraw to criticism. He gave me grounds. I had to follow my yearning in another way.

"Thank you very much," Philip said.

"For what?" I saw the bottle of sedatives by his bed and remembered what the doctor had said: "I give them the pills and let them make the choice. I warn them: 'Too many and you sleep forever.' But they just wait, usually until they have no choice. Stubborn—most men are stubborn."

"For entertaining Sandy, I mean taking her to the movies, talking to her—I mean everything, friend."

"Nonsense."

"Please try to be a little more gracious when I'm being grateful, pal."

My own history with him is not very pretty—a history of falling in with his schemes, taking his money (never as much as I expected), letting the con give me coffee nerves, and then walking out with cold parting shots and angry resolutions. Well, I couldn't just walk out on him anymore. He was in the thick of battle. He—not his words, not even his deeds, but Philip himself, the person hidden beyond all tricks —was telling a part of the truth, like all men, and more of the truth than many. Good-bye to the con. He was suffering. I learned some sour facts about myself from him; that's familiar enough in these days of prideful self-examination and self-laceration; but what was more common, traditional, and yet surprising, I was learning something about him. He struggled for control; he sought to master himself. He no longer thought of killing himself. The rest of life was precious to him, and not merely something he could use. He smiled handsomely, histrionically, and yet he was truly brave in his way.

The disease was marching through his body, consolidating its gains around his organs, receding, sending out marauding scouts, voraciously living off the country, blood, lymph, liver, spleen. First he felt weakness and dizziness, like a rapid elevator to earth, then seasickness and landsickness; remissions, illusions; then pain to breathe, pain around the heart, his body poisoning itself, drowning in its own fluids. This animal suffering he did not include in his public performance. He did not know how to use it; yet he was suffering atrociously. The horror of inexorable, irreversible pain is a great incitement to drama. He refused it. He suffered and left the suffering apart, as if it were the last holy object in his life.

His lungs filled with fluids. The doctors were making taps, inserting drains. They strapped him up like a sick tree and drew interesting substances from the trunk. "Did I tell you I was raised in Vermont?" he asked me. "Maple-syrup time again. Listen, we learned to say very little in Brattleboro, we learned to hide, and when I got garrulous those years in New York—"

"New York'll do that to you."

"I know. That's what I wanted. I never got good enough at it, was what I'm getting at. . . ."

He was in torment, and reconciled to the fact that this time he could not pass it on as gossip or conniving. Could there have been some joy in giving up the mission of promoter, of user? No, but relief at defining the area of no cop-out. Something. Anything. There must have been, I pray there was, some brain flash of discovery and relief. This was not borrowed pain, picked up on the free-lance market. It was his own, his personal creation; he had world rights to it. Once, or sometimes, or steadily through the new and terrible routines of his nights and days, he must have received the message, he must have gotten through to himself. Oh, surely he would have agreed to do without in return for ease, but it was offered anyway—that brain

flash, that ebb of sea over the meshed debris of depths, that withdrawal, clarity, and renewed confusion. An accurate, silent, perfect
recognition of himself! And still rich in confusions.

He had stopped leaving his room. The transfusions were no longer
perking him up; his body said no to the cortisone and mustard and
cell suppressants; the organs, the whole system was disoriented.

Now what? How long?

Last week propped lightly in a chair with book and glasses; sometimes shaving himself, sometimes dressed.

Now wearing pajamas and shaved by his wife or a nurse, saving the
strength for sitting and talk. It was too much trouble to turn face and
lift chin. He should let the gray-mottled beard grow.

"I'm going to sleep," he said. "Wait. Wait a sec." He was working
something out, his lips moving, racing the pills in his blood. He
smiled as if it were a game. He nodded. He had found what he was
looking for. "I'm carrying it by myself for the rest of the way—ah,
that's nonsense. Forget it. I'm sorry."

"For what? It's unnecessary."

Behind drugs and coming in after drugs and without drugs at all,
in the spaces wrought by disaster, he was finally exploring a territory
which was his alone, bordered entirely by Philip, traversed solely by
Philip, private beyond any despair or consolation.

"It's soon now," he said.

"Might be."

"First I'll sleep."

"That's fine."

"I'm finished promoting my last asset," he said.

"Shush, Philip."

The panic had left me. I too was calmed, as if for the first time
Philip were present in the room with me. The games were done and
there was no more advantage.

"There was something I wanted to say before I got confused by one
thing or another, but that wasn't it—the romance of my little situation. Not that. Oh, not that, buddy."

"No hurry, Philip."

"Yes, hurry, pal." He winked. "Didn't I do some bad things to you?
I seem to remember. I can't remember."

At the last minute, I was thinking, death might come to him as the friend he had always sought, or another enemy, or as an ecstasy of distraction; or merely as a new campaign and project—there was no reason to expect more of death than of life.

"Didn't I?" he asked anxiously. "Bad-mouth you one time? Put you on?"

"Never mind, Philip."

No, none of these. It would slip over him as it slips over animals and men—a diminution, a withdrawal, and an acceptance. He would be here like other men and then he would be gone.

"It was someone else then."

"Forget it."

"No, it was you *and* someone else. Plus a lot of others."

"I said forget it."

He shut his eyes. "Next year at this time I'll be a better person," he said. "You wait. This same time next year." There was an almost girlish, peaceful look on his face—eyes closed and mouth in a sensual, smiling pout.

I sat there, watching him, trying for my own sake to try to carry something away with me; and for his sake, too. Despite the drugs and vanity, the money and power and the cleverness, the common paraphernalia of hospitals and the special vaults of Philip's character, his body and soul were falling from him just as other men's do, and I had to meet my own abiding distrust of him in coming to see that he had a soul like other men's, like mine; and he did the best he could for his daughter and his wife, and if it wasn't enough to suit me, it was still all he could do; and finally he held the monster close, as every man one day must.

He seemed to be asleep. I tiptoed out.

"Bye-bye," he said. "Take care, fella."

I looked back, but his eyes were shut and I suppose he was sleeping.

A SELFISH STORY

Not long ago one of my daughters asked me, "Daddy, were you in World War One or Two?" At about the same time, a woman whom I consider as grown-up as myself told me that she remembers my war because she remembers the boots her father wore while washing the car. She was an infant on an Army post. And yet, for those of us who enlisted near our eighteenth birthdays in the early forties, the war is still immediate, our youth is not disappeared, and yet time and history have rolled over us, despite our will to give sense to the present and future in the light of the past. Now I must subjugate the past in order to tell about it. It turns out that I am still its willing groom, moving and mated to it.

In 1942 I embraced New York City. I had spent a year wandering on the road, living out a fantasy of rebellion from Cleveland, part of it in the flophouses of the Bowery and Bleecker Street, but now I had washed and scrubbed myself, turned seventeen and a half, and entered Columbia College. Morningside Heights was as far from my scrounging boy bum days as any place could be; Irwin Edman and Mark Van Doren replaced the gamblers and shills on Key Largo, the enraged, oversteamed chefs in restaurant kitchens all up and down the eastern seaboard, the hoboes, wildballs, and predators of the risky America I had pursued. Having so much eccentric fun made me morose and serious. I was an adjusted misfit.

The return to college structure was brief. We freshmen, turning eighteen, believed we might finish our first year before going to war. Autumn, black winter, reluctant spring. We read Homer, Thucydides, Herodotus, Humanities and Contemporary Civilization, and felt up the Barnard girls near the spiked metal fence on Broadway, and thought about our silver wings, our marksmen's medals, our future citations and press dispatches. We had no imagination for death, for our own inevitable future deaths, the death of everyone, and for the plain fact that a certain proportion of these readers of bloody Homer would be dead early, very soon now, before the end of the war.

However, there are fits in the process of growing up and imagining one's own mortality. Living is a flux and flow, but knowledge comes at moments. A serious illness is one start; the death of a parent is another. And sometimes even the incident of education can educate. By pure good fortune, one of these occasions occurred on a lazy late-winter afternoon in Hamilton Hall; the steam heat was boiling, there was a smell of chalk in the air, a seminar on "Lucretius and Time" was occupying a group of solemn freshmen and our professor, O.J. Campbell, a distinguished scholar of Shakespeare. Up until this afternoon, I must note, I had not formed any real friendships at school, although I admired the mad Cuban of Hartley Hall, who ran naked up and down the corridors, working out, and a boy with a Maine accent who wanted to be either a missionary or a dean, and an irritable young man from White Plains who felt misused because he was adopted into a rich family rather than born to it. Jack Kerouac was on the football team, a popular kid; I had spent a year on the road and felt cut off from him and the other middle-class youngsters making their way on squads and in clubs. I didn't even write for the *Jester*, the college review, or the *Spectator*, though I was a secret poet and journal keeper.

On that sleepy, still afternoon in Hamilton Hall, a crucial discovery was opened to me, and with it, I also made my first close college friend. Professor Campbell, looking out over the dozen of us slouched around a table, talking about time and time's end, life and mortality, suddenly remarked to this serious crew of freshmen, "I was dead once, and I came back. I was dead and I remember it." He had had a heart attack; he had gone under; then he had returned. "I was dead. I still remember it." The words were ordinary, but in the act of uttering them, he suddenly forgot to speak. He put his head down and remembered. Thick gray eyebrows, a heavy, handsome old head. A look of withdrawal, a look of the deepest seriousness possessed him. There was an uneasy silence in the room.

Ahead of my first risk in the war, ahead of my first dangerous illness, ahead of the first death of someone close to me, I suddenly had a premonition of what death might mean, beyond the drama of grief and mourning. My own heart stopped. There was the excitement of discovery and a terrible loneliness.

At that moment, and perhaps just as Professor Campbell began to speak once more of Lucretius, I noticed a fellow student, whom I shall now call Marvin Shapiro. Purplish hickey stood out in the pallor of his face. He was stunned by this reminiscence of death, as I had been, and he too felt that premonitory grief and loneliness. And then he flushed as the blood returned.

After class I approached Shapiro and we talked. We cut the rest of our classes that day, strolled the campus, ate ice cream, circled the track, told our stories, listened to our stories, and finally got around to the subject of girls. This led naturally to a number of pitchers of beer at the West End Tavern on Broadway. By closing time we decided we were lifelong friends, and so we were. Marvin was a skinny boy with bad skin, a deep voice and a surcharged Adam's apple, and a family in Brooklyn. He wanted to be a radio announcer, a physicist, and a lover of beautiful women. I shared the latter ambition, but aimed at poetry and philosophy as the means to this dreamed-of end. I also told him (me from Lakewood, Ohio) that he was my first Jewish friend. Marvin looked at me as if I must be crazy. He knew nothing about Lakewood, Ohio.

Expanding our horizons, we organized expeditions to eat eggplant parmigiana on First Avenue and fish at Joe's on South Street near the market. We were voyeurs who stopped at every doorway. And after we had peeked, we discussed what it all meant. The sting of prying was a philosophical lust, we thought; but also we were perpetually horny. Strolling through the fish market, we saw a child idly piddling his hands in a barrel of shrimp. It was a boy of eight or nine in a corduroy jumper-jacket; he had a bored, sallow, pretty, Italian face, and he was dipping his hands into the crisp pink shells and letting them spill through his fingers like doubloons in a pirate movie; he was watching the stand for his father. One withered leg was encased in a shiny paraphernalia of metal braces. Marvin's eyes filled with tears.

Disasters and horrors are familiar in the city. Only a few days before we had seen a dead man propped against a wall near St. Mark's on the Bowery. Marvin was shaking his head and tears were rolling down his cheeks. "What's the matter?" I asked him.

"That kid'll never get laid," he said.

Like most young men in those days, circa 1943, we had a sure means of solving all our problems with college, girls, boredom, and anxiety: We could be heroes in the war. When Marvin and I began to talk about it, however, it seemed different to us. Professor Campbell's eyes looking downward, looking inward, had changed our feeling about the days to come. We were infected by the beginning of the imagination of death, and it lay beneath our friendship as a shared battle. We too had been born twice.

In all friendships between adolescent boys there are curious contradictions, rivalries, and family difficulties. I was surely jealous of Marvin's great fortune with girls, whom he met and conquered in subway crowds, on campus walks, wherever he deigned to point his ardent, demanding eyes, his shiny beak, and his disturbed, acne-bothered face. He would take a girl for a walk and an ice cream, and not get back to Hartley Hall until his first morning class. Unless he lurked outside, imagining my envy all through the grimy New York night, I had to assume that he figured out someplace to go with the lady after the walk, the hamburgers, and the balcony of the Forty-second Street movie.

On the other hand, he envied me, too—my lack of "nervousness." In those days I seemed calm. To Marvin I was a rock, though I knew myself to be volcanic lava, in inexorable motion. Also, he envied me my year underground, hitchhiking, working at odd jobs on the

Florida Keys, escaping the Ivy League, as he called it, somehow including Brooklyn. No wonder I was calm, he told me; life had not passed
me by. All *he* had to his credit was satisfied lust.

Poor Marvin. I would have given up the life that had not passed
me by for one, two, or three—as many as the genie might allow me
—of the girls with whom Marvin strolled. Satisfied lust! But I would
offer them deep feeling, each and every one. He shrugged. They
couldn't resist him, he said, but that was not life. Every time he
traveled in a crowded subway he made a new conquest, and that was
not life either. That was just rubbing. Each and every one would have
been appalled by my morose deep feeling. They liked Marvin—cheerful rubbing.

I discovered, I think, why Marvin charmed women. It only *seemed*
to be mere cheerful rubbing. He needed them, he really needed and
wanted girls, this one and that one, each one in particular. He was
born for women. We walked around Van Am Quad, a little space of
brick and grass, endlessly turning in the damp midnight, while he
explained, "Some people are ambitious. You wake up and write
poems at dawn—"

"I kill myself, I'm so horny—"

"Shush. I wake all cold and gray and I know I'll die if I can't curve
into her body."

"Whose, Marvin?"

"So the next day I take a subway ride at rush hour. I find someone. I sniff it out and wiggle in, sometimes we never even look at
each other's face—sometimes we walk out together and go to her
place. . . ."

"What do you talk about?"

He grinned in the darkness. "I tell her how much I need her. I love
her. I desire her. I treasure her. I adore her. I'll do anything for her,
and more to her. Aitch-bert, when I talk like that, I'll tell you, they
always listen closely."

The bust of Van Am glistened in the diffuse gray of a globe lamp.
There were blackout curtains on the dormitory windows nearby, and
lights where the V-12 program Navy boys were doing calculus and
navigation problems. We walked round and round. Marvin contained
a famine which he offered up in tribute to womankind. He did not
hide his need. He surrounded them with joyous hunger. He gave it

freely, and thus they could forgive everything. He may not have been sincere, but he was desperate. Girls had the key; friends had the key; excitement and variety and new adventures had the key. Everyone was grateful to be able to do so much for Marvin. He responded with the tenderness of a gratified child. He could barely remember their names.

He also met a Barnard girl named Ellen who wore black woolen dresses, had long black hair, a long maternal figure; she wept when he took her into the cold bushes, wept when he brought her out, and wept all the way to her parents' apartment when they had left it empty for the weekend. Marvin reported, somewhat worried, that she was still weeping when they emerged on a fine, sunny winter afternoon. He had enjoyed the love of a good woman, and he found it wet.

For my own reasons, partly connected with the war, partly with the sag of midyear at college, partly with my lack of the love of a good or a bad woman, I began to figure on not waiting until the end of the school year to go into the Army. Casually one day I mentioned this to Marvin. He must have spent an unusually damp evening with Ellen because his answer was short and to the point: "Yeah!" The jukebox at the West End was playing, I recall, a song with this line: "Get outta here and get me some money, too. . . ."

It solved the problem of cuts in classes, the itch for adventure, the discomfort of school, the failures of successes with girls. We would go in together, and be heroes together. We enlisted together.

Before telling his parents that he was about to go into the Air Corps, he asked me to spend a night with him in Brooklyn. I expected to be bored—*parents*—but instead, I was amazed. No plump, dull Brooklyn lawyer, Mr. Shapiro was a jaunty man who wore a yachting cap indoors and liked to drink, eat exotic foods, and go out fishing. He had his own boat. He talked about mizzens and fore and aft; I was learning Latin and French but had no grasp of yachting. His face was weathered by Long Island Sound. I had never met a sailing Jew before. Mrs. Shapiro was a soft, sweet woman with a small, pretty, girlish face; she read good books and listened to Beethoven and smiled at her husband's jokes. He did calisthenics on a bar above the bed in their room. It was a jazzy household, unlike anything I had expected in that large, old-fashioned, furniture-filled house on a leafy Brooklyn street. There was also another son, younger than Marvin, to whom little attention was paid. Marvin was clearly the hope of the family, and Mr. Shapiro was delighted by his son's wildness. He twisted and dodged through life in a way which would have hurt him at thirty, but at eighteen he was a charmer. He had fun when I sought Meaning. He had style. From afar I admired a sense of luxuriousness. Even now, when rubbing up against strange girls in the subway does not seem very stylish, I carry the memory of a lively boy, with a swollen Adam's apple, a deep laugh in a skinny body, doted on by his parents and allowing himself all pleasures.

Marvin told them we were both going to war soon. This followed a discussion about Orientals in which we all agreed that there was something puzzling about the newspapers' descriptions of how to tell the face of a Japanese—sneaky, yellow, totalitarian—from that of a Chinese. The Chinese face in those days was open, smiling, friendly, and democratic. Marvin's father had a wild, high, energetic laugh at this. He said that the objective testimony of witnesses was sometimes inaccurate. He liked the way his son thought ahead.

"Aitch-bert and I are going to enlist," Marvin said suddenly. "It's time. Otherwise all the good jobs'll be taken."

His mother dropped a spoon; it made a little chime against her foot. Silent tears. His father clapped him on the back and said, "I knew it, why not? You'll tear 'em apart. They'll give up as soon as they get the news." His eyes glittered with envy. Marvin's kid brother looked adoring and pleased. No one fretted about his mother's tears until Marvin kissed her on the neck and she sobbed wildly.

The night before Marvin and I went to Camp Upton, we bought tickets for The Skin of Our Teeth, with Tallulah Bankhead. She wiggled and chanted the Joycean lines. If only she had known we were about to go off to die for our country, we both thought, she would have been absolutely indifferent to us anyway. The next day we shipped out, we were stripped naked, and began to put on our new lives.

As with girls, so with the war. Marvin seemed to have all the luck. His reflexes and his eyes were sharp. He became what both of us had wanted to be, a fighter pilot. I went to the infantry, and then to a school to learn Russian, toward a vague Army hope that I might help to provide liaison with our gallant Soviet allies. In the periods be-

tween drill, study, and fret, we deep Russian scholars continued real
life by drinking, writing letters, and chasing girls at the USO. Most
of us were successful at the first two projects, less at the third. I
corresponded with Marvin, with Ellen, and with Marvin's mother. He
was in England, flying missions over the Continent. I was in wet white
Maryland that next winter, doing maneuvers through an American
landscape—barns, churches, apple orchards—all traced and spelled
in Russian on our maps. O'er the steppes of Maryland I wandered,
dressed like a wolf, carrying a compass, a full pack, and a new vocabulary.

Marvin's mother wrote that she missed our coming out to Brooklyn
to eat fish on Saturdays. Her husband spent his weekends in his small
sailboat, digging salt fish out of the salt sea. He was also doing civilian
patrol work. She was worried about her son and wanted me to
reassure her.

Ellen wrote that she was crazy in love with Marvin and he didn't
write often enough. So she wanted to receive letters from me, since
I was his best friend.

Marvin wrote that the English girls were peculiar but cooperative.
He was now a first lieutenant, and what with his silver bars and all,
he didn't like to do it standing up in the alleys of Piccadilly. So he
had found girls who were willing to take him home. They liked
chocolate and they liked to rock with him as the bombs fell and the
sirens shrieked.

I remember this particularly now because it takes me back to the
time when prowess, position, and opportunity were the great issues
in love. It was technical and it was to be shared among men. Marvin
was collecting his reward for being a fighter pilot and a man. He would
dream of a girl in a flowing skirt, flowers and sunlight in a field, and
also admire the technique of the wife of a Pakistani colonel (or
perhaps he was an English colonel stationed in India).

Poor Marvin's mother, whose innocent boy was practicing the rites
of killing and lust.

Poor Ellen, who imagined him pining for her, needing her.

Poor me, crawling around in Russian in the snowbanks and slushy
mud of Maryland in winter. Our officers were combat dropouts—men
so ineffective at war that they were sent back to train future intelligence officers.

The only one not to be pitied seemed to be Marvin himself, handsome, his acne drying under doses of adrenaline, collecting missions and medals and the wives of our allies. He made captain. The boy quick into the bushes of Riverside Drive was also quick in the sky against the stubby German fighters. Ellen, his mother, and I all formed his audience against the backdrop of horror and destruction, explosions and fire, brandy and good jokes. Seen from our distance, the garish light lit his face and made it angelic, made it devilishly smile.

One winter night my group returned to Camp Ritchie, the intelligence training post in Maryland, after nearly a week of simulated war in marshes and orchards. We had been frozen and misled; we had been fired upon and tested; we had conducted a strange war among Maryland mountain people to whom we were not allowed to speak English. We needed shaves; we were jittery with stimulants; we smelled bad. Our mission had been a failure because our officer, who had been responsible for a minor disaster at Anzio, still believed that his own sense of direction was superior to that of a compass. He knew the way; could a compass think? Consequently we had been lost for three days in a prickly, cutover pine desert. I felt as if ice had been packed into my ears. We had the usual gripes against officers. They became the real enemy. We stood in our long khaki overcoats against a camp stove, smelling the chicken-feather singe as we tried to get warm, slurping coffee from our mess kits and reading the accumulated mail. Our officer went to sulk because north was not where north used to be in the Alabama National Guard. I tore open my little stack of mail.

A letter from Marvin described a weekend in London. What fun, what sparkle amid the blackout. A duke's daughter, he claimed; mentally I made him out a liar but read on, envying. She loved him, she really did. He cared for her a lot, of course, but not that much. Ellen was writing him weepy letters and he supposed he would have to close now in order to drop her a line.

Ellen wrote to ask if I had heard from Marvin. She was worried. He must be ill or something.

The last letter was from his mother. It was the most recent. Marvin had been shot down over Germany; others in the squadron had seen his parachute open, but it was being fired on. There seemed to have been a hit in the air. He was presumed dead.

I crawled outside into the snow as if I were seasick. I heaved and gagged and groaned because I had forgotten how to weep. I was too old to cry, and not yet old enough; later I would learn again. But now there was only this churning physical turmoil like seasickness, like jealousy, like lust and dread. The desire to run away or to deny was changed into an eating of the lining of my belly. I was simply sick, a trivial response to death, I then thought and still believe. I remembered Professor Campbell, his head down, contemplating the Fact. I remembered the awe Marvin and I had shared, which had been the foundation of our friendship before the matter of girls and career and the war came to give us the details of intimacy. I was appalled that I dared to feel my own body, even in sickness, when Marvin was simply without feeling, without soul, dead. I recalled with disgust Dostoevsky's denunciation of Turgenev: When he watches a shipwreck, children drowning, he feels only the tears running down his own face. And yet I now had only myself. In the midst of this unreal war which I was fighting and for which I was merely preparing, I had lost my emblem of vitality and true life, my friend. I was bereft. I was gagging in the deep, silent Maryland winter, with nearby slush piles and garbage cans and the debris of soldiering and, just beyond, a horizon of scrub and poor soil itching through the snow and a whiteness of hills and winter sky. The earth was an ache. This was the third death I had known in my life, and perhaps the beginning of the sense of my own death. I saw Marvin's face—grinning, acne-pocked, delighted by life—under his parachute swinging down and then exploded in midair as he hung between heaven and hell. I have seen him there for twenty years, and so he will be always.

Like Dostoevsky's Turgenev, I am telling a selfish story. After grief, how does the vain young poet survive? He writes a vain young poem, of course. It was a long elegy to the memory of Captain Marvin Shapiro (1924–1945) and I typed it in the company orderly room at Camp Ritchie, Maryland, and sent it to the *Atlantic Monthly*, 8 Arlington Street, Boston, Massachusetts. Presently it was returned with a long letter signed by a lady who had apparently been moved by this death in my life. I haven't seen the poem since the end of the war, but I am reasonably certain it was not a good one. I remember little about it other than its shape on the page and the rhyme scheme. I believe the editor wrote to me because I was a soldier mourning a dead friend and there was a war on. Shortly afterward I was shipped out and lost track of the poem. I carried the letter from Marvin's mother with me.

His body was never found. He had written to me that it was odd to have the initial on the dog tags that identified him as a Jew when he might have to parachute into Germany; but he kept the initial. Anyway, he was destroyed in the sky.

The class of '46, my class, mostly returned to begin college again as twenty-one-year-old sophomores. We counted our losses and secretly watched out of the corners of our eyes those with missing limbs or raw, still-healing, burned scars. Some of us were in line for plastic surgery; some were outpatients; many were on partial disability pensions. Our hairlines had changed. Moony faces were lean and loony. There was confusion, the GI Bill, and a host of babies who claimed to be college students, too. I could not take up school as I had before, in a dormitory, with a roommate. I rented a room off Broadway and thought to enter adult life after the three years of murderous limbo. Our bodies twitched with the unfulfilled destruction. How dare we live, how dare we not live. A friend and I jumped a thuggish heckler at a street-corner Henry Wallace rally. A group of us formed a klepto-bibliomaniacal society, stealing books, food, anything small and large. We called it the Book Find Club. Our motto was: Steal four books and get a fruit cake free from the A&P. We initiated girls into the sport. In their confusion they thought the war heroes must know what they were doing. They thought we were heroes and nervous. We were, in fact, nervous.

Around my thoughts of Marvin, on whose behalf I was taking certain revenges against the world, whom I was sometimes imitating in the subway, I came gradually to think of his mother, his father, and Ellen. Probably I did not know how to meet the grief of others. I was busy installing myself in the bohemian student life of those days, all of us in khaki, sullen, arrogant. But gradually, as the months went by, I decided to visit Marvin's survivors. At last I telephoned Mrs. Shapiro in Brooklyn and she reminded me of how to get to Avenue K by subway. I used to know the way. My ears felt different in the roar of the tunnel.

At the subway entrance I began to think of the smoked eel I had eaten for the first time at their house. Marvin had said, bragging, "We have eels all the time—crabs, lobsters, oysters, shrimp. Snails. Clams."

"Do you eat pork?" I asked.

"*Feh*, unclean," he said. "You know that joke?"

I remembered pausing at the newsstand to pick up a copy of PM. They were selling the New York *Post* with the same old headlines, and I thought it was the same man with the papers, fret on his face, hair in his ears, waiting out his time. Still alive.

I expected the house to be shaded, dark with mourning. Instead, it was light and sunny, with the curtains pulled back and the surprising winter sunlight filling the rooms. But it seemed empty. Even some of the furniture was gone. It was emptied of its men. After his death Marvin's father had enlisted, not as a lawyer but as an expert sailor, and had commanded a landing craft, and had fought as an overage captain through southern France. After the end of the war he had simply not returned. Mrs. Shapiro, smiling, told me that he had found a girl in Marseilles. I couldn't imagine what a Brooklyn lawyer would do in Marseilles—Jean Gabin yes, Mr. Shapiro no—and I saw him in a corduroy cap, on the waterfront, a handsome, stocky, make-out, middle-aged settler in France, with a young, high-breasted chick with wooden soles on her shoes. Mrs. Shapiro said simply, "It broke up our family. We were a good family, I think, but we needed Marvin." Her other son was now at Yale, going very white shoe.

She made tea. We talked about Marvin. Tea, raisin toast, orange marmalade, chocolate cookies. I thought of Marvin's hickeys—"zits" the freshmen now called them. She told me a little about her marriage and, I knew, would later want to tell me more. My need for a community of mourning gave way to embarrassment. I could not be husband and son to her, and when I slipped out into the deep early night, I tried to feel sadness and sympathy; I felt sympathy and sadness, and I felt relief to escape. Marvin was my friend in the past. What community I sought could not be built of nostalgia.

Still, I wanted to find Ellen. When I finally met her again, she was also in mourning, wearing an ugly, shapeless woolen dress, flat shoes, her hair untended, smelling of anxiety and poor caring. She was a graduate student and had a reputation for persistent moping. Never a very pretty girl, she had been a sweetly attractive one. Now at age twenty-three, she looked ravaged, as if she had been left out in funky weather. I had a bit more patience with her than with Marvin's mother. We took coffee and meals together near campus. She wanted to drink at the West End because Marvin and I had gone there with her so often. Three times, I think. She imagined for herself a deep love affair; she imported it backward into history, she imagined widowhood. At first I shared the play, stunned by her conception of him, which seemed so much deeper than my own. They had been truly in love, they had been deep true lovers; it was not wrestling in the grass, it was not couch work in her parents' apartment on Central Park West, it was an immortal passion; her hero had been blasted out of the skies by fate and she would treasure his memory forever. Marvin and Ellen stood in the great tradition of doomed lovers. She was a graduate student in literature.

After a few immersions in her fantasy of the past, I began to feel discomfort and then resentment. Marvin had been my best friend and his memory made me ache. But he slipped away in the tumult of Ellen's ardent dream. I found new resources of coldness in myself. I would watch impatiently for her to finish her beer and then deliver her to her room on West 113th Street. Once, when she managed to order another beer, I felt myself ready to groan with boredom. And when she wanted me to come to her room, tiptoeing past the other rooms, past the common kitchen, I felt as if I were being led into a trap. Her wet, beery kisses were not for me. I twisted away and cried out, "You're lying to yourself! Never cared about you! He had girls everywhere, in England, Brooklyn, everywhere!"

She started to run down the darkened hall. I caught her at the door, held her in my arms as she struggled, and pointed out that it was not my room from which she was running, but her own. She should stay and I should go. Be rational. Be logical. Make sense. I'm sorry, but it's the truth.

I believed myself to be proudly surgical, but also I was smelling the stench of a woman's hysteria for the first time in my life. Little popping explosions of rage and hatred were going off in my arms. "You think you can play God! You think you're God and my judge!" she shrieked at me.

The practice of playing God and Judge sometimes exhausts itself with time. I have the disease worse than most (*Ellen, wherever you are*).

I dragged her back to her room. Invisible ears were pressed to the shut bedroom doors. Community kitchen, community crises. Shush, shush, I said. The stringent, leaping sobs subsided; she was simply weeping; I put her in bed with her clothes on, covered her, and sat stroking her hand. Toward dawn she fell asleep. Cold-eyed I felt. I tiptoed out.

Back on the street, I saw a metal case of milk at the door of a short-order restaurant. For the first time in my life—not the last— I had spent a night trying to calm a woman made mad by something I had said. And for the last time in my life I felt that, well, it wasn't really my fault at all, I was right, I had done the right thing, I was right. So I told myself. So I told myself again. Still insisting, I believed that I had committed an obscenity. I stood at the doorway of the diner: CLOSED. GO AWAY.

They had no right to be rude. I was hungry and thirsty. I was a veteran. They were turning a veteran from their door.

The metal case of milk glittered in the early light. I looked at the bottles. My hand felt a premonitory sensual coolness, like touching a loved woman. It would be sweet to drink long, cool swallows from the bottle and then heave it into the street. I was thirsty and hungry and cold and feverish and I decided not to steal a bottle of milk.

I stood there, squinting at the metal case. I would leave it in a moment. I would leave without a bottle for myself. This was a new reaction for me. The night had brought me much that was new.

When next I saw Ellen, she had changed her hair, cut it stylishly, and her clothes looked recently dry-cleaned. Now she was a handsome, perhaps too-mature twenty-three-year-old woman. She was going with someone. She had a *friend* (stare, blush, angry stare). We met as acquaintances, not as friends. She made it clear that I had sacrificed our past friendship. But she bore me no ill will; she smiled and inquired about my doings. I had little to say to her. Our life together was all in the past. I had projects for the future. She was married within the year, gave up graduate work, got pregnant, left New York. Though I insisted to myself that I had done the right thing, she made me uncomfortable. It was much easier for me not to see her on campus.

Now the years have passed and I think of my friend who died when he and I were mere children. The event still seems real when I remember it, but like a reality glimpsed through a thick glass, without the physical heft of life.

Recently, however, an immediate grief seemed to break the glass of memory and Marvin came tumbling free and alive again. The distancing of history is fatal, and yet it can be reversed. I am accustomed to his death. And yet, when I needed an occasion to express my grief at something else, at something happening to me, in my own life, I found Marvin waiting like a boy, ready to play. I told the story about him to a friend who was a baby when he flew over Germany. "He was dead before he had time to lose his adolescent acne." I had no tears for Marvin's mother or Ellen, but now, telling it, I fought for control of myself. A peculiar humping under my palate.

My friend reminded me coolly, "Ellen has a child ready for college. Marvin's father, if he is still alive and eating eels, must be nearly seventy—more. Do you think he's still in Marseilles? His mother is an old woman. His kid brother is a middle-aged professor."

"At Williams College, I heard."

"So," she said. "So it was a long time ago."

Yes, child, that was mere history. Yet there are new wars for which we must prepare ourselves, and I am still ready. I am also ready to join the company of O. J. Campbell, remembering my own deaths.

A HAITIAN
GENTLEMAN

My *first and a coincidental meeting with André-Pierre Vilaire took place*
on a Panama Lines vessel, steaming southward along the North
American coast from New York to Port-au-Prince, just ten years ago.
I was bound for Haiti for a year of study in this odd paradox of an
Afro-French nation in the Caribbean; he was simply bound home. I
watched him pacing the deck, impeccable in a starched white tropical
suit, appearing quietly distraught, the lid of control tightly fastened,
an elegant tall black man with narrow features and no interest at all
in the vague efforts at ship spirit on board the SS *Harding.* The other
passengers—the ship was about a quarter full—were mainly depen-
dent families of men working in the Canal Zone, so I couldn't blame
André-Pierre for his determined abstraction. After he was pointed
out to me, I sought an occasion for conversation with him; he was
one of the people I had been told to look up in Haiti, and the

description I had been given made him seem a curious person. He was
the friend of a world-famous harpsichordist whom he had met at
school in Paris years before; he was the lover of an actress then
popular on the New York stage, and it must have been to see her that
he came to New York; he was a prosperous Haitian lawyer; and he
had that typical elite Haitian inheritance of divergent ancestry poured
onto the African roots—French colonists, a Jewish peddler (grandfather), and a Dutch businessman from Curaçao—so that in his family
there were those who sought to pass abroad as exotic Frenchmen and
those who, like proud André-Pierre, flaunted their blood and color.
To be sure, André-Pierre could not have passed, as one sister did, but
also it was not in his nature to try; he even stretched out his long legs
in a deck chair as the ship entered tropical waters and seemed to be
searching the sky with his closed eyes for a deeper suntan.

He did not invite conversation. He ate alone; he read popular
magazines negligently, and then flung them down; he walked inces-
santly, as if counting for a record number of turns around the deck.
There was no tranquillity in the man, though his striking appearance
made one think that such a person should be content to let the world
admire him. While the ship bucked and plowed through icy Atlantic
waters, he wore dress suitable to New York in winter; on the day the
weather broke, and the tropics announced themselves with a humid
calm, he began to wear that archaic starched suit which had been
crafted for him by his Rue du Centre tailor.

Also on that day, as if abruptly feeling at home on the ship, he
greeted me cheerily. My problem of how to introduce myself to him
was settled by his introducing himself to me. He seemed delighted by
my tale of having his name in my notebook—the small-world syn-
drome; he couldn't place the "mutual acquaintance" who had given
me his name, but he was accustomed to being noticed by American
women and did not think it odd that a dim stranger should describe
him as her friend. He shrugged and turned his hands out. He did not
dwell on it. "Mes-z-amis!" he said. "Quelle vie, eh? You do not know
what you are finding in Haiti. I warn you, you do not know!"

I told him I had read almost everything in English and much of
what was published in French about his native land.

He laughed richly at this. "You do not, do not know, my friend!
Cannot possibly!" My pedantry delighted him. When he threw back

his head to laugh, he radiated the charm—teeth, grace, open joy, desire to share it—which had led my friend to describe him as "the handsomest man in Haiti, perhaps the handsomest man in the whole world." I pitied her, since he had not even noticed her enough to recall her name; but this indifference to his effect upon others was also a part of his grace.

André-Pierre Vilaire was an atypical member of the Haitian elite, whose traditional business is cultivating lust and indulging pride, whether or not the occasion supports the fantasy. He was a little aloof from women, despite his famous love affair—or perhaps because of it—and he was barely curious about the ladies who stared after him. He made no lists and catalogues of his conquests, as other Haitians did. What he loved passionately, with a suffering and unrequited ardor, was politics; he had a desperate vision of Haiti, of the possibilities of life in the sovereign republic of Haiti, and frustrated by the succession of corrupt governments over a graceful, miserable people, he could shout and rant like a deceived lover. He talked of presidents, generals, colonels, and ministers with despair, with spite, with grinding hatred. With his hand on his heart he quoted "Haiti," by the murdered poet Massillon Coicou:

> Et pourtant elle est riche; et pourtant elle est belle:
> L'océan captive vient baiser ses pieds nus;
> De son plus vif éclat le soleil luit pour elle;
> La nature s'épand dans ses yeux ingénus.

Perhaps Coicou had indeed plotted against a corrupt regime, but have we the right to destroy (he asked me) the heir to Musset?

I answered no as loud as I could, but envied his raging pride. He pleaded the case of la belle Haïti with me as if I were her father; her sky and her sea, her sun and perfume seemed to absorb all the lust in the man; he spoke as if I were familiar with the intrigues of Cap-Haïtien and the Capitol. At first this was as strange to my palate as cassava or griots. With the passing days, I began to share his dramatic sense of the quarrels between mulatto and black, between Army and bureaucracy, between peasant and city dweller, between vodun and the Roman Church, between Francophiles and those who believed that American technique pointed the way to the future, among the admirers of Mexico and Jamaica and even the isolated circles of Marxists. These desperate struggles took on an intimate, playacting quality, since the elite class was so small that André-Pierre had relatives in almost all camps. He wanted to shoot his cousin. He had once been forcibly entertained for a weekend in the dread Fort Dimanche prison, of which another cousin was the commandant. He had a nephew in the cabinet and was convinced that the current government, that of the most illustrious General Paul Magloire, would again imprison and perhaps torture him.

Sometimes, however, he relaxed briefly and other matters could occupy our turns about the deck. He talked about his student days in Paris, when he had fallen in love with the daughter of the mayor of Marseilles; he had taken a Doctor of Laws degree. He believed Anglo-American jurisprudence to be more humane than the Napoleonic Code. The judge—the *juge d'instruction*—begins his investigation with the clear dream of revenge. This necessarily corrupts; it allows too much to the human; it gives privileges to passion, and passion in authority is the enemy of justice. ("They shot Massillon Coicou! They crucified Charlemagne Peralte! The best of us have been immolated!") He paced; he put his hands behind his back; he calmed himself before four o'clock tea on the deck. "I am the victim of my history—agreed? *Mes-z-amis!*" He shrugged and accepted his history, eager to change only the future.

I tried to lead him to talk about his plump Marseillaise, but he was uninterested in sex, it seemed, and uninterested in the handicap of his color. In the circles in which he moved abroad, he was more special for his good looks than for his espresso color, and both bored him. He never discussed the actress, other than once to remark that he had a friend in New York—"I am a man sometimes, am I not?" After knowing other Haitians, I found his refusal to gloat over prowess and success a miracle. He was unique in this and other ways.

And then suddenly one morning we lay at anchor in the sweltering harbor of Port-au-Prince, the ship pointed into the long, low, curving line of the shore, tiers of city rising into misty hills toward Pétionville, Kenscoff, and the faraway pine forests of Furcy, and the cathedral sticking out of one tier with its candy colors, and a confusion of customs and police and naked boys in hollow-log canoes, screaming at us to throw coins into the bay. I stood with André-Pierre and watched the flashing bodies cleave the water, come up gasping, the coin grasped between teeth, and then tucked into the cheek for another plea, "Aie! Aie! You! American! *Encore! Encore!*"

"My daughters will be here. You will stay longer in *douane*. My son will come with the pickup and take you to your hotel."

Busy with his homecoming, André-Pierre eased my arrival in Haiti, and then excused himself. Of course, he had much to do. Later we would take up our friendship again, continuing that shipboard good luck of intimacy which is often established but seldom sustained in the "real life" of land and habit.

My image of André-Pierre, from what I knew of him and from his manner on board ship, was of a very rich man, living elegantly, with aloof and indulgent manners toward his wife, children, and servants. He played tennis. He liked to lock himself in his den and build shortwave radios. But my conception was wrong. His house in the Canapé-Vert section of Port-au-Prince was modest and undistinguished; his Syrian wife suffered from his snappish temper, as did the servants; he indulged his two daughters and two sons, but they too got on his nerves. He would give them candy and tell them he had a headache. When he was nervous, he sniffed from a Benzedrine inhaler. He was allergic—to bougainvillaea? burning charcoal? bananas? to which of the many fervent smokes and smells of Port-au-Prince? Once I saw him dance the *merengue,* and that only for a few moments to entertain a foreign visitor, and never again. "Frivolity! This people destroys itself!" He had given up dancing, he said, as a protest against the corruption of Haitian life; in any case, it bored him. Sometimes he would go with friends to the Choucoune, where the blare of the orchestra eliminated all but the thought of the *meringue* or the mambo and the girls, and he would smile and nod; his friends received his smile, his mirthless laughter, his self-deprecating discontent; he would not dance; he was there only to confirm what he already knew. "*Mes-z-amis!*" he cried, laughing with chagrin for Haiti. "In such a world to dance?" And then he would tell me how President Sténio Vincent—or was it Lescot?—had stolen the bounty paid by Trujillo for the fourteen thousand Haitians slaughtered in a senseless pogrom.

My early sense of a man exotically endowed by fortune gave place

to pity, even to irritation; but in that familiar way, even his weak-
nesses contributed to our friendship. He snapped at his dowdy Syrian
wife. He listened impatiently to the prattle of his daughters, and his
sons sulked and avoided him. His law practice dwindled and there was
less money for his trips abroad. He never mentioned the famous
actress. Finally, in an access of gossipaceous curiosity—in Port-au-
Prince sex and politics were the consuming passions of the few who
had enough to eat—I brought up the subject. André-Pierre listened
pensively, with a bruised thoughtfulness. "You know of her?" he
asked. "Hm. Yes. Well, you know, my friend, at my age—"

"You're young yet." (He was forty-eight, with gray flecking the
short, curly hair which softened the angular planes of his skull.)

"But in this difficult life, *nos tristes tropiques* . . . So you've thought
about her all this time? You've been curious all this time? *Mes-ʒ-amis!*"
He laughed softly. "Sometimes you seem so young, like all Americans."

Sometimes André-Pierre seemed very young to me, open to the
world like an adolescent in his bruised idealism. Each new abuse of
power by the Magloire government outraged him afresh; he collected
dossiers on grafters, cheaters, and trimmers; he invited fellow dissi-
dents to his house, all of them risking a beating, imprisonment, or
worse. They knew it; their meetings had little point other than to
declare to each other their opposition; they knew it and they met
anyway. Since most business was connected with the government,
which was supported mainly by aid from the United States, André-
Pierre lay under a financial interdiction. He had few clients. He was
slipping down; he could not afford to spend. But sin made him howl,
and this howling gave him something like joy, and it cost nothing but
the danger.

An incident typical of the Haitian toy politics of the time took place
about one of these clandestine meetings in André-Pierre's house.
Word of the gathering had gotten to the police, and André-Pierre
knew that word had gotten to the police. To persist seemed a suicidal
folly. His friends decided to hold their illegal meeting anyway. They
would be arrested and take the consequences.

That week I had a friend visiting me from the States. He was an
oral surgeon, familiar with the mouth and jaw but unfamiliar with the

dreamy games of Haiti. I decided to give him a lesson. We drove his rented car to Canapé-Vert to watch the police raid. We stood in the street, waiting for trucks and sirens. This was adventure aplenty for a seventeen-day vacation; the cops would be carrying submachine guns. Within a stone-hot afternoon, with dogs barking and cocks crowing and donkeys crunching the grass, and the skinny black Haitian pigs darting and foraging in the ditches, and the shoeshine boys clacking and the sellers of lottery tickets shouting their lucky numbers —amid all the ceaseless animal teeming of Port-au-Prince—we stood at the corner and waited as the half-dozen conspirators entered André-Pierre's house. They peeked over their shoulders and dodged inside. We were watching dead men in tan suits, in starched white suits from the tailor on the Rue du Centre, with briefcases, smiling. They were men who had no need to imagine their own death—they were stepping forward to welcome it.

My friend and I loitered. We felt blindingly Caucasian on that nameless street in Canapé-Vert.

Twenty minutes later we heard motors. The police roared up in black Buicks. They sprang out, and then the major in charge caught sight of me and my oral-surgeon friend. The oral surgeon was a stranger in town. To the major he was not an oral surgeon—he must have seemed a dangerous, lounging creature. Could the American Embassy or the FBI or the Secret Service or the OSS or the CIA be interested in this case? Why were we watching? Who were we? There was an abrupt halt and a council among the raiding police. They peeked at us as we stood gossiping together in our Keds.

What if they made a mistake?

What if it turned out badly?

Internationally?

My friend blew his nose in a Kleenex—was that a signal to Foster Dulles? To Edgar Hoover?

The police decided to take no chances. Because of our presence on that corner, they piled back into their automobiles and drove away. An oral surgeon and a student had become factors in Haitian political maneuvering.

For André-Pierre the incident again demonstrated the absolute inferiority of Haitian political life. He seemed to regret being spared. After all, to be arrested was only an inconvenience. In those amiable days of the mid-1950s, the murder of political prisoners was not yet very common. Haitian coffee commanded a high price on the market, and more important, the one known Haitian Communist commanded a lot of anti-Communist dollars in aid from the United States. The government was corrupt, but the people were optimistic. There were enough beans, enough rice, plenty of mangoes and bananas. The songs about the sun of Haiti and the pneumatic Creole maidens and the joys of carnival, *rara*, and *bamboche* seemed more real than the grinding habitual poverty of Haiti's uncounted, unconsidered millions of peasants. "We could tell the truth," said André-Pierre, "except that things are real to us. We get hungry, we want things, we can't tell the truth."

André-Pierre was bored by vodun, as a southern planter might be bored by hillbilly music. The *loas* of vodun, and the *bakas* and *loups-garous* and zombies—the beasts of the Haitian hills—he had put away years ago, along with his childhood. If others believed, then others were foolish. "I have a degree from Paris, do you think I need to spend time on chicken-worship?" This sounded snobbish to me; I was fascinated by an exotic religion, folklore, and language; but on the other hand, hillbilly songs had found me a snob in the Army. André-Pierre had grown up surrounded by sounds of the drums in the hills around Port-au-Prince, and ceremonies often blocked the road when he had business elsewhere.

Once he had business in the dying provincial town of St.-Marc and I drove there with him, over a pitted road, through miles of barren mountains and gray sisal plantations, sometimes descending toward the blue and white waters of the bay which washes that island. In St.-Marc itself, the ruins of colonial architecture, thick walls and abutments, were surrounded by huts of mud and straw; the remaining coffee was loaded onto decaying docks, into iron-sheet sheds; sleepy peasants and a few sun-struck, white-suited old men wandered the seaside square. I saw one gentleman in a starched white suit, carrying a *coco-macaque*, the knobbed stick of the bourgeois, beating his way with tiny, arthritic steps across the street to the customs house. "Why does he dress like that?" I asked. He wore a high celluloid collar and button shoes. It was sixty years ago by his costume.

"He sees no reason to change his habits," André-Pierre said.

"It couldn't have been very comfortable when lots of people had those habits."

"They dressed like that in Madagascar, Martinique, Guadeloupe—in the French colonies."

"But Haiti has been independent for a hundred and fifty years."

André-Pierre then smiled as if his next remark answered all my objections. "It's my first cousin." He honked the horn and stopped the old man. He shook his hand in formal greeting. When I was introduced and took his hand, I felt the soft and womanly hand of a man who had lived in St.-Marc all his life and not yet done very much work. He did not take us to his house. He lived on pride; his starched clothes were his home, and he slept in what was little more than a hut. "Haitians are like that," André-Pierre said of him, said of many. "We are crazy—agreed?"

My friend's cousin would continue until the end of his term on earth taking his daily walk on vague business across the central square of St.-Marc, expecting deference from the peasants and soldiers who thronged the square, carrying bills, passes, receipts, orders, little slips of paper, and living on a few dollars a month—the rent of his land, the transfer of a few bags of coffee. He knew the town was dying; but he also knew he himself was dying, and he and the town awaited their fate together.

In Cap-Haïtien, Jacmel, Jérémie, and St.-Marc, my friend had relatives, or relatives of relatives, who lived like this. Once flourishing provincial centers, now the tramp ships only occasionally stopped in these places, unloading a few cases of Dutch chocolate, kerosene for the lamps, candles and medicine and mail. In Port-de-Paix, the one town of size where my friend knew no one, I was the first foreigner to visit since a woman anthropologist nearly ten years earlier. But when the mayor asked whom I knew in Port-au-Prince and I named André-Pierre Vilaire, he said, "Oh, yes! My wife's cousin is married to his niece!" And we played chess by flaring lamplight through a long evening which ended, I think, with my getting bitten by the mosquito that gave me malaria.

During the French colonial times, wealth poured through these ports along the crumpled shoreline of Haiti. In André-Pierre's youth, fortunes were still made by landholders. In 1954 there would still be a Café des Poètes or an Au Bon Boisson where, among a display of coconuts and dusty bottles, the old men might gather at dusk to drink their coffee by candlelight and discuss the future of Russia, the United States, Haiti, and Jérémie. A cousin to André-Pierre informed me that Haiti would be the third force to mediate among the other two great powers. But first, he said in this town without electricity, without sanitation, inhabited by illiterate and half-naked peasants and a few spirit-wounded Francophiles like himself, Jérémie would die. It would be killed by the predators of Port-au-Prince. He raised his fist and shook it in the dim air of six o'clock. Cursed Port-au-Prince! *Jérémie la douce,* as all the world knows. He ordered more coffee for both of us, and candles. As I met the friends and relatives of my friend throughout Haiti, I felt that I knew André-Pierre better. Kindness and courtesy and the deepest isolation.

On the drive back from St.-Marc, he honked furiously at a vodun funeral procession on the road. The mourners scampered and dodged, carrying the coffin zigzag as they ran, in order to keep the evil spirits from invading the body. Only evil spirits travel in a straight line.

"Fools. Idiots. Poor deprived people," said my friend. "Evil can move in as crooked a line as you and I."

When my mother visited Haiti, I expected the response of bewilderment. She had a conventional mistrust of Negroes, based on the habits of Cleveland, Ohio. ("Don't drive through Woodland Avenue unless you lock your doors, they'll jump on the running board.") But I underestimated her empirical character. She was charmed by André-Pierre; she was too old and too married to allow herself to fall in love, but she turned a bit girlish in his presence. Patiently he explained Haiti to her, controlling his exclamations of chagrin before the iniquities of the government, and later explained to me his affection for her: "My own mother, Christ rest her soul, was half-Jewish. She was a black nigger, but she had a nose—look at mine and see the shadow of it." He apologized for smoking in my mother's presence. She advised him not to use the nasal inhaler because it would not be good for his passages. They discussed, knee-to-knee in deep mahogany and wicker furniture, and saw eye-to-eye in some mysterious way.

André-Pierre poured himself into generous good-feeling with my mother; his striking appearance was a mere happenstance of his character; he did not depend on it. Sex occupied a trivial place in his life. Most Haitians had as many women as they could afford—a wife, one or several *placées* (semiofficial wives, whose children were often recognized by the father), plus mistresses, occasional unfocused affairs, drunken mountings. Their pride lay in possession, and unsanctioned possession was a demonstration of freedom. André-Pierre dwelled in his fierce dreaming against the government, his friendships, and little more. His pride was in being right. *"New-York, c'est fini,"* he once told me. The word *New-York* meant that famous actress; I envisioned a devouring love affair occasioned by sacrifice and passion and a dream of perfect attainment. Now he understood that there was no perfect attainment.

My mother kissed André-Pierre good-bye at the airport when he surprised her by appearing to see her off. "He's not the kind who'll jump on your running board, is he?" I asked.

"Hanh?" she said, oblivious to the indoctrinations of my childhood. "He's such a beautiful man—I mean, he came to the airport to say good-bye!"

During the nine years after I left Haiti, my mother asked me every time I saw her, "Have you heard from Andrew Peters?" I did hear from him at first, with the following messages: One daughter was married. Then a son was married. And all the time, the situation grew worse. In veiled ways, in case his letter was opened, he wrote with the intention of a drowning man: *Help!* He reported Roman Catholic marriages for all his children—to please his wife, to please them. "I attended," he noted ironically, as if he had a choice in the matter. Once he telephoned me from New York, but I was then living in San Francisco. It was the only time he visited the States during that period; earlier his habit had been to make the trip every six months. Money was becoming extinct.

During the past few years of the Duvalier regime in Haiti, I heard from André-Pierre not at all. My notes were unanswered. Was he alive? He would now be in his late fifties. Would he still have that graceful tread when he walked, that lean power in his gaze? And would he survive?

When the chance to revisit Haiti came, I was afraid of the news. Bad times lay heavy on Port-au-Prince—danger, morose suspicion, gusts of terror. Since the telephone system no longer operated, the only way to make contact with someone was to go seek him out. I directed the cabdriver to his office, *"près maison Morisseau,"* and found it boarded up. He no longer had an office in town.

It took me three days to find him. Most of his family were either dead or in exile. Almost by accident, I heard that he lived alone in a small house up the mountain in Pétionville, that he had suffered serious trouble with the government, that he had been imprisoned and hurt in an abominable way. The man who knew where he lived said with a grin, "He is obliged to be a philosopher one hundred percent. No more jigajig." This man was a *tonton macoute*, a member of the private militia of the ruling dictator, François Duvalier, who called them his "bogeymen" and let them roam the nation, administering the terror. He wore a pistol stuck in his belt. It pleased this *macoute* to hint at the injury done M. Vilaire.

When I found him, in the makeshift house in a courtyard where he lived, almost his first words sounded an echo of the *tonton macoute* who had snickered about the change in him. *"Eh! Mes-z-amis!"* he cried, stepping toward me in the doorway with delight, but not with astonishment, as if it had been nine hours and not nine years since last we had met. Then he put his arms around me and leaned back, squinting and grinning, as we performed that ritual mutual inspection of the damage and gain given by nearly a decade. Well, he was older, the tight skull a little less precise in its lines, the close hair nearly white now, but not really so very much changed except for a brutal scar at the side of his head, crossing just at the long line of his left eye. It looked as if he had been hit a glancing blow by a *coco-macaque*. "Oh!" he said. "They nearly expropriated my eye. It was infected, but you know my African blood, I thrive on disease. It healed without a doctor seeing it." He looked proud and then he shrugged. "Well!"

He was in a bathrobe. He wanted to dress for me, but I begged him not to move. When I found him, he had been eating rice and beans out of a bowl. On the table along with his lunch were bottles with Spanish labels on them—drugs from the Dominican Republic for indigestion, for calming, for stimulating. With a delighted smile he told me that he now lived alone in this *baraque*; his entire family was in the States, wife and children and in-laws. "But they won't give me my passport. They let me out of Fort Dimanche, but they're still afraid of me," he said. When he stood up again, I saw that he was as tall as ever, though with the soft weight added to his spare frame, the soft flesh flowing, he seemed less towering.

In ten minutes he told me his story. He had been held for five months in prison by the Duvalier militia. He told me with a smile. He had been brutalized, beaten, disgraced in the imaginative ways invented by a people slow to violence but with violence deep in their nature, as it is in the nature of all peoples. He showed his teeth delightedly as he explained what was happening to Haiti. Upon his release from prison—his eye had been damaged slightly, he had been forced to eat abominations and his stomach had been ruined, his manhood had been damaged—he went straight back to his conversations with the opposition, his sedition, his rebellion, as if nothing had changed. "Ah, *mais oui!* Now I must be a philosopher. But of course, I cannot travel anyway. And no money. Listen, this country is beyond disaster, my friend. Listen, we know grief now. Listen"—and I listened as he described the regime of a ruler mystically devoted to control of the apparatus of the state without any rational aim. The continuation of control by means of terror and grief meant a thousand instances of corruption, hatred, torture, and murder. Even the famous gaiety of the Haitian countryside was in ruins. Any stranger, even any friend could be a secret *macoute.*

The afternoon passed as he spent his pity upon this suffering nation. Then abruptly he paused and thought of his visitor. He gazed at me, confused suddenly by the time that had fled. "Are you happy, my friend? And you? Are you happy?"

"Pierrot, how can you ask that? What a question!"

"Ask *me*," he commanded.

"What do you mean?"

"Ask it me!"

His skin had a grayish tone under the espresso brown. "How do you feel?" I asked.

"That's not the question—agreed?"

"You can't enjoy being a martyr. Are you accomplishing nothing, Pierrot? What are you after?"

"My daughters are lovely. They became lovely girls. You knew them when they were awkward, but now they are lovely. They both live on the West Ninety-second Street near Riverside Drive."

"I'll see them when I'm in New York."

"But ask me! Ask me the question!"

Amid the desolation of that house of concrete blocks, with its debris of equipment, shortwave radio and inoperative telephone, photographs and piled-up magazines, bare bulbs hanging and disconnected refrigerator and a mess of half-naked children playing in the compound outside, I gave him his question: "Are you happy, Pierrot?"

He stood up with the tail of his bathrobe flapping. "Haiti has no future! I have said it and said it a thousand, thousand times! Now everyone sees the proof. We can no longer save ourselves. The power is gone. The sky is falling about our heads." He paused for a moment and flashed his delighted grin. "To your question: Yes."

MAX AND
THE PACEMAKER

Port-au-Prince has become an amputated town, throbbing in upon itself.
Grief muffles the rhythms of this Caribbean port city—tourists gone,
trade vanished, a crazed dictator pressing the Haitian millions into
misery. Still, amid desolation and dismay, the smell of ripe mangoes
is good, sun and salt are good, the sway of Creole girls as they go
about their day is a happy reminder of time that was and time still
to come—why not?

Or so my friend Max Liptzen the Fish Importer explained to me.
Someday the walls of the Fort Dimanche prison would be torn down
and *bamboche* would take the dancers once more. And then, he said,
the living will regret giving up life before they have to. "This is a
country for people with juice in them. Let's squeeze the juice, kid."

Convinced by Max's argument on a particularly sweet and humid
evening, I wanted to pay a visit to the house of flowers known as the

Flamingo, just beyond city limits in the district called Carrefour. I suggested the expedition partly to distract Max, who was one of the few foreigners to remain in Haiti after many years of the capricious and brutal regime of François Duvalier. The phrase *house of flowers* is a sweeter name for what in other places is called BAR! DANCE!! GIRLS!!! A place for talk, dance, and putting away the cares of the world; also a place for catching an assortment of penicillin-resistant diseases, nostalgia, *Weltschmerz*, and weariness with the self. Max needed distraction for the long night stretching ahead. He didn't answer me.

Because of the general decay of life in Haiti—roads, electricity, telephone, police—Max had given up his house and was rattling about the Grand Hôtel Oloffson, as was I. The tourist business was moribund. We became rapid easy friends, in the fashion of travelers on shipboard or marooned in hotels, but this night was a difficult one for Max Liptzen: news by cable that his mother was dying in Brooklyn and the next flight out of Port-au-Prince was two days away. He needed to survive until then. A broad-faced, deeply tanned man— that mahogany weathering of the dweller in the tropics who has retained his northern love of the sun—Max had played football for the Texas Aggies (scholarship), spent the war in the Marines (sergeant), wandered New York looking for a crevice in which his lazy, free-swinging spirit might pass its time, and finally cast himself up on the beach in Haiti. There he found play for his talents—a bit of business, a bit of monkey business—and lived easy and hard, married several times, and gave the world a number of children in assorted colors. Two of his children were now in school in the States, living with their separate mothers. And now his hair was thinning, too much salt water, too much sun; and he blacked what remained with a Dominican product guaranteed to restore youth. The heavy shoulders were sloped with flesh; belly pressed over and around belt, no matter how he worked at the Royal Canadian Air Force exercises. And his mother, to whom he remained faithful as only a lazy, playful New York boy is faithful, was dying far away and out of reach.

"I thought heart is for men?" he asked. "Isn't it usually cancer for women, or the sugar diabetes?"

"Well, not much difference anymore."

"Not much difference between men and women?" He threw his head back and roared at his joke. The ritual laughter was called up by the idea of a joke; nothing to do with his feelings.

1804), and the single-minded intentions of its women. Many find favor in the bars along the Carrefour road. The best of these village girls have high rumps, jolly natures, and avaricious hearts—they are self-respecting whores. The jukebox boomed out its Chubby Checker beat; the ladies, who take their English neat, were mouthing the memorized words; Max was buying surcease from sorrow, rum and soda; and to keep from being hounded by a pack of ladies, I had chosen one of them to be my very own. I discovered, as my head filled with smoke, that I was dancing the twist.

"Tweest! An' tweest again!" my partner sang. "An' tweest wan more time!"

All this for us? I recall thinking. Naked bar boys running, girls chanting, sweat rolling, rum bottles clinking. On the wall the portrait of Dr. François Duvalier, the swollen owl's face in black horn-rimmed glasses and topped by a homburg, like a voodoo priest, gazed down unblinkingly upon us. "The Great Protector," I said to my dancing partner.

"Ah *oui oui oui*," she said.

"Everyone has him on the wall," I said.

"Of course, he is the Great Protector."

I led her toward him by the arm, making as if to press her face against the photograph. "I've seen him on lots of walls," I said, "but I've never seen anybody kiss him."

She collapsed with the giggles. In Creole she reported my remark to the other girls and the barman. The girls howled. One cried out, "He never kiss me either," and the shrieks of laughter mounted afresh. The barman frowned and brought me a rum-soda on the house.

Max said without conviction, "You want to get me expelled?"

"Tweest again?" said my date. "An' we tweest again?"

The jukebox took off in stratospheric answer to her question. I went along for the ride. Watching her deal with the problem of weightfulness, I nominated her for lady astronaut. When the record was over, we held hands back to the table, where Max was deep in conversation with another girl, a girl of about fifteen with a healthy high pout to everything, rump, breasts, lips. "We talk," I said to my lady.

"No no no! We go upstairs!"

"Talk!" I said.

"No"—and then with sudden suspicion: "You seeck?"

"No."

"You t'ink I seeck? I no seeck. Fresh young t'ing. Inspection by *docteur* evair mont', and no jigajig busi-ness zis mont'. *C'est la pagaïe.*" She gazed at Max, who was busy downing one rum after another and talking, talking, talking to his lady. "He seeck?"

Perhaps unnerved by the music, the noise, the expectation of direct action, I told her that his mother was very ill in New York and that he was awaiting the plane to take him there. She advised me to advise him to go upstairs with his lady in order to while away the hours of waiting. This is the remedy for most problems, especially the ones for which there is no other remedy. But when the girls knew that we had come only to drink and talk, they made the best of it. They drank. They talked. Max was getting very drunk as he explained to a lady who spoke about twenty words of English, all learned from sailors, what the pacemaker does, how heart surgery has developed in recent years, and where New York lies in relation to Port-au-Prince, Cap-Haïtien, Jacmel, Jérémie, and Port-de-Paix. Further north it lies. The pacemaker can lie to the north or the south of the heart. But it keeps the heart going with an electrical impulse conforming to the heart's own rhythm, the rhythm of a mother who loved her youngest son though he gave her no joy, only a succession of daughters-in-law and grandchildren—the grandchildren scattered, the daughters-in-law scattered, the son lost in a strange land with a business that bore no looking into. A fish business, but what kind of a fish business? A fishy business, she always said.

The girl sitting with Max asked him, "You like maybe my sister?"

I was telling my own lady about the United States. I was keeping an eye on Max. When she asked if I would take her to the United States, and I said maybe, she laughed scornfully. She didn't expect to get taken to the United States by a man who bought drinks but paid her no serious attention. She didn't even expect to get taken from Carrefour to Port-au-Prince, or from the Flamingo Annex to the Flamingo. She expected very little from life, and knew she would get less than she expected.

Then suddenly Max turned away from the girl listening with her elbows on that wobbly table and began to talk to me. "I've been married four times," he said. "My mother is dying. I make about seven, eight thousand a year here, but it goes as far as twenty in the States. Maybe about that far. And in the good years I made more, sometimes twice as much. But I could never keep up the support payments too good. My kids don't see me. I can't visit them much on what I make. I can't bring them down here. My mother, I always wrote to her, though. We kept in touch. We kept in touch. How can I keep in touch now?"

I asked if he would like to go back to the Oloffson. I offered to drive.

"No," he said.

Tears began to flow down the furrows of his sunburned cheeks.

"Yes," he said.

The girls followed us to the door. He was having trouble keeping on his feet. He was cursing the government of François Duvalier because Pan Am only flew out of Port-au-Prince three times a week.

Now I saw the same tears that his Syrian girlfriend had discovered on his face. But he was not ashamed of them. I was a stranger to him; the girls were strangers; they chattered and clucked and helped to push him into the jeep, just as if this were their customary job—to pack away a weeping American. "I been married four times!" he said to one of them.

She understood a little English. "In one night?" she asked. "Oooh, you beeg man. You come back when you feel better, yes? Gran'bamboche, we marry you four time in one night."

There was the smell of charcoal smoke and rotting mangoes on the road.

Max asked me, "What if my mother knew how I spend my time?"

I told him not to worry about it.

He turned to me again, seeming nearly sober in the darkness, first sticking his head out into the midnight coolness of the bayside road. He was giving thought to what the girl had told him. "Listen," he said, "if you're really in love, there's no limit. You know what it's like —really in love? Listen, if it's true love, hell, you're a man all the time. 'Be a man,' you say to yourself, and you're a man, just like that. When she looks at you with that look because she loves you. When you want to." He ran his hand through his thin hair. He looked at it in the dark as if the blacking might smudge his fingers. "My mother used to fly down sometimes for the home games," he said, "you know, in Texas there. Of course, the school paid her fare. They knew I liked to have her in the stands. I played better with her watching me."

"I know."

"Listen!" he said. We were stopped at a barricade by the ragged militia known as the *tontons macoutes*. They pointed their guns and shone their flashlights over us. Max held himself with dignity and let me do the talking. I paid the toll. Then he continued, dead sober.

"Listen," he said, "this is how I spent my whole life in this place. Since the war. Since 1948, that wasn't so long after the war. Since after I got done bumming around. I figured out how to import fish in barrels from Canada. Started with Norway, ended up with Canada. Dried. Salted. Industrial quality, it won't kill you. Okay, it made me some money. I didn't have to work much. Just organize it a little. Listen, I got married a lot. Kids all over. A couple brown kids, too. Now I can't fall in love anymore. Ma gets her pacemaker, maybe she'll be all right, okay? You think so? Oh, Christ. Oh, God. I get out on Pan Am, Montego Bay, Idlewild, my brother meets me. Straight to the hospital and she'll ask me—oh, God in heaven, keep her alive. But I don't know how to answer her. You know, kid? What I started to tell you about falling in love: *This is a place for hiding out*. That's all it is." He paused once more, trying to make his discovery for me so that he could make it for himself. "It's like this when you're in business all alone, like I am. You bite a lot. I'm a tough fellow. You get bitten. So my mouth been bitten by lots of girls, but no one has bit *me*. How do I answer my mama when she asks what I'm doing? How do I lie to her when she's needing a pacemaker? But how can I tell her the truth?"

WAITING FOR THE FORTY-ONE UNION

There was this girl, Peggy, he could call anytime. They had an agreement,
Karol and Peggy did, they were old friends. "You get the night frights,
you telephone, we'll talk," she said. "Any hour, I don't care. I can
talk you up, I'm really good, Karol. Up and out of it. And if talk
doesn't do, we'll cuddle together, okay? I won't even ask you for taxi
fare, okay? I'll just throw on a raincoat over my nightie—"

"Thanks, Peggy." Good old Peggy Something.

"Um."

"Yes, Peggy."

"I get the night frights, too, sometimes, Karol. Oh, bad. That
means, um—"

"I throw on the raincoat over the nightie and—"

"Yes, Karol."

So Karol never took Peggy up on her offer. Down as he sometimes slid, he knew enough to know her downs were oftener than his, and pretty soon he wouldn't have a night to call his own. Good Peggy, nice and pretty Peggy; but Karol valued his privacy, his sleep, and even his sadness too much to shuffle through them with cuddly sex from a sweet and friendly North Beach chick whom he didn't want to carry around with him through a difficult life.

Nevertheless, when the bad nights came, they were very lonely and bad indeed. Who and what and why am I? he asked the Alcatraz foghorn, the maroon fog glowing with city lights, the outcries from the Broadway strip and Chinatown which drifted up Russian Hill to his whitewashed little studio. And the answer to the question was lacking. Perhaps the question itself was not clear. He had lived with it so long that it was almost an esthetic question now. Just as he couldn't paint dream and horror by smearing ink or a little wash over his vision, so he couldn't answer the basic question by asking it in this outrageously vain manner. Me, myself, and I look out at the glowing dark? I don't want to paint, I don't want to pain, I can't sleep or think, and why?

Selfish questions.

Worse: unclear questions all rolled up into one bad question.

Noisy head!

Not finding the answer in bed, not wanting to find it in Peggy— in fact, certain it was not to be found either in bed or in Peggy—Karol arose swiftly and put on the clothes not meant to be worn until morning. Modestly, as he dressed at midnight, he turned his back on the table, a flush door on horses, on which he was carving a wood-block of his friend Lew the Poet. He didn't want half-born deadwood to see his misery and look chips of sawdust and curly filings at him.

He snapped the light and felt wide-awake. He need never sleep again; perhaps it was only that. He heard his shoes on the concrete stairway and hoped he didn't wake any neighbors, or if he did, that they thought he was a serious person with serious business at this hour. Well, in San Francisco, they don't worry; this was no longer Evanston. Rioters, burglars, cops, kids, transvestites, even artists and nobodies and semisomebodies wander the night, and only when the stockbrokers come stalking down the hills at dawn in time for the opening of the market, three hours earlier by Pacific Coast time, do the sleepless wander home to bed and leave the night world to a few

vendors of the Berkley *Barb*, skipping on speed as if still alive. Down
the hill toward Broadway. Past the haunted house: This time he
wouldn't do it, wouldn't, wouldn't.

But he did.

He saw the girls dancing in the window, as he had seen them three
years before on New Year's Eve, when, reconciled with his own lady,
with loins exhausted by reconciliation, they headed this way to a party
and he glanced into the window and saw the girls jerking like ma-
rionettes—no strings, no music—jerking and swimming and smiling
and silent, flying to a rhythm he could not hear, with men he did not
see, early celebrants with the joy of girlishness frantic on faces, hair,
lips, teeth, shadow of neck. Now it was like a slide inserted between
his eyes and his brain each time he passed that window, an image of
hope and desire, youth leaping to unheard sounds, girls deafening
themselves with dance.

He moved on by and it flicked off. Thank God; relief; the panic
subsided. They were so lovely, and he feared them so.

If the real girls of three years ago still lived there—stewardesses,
were they? secretaries? students?—he could have charmed them and
known them and finished with them. But there was a parade of
tenants in that building and he was caught with a memory that could
never be tampered with by reality, silently dancing on a New Year's
Eve which never ended in a new year. He never saw them afterward.

The night air made him feel fresh, lively, almost grateful for insomnia. Down Broadway he strolled, to the corner of Columbus, where
the barker for the Condor stood hoarsely importuning sailors, salesmen, and conventioneers: "One drink sees the entire show! One
drink, come on in, only one drink and see the famous San Francisco
bottomless!" A police car, two lounging cops grinning, was parked in
the bus stop. One officer had a clipboard in his lap, but he wasn't
looking at it. A voice cried out: "Karol!"

It was Harry Cameron, a day stroller whom Karol knew from the
street. He had been a doorman, manager of a defunct rock band,
postermaker. Lately he said, when asked what he did for a living, "I'm
getting healthy." But now he was standing at the bus stop, jiggling up
and down, and shouting at Karol though Karol was standing right
next to him.

"What's the matter?" Karol asked him.

"Wait! Ing!"

"Waiting for what?"

"Wait! Ing! for the Forty-one Union!"

But the bus had just pulled up, lying clumsily out in the street to avoid the police car, and Harry didn't move for it. It smoked and rumbled and the gears shrieked.

"There's your bus, Harry."

"Still wait-ing for the Forty-one Union!" Harry sang, letting the bus by. He hopped and jiggled, and his beefy face was purple in the reflection of lights from the Condor.

Karol hadn't known that Harry used speed. Now he also guessed what he was doing out on the streets all day. He was dealing in the product.

"I thought you were getting healthy," Karol said.

"Getting healthy on the Forty-one Union! Getting healthy tomorrow! Getting healthy is a state of mind! Getting healthy—"

He was still discussing his coming good physical and spiritual organization as Karol moved off. Karol was sure he didn't notice that his friend was gone. Future health on the bus out of North Beach was of primary concern, and Harry was still making points in the agitated neon air as the cop ate his sandwich on a clipboard tray.

Karol decided he would get hunger taken care of as his own way to a good night's sleep, even if it turned out to be a morning sleep. He turned down Grant toward the Hui Chao, an all-night basement mirror-and-steel restaurant. Beef and tomatoes and noodles were cheap and provided everything a man needed to live healthy, though none of the late-night diners confirmed this theory by their appearance. Well, maybe they were young Red Guards eating raw fish, old, toothless, and used-up refugees from Hong Kong and Taiwan eating only noodles or soup. No one stared in the mirrors, which reflected Hui Chao basement within Hui Chao basement within Hui Chao steel, chrome, and mirrors and scrunched-over-eating basement. It was a mistake. He felt healthy now, but depressed, lonely, and artfully horny. It had been harmless to be a jittery insomniac; there was trouble in being a sleepless night wanderer. If he could have used electric light to paint by, he'd have been better off to try working. That's all right; he didn't want to be better off.

He paid his $1.75, which included the rice and tea, and moved past the splintered crates at which an old man, stoned by age, not opium, sold scraps of Chinese newspapers which looked as if a new one hadn't been published since he came to town. Back out of Chinatown to North Beach, through the alley past City Lights and Vesuvio's and onto Columbus, where he saw a girl he knew. She was the friend of Stan Wong, she was blond, she had a baby, she was crazy, she had traveled with the first acid freaks; she didn't remember his name, but she knew she knew him; she came up and said, putting out her open hand, "I want to lay this on you because I love you."

There was a pill in his hand. And then again, it might be only a Rexall aspirin.

"What is it?"

"Because I love you," she said, chattering something else to an invisible companion as she hurried down the street, pulling her two-year-old by the arm. The kid needed to have his nose wiped. And it probably wasn't an aspirin. Karol only took aspirin when he needed to deaden a cold, when his nose was blocked and he was dead already and needed some additional deadening to forget his sinus and brain; and what it was she had given him, whatever it was, he was pretty sure he had never taken it before. And wouldn't now. And the nighttime North Beach street smells were alive and whirling in his network of sinus which was merely an extension of the fingerprint whorls and swirls of his brain.

What was her name again?

Maria Something—yes, that's it. Maria. Maria Velveeta, they called her.

She and the kid, sleeping on his feet, disappeared up Columbus. The kid just hung like dead fruit from a tree, waiting for a breeze for its excuse to fall. Well, he could always call Peggy.

The speed freaks were rushing in and out of the Dante, the Swiss-American, the El Dorado hotels, slamming doors, stumbling against one another, in a hurry, heads busy. Constricted blood vessels made their nerves squeak. It must have been about three now, because the go-go dancers, the topless and bottomless artistes with stars in their eyes and spangles in their orifices, miraculously transformed by closing time into sallow and spine-sprung dropouts, were being met at the sidewalk by their old men and guardians, sharpies hoping to leave pimping behind them on the golden road into show business. They

would have coffee and eggs at the Ferris Wheel, or omelets and
potatoes at the U.S. Restaurant (spinach omelet the specialty), and
the fellow would have to listen to his client's tales of a hard night on
a hard beat. The Filipino guardian at Enrico's was watching over the
sidewalk, saying, "No, closed, too late, no." A pair of cops were
frisking a girl in a cape at the Kearny steps. They looked in her hair
and pulled it off. It makes a ripping noise. Well, they had known in
advance, with the deep intuition of cops, that it was a boy in a girl's
wig, not a girl in a girl's wig. The city had recently declared war on
transvestites who didn't pay off (confused so many sailors recently
home from Vietnam).

Karol had the taste of noodles and tomato sauce in his mouth. He
could see the sailors waiting up the hill for the cable car. That was
something to do: Walk up the hill and let them know the cable car
had stopped running for the night; a little patriotic deed for which
no one would thank him, only the sailors, not the government, the
president, the Congress, or Peggy, unless he telephoned her. But he
was not willing to incur this debt. He stood in despair, but he thought
ahead. "Hey, fellas! Doesn't run anymore!"

"Don't mess around with us," a sailor said, strolling toward him
with hat tilted over one eye.

"No, I just wanted to tell you the cable car stops for a couple
hours," Karol said.

"You want to mess with me?" the sailor asked.

Karol retraced his steps down the hill. The sailors, waiting for the
car, yelled and dared him to come on back up.

The sailor reminded Karol of Peggy again. When you get the night
frights, that's what you should do: Think of messing around with
Peggy and get happy. But he didn't want easy oblivions. Like the man
waiting for the Forty-one Union, he preferred to work it out his own
way, looking for the magic lady, the dream lover who would be
looking for her magic man, her dream lover, himself.

The sugar was diminishing in his blood. The spurt of energy, three
o'clock closing time in North Beach, was closing down. A few drunks
rambled; a few freaks stood in doorways, looking for sales or buys. A
dusky orange glow was reflected in the fog, the early false dawn of
cities. A truck dropped a bundle of newspapers at the corner, twisted
about with wire so that only a kid with wire cutters could mess in
them.

Karol knew what he needed to do now. Just keep walking until there was nothing for it but sleep. Tire himself down into sleep, like a good boy, breathing easy after his tantrum. Down Broadway toward the Embarcadero, down the slope toward the warehouses and show-rooms. As he paused for the light at Sansome, he heard someone giggle. "What?" he said.

A giggle, but he saw no one.

"Who is it?" he asked.

Morning commuters were already heading onto the ramp, sleepy chaps locked into their cars with the weather-news-music breakfast to keep them steering straight. Later there would be coffee carts in the halls.

"I been following you," Maria Velveeta said, stepping out of a used-car emporium doorway. She didn't explain how she could have followed ahead of him, but perhaps he hadn't noticed or perhaps she hadn't really been following him.

"Where's the boy?"

"You're the boy."

"The boy."

"Oh, him. Beddy-bye time. I dropped him off at . . ." She shrugged. "Left him home," she said. "Hi, King Karol of Rumania."

"How did you know?"

"Just guessed it. Take that pill yet, which will make you a king?"

"How'd you know?"

"Oh, I know, I'm a friend of mine, I'm not as crazy as I let on."

Karol extended the linty bit of stuff. He had rolled it in his fingers, stuck it in his pocket, and now he offered it to Maria. "I don't know what it is," he said. "I don't want it. Here, have it back."

"I don't know what it is either," she said. "I want it."

He watched while she rolled her tongue around to moisten her mouth. She grinned and made a jerky lifting gesture of her chin, and her throat rippled. Down, like a chicken eating corn.

"It'll take at least twenty minutes for whatever it is," she said. "Maybe it's an aspirin."

"We got twenty minutes to be straight in."

"You got a whole life to be straight in. Me, I got twenty minutes."

"I'll bet it's an aspirin."

Maria looked hurt. "But I said I loved you when I gave it to you. I wouldn't lie like that."

"You can love someone and give him an aspirin."

Maria looked at him as if to say, "You're deep, you're heavy, what a trip." Who could tell what she was thinking?

They stood at the chilly corner. Maria sighed.

"Listen," she said, "before my straight twenty minutes is up, let's."

"Let's what?" he asked.

"Let's," she said. "Right now. I want to."

He stood waiting in the dark as the headlights swung over them, then up the ramp.

"Okay," she said, "just let me." She pushed him into the doorway. It was still dark. It would be dark for a while; then it would be tomorrow. The headlights up the ramp just flicked across, climbing their bodies, nothing more. She grabbed him and held him to her coat. He smelled leather, suede, grass, patchouli. "Oh, that's good," she said, "good." She undid him. Rapid handwork. "Oh, good, good." He was saying nothing. He was pressing his mouth against her hair. "Now let me," she said.

They were leaning against each other in the before-dawn glow of fog. A cop car passed slowly but didn't stop.

Karol was slipping and sliding. He was standing up and leaning. He remembered Peggy. He remembered someone else. Her hair. He remembered nothing. She was guiding him. Strain in his thighs. Yes, he was allowed to help a little. Leaning back and riding, lifting, riding. "Oh, do it, do it, do it, let me," she whispered ferociously into his ear.

Oh, good.

She patted him, stroked him, shook him.

They leaned against each other. Karol tried to think tenderly of her, but thought only of needing to walk back up the long slope of hill.

A flashlight beam caught them. Two cops crossed the street. They had been watching them from another doorway. "Hey, you two kids—"

"Naw, they're over twenty-one," said the other cop.

"We were just talking," Karol said.

"Oh, boy. We didn't hear you talking." He shone the light up and down their bodies. "Christ, and you're not even kids," he said. "Go on, just don't pee in the doorway."

And the cop switched off his light and the two of them moved on heavily, back into their car, laughing and breathing and off to their breakfast breaks.

Karol stood there out of breath and frightened.

"It's okay," Maria said. "Are you nervous again? Want to do it again?" And her hand finding him.

"No! I mean, no thanks."

She patted him sweetly. "That's all right. Excuse me, will you? I got to go look after my baby. Sometimes he wakes up early and I left him without a sitter."

"You'd better," he said.

She didn't move. There was more on her mind. She said, "Oh, by the way, there was something I meant to ask you."

Now she'd put the ask on him—rent, food, the kid. Okay, he had it coming. First crumbling pill and she loved him, then crumbling against her in a doorway. If she weren't a good girl, he'd have said she was setting him up. Sure, he could help her out, five, ten, probably no more than that. "What?" he said.

"Anything?" she said. He wasn't sure if she was coquettish or anxious. "Okay? You will? Promise?"

"Depends. Yes. Go on."

She sighed. She said, "How old are you?" and then turned away without waiting for the answer.

And he was standing alone in the doorway, shivering. Call Peggy? No, he wouldn't call Peggy. He looked across the street at the empty warehouse, a dusty window and a LEASE OR SALE TERMS in red, white and blue; and behind the sign he suddenly saw two girls silently dancing, fingers raised, hair flying, smiles of ecstasy on their faces. He hurried out of the doorway.

By the time he got to the corner of Columbus and Broadway, the sun had already begun to glint over the Bay. There were diamonds of light on the windows ahead. Harry Cameron was still waiting for the Forty-one Union. Up the hill, past the retina confusion of girls doing the insane jiggle forever, grinning and lovely, ghosts leaping behind diamonds of sunrise; and to bed now, this time to sleep.

WINTER OF '73

It's cold up and down Van Ness Avenue in San Francisco, where they sell the cars. It's raining. There is never any snow, this is San Francisco, but the people are surprised to be shivering. The showrooms through the great plate windows look cold, despite the circus slogans painted on shimmering glass. It's also cold on Van Ness because they aren't selling many cars this year. The flow of oil has been tampered with, unclear exactly why. The Arabs say the oil users should take a turn as colonies, subject to cold winters.

My wife has invited a friend to have lunch with us. The other lady wants to discuss her recent separation from her husband. Since my wife has heard the story several times already, she thinks it only fair that I also hear it and give the lady—whom I like, since she is pretty and bright—the benefit of my useless advice.

It is raining. Or perhaps it is only a heavy winter fog. Sloppy, shapeless droplets stain the debris along the curb. I drop the lady and my wife at the Haven, seminatural foods, and find a parking place on the street in front of an automobile agency.

As I get out, I am careful to lock all the doors of the car. I didn't always do this. A few years ago I began. Standing nearby in the rain, wearing a blue blazer and neat gray-flannel trousers, a tall, slender, almost-distinguished man—a golfer's looks—was ignoring the heavy fog seeping into his flannels as he shouted at a young man on the street, "Why don't you see a psychiatrist?"

"All right, I will," said the young man, turning.

"Right away!"

"You too," shouted the young man.

Odd conversation early on a Saturday afternoon in the heavy fog of winter. The young man was wearing jeans and a leather vest over no shirt—probably a clammy feeling, unless you're doing it out of moral principle and a local sense of beauty. The conflict between him and the man from the automobile agency was loud but entirely verbal.

"Stoo-pid!" shouted the automobile man. (He wore a tag above the pocket of the blazer.)

"Idiot!" shouted the young fellow in the leather vest. He was moving backward away, and as I finished locking the doors of my station wagon, I thought to ask the salesman what this post-flower-child trouble might be.

"Goddamn Jew!" shouted the salesman at the hippie.

It took no particular thought or effort on my part quickly to substitute for my question about the source of the difficulty the following statement: "You asshole, shut your fucking mouth before I rip your tongue out."

The automobile salesman whirled toward me with something like real despair. "What'd I do to you?" Here he is, trying to make a living in a sick world, and strangers come to abuse him from everywhere. "What are you yelling at me for?"

"Because you called the man a goddamn Jew—"

"But I don't like him," he wailed.

"Well, I'm a Jew and I don't like to hear you talking like that."

"But I think he's a goddamn Jew and that's what he is." He was regrouping himself after my surprise attack.

"And you're an asshole."

He moved toward me, shouting, "You can't call me names." I waited. He paused nearby. He was genuinely puzzled at the sight of me. "Or I'll call the police."

"Call. I'll wait, asshole."

Van Ness is well patrolled, and it happened that a car—black and white, extinguished red Cyclops eye atop—was passing and the auto dealer shouted, "Police, police!" He looked proper and neat in his blue blazer, although his voice was a little anxious and hurried. Bearded, in corduroy jacket and jeans, I wondered how the police might respond to me as two of them came sauntering out of the car, measuring the situation in that wary, professional way. My car dealer started to sell his case to them. "I was just yelling at that Jew up the street when this one came along. I wasn't even talking to him, and he said something dirty to me, he won't apologize, I want him to apologize or put him under arrest—"

The two police divided themselves up. "I don't like that word *Jew* used in that way," I said to the one who chose me.

The one who spoke with the car dealer said to him, "Okay, okay, why don't you go back inside and sell some cars, okay?"

The one who spoke with me said, "Where were you headed?"

"To lunch."

"I don't blame you. I'm kind of hungry myself. Why don't you run along and have a good lunch?"

"I want an apology from that Jew!" the car dealer cried.

"Do you want me to wait around? Would you like my identification?" I asked the policeman.

"Actually, I'd prefer you just cross the street now and go on to your sandwich and soup, it's getting kind of late," he said.

The other policeman had his arm around the car dealer's shoulders and was guiding him toward the door of his agency. He was asking him a question: "What'll you take for that '66 Rambler I saw back there in the lot?" I waited for the light to change and crossed the street.

Although the fog was heavy and chill, I felt hot and winded, as if I had been running; not jogging but running. I walked up the long block to the Haven, where my wife and our friend were waiting at a table.

"What's wrong?" my wife asked me.

"What's wrong," her friend answered, "is that marriage just can't work in this society, when women have to make their own place for themselves, they can't just say, You're nice, you're great, you're a big strong hunk of man, if the slob is doing nothing for them but bringing home six-packs of beer and the *TV Guide,* so I say out is what I say. My husband has bad habits."

"I'd like to hear your story from the beginning," I said.

"What's the matter?" my wife asked me again.

"There's a long winter starting out," our friend said, starting on her minestrone and sandwich on natural bread with sprouts. She looked up at me, knowing that I need to think about the meaning of things in order to keep interested, and wiped a piece of macaroni off her chin. "I sometimes think—don't you?—that war is the natural condition of things for settling disagreements. Too bad Phil and I have only marriage to go to war about. Since we don't get along, we have to go to war."

A DARK
NORWEGIAN
PERSON

When he heard that his former student Rodman had died on the rocks down a cliff where the sign read FORBIDDEN TO SWIM FORBIDDEN TO CLIMB STRICTLY FORBIDDEN, his first thought was: *Dummy.* He remembered the young man as the kind of sixties pushme-pullyou for whom the Revolution and ardent courtship of his teachers were both part of the same program—the aggrandizement of Rodman. His old-fashioned ambition had dressed itself in the new manners, but the last time they had met, in Paris one summer, Rodman had run up to him, saying, "Dan! How you be, man? Listen, you got to meet my wife, my Norwegian wife, man, I dug up the daughter of about the only Norwegian nonshipping millionaire. Which you wouldn't expect: fantastic in the sack, too."

"This is a big city, Rodman," Dan Shaper had said. "You pick one bank, and I'll take the other, and we don't ever have to see each other, okay?"

"Aw, Dan, why you so uptight 'cause an old disciple made it?"
Dummy.

But his distaste had gotten through to Rodman at last, it seemed,
or perhaps Rodman simply had no further use for him. Although they
both lived in San Francisco, there were no more attempts at buddy-
hood, and they never spoke again. The joke of it was that Shaper
caught glimpses of Sigrid, the dark Norwegian wife of his student, and
wished he had met this beautiful tall slim wife with fine straight black
hair, a fine straight long nose, pale cheeks with a few girlish freckles,
the slow grace of careful tall girls when she moved; occasionally he
saw her laughing at Rodman's jokes in a restaurant, in the lobby of
a theater and once on the back of a motorcycle—a rapturous flashing
smile that he remembered and carried with him like an antique
postcard from some rare wonderful unvisited place of pleasure. The
wife of his student who was enjoying a man's games. The wife of a
man who proved his revolutionary fervor by climbing on a private
cliff; small, curly, ever-smiling Rodman, sliding, still smiling and
scrambling, until he smashed on those foam-covered rocks where the
sea lions honked at low tide, where even the ghetto kids knew it was
no place to play macho-man games. The widow of that dummy.

Shaper did not wait past hearing the news. He wrote her a note
expressing his regret and that perhaps Rodman had mentioned him
and that he would call. He telephoned the next day, and her laughter was light and high for such a tall girl: "You do not bide your
time, do you, Mr. Professor?" But before his heart could quail, she
added, "I must some rest of this business. I might very much like
dinner with a person who is not involved. Tonight would be best
for both of us, would it not?" The laughter again: "You because you
are so impatient. Me because I do need distraction, dear solicitous
kind friend."

When he came for her, it was not a house of death. The color of
mourning was only in her hair; her dress was white, a dazzling crocheted material that clung to the long limbs; she wore no jewelry—
perhaps out of respect for her husband—but the effect was to empha-
size the brightness of teeth, the caves and shadows of breasts, bones,
sea-colored eyes, even the faint pale down of her arms glimpsed
through the long, loose sleeves. Of course, she still wore her wedding
band.

"Sit." He perched. "May I offer you some wine? I don't know what I'll do with all the wine our friends have brought me."

"No thank you," he said.

"Perhaps you would like a bottle or two to take out for your own cellar? German wine, Rhine wine, May wine, I seem to have a great many sweet wines in stock these days."

"Maybe you'd just like to get out," he said. "I mean—"

"It's all right. Look around you." And as he followed this order he saw very little sign of Rodman. There were spaces on the walls; there was the sense of a roommate having recently moved. "I asked his friends to take souvenirs of him. I called the Goodwill for the rest. Naturally I have kept a few books, some pictures. But what else should I do?"

He did not answer, and she shrugged.

"Before you express your condolences in the manner of some of his friends, let me say that we were about to separate, I wanted a divorce, I didn't know how to make him give up. And I know you didn't like him, he complained about you, you were a toothpick in his arm"—odd expression—"and that's why I accepted your invitation. Please, Mr. Shaper, no bullshit."

He focused on a floating mote. He did not know where good manners would place his stare.

"Not that I am not sad. Of course, I am sad for the poor soul, poor selfish lost soul, poor poor sad silly boy."

Her eyes filled with tears. The tear in each eye seemed to swell like a gigantic contact lens, without falling, and abruptly she stood up, and her long, sure stride took her to the bathroom. The water ran. When she returned, her face had been scrubbed, her cheeks shone, she was smiling. He had been in love before he saw her. It was not love, of course, it was infatuation with beauty, perhaps complicated by spite for an irritating young man with unmerited good luck; Dan Shaper, himself, considered his fate in marriage to be unmerited bad luck. But what he felt for her now was respect for her lack of hypocrisy, admiration for her straightforward honesty. He desired her. He even felt some grief for the suffering she tried not to allow herself. It welled up in her anyway. He loved this woman.

He remembered a sabbatical visit to Norway, all those fine-haired, fine-eyed people, friendly and polite until they got drunk, and then the bloody fights over a taxicab while wives or girlfriends huddled and watched, and then either the police screeched up in little black patrol cars to haul them away to sleep it off, or they simply picked themselves up off the street, bowing, shaking hands, offering each other a congratulatory drink for a slugfest well slugged. Crazy people in their sensible way. Of course, he had not met a girl of Sigrid's worldtraveled, moneyed class. She might be crazy in her own way, he thought as they talked through a fish dinner at Scoma's (petrale, salad with just lemon, a bottle of white wine, fruit and cheese for dessert —a light dinner for the recently bereaved), but she also seemed to him the sanest person he had met in years. As for craziness, Shaper could supply all they needed. It was crazy to feel what he felt for her, like a boy. It was crazy to admit it to himself and, given her sharp eyes, to her. It was crazy not to care that he was crazy and to take such satisfaction in it.

She enjoyed laughing at him.

"Rodman," she said, "he was so jealous he wanted me to stay in the room while he composed. Have you ever sat for hours, days, while a songwriter picked at a guitar? A Zen Buddhist country-rock composer? A ballad in favor of saving our waterpower, adopted from the original Japanese rockabilly tune? An untalented ambitious clever boy?"

He touched her hand.

"And have you ever had a lover who wanted to keep the bathroom door open for conversation? To talk to you? At least I hope that's why. He even took the lock off the door. Maybe," she said, wrinkling her brow, "maybe he liked to watch. . . . No, I think it was just Rodman's jealousy. Perhaps was I hiding something in there?"

When he touched her hand, she squeezed his fingers with her own long warm slim ones and did not hurry to let go.

"I'm so sorry for him," she said. "He found the wrong wife, the wrong way of life, the wrong death. He admired grand suicides, you know. Very romantic person. I think his death was not even provisionally grand. And even," she said, he waited, "I even believe it was mostly an accident. I am going on that assumption."

"You're a firm person," he said.

"I try my best. I do what is required. I deeply regret some things in the past. I do my best to go on."

There was no question about where they would go or what they would do after dinner. First they had a little walk by the Bay, along the Embarcadero. For Shaper it was a good augury, no particular reason why, that they saw a Norwegian freighter shining, a bit scummy, in the late summer remnants of daylight-saving daylight. The disappeared sun, still reflected in the low rim of fog through the Golden Gate, made faint diamond glints against the portholes. She took his arm.

They drove to his flat in an old house on the steep, quarried slope of Telegraph Hill. Women sometimes commented on how lucky he was to have found such a place, and then he had to say it was hard to carry groceries up, but, yes, he was lucky, and then they would talk about fireplaces, about books, about views, about the pleasant detritus of a fairly long life. She skipped all this. They stood and looked back at the darkling city, and then they looked at each other, and then he led her into the other room.

No, it seemed as though she were leading him. "I hear your heart!" she said. "Please, don't be nervous. Please to please yourself, sir, and you can be quite sure I will be happy. Please!"

Because he seemed so nervous, she slipped off the tiny filmy bra first. He helped her with the dress, she said, Ouch!, and she laughed, and he laughed, and they both laughed when she said, Wait! as the crocheted material caught on one erect nipple.

His nervousness passed.

The night passed.

In the morning, when he awoke, she whispered to him—she must have been awake awhile already—"Poor Rodman. This is what he feared, he so much dreaded." She touched his lips with her fingers, fingers that smelled slightly of their lovemaking, and he kissed each finger in turn. "But not with you," she said. "You were one he never feared, he only wanted you to like him a little. Perhaps now you do."

Since his divorce, since his loss of the wife he had mourned so long, Shaper had treated lovemaking as a way to say good-bye. It eased him. It said, Okay, so go, to that lost wife. Lovemaking should not be a way to say good-bye, but that was how it was for him.

His first lovemaking with Sigrid was a hello to something new. It was only a beginning. He thought of her. He thought of no other woman. Ah, perhaps he thought a little of himself and of Rodman, but only because poor Rodman had led him to Sigrid, and Sigrid had led him back to himself. And the spiral was complicated but complete. He could forget himself and think of her.

So far he could not tell if she thought of him. When love is fresh, or so it seemed to Shaper, that does not matter so much. Eventually it matters very much. It matters the whole world. Eventually it was a matter of life or not life, life or what Shaper had been living until he met Sigrid, that she begin to love him.

Pillow philosophers sometimes write that the important thing is to love, not to be loved. They emit a steady hum of benevolent nonsense, advice for self-help manuals, framed, fake parchment sheets, the poesy of broccoli-headed teenagers. I'm running on, he thought. What's the subject?

Shaper's avid hunger had been reawakened overnight. After the famine and fast and the years of stolid acquiescence in a poor regimen, he wanted once again what everyone wants. It was good; he was sure of that. It even allowed him to feel kindness for poor Rodman, a little pity for his loss, something like human respect for the boy. And one hell of a lot of gratitude. Inadvertent favors may be the best ones.

They spent the day together. They went to a museum in the morning, like kids courting: French impressionism plus not enough serious looking to tire their feet. He felt light and floating; the morning's cold shower lasted all morning. Then they sat at the counter of a shellfish bar and ate clams, shrimp salad, drank little bottles of cold beer, and she said it was like a Norwegian lunch, except there were no little squares of buttered bread. No matter. They ate little crackers and broke off chunks of sourdough French bread. Then she had to see her lawyer, something about the will, something about taxes and probate, and he drove her to Montgomery Street.

Now the shower was used up. He was sweating with desire for her —her athletic back and long legs rapidly retreating into the foyer of an office building—and it was good to have an hour to catch his breath. Finally he remembered to call the department secretary at the university and tell her he would not be meeting office hours today. Suddenly, in her absence, he was gasping for air, as if they had run a race, as if he had drunk a whole thermos of black coffee; it was no rest at all to be without her.

He remembered that she had wanted to divorce Rodman because he could not live without her.

When she returned, smiling and easy and carrying a legal-size envelope, he smiled back just as easily and welcomingly. He felt cured.

"You always smell so sweet," he said. "You know what someone said about the California blonde? She can ride forty miles in the back of a pickup truck and still smell delicious."

"You forget I was born in blond country," she said.

"You smell that way."

"But we dark ones have to work at it, I think," she said, laughing into his eyes and poking at him. She took a fistful of his hair and pulled. "You're dark, and you don't bother."

"Where's your truck?"

"Tak tak tak," she said. "It's not fair, but thank you. Now let's have a nap. I need—after the lawyer, such questions!—I need a dream or two."

"All I can promise is one," he said because he wanted to hear her laughter, and he knew he could promise her and himself all they required, all that was necessary to forget lawyer and probate and Goodwill, all that was past and painful and insignificant; he felt strong enough with her to provide all the sweet dreams in town. Life was intended to be this garden for those who made it so.

A week passed. They spoke of Rodman. She didn't want to meet Shaper's friends. "Remember I'm in mourning," she said.

That was all right with him. He wanted her all to himself anyway. He didn't mind if she spoke of Rodman at odd moments. It was natural; it was touching; it was sad; it had brought them together. Once he peeked in a closet and saw that, indeed, she had given his clothes to Goodwill. A few hangers clanged together like a broken piano when he brushed them. When one fell, he saw a single, forgotten sweat sock in a dark corner. Poor Rodman. Lucky Dan.

He spoke a little of his former wife. She listened patiently. He admitted he had loved his former wife. She listened patiently. He told how he had suffered when she needed her freedom, she needed to change her style, she needed up, out and away. Sigrid listening patiently.

He caught on, being reasonably intelligent, to the fact that none of this interested Sigrid in the slightest. It had not brought them together. It was stale news. It had nothing to do with their lives now, or so she thought, however important he might consider it. He was not too stupid. He shut up.

One more time, and it was only in the dark, near four in the morning, he found bereaved widow's eyes staring at him across a bleak snowfall of sheet and pillow. When he started awake to comfort her, she shut her eyes and seemed truly to be asleep. He was not sure if it was his dream or hers that had awakened him or her.

That morning he watched her pick up the snails in her garden and throw them into the street. "They'll sneak back at night," he said.

She shrugged. "Then I shall have to throw them out again. Do you like my garden? I don't grow vegetables, only mint and flowers."

He liked her garden.

At the end of the week he had to make a three-day trip to Denver for a meeting of experts in his field. It was not the usual airport conference to exchange reports, papers, and expense accounts. "It is," he said ironically, "an in-depth three-day meeting. I'll miss you."

"Yes," she said.

"Will you miss me?"

"Why else would I be here?" she asked. They were in his bed; no, they were in her bed, the bed she had shared with Rodman; of course, she cared for him.

Don't press, don't press, he thought.

"That's nice," he said.

A little later, stroking her back, kneading the long skier's muscles, he asked, "Will you miss me?"

"That was nice before," she said. "Turn over, and I'll do for you, too. Come on, turn over, your turn."

He submitted to those long strong kneading fingers. Oh, good, good, good. How cleverly she had guided him into not insisting on the wrong question, the wrong prying, and yet gave him what they both wanted. How intelligent. How good.

"It's all right I'm leaving for a few days," he said. "It's important. It's too much otherwise."

"Shush," she said. "Just feel what I'm doing with my hands. Let your back be alive, and that's enough."

"I never thought I'd feel so good again."

"Shush."

"I don't remember anything like this. I don't remember anything before you. Why am I going to Denver?"

"The Brown Palace is a beautiful hotel. I love the light in the central hall—you call it central hall? You will do good report and answer other people's questions. Now turn a little this way and shush."

He lay in silence awhile.

"See," she said, "you are you, and I am I. That is very good, dear."

"Everything is good now. Use my name. Don't call me dear. Speak it."

"Now I relax your legs like so. Shush."

"Speak it. Use my name."

Silence.

"Speak it."

From down below where she was smiling and pulling at his legs, pressing her thumbs against the inner slab of thighs, bending, letting him feel her long hair brush against him, her warm breath, she said stubbornly: "Dear."

Nevertheless, he separated himself from her, scraped clean inside with joy and also exhausted and nerved by desire, his body trimmed down and tensed by the effort of pleasure. He had expected nothing more like this in his life. Stan, an old friend, a colleague of other expense-account festivals, a veteran of two marriages, looked at him at the conference registration desk in Denver and said, "You've changed! Oh-oh, one more gray hair, but you look so much younger —you look like a kid!"

"I've found someone," he said.

"That'll do it every time," said his pal. "God's stacked deck. I think I've paid for that mistake by looking younger a few times, too."

"No, really."

"I agree it's wonderful. I do. See me turning moldy colors? Hey, pal: Getting married? Living together? What's happening?"

"I just met her. Her husband just died." Unwillingly he added, "He was a student of mine a few years ago."

Stan sent him a pitying, sarcastic, jealous stare. Out of his own hunger, in a lobby full of people peeling off the backs of their identification labels, he gave him this naked look. Stan said, "What's good is good. We'll see. You are pure enchantment, my man." And he slapped his label to his jacket above his heart.

Shaper took the elevator to his room in the Brown Palace Hotel of Denver and wrote a letter although he would be home to her by the time she received it. But he wanted to tell her about meeting Stan, poor, funny Stan, who hadn't gotten over an infatuation with blacks, natural sense of rhythm, a graduate-student disease; no, he wanted only to tell her about her long lean gawky legs, her graceful, skinny arms, that lank fine black hair, the lemony taste of her kisses, the damp cool warm idiotic peace of his dozing against her back, her belly, the curve of her throat, wherever he tumbled, of what his friend Stan the Spoiler tried to say to him, of his final triumph in not looking back to his wife, of his even greater triumph in not looking forward to any plan at all for the future, only for tomorrow, the day after tomorrow, the day after that. . . . Perhaps she didn't know all these things. It was unnecessary to sort it out. Perhaps she had other matters on her mind—of course she did—and didn't need to be called to order.

Careful, he thought.

He actually wrote the letter and carried it downstairs to post so that, with luck, she might receive it on the morning of his return.

He was smiling and clever and useful at the meeting in the Rocky Mountain Room of the Brown Palace Hotel. Stan and he had no further conversation about anything but Stan and the conference. This seemed wise.

He did not drink with his colleagues after the meetings. Leaving, he received a blessing from Stan, a tap on the left shoulder, *I dub thee Sir Dude Courageux,* and he proceeded to bed upstairs of the raucousness and slept as easily and calmly as if her lemony breath had been breathing into his mouth.

He took the early plane home.

There was no answer when he telephoned her. Well, that was okay. He hadn't told her which flight he would arrive on. But nevertheless, he was disappointed because he had funny things to tell her, and now they seemed stale. He had bought a book of rodeo drawings at the Denver airport, and it seemed stale. He had written a note to her on the back of a postcard showing a rope-twirling contest at the University of Wyoming and put it between the pages of the book of rodeo drawings. "Higher Education in the Far West. B.A. in Broncobusting, M.A. in Corral." Stale.

He called an hour later, just before dinner time, no answer. If she had an appointment with a lawyer, it should have been over by now. But of course, she had lots to do. Surely her friends were keeping her busy. He knew nothing about her friends, of course.

He imagined one of Rodman's grief-stricken friends putting an entirely natural make on her.

He called later in the evening. He let it ring although that was foolish. When he put the phone down, it went on ringing in his head, and his joke about higher education in the Far West seemed terribly stale and foolish and Stan-like. And this was reality. Such was really the case about his attempt to be young and cute for her.

He called at midnight.

He decided to not call again till the next morning, but he called at 2:00 A.M. and let the phone ring and ring.

He went to the bathroom and looked at a haggard face in the mirror. He slapped his cheeks lightly. He tried to think of his former wife and the pleasure they had once taken in each other. It was like remembering a favorite movie, finally seen once too often on a late-night channel. He thought of Sigrid, but there was very little to remember, it seemed, very little to think about, and yet he could think of nothing else.

He looked for something of hers in the bathroom. Nothing. No, a shadow of her—a fine honey soap she carried in her purse the first time. For the dark girl who smelled sweet in the back of a pickup. It was dry and barely used, and the indentation MIEL D'OSLO was sharp.

She didn't answer in the morning either.

That day he finally awakened her at noon. Her sleepy voice. Her lemony breath. Even over the phone he could taste her breath. So there were other things to hold besides the honey soap.

"I've been calling!" he burst out. "I've been calling!"

"Hi. I suppose so," she said sleepily.

In a spasm of sanity he said nothing and waited.

"I'm sleepy," she said. "It's so hard to explain things when you're asleep. My husband died a week, no, I guess it was almost a month ago. Time passes so fast anymore."

Episcopal priest, and he gave lectures now on his mission to the
Tenderloin. The band that played had never quite made it during the
rock era; they were angry about this and played angry Frisco rock.
The San Francisco Chronicle's porn editor covered the ceremony. He
remarked that it might last as long as some of the marriages he used
to cover for what was called the Society, then Women's, now People
pages.

They all floated in their various highs in a meadow far up on Mount
Tamalpais, the magic mountain, where the ghosts of extinct Indians
—measles? syphilis? drink?—watched over the peacefully browsing
Harley-Davidsons and BMWs. Insects thrummed. Birds twittered.
Couples coupled.

Although her heart was broken, Linda attended the party afterward. That was brave; it was good form. Her friends expected it of
her, and Willi suspected she might. Okay, so what? So although her
heart was broken, she didn't want to miss the party. She had rejected
an offer to be matron of honor, since she was an Orange County girl,
raised in the tradition of decorum, where a girl doesn't preside over
her ex-husband's marriage to another man, but she wished the new
conjugation well. However, she remarked to the leader of the band:
"My heart is broken, man. Say, you know I worked as girl Friday for
John Lennon when Yoko and he were holed up in the Miyako Hotel.
Say, some people think she has like big hairy hands, but they aren't;
they're just strong. I really liked her, man. I used to take them fresh
OJ."

No matter; the red splotches under her eyes remained; broken
heart leads to broken capillaries. Her nostrils were red, too, so if she
was up, she wasn't really up, just sniffing a little coke so as to make
it through the pastoral afternoon in a meadow on the heights of
Marin, nearly thirty motorcycles plowing around, noise, distraction,
the full 1973 Angels' Nazi production. There were no human sacrifices today, for the message they brought was love.

I was her date for the afternoon, with hopes of keeping her from
despair even if her heart was broken (that's only a mental thing, it
heals). I had to get used to the fact that she was completely confident
of me but needed a little coke to make sure.

To enjoy the music of thirty motorcycles tearing up a meadow, driven by wild greasers stuck all over with swastikas, leather, and metal, you might tend to ask a little chemical aid. I made do with only a deep-seated masochism. I suppose there was a time when I imagined joyful tumblings with Linda, because she seemed to be cute, essence of cute—quiddity of essence of cute—but now I traveled with her in a state of bemusement, merely surprised most of the time, and settling merely to find someone to surprise me. Finally I understand why girls resent men who grab at them first off, demanding bed as the reward for passing their valuable hours. The reason is that they suspect a man can be happy with a Linda, too: just because it's fun to be in her company; or, if not fun, lively; and every man seeks easy friendly funning, too, although he may settle for the distraction of a sweaty roll in the sack.

I didn't give up the idea of sex. I was merely willing to postpone it.

I wondered if I had postponed our lovemaking past its natural moment. I was willing to think of her as a friend first, but maybe she required an immediate kink. The kink who waits becomes a paternal figure—too bad for me.

Or maybe, I prayed, a paternal kink.

It wasn't all one-sided. She gave me a kind of wake-up generosity. As we were leaving the meadow, one of the Angels throomed up on his hawg and grunted, "Hey, Linda. Jump on." Ungh, ungh, ungh.

"I'm with Frank here."

Ungh!

"Dump that creep. Jump."

"Frank's my new old man," she said, hugging me.

He stood there with his eyes bulging as if the leather thong around his neck were too tight. Probably that's why his eyes were bulging: that, plus a little deal with thyroid his metabolism had going; plus maybe the fistfuls of pills he swallowed to inspire his endeavors. He was still leaning there with one pointed hoof prodding the ground.

Linda said sweetly, "You'd have to grab and rape me, and I'm sure Frank wouldn't stand around for that. So you'd have to kill him, too. I know I'm nice, but am I worth it?"

The Angel stared morosely. I could see the motes swimming across his eyeballs. The eyes seemed nearer my head than his.

"Well, I never rape a girl unless she wants to be raped," he said.

"Well, see you, then," said Linda, and she turned, still holding my arm.

How is it not probable that one would be charmed by a girl with such marvelous logic?

Ungh!

"Hey, man." The Angel was calling me. I stopped. Always polite. Linda took my elbow like a school guard and moved me across the daisies.

"Hey, man."

Even she couldn't move me now.

As I looked back, the Angel was smiling and touching himself. "Hey, hear the news? The one-star final, man? Someone died tomorrow."

We went back to her place for a drop of tea, herbal tea, rose hips for a possible nasal congestion. Linda sat down with two chipped mugs and asked nobody in particular: "I wonder if he ever kills a dude even if the dude doesn't ask to be killed?"

"You think they did in that dealer from Texas?"

"I didn't know him personally, Frank. Actually, he was from Oklahoma, if that's where Tulsa is."

"The jury cleared them."

"Then they must be innocent, Frank. I believe in the American judicial rip-off system, don't you?"

Her eyes, if you could see them, were filled with faith. Perhaps it helped to know I was devoted to her, too, just as she was devoted to the jury system. The teller of this story was devoted to Linda because she enabled him to tie in directly, without paying tolls, to the lower levels of his brain, where he smelled girls, sent the blood to sudden anatomy lessons, knew that his throat would fill with blood because of the mental stroke of love. She gave me reality because she was so strange. She kept me in touch with triviality. She dispersed a regular dose of crisis. I wanted to be a disgrace to the life of the mind. Perhaps a good therapist would also receive the hint from all this. Often I just wanted to die. It wasn't just in the middle of the night. It lasted whole weekends or perhaps a whole year.

He.

All this happened to him.

Next thing he knew, they had spent a night together. They; we. He discovered groans within his melancholia that no one had told him about. He discovered an ache of desire, and her chilly jokes only made him laugh, they did not discourage him, and he felt very powerful. He smelled the bed, the mattress, her arms. He sniffed and followed his nose. He levitated. He sighed. So now he was a man. He had taken charge. There was no doubt she would love him.

He took her home in the morning. There was an ache of exhaustion, but that made no difference. He slept. He had won something. He telephoned her and there was no answer.

He kept calling and her phone kept on ringing.

Nobody. Nothing.

She disappeared.

Nowhere.

In three weeks, when he had almost given up trying to find her, he discovered that she was living with Van Dixon, the guitarist, in Mill Valley. A redwood house that had been featured in *Rolling Stone*, along with its dripping eucalyptus and mass bathing in the redwood tubs.

He didn't feel jealousy. He was still a different man. No jealousy. He only felt a terrible loss, a blackness of loss; not even desire; just failure, dread, loss, grief.

When he finally decided she was never going to call him, he tried one more time. Finally she spoke with him. She didn't seem embarrassed. She was fine. He was fine. "I'm okay, you're okay." They were cheerful together. "I just came to the conclusion," she said, "a few days in the country would improve my color. I was kind of pale. I should get my energies together. You know, it's kind of freaky, paranoid, in the city. There is a *living space* out here. Not just the trees and all. The aura, man, it's different. So the days just run into the weeks, man."

She didn't mention that what she was running away from in the city was him, was love, was his ignorance. She was talking and confiding how she liked the country and she never seemed to remember that *he* had driven her out across the Golden Gate Bridge; this being-in-love thing, that great night together, they were what finally wiped her out and made her discover a distressing paleness.

At that moment, he knew no other way to be than icy.

"I hear you gave him the clap," he said.

In fact, he had heard they came to the city only to get a shot of penicillin, Van and Linda, together in his Mercedes sedan, both bending over for the needle.

"What?"

"I hear you gave him the clap."

Her sweet laughter. "That's not true," she said. "I didn't give him the clap and he didn't give me the clap. It just happened we both had the clap at the same time."

When next he heard of her, she was carrying orange juice to John and Yoko again when they returned to the Miyako Hotel—temporary help; and then she was the girlfriend of an actor who used to be a star, three years ago, and now was only the lead in a TV series, shooting mostly in San Francisco—she was his San Francisco girl; and she had given up organic waitressing.

He saw her having dinner in the Natural Sun, where she used to serve. She had lost twenty pounds, her nose was red, and she was just smearing the avocado on her plate, making green tracks with her fork. "I can't eat in this place," she said. "He ripped off my customers."

"What're you selling? Speed?"

"Oh, no, a dirty rotten lie, speed kills. Coke."

"You need to eat. You're sick."

"He ripped off my customers. This place is just a front for coke. I told him about my customers and he ripped them off. I can't eat here."

"You don't look like you're eating at all."

"I can't eat anyplace. They all rip me off." When she smiled, her teeth were yellow, her gums were showing, there were spaces as if her teeth were subtly shifting. He remembered those perfect doctor's-daughter teeth. But the smile was the one she used to dazzle him with and make boredom unboring with. "I'm sorry I ripped you off, Frank," she said. "I gave you a bad time. I don't know how I could, since I'm not worth it, but I guess I did."

"You did," he said.

She waited.

"That's all right," he said, "you're worth it."

He meant he was willing to be ripped off.

"Brave boy," she said. "It was still fun, wasn't it?"

Finally he didn't like being played with. These were words from a scenario and he didn't like them. Not liking them stifled pity. He just got out, leaving the rose hips tea on his table and the girl who couldn't eat still not eating.

The next time he saw her was in response to a telephone call. "Frank, he's killed me."

When he got there, she was lying on a bed that hadn't been made in months. The place looked as if six Angels had been camping in it, but there was only one, the friend from the wedding, standing over her and holding a glass of water. It was the friend who didn't rape a girl unless she asked to be raped. He looked wobbly. Linda looked as if she were fading in and out of shock.

The Angel glared at Frank with that leather shoelace still tight around his neck. He said: "I told her to call you."

"My father's a doctor, I know what he did to me," she said. "He broke some ribs."

"She was comin' through all over me. She was, I was tryin' to stop her, what she was doin'. Listen, man, it takes a powerful woman to make me so mean—you calling the pigs?"

"Doctor," Frank said.

He stood there till the doctor came. She would probably be okay if a rib hadn't punctured a lung. When the buzzer rang, the Angel's eyes gave a little extra bulge and he went out the window, just in case. Okay, better that way. Frank could handle the explanations.

Linda was finished as a pretty little thing. Whatever came next, it wouldn't be pretty. Frank could go back to saying I about himself.

BLIND, BLIND DATE

"I'm not used to blind dates," I said.

My good city acquaintance Merrill was telephoning an offer to fill an evening and perhaps, whoever knows? the rest of my life. "She's a folk-rock singer," he said, "hasn't found the right group yet."

"Blind dates, that's kid stuff," I said.

"So that it shouldn't be blind, my dear friend, let me tell you. A folk-rock singer, part-time professional, good voice, great guitar, plus speed typist, a hundred ten accurate words per minute, very much in demand as a temporary legal secretary, plus she's been burning—well, why should I seek to flatter you?—*burning* very much to meet you."

"Uh. If she's got those talents—"

"Plus a high IQ. Reads everything. Keen, logical mind."

"—then what does she look like, how old, you know?"

"Looks good to me. Tall, nice. Haha, you want to know what she

229

smells like, too, my dear friend? You are really into caution and curriculum vitae, aren't you? Clean. Hahaha. Thirtyish."

"Ish?"

"Maybe lateish. But lovely skin, graceful, look! Don't hassle me. Very nice, my friend. Come to dinner."

Okay, though my good acquaintance Merrill was probably not the ideal judge of my needs in blind date—true love forever plus a lot of fun—I could pass an evening with him and his friend Brad and this lady. . . . "Her name?"

"Louisa."

A nice slightly old-fashioned semipro folk-rock speed-typist sweet-smelling high-IQ sort of name. And Merrill was said, by himself and others, to be a gourmet cook. And he deeply desired that I share his pleasure in the new Twin Peaks manse he and Brad had taken to celebrate their seven glorious, trouble-filled, problem-solving years together. They had hacked it. The itch for change was eased by a new house hooked up with advanced equipment for sound transmission and ethnic cooking. I could use some thirty-two-track Berlioz. Even more, in my wan state, I could use some wok-seared vegetables with unbruised health, vitamins, and good intentions.

My hair had actually been wet with water, as I used to do on my blind or at least nearsighted dates in Lakewood, Ohio, so many years ago. While we waited for Louisa, Merrill and Brad showed me the house, upstairs, downstairs, garage, closets. I sniffed the air with appreciation, but there were no signs of cooking. "I decided to take us out to this little bistro in Mill Valley," said Merrill. "I want you to try my new Caddy Eldorado, too. We'll have drinks here first. Louisa hasn't seen the house since we finished the kitchen."

The doorbell tolled its Swiss melody, electronically amplified throughout. Merrill ran to greet Louisa, calling behind him, "We had the bell hooked into the stereo."

A nice touch, I mentioned to Brad. Brad said, "He's taking her bag. She's hanging up her coat." Then Louisa entered and shook my hand and blushed. Unusually nice, smooth, delicate skin and unusually large hands and feet. Somehow I knew at once—the truth came to me!—and was thinking with inelegant panic: A restaurant in Mill Valley where my former wife will surely walk in with some sterling chap . . . "Why, both of you are blushing!" Brad cried. His voice echoed from Formica beams in the lodge ceiling. "You'd think they never had a blind date before. But that's how Merrill and I met, seven years ago, and not even through good friends—"

"Through an advertisement in a Laundromat," Merrill said, squeezing his hand, "and weren't we both embarrassed? But we got over it."

"You're working on it," Louisa said, laughing a delighted little trill. She winked at me, the first of many winks.

This little Provençal bistro in Mill Valley was layered with warm and friendly aromas of onions, tomatoes, peppers, eggplant, and perhaps a soupçon of garlic, and they had somehow found the water to keep the ferns oily and fresh. It used to be a Porsche garage before it got to be a traditional Provençal bistro, Merrill told me; he knew the owner, who greeted us with ecstasy, with raised pencil, with a round of drinks on the house. Brad suggested, motion seconded by me, made unanimous by Louisa, that Merrill order for all of us.

He put on his other glasses. "Food, food," he murmured. "Let's see the wine card first. I don't think a French tonight, strange as that may seem, a California. I've really gone bananas over the great Californias since I sold my condo and purchased my home." After careful reading he slipped off his other glasses while the steward waited, slid them into the breast pocket of his suede jacket, and put on his original glasses to tell the steward what we wanted.

"Excellent, outstanding choice," the steward murmured, rubbed himself, made himself vanish.

Merrill smiled and clapped his hands. He took off his glasses again and put them in a different pocket. He gazed at Louisa and me through naked eyes, frankly pouched with difficult living. Merrill was a large, bearded, hearty, booming-voiced man with a delighted smile growing delighteder as he beamed upon us. "Ah, good friends," he said.

The wine arrived, was tasted, was good if not great, was offered in clicks to friendship.

May I now skip the food, trusted reader? There were garlic, peppers and sauces, aubergine, veal, and chilled salads, nothing wrong with the food; there was a duck with orange sauce for Louisa; but this is not a gourmet story. This is a story about hope, faith, charity, and the lack of charity. "When I joined the church and had my operation," Louisa said.

"Which church?"

"Roman rite."

"Which operation?"

She blinked at me, her heavy mascara shredded on her eyelids. Well, she herself had brought up church and operation. "I don't keep secrets from my friends," she said. "They're like family, closer sometimes. I lubricate. I'm normal in every way." She gazed demurely at my lap. She touched my elbow. I was eating. It was the touch on the elbow of a person making a political or literary point, or of a relative, or of a normally insistent believer. My eating was the eating of a skeptic or of someone in a state of unease for whom eating is a demonstration that life will go on, no matter what life does to itself.

"I lubricate normally," she said. "I find you very intelligent."

"He has a wonderful, keen sense of humor of his own," said Merrill of me as if I were a visiting Japanese, "but you have to learn to dig his form of levity."

Merrill blessed us all. He had an old-fashioned brown mole athwart his cheek, with three irregular-sized ash-colored hairs growing from it. In California they change such things by removing them. It looked like a badge of some rare genetic distinction. I didn't really want him to praise me. Louisa's gaze into my lap, where a red napkin lay like a limp shield, was demure but insistent; it was a look of heavyweight wistfulness.

One can be encouraged in adversity. I realized, thanks to Merrill's praise, that my sense of humor might be on trial. I should rise to the vision of my former wife coming in with a heck of a young man and finding me crowded into this cozy booth with Merrill, Brad, and large-featured Louisa. I was ready for the test; the fear was now declared defunct. But I sincerely hoped it would be heeded.

"Are you Jewish?" Louisa asked. "Because the name, you're quite attractive and all, but the name—"

"Yes. Are you?"

"My parents, true," she said. "Me, not. I hope this doesn't hurt your feelings."

"It's foolish to judge others," I said. "But I have a tendency toward foolish. Are you running away from something?"

"Oh, dears," said plural-minded Brad. "Like yourself. We're all super people."

"I lubricate normally," Louisa said.

"I only learned I'm soopah recently in my group, but I really learned it; now I know everybody is soopah," said Brad. "Even if you didn't lubricate, what's wrong with a little K-Y jelly?"

"But I do!"

"That's reasonable," Merrill said.

"*Reasonable?*" Louisa demanded angrily. "Cost me eight thousand dollars for my birthright, and that's reasonable? Do you think Medicare would handle it? God, I had a fight on my hands from beginning to end."

I said soothingly, "I had a daughter in an incubator for a month. And twin sons all at once, too. Everything costs."

"I had to go to Stanford Medical Center, the doctors there. My shrink here said there was no doubt I was a woman where it counts, in the soul. Also, I had something like a woman's bladder to begin with already. You could build from those. I said to those docs in Palo Alto: I demand to lubricate! Fuck the expense, excuse my passion, I'm young and horny, I want to be perfect."

"You look good." This is the comment one cannot help making under such circumstances if one has any responsibility to the needs of others. I have such.

"No beard," Louisa said. "Smooth. Here, feel." Her paw seized mine and guided it. Smooth chin. "My shrink discharged me. Said I'm normal, bladder, the works, anybody in his right mind knows that."

Nevertheless, I felt like arguing certain points. "Not normal," I said, "not to be Jewish if you're born one."

"Try the cold zucchini vinaigrette," said Merrill, "here, you haven't sampled it, so how can you know?"

"Yes, yes," said Louisa. Her look of scorn said: *What's important? I spit on K-Y jelly.*

I was all this old, with five children, unmarried again, and brought to this single swing in a Mill Valley Provençal former Porsche garage with ferns and a headwaiter talking about his back trouble—"an old badminton injury," he said. "Plus I twist sometimes in my sleep and wake myself up. If someone happens to be with me, they say: Stop twisting."

"Have I got a doctor for you," said Merrill. "He studied chiropractic and nutrition with a Korean master in Seattle."

"Personally, with all due respect to Merrill, whom I respect as a person to a maestro, I'd join a group," Brad said. "So many of these things go away if you have a really caring, nurturing relationship or ships—"

Louisa was drumming her fingertip or tips on the table. We had gotten off the subject.

"—in an up-front and caring group. You should have been there when we all wrote postcards to Florida orange juice."

A vigorous smell of healthy flesh, busy with its metabolism, arose from Louisa's shoulders. This is a smell, like a tropical courtyard in the first flush of thunderstorm, sheets of feeling pelting the earth, which I loved in the Midwest, in France, in Haiti, and now should politely learn to love off Louisa's perfumed arms, although there was also a back-alley scent of anxious mobilization. I didn't love it yet.

"One thing I thought before isn't true now," Louisa said. "It's still hard to find a man who's not hung-up. The really twisted ones, I mean dumb kinks, should do what I did, but instead they—" She stopped and gazed at me.

Yes, some dumb kinks dream of sweet girls who welcome without demanding, without sleek back-alley anxieties; whose gazes are equal, kind, and inciting; who take pride in what they are and in what they might be. Louisa had evolved to a new level. She had radically abolished her circumcision; she no longer dreamed from memories; she wanted a purer invention. "So are you a finder or a seeker?" she asked me.

"I don't know. Those are categories."

Merrill, mighty, bearded, high-colored in the cheek, looked happy at the serious conversation of serious people. Brad looked bored at this turn from interesting conversation but did his best to arouse his own interest: "I'm both a finder and a seeker, I'm me."

Merrill's laughter boomed out. "I don't have to look, I found it. If you're ready in your heart, you can find it in a Berkeley *Barb* ad. "Adventurous Male Likes It Every Day. No kooks.' "

"You're kook enough for both of us, you're just a hunk of kook," Brad fondly stated.

"It's stood the test of time," Merrill said.

"You see, you see, you see?" Louisa demanded of me.

"You have to allow me my own way," I said.

"Of course, of course, of course," said Merrill.

"Really," said Brad.

"So long as you're not a pothole, what I call," said Louisa.

"I'll strive not to be."

"Whatever's right," said Merrill. "Louisa, you said you had high hopes."

"Oh, not without reason." She lowered her eyes. "There is so little time in life, our hours must be festivals. So I got this friend in the auto license bureau. How could I spend this soiree with you if you were, I don't know, a pothole, a Capricorn? Please forgive me, dear. He told me birthdate, color of eyes, hair, violations. Forgive, okay? There's only so many soirees in the week."

"I feel the same way."

"I like you. I thought I'd just throw that out," Louisa said.

"Thank you."

She steadily tossed zucchinis from her plate to her mouth with the fork as intercom, and steadily she continued this forward march of her liking. "Today I'm happy with my body. Meeting you, I'm happy with my bod. I thought I'd just throw that out."

"Thank you again."

"My feet were killing me—those new heels. But I feel fine now, good food, good conversation, good company." Brad and Merrill were hushed and watchful as I said thank you. "Oh, I know you've had your full share of midnight tears. I thought I'd just throw that out."

I believed I could believe her, since she had already thrown out so many things—her history, her Jockey shorts—and had somehow also trashed her circumcision in the process, converting the trembling and unsure instrument into a steelbelt-radial, industrial-duty receptacle which becomes moist on demand. The buck stopped here. She thought she wouldn't just throw this out.

We drank more California. We nibbled at crusts of sourdough French bread. We had perfect little cups of espresso with little twists of lemon in them. Louisa bit her lemon rind with her front teeth, staring at me, to release the flavor.

I should have been carrying my sleepy sons in from the car after a day in the sun. I should be helping my daughter with her French. I should be writing to my old parents. Instead, past the middle of my life I was having a blind date with a Taurean hairdresser, an aerospace engineer who knew what he liked, and a lady who was like a new foreign sports car, with a superlative sealed system, self-lubricating. She touched my arm. I longed for my sweaty, squirming, sleepy sons.

"Some people," Louisa was saying, "you kiss, and you get that tingle. You know what I mean? That tingle? Well, my friend in the auto license bureau I was telling you, I don't get that tingle. But I do get birthdate, color of eyes, height, weight, age, and I can tell if you're a hunky guy. And sometimes, Herb, you can use truth better than a tingle."

"I know what you mean," I said. Calm. Life must be a festival. My children were asleep by now anyway.

"You're warming up," Louisa said, and guided my hand to touch her chin and cheek. They were smooth, no growth at all. Not silky, but definitely in the range of Smooth.

"It's the wine," I said cheerfully, breaking contact of hand and cheek, "plus I feel good. I'm not having the glooms like sometimes. I just feel good, and we can let it go at that."

"It makes me truly happy."

And so I would just smile if my former wife walked in with some fine fellow, easy and comfortable; she would smile back and wave. I could get up early next morning, suggest taking the kids to the House of Pancakes. Soon my sons would be too big to carry, but I still liked to carry them. In the evening, sleepy, they liked it, but in the morning they would dash shrieking over the hot asphalt of the House of Pancakes parking lot—French toast, waffles, or blueberry pancakes, plus ice cream, plus syrup down their tee shirts.

Merrill beamed. He was mighty and broad-shouldered and kept his mole. Brad batted his eyes at Merrill, their evening's work done. A smell in my nostrils like a wet, extinguished fireplace.

"So let's go," said Merrill. "Did you really love the duck in orange sauce?"

"We liked the pecan roll, didn't we, Herb?" Louisa said. "And the wine was really a la carte."

As we swung, satiated, out of the Provençal Porsche garage, good-byes from the badminton-playing headwaiter, good-byes all around, nice duck, nice duck, Louisa gaily took my arm. Not since long ago had I been a single; not since long ago had I enjoyed such a really boss, dynamite sinus headache. Feeling my arm stiffen, Louisa said: "I can't just do this all by myself cold turkey, Herb."

What's to become of the gray-bearded lad now?

Which might have been the end of this account. But Merrill telephoned the next day to talk about our evening. "You know, you understand surely, that Louisa hasn't many good friends in this world. She works the White Glove typing pool, but that's got to be temporary. You don't make good friends in the typing pool. She thought everything would be different, but there aren't many real persons around this world."

"I know. I'm sorry," I said.

"Not that you were anything but a gentleman."

"I understand."

"I don't really meddle. Brad always says that's not my way. Ride with the flow is our rule. I had hopes for you two, but I suppose I should have told you first."

"I figured it out. It's okay."

"You did?"

"It was clear."

"It was? So lonely. And me so sad about it. Louisa is all alone now, and there should be such sweetness in life. I'm kind of distraught about her. She used to be, when she was a man, my wife."

CHILD OF EMBASSY

"Yoohoo! Yoohoo! Meester Jo-nez! You have vees-i-tor, Signor di Jones!"

Her song stopped him in his measured, therapeutic crawl back and forth across the pool of the Grand Hotel Oloffson in Port-au-Prince.

"Yoohoo! yoohoo! Indeed I say yoohoo to you, kind sir!"

He knew at once who it must be. He descended like a timid fish toward the bottom of the pool to think on it in privacy but, owing to the limitations of his lungs, found himself climbing, huffing, up the ladder a few seconds later. She was smiling and offering him a slice of mango from the plate. Her teeth were pink from her lipstick. It was his own plate of sliced mango she was offering; she was nodding and smiling and bidding him welcome with dauntless cordiality amid the scaly bark and fernlike leaves of tropical trees.

A verified lovely Chilean lady in Washington had told him to be sure to look up her best friend, a lovely (not yet verified) Spanish

239

diplomat who was now first secretary of the embassy in Haiti. On his coming trip, he promised to do it, and now it seemed to have been done for him. At least he knew something about the flawless Chilean beauty and the odd procedures of friendship between one woman and another.

Nearsighted, he recognized the beckon was for him. This long female person with sparkles of sunlight behind her was waving at him. This person accompanied by leather carryall, string shopping bag, and child hiding with beach ball behind her had come for him.

"How did you know I was arriving today?" he asked.

"Oh, I knew, I knew!"

She was collecting him at the hotel, forewarned by the international Chilean communication system. *Yoohoo, yoohoo.* It was his first afternoon and he had been cooling and straightening the kinks of the flight by stretching himself in laps at the pool. Now he had to be nice instead.

Many women are not good judges of what a man might like; of course, many men are not good judges also. But Estrelita da Costa da Martínez y Jalisco seemed early on to be one of the great errors of Chilean conclusion. She was clumpy, clumsy, overendowed with hair on the arms and cheeks, shrill of voice; not a lovely Spanish lady at all. Surely she had important qualities of generosity, intelligence, and depth which would appear in due course to justify his Chilean adviser. Surface defects are not enough to condemn a friendship, especially the rapid, lonely, needful traveler's friendship.

He came dripping out of the pool into her appraising glare, feeling naked before this woman with frock, neckerchief, rings, Gucci bag, his own plate of sliced mango, and beach ball-bearing child. There were towels in the bag. Why the devil the towels? Why the beach ball? Why his mango? He was thinking profoundly and drying his eyes on the hotel towel. She was wrapping him in charm. "Allo allo, Meester Friend from Afar," she said. "You are so feet"—she meant fit—"as my dear kind friend tell me you are. And what we do besides swim today? What appointment you have, you want me to make for you? I know everybody in this little country—" *Thees leetle contree.* "But first perhaps Bruno, my only son, would like a deep."

The boy plunged the knuckle of his big toe into the pool. He waited for further developments, a warming trend.

Mr. Jones shook his hand formally. "Please, Bruno. Would you like to swim?"

The boy looked at his mother. The mother was looking at Mr. Jones. Mr. Jones said: "He's a fine little fellow, isn't he? May I order you a drink?"

"Oh, in this climate!" she cried. "No, no, thank you. Just a margarita perhaps—for the salt."

Travel alone, Mr. Jones noticed, produces new passivities to add to the familiar ones. The visitor to a strange place is vulnerable to temptations of help and expert knowledge. Young women are vulnerable to the local men, in and out of national costume, who pose like hawks midair, waiting to pounce, or like hummingbirds, waiting to dig deep. Mr. Jones also partook of the weakness for company and comfort. Bruno swam and pushed his beach ball and, once, splashed both his mother and Mr. Jones as they were getting acquainted, she affixing dark glasses and slipping off one sandal in the sunlight, he listening to an agenda of introducing him, driving him, feeding him, helping him. "All thees"—skip the accent—"because my friend in Washington, D.C., write to tell me how you are so nice. Bruno! Bruno! Attention!"

"Nice, she said, did she?" asked Mr. Jones. "I thought she knew me better."

A trilling laugh ensued, and at its conclusion the first secretary said, "She always like strangers. I too." There was a little cooing sound of recovery and a roundness of mouth. "Strangers, you know, can be so nice."

She snapped up the last piece of mango, chewed, and fell to smiling and nodding. She brooked little opposition. She was worthy of the diplomatic service of a mightier nation, Mr. Jones decided, perhaps one with advanced hydrogen weaponry. "Nice," she was saying, "very, very nice when they so choose."

The thoughts of Mr. Jones were not so profound and secure as he would have liked: *Oh, no, oh, dear, oh, my*; but for reasons of laziness and floating in the tropics he was accepting her invitations and telling himself: Well, there will be other people, I'll be seeing the country,

I can meet different people, and she knows her way about. I'm not taking advantage of her, he thought. She is offering.

Madame da Costa took him to an interesting reception at the Italian Embassy, up a flowered road in Pétionville. "Call me Estrelita," she said.

Estrelita took him to the Iron Market in dusty dirty amazing downtown Port-au-Prince. "Call me Lita," she said.

Lita took him to a voodoo ceremony, almost an authentic one, at which a goat was sacrificed to Ogoun Feraille, the god of war. "Would you like now nightcap back at my leetle house?" she asked. "Bruno ask so much to see you. And then he will sleep. . . ."

She took him on excursions, and when he went out alone, she seemed to discover where he would be, or when he would return to the hotel, and she would appear with some interesting idea or tidbit of information or proposal for an outing. She was very helpful. It wasn't worth it.

The first secretary suffered from an obsession which tended to obscure her possible excellent qualities. She was a woman with a demon scratching at her. She summed up all the horniness of the Iberian Peninsula in her hot-blooded, Foreign Service person. Mr. Jones found himself making the excuses he had heard from many women during his long bachelor life: a headache tonight, a disturbing letter from home, a friend back someplace, the tropics, this is so sudden, want to get to know you better . . . I'm not that sort. . . .

Nevertheless, he had the habit, shaped by her, of not finding his own way. She surrounded him. It made him think of marriage, although he was not married, not father to Bruno; it made him think of sex, though there was none between them; it made her think more of sex than of anything else, as if he were a reluctant girl afflicted with headaches, scruples, habits of teasing, times of the month. She pouted when she let him off at the hotel and he ran with small, finicky steps into the safety of the lobby and then turned and graciously waved good-bye as she sat in her Volvo, watching him speculatively, wondering when he would give up and say: Now I know you well enough.

Why, he wondered, did he trot up the steps into the hotel—was it new shoes, the climate?—when normally he took a long athletic stride? And could these few days of *faiblesse* be doing harm to his character, which had been established these forty years now? Could saying no to a hairy Spanish diplomat hamper his nerves, his metabolism, his posture?

He promised himself to behave better, in line with his possibilities, without violating his own instincts. Bruno was a place for his traveler's good nature. He missed his own children, who lived with their mother in one of the farthest suburbs of Washington, while he kept to his lonesome in an overcrowded, overdecorated, overcleaned flat in Georgetown. His fondness for the boy might mean anything; no use to question that; he was genuinely fond, and he hoped that he and the mother could share this warmth. That was something he could return to her, was it not? And without discomfort to himself?

So he brought not flowers to Estrelita but toys and ice cream for Bruno. He was flattered and touched by the child's adoration. Bruno had a clever, quick, sharp-featured moroseness about him which broke into sudden hilarity when Mr. Jones paid attention, told him a story, made him a face. It was pleasing to Mr. Jones to be so powerful. He showed his tricks: the penny disappearing trick; the mechanical toy trick ("You mean you're a robot?" the precocious linguist asked); the riddles and jokes from America. Bruno said: "Why don't you stay with us while you're in Haiti? I asked Mama and she said you could save your money, free of any charge."

"Shush! You didn't ask!" Lita cried.

"I asked, Mama, and you said maybe."

She gazed at Mr. Jones expectantly, with sparkling good humor, a pulse throbbing in her throat. This was normally a sign of life which Mr. Jones found enticing, even moving. Her look said: Well, since the boy has brought it up . . .

"That's very kind of you," Mr. Jones stated formally, addressing Bruno in his embarrassment. "But you see, there are things I need here at the hotel—my mail, the phone—uh, what a nice thought that was, Bruno." He turned to the mother. "I'm expense-accounted anyway, and I hate to put you out—"

"Oh, we could stay, too!" Bruno said. "It's a big, big house!"

"He doesn't wish to," his mother said sharply. It was like a slap in the child's face and he reddened. Mr. Jones was not sure if the pain he saw came from the mother's voice or his refusal of the invitation. He invited them both to lunch by the pool and a swim at the hotel.

He picked Bruno up and said, "What amusing eyes, what a nice color, what a big boy," until the boy smiled in that black glinting grateful girlish way he had. Mr. Jones thought he saw, in the childish face, its pouts and pleasures, the future young man who would run insatiably, in a certain Latin manner, from woman to woman.

Bruno's mother invited Mr. Jones to drive to Jacmel and spend the night. Jacmel is a town on the coast a few hundred miles from Port-au-Prince, and the roads are not easy, and foreigners might not like to drive in Haiti, and the guides or chauffeurs are unreliable or difficult or expensive, and to fly misses the whole sense of the countryside, which is much more Africa than Spain or Virginia. Mr. Jones said yes. Then he added, "But we'll take Bruno, too."

"I can leave him with the maid. I shall even have leetle friend stay overnight with him for company."

"Bruno," said Mr. Jones, calling the boy from the pool, "wouldn't you like to drive to Jacmel?"

The woman took any abuse. She knew not to sulk. She said, "Bruno, you can swim on the beach at Jacmel."

"I don't care," said the boy adoringly, "I want to go. Thank you, Mr. Jones."

The road, in fact, was not too difficult. It was a new French road, built by a French company, *la Route de l'Amitié*, and only beginning to wash out at certain turns and bankings. Estrelita was a terrible driver, weaving across the center onto oncoming trucks, the "tap-taps," changed into mass rural buses, filled with chickens and pigs and people, and Bruno and Mr. Jones would shout, "Watch out!" And Mr. Jones said, "Why don't you let me spell you awhile?"

"Spell me? E-s-t-r-e-l—"

"No, take turns driving, my dear."

"I think," she said flirtatiously, "you do not trust me. I am beautiful driver. But sometimes I am thinking, oh, *roman-tique* thought. . . ."

"Think vehicular thoughts," said Mr. Jones.

"Mama!" the boy screamed. "A cow!" The man and the boy shut their eyes.

"I missed it, you see?" she asked.

Mr. Jones turned around and winked at Bruno. "Moooo," he said. "That's American for cow. What do you say in Spanish?"

"Mama! Mama! Let Mr. Jones drive now!" They successfully skidded past a United Nations jeep with its passengers howling curses at them from the ditch at the side of the road. Bruno sighed and said, "*Vache* in French—Mama!"

She had said Jacmel was two hours away, but somehow, even with her wild driving, it was longer and further. She had made a picnic. They stopped on a hillside with a view of mountains, of Caribbean. She had brought a bottle of Spanish wine, cold chicken, and a red-checked tablecloth in a straw basket. The boy ran off to choose rocks, throw ardent gazes at cows, study corn growing on a precipitous slope. It should have been delightful here. "I have *roman-tique* thought about you all the time, Meester Jones," she said. "Do you sometime begin to have *roman-tique* thought also?"

He was miserable. He knew he had gotten himself into this. He had not sought her out, only happened to be there when she came by his hotel. But he had submitted, and now he was here. And soon they would be spending the night together in the Pension Craft in Jacmel, a little fishing and trading town in *roman-tique* Haiti. It was not delightful.

The dusk was filled with shadowy figures by the road. Candles burned and cooking fires smoldered as the Volvo hurtled into the village.

The hotel was charming. There was a café open to the street and cast-iron balconies on the upper floors. "Park the car," he said, "while I see if they have rooms for us."

Her mouth made international astonishment signals: round, wet, mute.

He ran up to the proprietor, a man leaning against an espresso machine with the distinct worried satisfaction of Owner, and said: "Two rooms. *Two* rooms."

"Yes, sir, one for the child?"

How had they gotten in so fast? The boy was carrying a shopping bag. Estrelita was carrying three suitcases and a net sack.

"One for Madame and the child," said Mr. Jones, "and one for me."

Estrelita's mouth was a perfectly discontented mouth.

They ate a silent dinner. It was a good dinner, but a silent one.

Estrelita was putting the sleepy boy to bed. Mr. Jones was standing in the road in front of the hotel, listening to the whispering and laughter of evening gossip and wishing he could be a part of it. A woman in a turban came up to him and said in English, "You alone?"

"No."

"You are with a friend, some kind of friend?"

To get rid of her, he said: "My wife."

"Good," she said. "I have ways to amuse both of you. Tell me your room number."

He shook his head no as she smiled and smiled and finally began to laugh at his unease. He didn't walk away because he wanted to stay near the hotel. He didn't go inside because he wanted to stay away from Estrelita. But then Estrelita was standing behind him and he didn't know how long she had been there, listening, waiting for him to finish his negotiation with the woman in the turban and the African robe. When he caught sight of her, he asked: "What do you want?"

"Bruno wish to say good night to you. He will not sleep until he say good night to you also."

Mr. Jones felt a small tremor of pride in this affection from the boy. He pushed past Estrelita, who was staring at the woman in the turban. He ran upstairs to the room of the mother and child. The curtains were pulled; it was dark, with only a thin starlight from the unlit street.

"Bruno," he said, "are you asleep yet?"

"No, no, stay here."

"I will for just a minute."

The boy held his hand. He whispered, "I never seen my father, never even seen a picture of my father."

Estrelita had slipped nearby to listen. "Is that correct English?" she asked. "No, it is not. Tell him, please, he must make special effort to grow up speaking correct."

"You're a good boy," said Mr. Jones.

The boy smiled. "You stay here tonight. I want you to stay here tonight. Tomorrow morning I want to take a picture with my camera."

A KARMIC LOVER

"Why bother with me?" he asked with genuine concern of the poor, strangled, adoring voice coming at him by telephone from the Rocky Mountains.

The distinguished writer was middle-aged but knew he would be forever young. To be the chosen of a few women and the envy of a few men was enough for him; he was different from other writers; he needed very little in the way of heaped-up riches, fame, or ferocious followers. He needed only a minimum of honor to keep him feeling easy with himself on unavoidable social occasions.

His joys lay in contemplation and movement, the play of daydreams and night fears translated into daydreams. He loved to imagine stories and to tell them. When I grow up, he sometimes thought, maybe I'll be a camp counselor. While waiting for this career, he gazed out of his window on Perry Street and never tired of the madness of the streets, the orderly sorting of his words on the page. He had now spent a generation at this window. An interviewer once described him as the oldest young writer, the youngest old writer in Greenwich Village—he liked that. His mornings were set glowing by the mixture of half-remembered dreams, the loyal companionship of coffee (his marriages tended to wear out, but coffee was a faithful friend), and the sharp elbows and mysteries of Manhattan.

"It's much too far to drive for a school paper," he said to the timid, insistent, stammering voice from Boulder. "I can assure you I'm not worth it."

Praise and achievement are both passing things; he knew this. Appreciation touched him only a little; flattery amused him. He was not ordinarily vain. The time he spent contemplating one of his own achievements, a nicely wrought book, say, was not much longer than the time he spent relishing a surprising good luck in his daily routines: a woman, a phrase, a meal. Under his breath he might say, like one of his many children by his three wives: Yummy.

He also enjoyed his children, except for one angry grown son, and most of his wives most of the time. Of course, a wife, and this is even more true of a former wife, is not to be steadily enjoyed, like a self, which never gets to be a former.

Cheerfully he sat down to his long legal pad and his pen swept like a busy broom over the pages, piling up little improvised mounds of words. He disliked the typewriter, too fast and impersonal, but with the new felt pens, he could go almost as fast, silently and rapidly sketching the lives which spilled out almost of their own accord. Other things, money, family, friends, occasionally let him down, but his health was good, and he had a stock of paper, lots of felt pens. There was so much to say and plenty of time. He was not even vain about youth (gone, of course) or old age (at bay forever). People who knew lots of writers told him he was the only happy writer they knew.

"Don't bet on it," he replied with a mischievous, boyish smile.

And so on this late September morning, when he received a telephone call from Boulder, Colorado, he smiled as he talked to the young woman on the line. "Why bother with me?" In his healthy endless middle age, still tanned from the summer at tennis and beaches, not yet pink from the winter's skiing—he did other things besides write—he saw no reason for the nice and kind young journal-

ist to drive all the way from Boulder to New York. She wanted to
interview him for the university newspaper, or perhaps it was a magazine, of which she was the new poetry and literary editor. She said
she had an uncle in Connecticut anyway, and she would like to visit
the East. "All right," he said, "you have a nice voice. If you're coming
anyway, call me when you arrive and we'll have . . ." A drink? a joint?
lunch? He made his choice and said, "Tea," trying to put a twinkle
of humor into the finicky English literary-person invitation.

"I don't use a tape recorder," she said, "but I remember everything.
I haven't forgotten a word you've written."

"You're way ahead of me then."

"I'm sure, Mr. Carmel, you're the medium for a knowledge you
don't even need to understand very well."

"Well, I'm sure we'll talk about this when you get here." He was
eager to get back to his yellow pad. "This is costing you money."

But she had already hung up.

Perhaps he was as far-seeing, clairvoyant, prescient, and sensitive
as she thought him to be, for when he heard a powerful small motor
churning outside his building, he saw in his mind a red Alfa Romeo
sports car and the lady with total recall from Boulder. He was right.
Except it was a red MG (he was neither perfect nor a sports car
expert). Also, he had not anticipated that she would be lovely: tall,
slim, intense, a Greenwich, Conn., fashion model somehow trans-
planted to literature and Colorado, with small, violent, perfectly
shaped features—not perfect, of course, a little compressed and tense,
and a truly distressing slime of anxiety covering her face and wetting
her blouse under the arms. Pity, he thought. This old-looking girl had
violet patches of insomnia around the eyes.

"Did you drive all the way nonstop?" he asked. "Did you drop out
of school?"

"I'm on a special project, you're my honors project, it's so silly,"
she said.

He put her at her ease; that is, he practiced the skills which usually
put girls and women and even men at their ease—a smiling, generous
bustling, a pot of tea, crackers and cheese. "Maybe you'd like a
drink?" he asked.

"No, no, no, I don't, I can't, of course not."

"Slow down, my dear. I'm delighted to spend this hour with you."

"I won't take more than an hour of your time, Mr. Carmel."

"Please. It's of no matter."

And he realized she was not what she seemed; or more precisely, she was what she seemed, but not what he anticipated. She did indeed know his every word better than he knew them. And she knew what they meant. She knew more than they meant. Her interpretations extended beyond the fun of his stories and novels toward magic, myth, ritual, and the deepest truths. In principle, he had no objection to such interpretations. He recognized that the imagination is a vehicle for more than the mind knows. But it seemed to him that she rushed too soon from the surfaces to the depths, and then to depths beneath the depths. She saw him as the unconscious bearer of the darkest tidings. It wasn't so much that she had read Jung and Laing and the Indian mystics, although of course she had. She was also a little nuts.

Pity, he thought again. This was a word he used to execute a friendship, love affair, or wife. Sometimes he caught himself even mouthing the word aloud, like any other man who lived alone.

When they had finished talking about Nietzsche, Berlioz, Rimbaud, Andreas-Salomé, Rilke, the Yoruba rites—a few of her subjects—and driving conditions on the interstate (one of his subjects), plus whether he worked his stories through in advance or just let them unfold out of daymare (her subject) and whether she was a senior and what her plans were after college (his subject), an hour had long passed. It was nearer to three hours. In some such cases, Ward Carmel might have brought the interview to a graceful conclusion with an enjoyable early-evening roll in the bed, in which he would certainly give as good as he got. He was not selfish and exploitative about enjoying sex with admirers. But he was not an idiot either. In this case, he knew enough only to pat her hand, to steer the lady gently to the door, and then down the stairs and into her red MG.

As he waved good-bye, and the troubled motor flared up again— get a tune-up, please—she looked like a dreamily lovely young woman, with rich hair and a profile of intelligence and breeding. If he had seen her drive past, he would have suffered a pang: How ever does one meet an adequate supply of such young women? And now he had met her. Pity.

The essay in the *Mountain Sunburst* astonished him. It was complete, knowledgeable, eloquent, with a touch of wit that reminded him of his own; it had balance in its concepts, although emotionally it tumbled very far toward overpraise of his gifts; the mystic probing was there, but perhaps not too obtrusive for Colorado in the late 1960s; the words were even spelled correctly. It was just a little too deep for his taste. The only thing that really disturbed him was the photograph. It was a good picture; he was striding past a black Frisbee player under the arch of Washington Square; he looked smiling, vigorous, and content. But he had no idea when the picture was taken. He had not seen it before. Had she been following him on his little trips to the grocer, the bank, the post office? The privacy and anonymity of Manhattan bustle had always been an essential ingredient of his good happiness.

He shrugged. No matter. She was far away in school again. And what's so bad about having a fanatic admirer? He was even lucky in her; she had revealed herself sufficiently. It might have been nasty if he had laid more than a finger, such as the rest of his body, on her. So his conscience was clean. And the idea of this devotion both present and conveniently far away, intelligent, passionate, and, above all, absent, invigorated a middle-aged party who knew about the menace of boredom and how to defeat it. The occasional thought improved his afternoons with the schoolteacher in the building, a rather morose, unhappily married young woman.

Once, crossing the square, he spotted the Frisbee player, still playing Frisbee, gracefully running toward the fountain—years ago it was called the Beatnik Naval Basin—and he said: "Hey, man, I got a photo of you."

"Well, you bring it next time you in the square," said the player. "Maybe I give you little something for it."

There was a problem with this invigoration. Suki was in danger of becoming real to him. Her letters had, how to put it, an odd gift of one-way intimacy. They asked nothing of him. He seldom replied, and then only with a sentence or two. Yet he opened them first in his mail. She rambled, she honored him too much, she credited every syllable and reference, she interpreted his stories as they appeared; she wrote the best study of his new novel—only in a letter, alas. She got what he didn't know he was after. She touched a nerve. She knew him.

balding," he suddenly thought: What will Suki think of this one? Is she still out there in the unreal world? And if so, she must be nearly thirty by now.

She had been merely busy.

> . . . Beware of a Viennese Druid who tries to unstring
> the queen Diana of Dionysia's raveled skein of perfect
> knowledge of the Perry Street Poet's secular confusions.
> Take care. Take care. Take care. The Children of the
> Mystery have begun to pray for you once more. They
> never stopped, my love, my only true love, my dearest
> soul. . . .

In addition to a career organizing her thoughts about him, she had become a fashion model, evidently an occupation in which there was enough craziness already so that she could pass unnoticed, so long as she had the right look and came to her appointments on time. On the far East Side of Manhattan, among models, art directors, photographers, cooks for cooking setups and dressmakers and the children of divorce playing house with their single parents, she had made a life for herself. She was good and she was smart. She had enlisted a little group of worshipers in the cult of Ward Carmel, and their analysis of the secret meaning of his expressions began to come to him in poems, essays, telegrams, letters, and gifts. He was not surprised when the phone rang one night—of course, it would be three o'clock in the morning, when witches and sorcerers come to their important decisions—and she said: "It's time."

"It's three o'clock, my dear."

"For us."

"I realize you have the privilege of organizing your thoughts according to your own devices, my dear, and your career permits a certain indulgence—"

"Are you asleep?"

"No. Do I sound asleep? But I *was* when you called."

"Because when you get nervous, your anima is pompous."

"Forgive my anima."

"It's no good pretending," she said. "We must complete the circle. I'll come to you at noon on Monday."

And she rang off. He had never kept her telephone number when she had given it to him before. Her number was unlisted, and the telephone company wouldn't listen to reason. Did *she* have unwanted callers? Could he just go to a museum at noon on Monday?

The museum he liked was closed on Monday. And if the truth be told, he felt a small thrill of anticipation, an almost welcome excitement. After all, she understood him; oh, perhaps she *over* understood him. She valued him. She adored him. Perhaps she even loved him. She had read him as no one else did. And when he thought: She is also beautiful, he also decided: Perhaps there is some sort of fate in all this.

Karma, anima, the eternal return. Who is Ward Carmel to deny the possibility of miracles?

Well, by noon on Monday he could get a few paragraphs tucked away, and the mail read, and then he would be ready for her.

But he knew he would be able to do nothing Monday morning but wait. He might try to do his Monday's work on Sunday night, which was usually devoted to the New York *Times* at the Laundromat—the New York *Times* and the notices about Swami Muktananda and reliable apartment cleaning. He was a person with habits, but not rigid ones.

Sometimes, after traveling, due to jet lag, or after a bout of flu, due to insufficient exercise or fever or going to bed too early, Ward suffered insomnia. It was a wonderful opportunity. He would walk Eighth Street and over as far as St. Mark's Place, eat breakfast at the early-morning taxi drivers' café on Second Avenue, where the drivers and the speed freaks went; he dreamily floated on the night life and dawn life of the filthy, imperial city. He enjoyed his insomnia; it varied the routine; it was a vacation from enjoyment of his days. There were so many of them.

But these nights he could not sleep and he wanted to. He could not walk the Village because he didn't want to. He was as tired and as fretful as a child. He was impatient for one particular day.

Young men were screaming and fighting and lighting fires in trash cans outside his window all Sunday night. They may have been gay, or they may have been antigay, or they may have been an unstable mixture of the two. A little excitement—the police came twice—was

part of his whole deal with the city. But this time he needed his sleep
for Monday, he was greedy for it like an ordinary insomniac, and he
felt as uneasy as if he had forgotten to write in his journal the night
before.

He did not dream of Suki. He was the one who gave *her* dreams;
he felt it important that he not be the dreamer in this exchange. He
wondered if maybe his will did not control the matter and he had
buried some treasure out of reach. Well, this had gone on a long time.
When someone thinks she has a map, knows it absolutely, she ends
by making doubters want to give her a chance—laetrile, UFOs, Atlan-
tis, the Bermuda Triangle. *Might be* is one of the ways human beings
differ from other beasts. It was Ward's business, too. And if one is
adored long enough, one ends, no matter how sensible, in feeling
some wound of commitment. His head this morning felt like the
burnt-out trash can in the gutter across the street.

For Suki, surely he was a dream lover through and through. For
himself, she had not begun as any lover at all. She had begun as a
lovely and amusing pest. But now he recalled the excitement he used
to feel in anticipation of a cozy afternoon with a secret lady, and he
had not felt it in a long time; this part of his life, mainly with the
depressed teacher on the ground floor, was steady, sexually inventive,
mutually convenient, and staid in the newest fashion. He tried to
think: Pity she's a pest; but all he thought was: Only a few more hours.

It was less time than that. She arrived nearly an hour early. He was
ready anyway. "Oh, hullo," he said, opening the door, and she answered:

"You must get out of my body."

"Pardon?"

She stood there swaying, her hair lank with sweat, her eyes wild,
and yet he could still see the American beauty that she showed in
photographs. Her distracted skinniness photographed neatly. Neuras-
thenia was high fashion. Now she seemed nearly emaciated, and he
wondered where there could be room for anyone else in her body.

"There's no room for anyone else!" she said, sobbing.

He had straightened up the place for a visit. She brought disorder.
"How can I do what you ask of me?"

"Push, push, push!" she cried.

"Pardon?" He felt stupid and talked stupidly.

And now she entered, shoving him aside, unbuttoning her blouse, starting to unhook her skirt, saying, "Push your soul out of me, press your body in and push your soul out, you must!"

"What the devil are you doing?"

"A man loves me, a decent normal man, I can't marry him until I get rid of you. You must help me, please! Won't you help me, please, please, please?"

"Not this way I can't," he said (he uttered), and he started to hold her skirt, to try to button her blouse, to push it back on her arms as it slipped off, flimsy stuff; and he felt her thin, hot arms, like a sick child's without clothes, her narrow squirming feverish body, and then her mouth fastened on his and her teeth were biting into his lower lip.

He slapped her.

She fell back, gasping and holding her jaw. And then she said: "This is a nice little place. It hasn't changed since the last time."

"That was eight years ago."

"Now that you've hurt me so much, will you make love to me, just one time?"

He had no habits of beating women. Women sometimes attacked him, more with words than with their bodies, but he was not used to brawling. He had heard about the calm of some hysterics after a fight.

Nevertheless, he was also no longer tempted to make love. He was tempted to try reason with her again, despite reason's poor reputation as a remedy for pain. She was struggling with tears. "You don't understand," she said softly; she swallowed, she choked, she calmed herself. She touched his thigh. She kneeled before him, kissing and pulling at his leg. "There is this man, a lawyer, I love him—he loves me, anyway—and if you let us, we could marry, we could have a child —" And she was softly caressing his knee; she was running a finger up the seam of his jeans; she was reaching tenderly, worshipfully—

"My dear! Impossible!" he said, and wrenched away.

"It's my only chance! You must save me!"

"No," he said.

"Has it ever been in your power to be the salvation of a person?" she said. "I am the only soul you could act to save, the soul you damned. Am I not worthy?"

As often in his life, laughter saved him. He did not laugh aloud, but this plea—am I not worthy?—touched the history of amusement in him. Even grief can be pompous. He was in control. It was real again. He would get her away and figure out what to do next.

"Where are you living? On York Avenue, isn't it? Let me think, there's never a rush about salvation, is there, my dear? Give me time."

"Will you call me?"

"Give me time."

"Will you call?"

"Yes."

"Then you promised." She had gathered her scattered clothes— an umbrella, a silk scarf with a designer's name on it—and she was gone. The maelstrom swallowed itself up. He was alone and he gasped for breath.

Now what a rational person does in a situation like this, once he has got his senses back, is to continue to act rationally. He remembered her family's name in Denver. She had parents. He telephoned until he found her father (her mother was dead). It was not easy, and he made a number of calls, and finally he reached the man at his office. He was the president of a steel fabricating company. There was money.

"I'm Ward Carmel—"

The man interrupted. "I know, I know, Mr. Carmel. First of all, I want you to understand that I do not hold you responsible."

"Responsible? Responsible for what?"

"I know my daughter's feeling for you, and I do not blame you, sir."

"I don't blame me either! But that's not what I'm calling about. I think she needs help, I think she's a danger to others and possibly herself, I think you must—"

The man's voice was very assured and a little amused. "Calm yourself, sir. Suki has been my daughter for a long time. I'm used to her exceptional ideas. I appreciate that you are an artist and your emotions are very precious to you—"

"What is she haunting me for?"

"In New York? *Haunting*, sir? Well, I suppose she has developed some ideas about you—"

"Get her out of here!"

The man paused. His patience was wearing thin. "She's a grown person," he said. "I imagine this has seemed to be a wild-goose chase. I'm sure she has appointments for the week and she will go on as usual. I've learned not to try to control my daughter—it was not easy to learn. That's my best guesstimate of the situation."

Guesstimate, Ward thought.

"But I'll tell you what. Let me make a suggestion if you feel unable to deal with this young woman. If she comes to your offices again, please have someone on your staff detain her a moment and call, let's see, please give me a ring. Next time you can call collect, Mr. Carmel. Let me give you my private line."

So these were the corridors of money and power. Ward wanted out of them as well as out of the concentric circles of karma and anima. The conversation ended in an exchange of numbers. Ward hung up. He waited for the worst. He had forgotten the designer's name on Suki's pale green silk scarf.

The worst seldom happened to Carmel, although he knew eventually it would. He waited for the woman to reappear. But like the worst in life, she never came back until the day when she did. It was only a week later. She stood at his door and made no move to enter. She was carrying a small suitcase—elegant pale green fabric luggage—a taxi waiting; he didn't expect that. She wore a hat. She wore a trim woolen suit. She could have been a handsome young matron on her way to a weekend in the country, and perhaps there was a young man patiently waiting in the cab downstairs, and her face was calm, and he thought with a peculiar pang: Cured. Pity.

Good-byes were not her business. She had one more issue to settle with him. "You dared appeal to my father to settle things between us," she said. "Wrong, wrong, wrong, Ward. I don't love you now. I had my reasons. I was foolish, but that's how I knew you. I'll never love you again. Nor will anyone."

There were no grounds, he thought, for her to know the truth about him.

She turned to leave, and then suddenly turned back, and for the first time he saw a smile on her face, a sweet and easy smile of pleasure. "Perhaps I seemed a little odd to you," she said. She winked. "You seem odd to me, too."

BART AND HELENE AT ANNIE-AND-FRED'S

It was a party to celebrate the coming together and going together of two lovers who surely deserved a good time after their recent bad times. Fred's wife had left him for the organic baker down the street. Annie's husband had not left her, but he really should have made the decision she finally made—he forced her to make it—leaving him for Fred, who hung about the village library after his wife's defection. Fred had moped a lot until Annie consoled him. Now they were happy and everyone was eating grape leaves wrapped around meat and bread crumbs, and drinking white wine, and the party looked like a party for slightly thickened college kids. They were no longer college kids. The thickness was mostly not in the bodies, only in the faces and jaws, since in California one jogs, one plays racquet sports, one skis, one keeps fit. Annie and Fred were a fit, newly happy couple.

Bart was glad for Annie and Fred. He sat on a pile of foam covered

261

with fur, leaning against the wall and fingering the extruded nipple of an empty plastic wineglass. He would have risen for a refill, but he didn't want to lose his place on the improvised couch. He was pleasantly bone weary from a late afternoon at racquetball and he was interested to talk with the very tall, excessively broad-shouldered outdoor goddess seated next to him. She turned to offer him wine from her glass and they got through the introductions, professions—he a lawyer, she a psychology instructor at the community college—and the first affable joshings and seriousness. She was a fine-looking woman with heavy sunlines around the eyes and on the forehead, skin etched by sun. He liked her; he wasn't interested in her, he felt at ease with her; he would just drop here for a chat.

Helene told him she had spent five years in the Peace Corps in Brazil. Bart told her he was the oldest man at the party, an observation he freely made these days, and she replied that she was thirty-nine. He said, "You look it, but that's good," and she laughed, and he said that anyone under fifty looked young to him (not true), and he told her he was forty-seven. And thus they fell to talking about being alone at night, or on the party circuit, or having trivial—*quadrivial, madame!* he said—connections at their ages.

It didn't even seem odd to be so frank with a stranger—"You're the only stranger I know," he said.

She said she was tired of "boys"—men little older than her students, "sensitive" sometimes, but not knowing very much, or not enough, so that after she finished her days as a teacher, she spent her evenings teaching, too. She ended these relationships after a trip to Hawaii or into the desert or up a mountain or anyplace, she said. They didn't survive more than a few whole days together, even with some active sport to bring them together.

"I know," Bart said. "I don't live with women now. I travel alone —that's your mistake. I confine myself to . . ."

Helene smiled.

"A few hours at a stretch," he said.

Helene didn't seem very sexy to him, but he found himself making erotic insinuations to her. He didn't mean to tease. It just came out like that. He felt a little tired in a pleasant way. She was a nice stranger.

Everywhere else in this cottage on a hillside, filled with furniture scraps and people, unfurnished because other spouses still had custody of such things, other new couples and new noncouples were eating folded grape leaves, drinking white wine, making jokes, constructing plans for later, all pleased for Annie and Fred, whose finding each other they were celebrating, all interested in what erotic surprises such a happy occasion might bring. A few talked about their businesses and the economy, their professions and the economy. Annie and Fred circulated with plates and jugs, Annie's face visibly flushed with pleasure despite the discordant disguise of disco makeup, Fred's face quite pale and worn with all the joys he was suddenly being forced into; they made a nice pair, one so determined and strong, the other so recently unhappy and now gratified, being taken care of. Once Fred tried to refill Bart's plastic glass and Bart said to him, "Buddy," and Fred answered, "You told me, Bart, you told me everything would be all right, you were the one who told me."

"Your attorney wouldn't lie," said Bart, "that would be unethical."

He didn't express, however—though he might to Helene in due course—his doubts about a recent wife who took up with her new true lover and yet kept herself hidden behind the makeup strategies of a punker. *Maybe she's insecure,* Helene would no doubt reply.

Fred moved off with a pleased wan smile at Bart and Helene, at his friend and Annie's friend, who were so obviously and seriously exploring the worlds of hope and possibility on the temporary heap of foam.

Helene and Bart found themselves making little alternating speeches about their experiences in love. Bart had the comfortable sense that these were not serial monologues, plaints, and brags, but rather a sort of leisurely dialogue. He was interested in her story. She seemed interested in his. When one interrupted, the other waited, answered, and completed the story.

She had had a serious lover in the Peace Corps, another her first years in Berkeley. Serious love affairs break up as shatteringly as unserious ones; more so, of course.

"Of course," he said. "I've had that experience."

Patiently and kindly she waited to see if he wanted to take the initiative with his own story. He didn't yet. She went on to describe the increasingly unserious love affairs, unserious at least to her, in which she led young men on pedagogical expeditions and felt lonely after the strong smells of athletic boys had been aired out of her flat.

"That's not unserious," he said.

She waited and he waited, so she gave him an example—the lad with whom she had just broken up. He didn't read worth a damn. She thought he was bright. But he was just "into music," and nothing she could do—

"I find it's a mistake to try to educate the young," he said. "Better to accept them simply, without trying to be one among them, of course."

"Otherwise you become a parent," she said, smiling.

"Or a teacher," he said, smiling.

They smiled upon each other. They were holding hands. How had this happened? he wondered. He wasn't really interested, though he liked her a lot just now and it was cozy here with her on the pile of foam, being ignored by the standing and shifting bodies that filled the room.

It would be rude to let her hand go. Her hand was dry and warm and strong and nice, even if he wasn't much interested in more than resting here after his recent exertions at racquetball and talking with a canny and sad woman going through some difficult times in life. He too was going through a difficult decade or generation or, anyway, something difficult, without necessarily being wise. He was just himself, and that was what he had to work with.

She smiled expectantly. She was looking at him with sun-crinkled, sun-washed eyes that asked, And now you?

He disengaged his hand from hers, reached for her glass, and took some of her wine. The gesture felt like a necessary apology for what he was about to say—a gesture of friendly intimacy in advance.

"I like young women," he said. "I like their smell. I like their expectancy. But mostly I like that they haven't been hurt. I think I could like older women, too, because I know some I like, and they smell sweet, too, but the older women of that sort, the great ones, are all claimed. They have men. And the ones that don't—"

"You don't want to live with their bitterness," she said.

"I don't have to, so I don't."

She did not grow angry. She went on smiling as if this were the nicest thing in the world to hear, what she had always wanted to hear. "Naturally you want only the great ones," she said.

"One great one would be enough."

"So lacking her—"

"It's easier for me," he said, "than it is for older women. It's simply a fact that I'm not disqualified. You're not either, you're special, smart and talented, but it's easier for men. We don't have to be special to be in luck, in a kind of luck. Which doesn't mean, of course, that I haven't had some miserable spells of grieving over women— over one woman, as it happens in my case—only I've given up grieving in public. In public I've developed good cheer."

"Imitating good cheer tends to mean you feel it."

"Thank you, Professor. Yes, you're right—"

"William James was right."

"Both of you. Cheerfulness spreads, that's right, to the inner being from the outer action. Hypocrisy turns out to be more valuable than we used to think in the Summer of Love."

They toasted hypocrisy, she with her plastic glass of white wine, he with his clenched fist. She drank first; then he took the offer and drank again from her glass. He got up and refilled her glass and a fresh one for himself. When he returned, he said, "The main thing I notice nowadays is I don't fall in love anymore, I don't get infatuated, I just enjoy the young women who can put up with me. My kids—children —take a lot of my time. I even enjoy good relations with my former wife. If love is an attempt to complete the inadequate in ourselves, well, I seem to be reconciled to my own inadequacy without love. Or at least to the fact that love won't cure it. And so—if you'll forgive the vanity—I give the impression of security. I don't care. I don't care enough to be insecure, but I like the good tastes and good natures of some young women."

She smiled to indicate that she forgave the vanity, perceived the inadequacy, liked him. Her teeth were large, squarish in front, regular.

"My lovers are all looking for mothers or teachers," she said. "I think some of them mostly like eating my food, using my washing machine for their tee shirts and jeans." He laughed. "I'm not kidding," she said. "They like to save their quarters for records."

"You're a nice person," he said. "You're grown-up. You're intelligent. You're decent. You're pretty."

He meant everything but the last, though she had a kind of appeal

in her large boniness. Her hand tightened on his. He wished for her
to be his friend, even very briefly, even for the time remaining before
he would head home. To say she was pretty was not a reprehensible
lie. For some men it would not be a lie at all.

He looked at his watch. He had expected to leave before now. She
was keeping him up late. She caught his eye and smiled. They were
leaning against each other. Her shoulder radiated warmth. "It's later
than we think," he said.

She sighed.

"No one is interrupting us," he said.

"They think we're together."

He sighed, too. He stood up. He said, "It really is late. I played
racquetball. I have to be up early to take my kids to, you'll not believe
this, Sunday school. Honest."

"I understand," she said, and she understood.

Because they were honest and understanding with each other, he
did not ask her telephone number. He saw no need to imply any lies.
He would not call her. He had already forgotten her last name. He
held her hand as she remained seated and he said, "I really liked our
conversation. It was good to talk with you."

He had no idea what she was doing when he walked away. He
didn't look back till Annie and Fred came to thank him as he thanked
them for having a good time at their party. Helene had already
vanished from the foam temporary couch.

CHRISTMAS
IN DAKAR

What luck! Every Jew with a Yuletide weakness for slipped soul, a melan-cholic whiplash in the goodwill aura of department store Santa Clauses, Handel's Messiah, and rosy-cheeked family turkey sacrifices, should get the chance to spend the holiday season in West Africa; the republic of Senegal, removed from all average memories, will do nicely. Probably frazzled singles, widows and widowers, and lifelong dignified bachelors and spinsters might also want to join the ranks of the Jews in this salvation from Christmas depression.

Bless my good fortune—sent on a writing job to Dakar. The assign-ment was to do a piece about this peculiar corner of Africa, jungle and desert and a jutting horn across the Atlantic from Brazil. The secret agenda, my own, was to white out the season with some busy unconnectedness. And with a serendipity I did not deserve, a friend happened to call—an acquaintance, really—bearing the name of a

bright, pretty, "severe," he said, young woman who worked for
UNESCO in Dakar.

Would I give her his greetings? Would I ever? I'd staple my own
greetings to his; who knows what longings for home she might be
feeling at this time, and what a miracle that I just happened severely,
but with a crooked smile, to turn up at the right moment?

Call her Patricia Neville.

I tossed my bags on my bed at the Hotel Teranga, which means
"Welcome" in Wolof, looked out my window at the bank skyscraper
designed in the shape of a baobob tree, looked at the ocean and the
island of Gorée, through which thousands upon thousands of slaves
passed on their way to America, meditated for three or four seconds
on the many varieties of slavery to which we are fated, looked at my
finger, which was dialing for an outside line. The UNESCO office
happened to lie across the Place de l'Indépendance from the Hotel
Teranga. When I couldn't reach the lady by phone—purgatorial
telephone lines are one of the great traditions of French civilization
—I showered, dressed, and decided upon a little stroll across the
square to get a first impression of Dakar. Beggars, salesmen of primi-
tive carvings and original Swiss watches from Taiwan, tribal cos-
tumes, screeching taxis, and what's this? Why, it's the office of
UNESCO looming up in front of me—another great coincidence.
Why not just go in and say hello?

Recently an African village, Dakar is now busy becoming a metrop-
olis of a million people, "the Paris of Africa," which means that the
elevators don't work. I climbed. I arrived at the floor for UNESCO
and found a door with P. NEVILLE printed on it—a severed form of her
name living up to advance notice. She had a Lebanese secretary, a
sharp-featured, brown-faced, straight-haired little person, who said
Mlle. Neville was in a meeting, but she could take in a note from me.
I scribbled. The secretary took.

The lady emerged from her meeting. Indeed, she was elegant, tall,
very slim, wearing some kind of mitigatingly delicate Indian gauze
shirt, with a hawk nose and dark blue eyes accented by makeup.
There was a bead chain of sweat on her upper lip, which somehow
caused tender feelings in me. My clothes must have been nearly
transparent from my exertions. She stood near me but did not suggest
that either of us sit. I quickly ran through my credentials for taking

her time—friend of a friend of an acquaintance—and apologized for interrupting and suggested we meet for lunch or a drink or . . . "I'm rather busy these days," she said, "a year-end report, and my parents arriving for the holidays."

Her voice was clipped and cool. Well, I'd been told *severe*.

"Of course. I'll be here at the Teranga for two weeks; maybe if you have a moment sometime . . ."

She seemed to relent; she smiled with a sudden dazzle of healthy teeth—it was a smile of charity and forgiveness. "But please keep Christmas Eve," she said. "I'm having my annual Christmas party. Do come."

That's a start, I thought. Fair enough. She did legitimately seem busy, too busy even to wipe her upper lip, and what right has a passing stranger to demand her time? She would no doubt get in touch to inform me of time and place for her annual Christmas party. The line of wet on her upper lip, like the blue mascara on her eyes, made her seem vulnerable. She was making herself into something other than what people expected of her. She charmed me in my Christmas need.

I was far from home. I knew no one. Jet lag turned the day around. I awakened in the night, nowhere to go, nothing to do, no sleep, no proper alertness, either; longing for an answer to the meaning of life, but no bars open. I too was trying to make myself into something other than what I was at Christmastime.

I would leave it to Miss Neville to contact me if she had time.

The next day I got busy with my explorations of Dakar and of Senegal. That's the ticket—thread my way through the season; work. I was ready to override even stomach trouble. Love, the meaning of life, and the community of lonely souls would have to take care of themselves while I did my job amid the distractions of homesickness and coli bacillus unfamiliar to my inner being. I brought my emotions and stomach into line by pure will, plus drinking only bottled water and eating no uncooked vegetables.

One evening I reluctantly returned from a stroll on the Boulevard Georges-Pompidou, where I watched a Wolof Santa Claus with white cotton clown gloves in front of the Chaussures Bata shop. My other entertainment was listening to the kids shouting at him: "Khomeini! Khomeini!" Then there would be the lobby, the elevator, and my

room with its view of sea and bank. There was the bar, of course. I
hated to go upstairs again. I dawdled, and then I saw her. She was
leaving the hotel alone and about to step into a taxi. "Miss Neville!"
I said.

"Oh, hullo. Sorry to be in such a rush. I forgot to ask you about
the Christmas party—you do sort of celebrate Christmas, don't you,
Mr. Gould? As a cultural phenomenon?"

And I stood there in the Saharan heat, the red Saharan dust, as
her taxi carried her away. What a question. Mr. *Gould!* A blanket of
dumb misery sank over me, the insecurity blanket recalled from
childhood, a nearly forgotten exclusion, associated with the whispered word *Jew* sent my way in Lakewood, Ohio, which marked me
off from everyone. And in rage and disgust for my own need, for this
stupid past which could be revived even in middle age, in Dakar, by
a tone and a mispronunciation, I turned around and walked back
through the evening dust and swelter to the closed-down ferry to
Gorée, stood gazing in the night at the *Blaise Daigne,* the battered
motor launch which carried visitors to the site of slave shipments, my
head boiling and my nose itching with red grit; and thought, No, no,
this is too dumb; and walked beneath starlight and a discolored moon
till I was worn out and could sleep. Bathed and slept. Bathed, turned
off the air conditioning, covered myself with a sheet, stared out across
the harbor toward Gorée, and in the tropical night dreamed and tried
to sleep. *Sort of celebrate, don't you, Mr. Gould?*

The next morning, at the swimming pool, a short, elderly man with
a mat of gray hair on his chest watched me swimming laps. I thought
his muscles twitched a little, as if he too were about to dive and swim;
and since he was still watching me when I had finished my *Herald
Tribune,* I offered it to him. He had been reading the London Observer. He did not offer it to me. But when I introduced myself, he said,
"Oh, yes, my daughter mentioned you."

"You're Mr. Neville?"

"Must be," he said. The plump pink blond lady by his side was
Mrs. Neville, and she smiled toothily, waved four fingers, and then
blinked and went back to sunning herself. "What brings you to
Africa?" he asked.

"Writing something," I said, "and you?"

"Oh, I've lived here for ever so long. Economics, y'know. I was economic adviser to President Mobuto, and before that in the Congo, and you'll get used to it, I'm sure, if you're having a little stomach. Wouldn't do without it at all. Best not to drink water or eat salad, y'know."

"Are you American?" I asked. "Your accent suggests English, but—"

"Ottawa," he said. "But I've spent most of my days in Africa for so long now."

"I've never met anyone from Ottawa."

"Well, I'm really out of Zaire, y'know. Here for the holidays is all. Dakar. A little R&R, as you might put it, sir."

I didn't like him. I didn't like his daughter. I had nothing against the pink wife half-asleep by his side. I said I needed another swim, and then I had a meeting in town, and he nodded farewell, folding my newspaper between his heavy gray arm and the thick gray chest of a powerful old guy. Having escaped Christmas in the States, here I was by the side of a pool in a luxury hotel in Dakar with a nagging wounded grief in the sight of this muscled little overweight and gray-matted person.

It began to seem funny as I went about my routines. I heard him advising, "Don't push too hard in this climate, old chap," and I thought I'd ignore the belly pains from the water or the unwashed vegetables and be very, very cool and easy for my morning swim at the pool, not pushing at all. I would not ask if he had ever been economic adviser to Idi Amin or the emperor Bokassa. Neither making friends nor picking quarrels was the solution to the Christmas season. Poking about in Senegal would keep me interested in other things.

The invitation, time and place, to the Patricia Neville Annual Xmas Party never came, but it happened one day that I was invited to have a talk with the president of Senegal, Léopold Sédar Senghor, and was waiting in the lobby of the hotel for the car sent to pick me up. I was wearing, as instructed by a protocol secretary, my best approximation of tropical formality—tie, jacket, water-slicked hair, with the effects of a bit of money disbursed for a rush cleaning and a proper pressing of the khaki pants. Mr. Neville came strolling through the lobby, saw me, started, and said, "Ho! Going somewhere, Mr. Gold?"

I told him.

"How did that happen, sir?"

"I was invited," I said.

He looked at me for a moment with a sickly smile. "Having a bit of the stomach myself," he said, "but do you play tennis? I'll be better tomorrow. I have access to the club—"

I explained that I was very busy, working actually, and just took a swim after breakfast—

"Understand, understand perfectly," he said. "Maybe we should have a drink tomorrow and you can tell me about your meeting— fascinating, I'd guess."

I clucked unhappily. "Some people to see tomorrow," I said. "Actually I'd have loved to chat with you, and I was supposed to go to your daughter's party, but she neglected to send word—"

"Oh, Patricia, Patricia! She can be so careless, that girl! I must speak to her at once and see if we can arrange something all together, perhaps a little dinner or a late supper if you're not too occupied—"

The weeks went by. I made acquaintances among the Senegalese and tried to puzzle out the meaning of this West African nation which is lacking in the normal turmoil, tyranny, and police brutality. When I traveled, I returned to the hotel after a few days to find Mr. Neville ardently greeting me, irked that we couldn't seem to get together, still trying. I disliked him; I disliked his daughter; I had no grudge against his wife; I was polite and busy.

One day I noticed him not sunning himself, reading his English papers, reading his computer readouts, whatever he did at poolside; not doing any of it. The spot was empty. No London *Times*, London *Observer*, no *Economist*, no papers and pencils and sunshades and tray of drinks and peanuts from the bar. I did my swim and started back up the flowered slope toward the hotel.

"Oh, sir! Sir! Mr. Gold!"

It was Mrs. Neville in her flowered print bathing dress, running toward me from the bar entrance to the pool.

"My husband is confined to his room! Not well, not well at all!" She was slightly breathless. "He was asking, he wondered if you could come and have a little gossip, come to keep him company!"

I explained that I had an appointment but politely inquired about the trouble.

"Stomach!" she said. "It's just been coming on him so! But he has refused to admit it, refused to take the precautions with diet and medicines, refused to take care! I'm sure you understand."

"Yes, I had a touch of it, too."

"No, no! The way he is? When you asked about his accent, I saw that you recognized him."

"Your husband has a particular style of speech—what do you mean?"

"Ah, he hates to admit anything more can happen to him. He's a survivor! You recognized, of course, he survived the concentration camp, so now he doesn't like to admit anything, anything at all—"

PATERNITY

The sun burned through the summer dust of Port-au-Prince, road grit and
charcoal smoke. The consoling sway of palm was stilled at midday.
With total confidence Fritz emerged from the shop and set an un-
wrapped quart of ice cream on the floor of his Fiat. It would go too
fast for mere melting, I said; it would explode—fissionable chocolate,
the first Haitian atomic bomb.

"Wrong again, my friend," he said. "It's mocha. And I know from
experience of my many years how nicely it will last from this creamery
to my villa."

In the back seat the child, Marie-Claude, said: "*Jou-jou.*" Toys.

"It is every Saturday like this," Fritz explained. "Only usually not
you or any other friend, although sometimes her real father comes for
a sandwich at bedtime on Sunday. I keep her toys at my villa, a
bathsuit, a bathing suit. Now she must bathe at once. She smells"—
sniff!—"*chérie, tu sens le pipi.*"

275

"It's just a little-girl smell," I said.

"I suppose you would be the expert, dear friend."

I have known him for twenty years now. For Fritz, tall, elegant, a blond, blue-eyed, coffee-colored Haitian who has delighted three continents and many islands with his lazy grace, adopting this lovely black child seemed very odd. It was a responsibility, and others had always felt responsible for him, for the pleasure he gave, for the sweet lightness of his smiling presence. Responsibility had never, in Paris, Rome, London, New York, or Port-au-Prince, been one of his fields of endeavor. It seemed to me like the end of something, the end of the last boy of my age, but he was not in mourning for himself. Once again he was happy. He loved her. She was four and three months, he told me, more than four years, and he had adopted her legally. It was the beginning of something for Fritz, a new life with his delicious daughter. Already she knew enough to speak French, not Creole, with him, because although he sometimes became angry in Creole, he always smiled upon her in French.

"You'll like my pool," he said. "Well, you will tolerate my pool. I share it with three others of my sort. We live in Bois Verna." He lifted his shoulders in the classic international driver's shrug at the impossibility of life, of traffic, of the heat, of time passing. "My pool is cleaner than it looks. Filtered. Chérie! Don't touch! No fingers! You'll have cream after your bath."

And to me: "Don't worry. I'll explain. And the ice cream will endure, my friend."

We sat by the pool. His cottage reminded me of the brave, seedy, plaster-and-stucco digs of poor writers and actors in Los Angeles— falling apart and the envy of millions. There were bougainvillaea, great carnivorous red blossoms, darting hyacinths, palm trees shedding, and a mass of tropical plants I couldn't identify. The water in the pool was gray-green. Lizards slipped across the cracks of concrete, swelled up their necks, darted at mosquitoes. There was thunder from far away, perhaps Kenscoff, but it wouldn't rain here today. The child played, murmuring softly to herself. Like a good father, Fritz didn't press at her shyness at the beginning of the weekend, at her father's strange visitor. And he said he would explain and he did.

"Since we are such old friends and I know how good we are friends,

I tell you the story. The grandfather of this child was a famous beauty. However, when I was a boy and first learned who I was, he had already become, perhaps, a little less beautiful. His hair, you know, as mine now. The forehead in a beautiful person should be a little lower."

He touched his crown. I mumbled but didn't really know how to console him. He still looks like one of the tall, straight, tennis-playing young leading men of the fifties, with only that creamy skin to say he is Haitian. But he didn't need my diplomacy: He knows what he is and how old he has become.

"So when the grandfather have a good chance to travel to Italy with an Italian count, naturally he seek to achieve this wish. The Italian adored him, and I was only a child. We never consummated his desire for me. I was too proud, I think. Then, in a few years, the grandfather returned to Port-au-Prince. He married. He had this son, Marc-Albert. And I watched him grow up. First he was pretty; then he became an angel. However, he loved mostly women, although naturally he took his pleasure sometimes like his father. He was so immature. I watched, I waited. He was capable, I thought, of pleasure but not of passion, and I waited. I loved him so, I wanted only passion when finally we met.

"It did not happen. We were friends only. He knew, but he teased me, oh, very bad, and then he married. He had this child. The mother is crazy and beat her. Marc-Albert found a new woman. Oh, he is less beautiful now anyway, but I still remember and perhaps I no longer even feel desire for him. But I love him. He is nearly thirty now, you know, and I am nearly fifty."

He offered me a rum-soda. He showed me the crisp nut from a nearby tree and told me its name in Creole. He watched Marie-Claude making tea with water from the swimming pool in her tin tea set, and carrying it back and forth, spilling it out, making more tea. She was at home here. She called him Papa. Her hair, the color of mahogany, very curly but long, was held by pink elastic with little bells jingling. He had dressed her in the pale green swimsuit he kept for her. During the week she boarded with friends—"it is good she have a kindly mother, it is good she have many fathers"—but during the weekends he gave up his other lives to be her father.

"So since I was neither enjoyed by the grandfather nor did I enjoy the father, I adopted the child. A girl," he said, smiling, the winking, amused shrug of a man bent on joy who has become a kindly ironist because what else is there at this time of a life?

What else to do was to set the table for the two of them. I was not invited for dinner. Two plates on two straw mats, under a sun umbrella; forks, spoons, knives, cups, and a red flower floating in a glass. He admired her preparations. He straightened the mats and touched the flower so that it turned slowly in the water.

"How lucky I have always been. And now to participate in history like this. How happy you must be, dear friend, at my good fortune. To have a descendant, and this sweet little person, who reminds me of so much." He looked at me with his hands clasped in front of his bikini and his shoulders slightly stooped, in none of the stop-action displaying postures which his body still often took. "It is rare to be so fortunate, to give pain, to suffer pain, and then to receive nothing but so much pleasure as this child brings me."

"You'll find being a father brings other things, too."

"I believe I am ready, my friend."

The child played sweetly, we watched her, it was very peaceful under the palm trees, we had a swim in the pool. That inevitable male sagging at the middle—two plump creases when he bent to give Marie-Claude a kiss on the top of her head—was his only visible mark. He could still have passed for twenty-eight, and I thought of telling him. But I recalled that he thought this another age of loss and decay.

We returned to our chairs and he counseled me about Haiti. "I am not stupid," he said. "I left for New York during the worst times of Papa Doc. And then I knew when to come back." He described the decline of the golden elite, and particularly of his subclass, the clever boy-lovers. They had always had things a good way for them, a way that did no harm. They treasure boys of deeper color than their own. They search des numéros, des grains, as he called them; perhaps it could be translated "numbers," "trade." All young men are for hire in Port-au-Prince, he assured me; all are available for money; this is easy work and it means nothing to them. He was speaking of the poor, and of those smiling angels who sometimes emerge from the slums of La Saline or from the caille-pailles, the mud-and-straw houses which fill the interstices of the city. "We have all the advantages," he said, sighing his acceptance of this minor social injustice.

But now the rich Americans have discovered Port-au-Prince. They come to steal away the sweetest grains, and take them back to Manhattan to walk around nude in steam-heated, well-decorated apartments, and give them Haitian goatskin drums to play with while the master works in his advertising agency or design studio or airline office. The master invites guests to envy him; not everyone possesses a Haitian boy. No one through flimsy American walls complains about the sound of the lonely drum all day, because in fact, the boy never touches it except when the master has guests. He is busy with *The Guiding Light*, the storm door, and Brillo advertisements, the white magic of daytime television. Then next winter he develops sinus trouble, homesickness, he steals a shirt when the graphic designer would be glad to give him all the shirts he can wear, his nose runs, he runs away. Fritz emitted a short angry laugh. "It's an old story. Nobody can help."

My friend sighed. "I am now out of this combat, thank God," he said. "I love this child more than anyone, she will be my heir, you will see how she speaks French like a little French doll. Six months ago she spoke only Creole. Now, you will see, she goes babababa in French. Only she is a little shy with you, *blanc*."

I think we dozed in our chairs. Marie-Claude was touching my arm. She offered me her tea made of swimming pool water and mud. I pretended to drink. "*Merci, merci, ti-moune*," I said.

Fritz awoke with a start. "Oh! Marie-Claude! *Que tu sens le pipi!* First you will bathe, you will see, and then you will have *crème, tu comprends?*"

She was afraid of the pool.

"Must!" he said sternly, and arose from his chair with that lazy grudging gesture of the dutiful father. He seized her arm and pulled her with him to the pool. "*Un, deux, trois*," he said, "you're ready?"

She smiled with a sudden brilliant submissive pride which this man had loved now through three generations. "*Oui, papa*," she said.

CONTINGENCY PLANNING

In Jerusalem a joke arrived just at the middle of the war of October 1973.
Hadassah Hospital was filled with burned tankers; the plastic surgeons and orthopedic surgeons and anesthesiologists looked haggard
with overwork, with what they saw, with what they did; but a new
joke appeared, as one always does. The song which commemorated
the Six-Day War was "Jerusalem the Golden," usually sung by a
triumphant lilting soprano.

"Now should we sing Damascus the Golden? Cairo the Golden?"

The joke fell flat as it went its rounds, of course. People didn't really
want to go to Damascus or Cairo. But the people of Jerusalem, as the
news of their dead and wounded and missing came in, wondered what
new mysteries the times had in store for them. And to get the jump
on history, they tried to make jokes.

The man I'll call Jacobi anticipated history in another way. He was

281

returned to duty in the Army as a member of the Committee of
Contingency Planning. Things have to be thought out even if they
are nearly unbearable, and someone has to think them through, in
the Israeli world of what-if: What if the Russians send troops? What
if the United States abandons us? What if the Arabs break through
to Tel Aviv? What if poison gas, atomic weapons, Soviet naval bom-
bardment? What if the worst comes to pass; what then?

Jacobi, who was thirty-two years old, came home to his wife and
children distracted and glum. They lived in a light, high, airy apartment, in a new quarter of Jerusalem, and they had a girl of four and
a nursing boy, and they loved each other; and Jacobi was safe in his
Army assignment, as many of their friends were not, but nevertheless,
his wife found him needing consolation and unwilling to accept it
during the evenings when he could come home.

"Don't worry, I'm doing okay, I'm doing my job," he said.

"That's not what I'm worried about."

"I only act like this at night. During working hours I'm fine."

"I'm worried. I'm sad," his wife said.

He was too tired to roll and hoist his daughter in the air, as was
their habit until recently. He sat in his chair and waited for her to
hug him; then he would hug her back; but this was not what Sidra
liked to do with her father. The war had suddenly broken into many
comfortable ways.

Jacobi is a scientist in a research institute when he is not a contingency planner. His wife, Hannah, is one of those lovely Jewish flowers,
both delicate and opulent, very dark, serious, humorous, shapely. In
America she would be worried about her role as a woman. In Jerusalem she was nursing her baby, taking care of her other child, worrying
about the war and her husband, and waiting till later to think about
her role as a woman. In her present contingency, October of 1973,
she tried to keep fresh flowers in her house, and to keep her baby well
fed, and to please her husband as best she could.

She worried that Sidra, her elder daughter, was suffering from
rivalry with an infant and the war. And was unaccustomed to her
father's being away on many evenings, and sitting so quietly, looking
at her from his chair, waiting for her to hug him, when he managed
to come home before her bedtime.

What if Qaddafi comes to Jerusalem, and only the French are

present to moderate his ideals about holy war? No one believed such a thing possible, but everything is possible in a world in which every disaster has already shown its tentacles more than once in history.

What if oil, and only oil, determines men's actions?

Sidra couldn't know about her father's preoccupations, but she knew her father was preoccupied. Hannah believed her children were lucky. Other fathers were dead and dying; Jacobi would surely live to plan other contingencies first.

The jets snarled like angry cats overhead, going or coming from the Golan or Sinai. In such a small country, the passage to war was everywhere, even if for the moment the war itself was elsewhere.

A short walk away men, covered with war dust, leaned their heads against the Western Wall and prayed. But the mail was delivered; the telephone worked; eggs were in short supply, but there were enough chickens. Men with minor wounds, furloughed from Hadassah Hospital, were attended by their families and urged to eat, eat darling, eat more, in the restaurants of the King David Hotel.

At night, in scenes like sporting events, Israelis watched television, and saw their men encased in steel, lumbering over the desert, killing other men encased in steel; saw their men floating on the waters nearby, flashing rockets at other floaters and cheering as the enemy exploded under the waves; saw the blazing jets snarling at each other, and saw one explode; heard the infantrymen, leaning against armor, tell of the day's battles. Helicopters, ambulances, bottles of plasma held over stretchers—but they were careful not to show any faces of the wounded and dead on Israeli television. The silence was extreme in the watchers of these events. Hannah tried to put her daughter to bed before the evening news; but in her own distraction, she didn't always succeed, and the little girl often silently crept out of bed to join her mother and the adults at the screen. In any case, there was no place in Israel, not even in the nursery schools, where anyone could escape the war.

Sometimes, in exasperation, with a baby to nurse and a battle to watch, Hannah would send Sidra to her own room to play with her dolls.

She told me of a troubling accident which occurred one of these times. The child was sent, was silent, was alone in her room. Hannah finished nursing the baby, changed him, dusted him with powder, put

him to sleep. Then she went to Sidra's room. The child was standing
in the corner with a wrist lifted to her mouth. She had taken a scissors
and cut off the legs of her dolls and thrown them around the room.
Straw and plastic protruded from stumps. She had sawed off arms.
Pieces of doll were flung at the walls. She had plucked out the eyes.
Like marbles, they were scattered and one was still rolling on the floor
when Hannah opened the door.

"Sidra!" her mother said.

The child seemed not to hear. She didn't answer.

"I have to talk with you about this, Sidra."

She said nothing for a moment. Then she said without looking at
her mother: "I want to see my daddy. I have to talk with my daddy
about this."

Please forgive my not ending this history with a blotch of complaint
from a child, but rather with Hannah as she looked at her first child
in the brilliant dry evening of a Jerusalem silenced and blacked out
in the Yom Kippur War.

She remembered the stupor of evenings with her own parents,
where she sat merely waiting to grow up, and was grateful for the
present vividness of her love of her husband and her children. Even
the griefs of war—the dreads, the excitements, the mourning—did
not tire her. Perhaps weariness would come later. In the meantime,
she thought herself fortunate to be a young Israeli woman with a
husband who was very bright, respected, mustachioed, an excellent
chess and tennis player, agreed by all to be handsome. She knew she
was beautiful and that pleased her, too. She used a new eye makeup
from France because the war did not mean she should sacrifice every
pleasure, and she was a young mother with a husband often away. A
brownish tint to her thick lashes. And when there would be peace,
things would be even better. When the war was over, Hannah and
Jacobi thought they would return to the ways of peace—six ordinary
days a week, followed by the blessed day of the Sabbath in Jerusalem.

A visitor could admire this young woman without feeling an obligation to please her with anything but his admiration. Lovely lady,
sweet children, sad husband. Things might be better someday, and
the torn dolls repaired or hidden away, and new dolls to console Sidra
for the suffering she could not understand. Hannah stood vigil over
her in the dark, feeling no wiser than her daughter, silent.

A NINETY-SIX-YEAR-OLD BIG SISTER

When I last visited Cleveland, Aunt Anna was ninety-six or maybe only ninety-five years old and asked to be reminded: How many children you got, Herbert?

Five.

You married?

Not now.

Herbert! Did you say five? Are you going to have any more children?

I held her hand and looked into the milky, tensely squinting eyes. The hand was hard, dry, small, and firm, and it gripped back. The hair was thin. The attention was complete.

Herbert! You deaf? I told you: You going to have any more kids?

I won't if you won't, Aunt Anna, I said. She held both my hands to keep from falling as the laughter vibrated through the wires and filaments of her body. Her children—a retired doctor, a retired law-yer, a retired teacher, a retired businessman, a widow—pushed around her.

I'm only laughing and choking a little, she said. Go away. Leave me alone to laugh with this boy.

My mother, who is eighty-two or so, talked with her every day on the telephone. They exchanged the gossip of an enormous family—births, deaths, marriages, quarrels, wills, children, children, children unto the third or fourth generation, spreading out from Cleveland and beyond, ripples on a gigantic pool. These years there is a great deal of complaint about the problems of other people's aging, not theirs.

Aunt Anna's children worried about her living alone. But she refused to move in with one of them or (out of the question, you crazy?) into a "home." When they hired someone to stay with her, she fired the woman—Who do I need a cleaning? What do I need a cleaning? I did all my life for other people, I can't do for myself?

Someone in the family went to the market and visited her daily. She consented to these attentions.

I want my independence, she said. At ninety-four, I can't do what I want yet? I still got to watch out for other people?

You said you were ninety-five, Ma, the retired lawyer said.

So you tell me. I know different. I don't feel ninety-five yet.

You don't look it—does she? the retired teacher asked.

A family consultation, she remarked. Kids wet on my shoulder and now they argue I'm too old. But they retired, I didn't retire. I can still do my floors—what can they do?

She had always been small; she shrank as if time were a zinc tub and she were wool and washed in hot water. The family worried about her eating. At a country club wedding for the daughter of a niece, we sat gathered at one large table. My mother and Aunt Anna were shouting the news together. The retired children urged her to eat. I returned from the buffet with a plate of scallops and Aunt Anna found them, began to pluck them up, and chew and swallow, one after the other. She sighed. Her fork got busy. She had never eaten shellfish in her life, but this was the sort of country club where the Jews eat shellfish on weekends or special occasions. Her fork flew like the needle on a treadle-operated sewing machine.

Her children watched in that state of dilemma which is akin to horror in people who normally find the rules congenial, following them with comfort in the good sense of traditional regulations. They worried about her eating. They worried about her nourishment. They liked to see her doing justice to her plate. They begged her to eat as, many years ago, she had begged them to eat. But they knew she would die if she learned she was eating shellfish.

She finished the plate of soft, squirmy, sweetish, nonkosher flesh.

She turned to my mother, scraping her fork around and finding none left on the dish. She said: Frieda! You like to get me some more of those nice noodles?

An immediate high-level family treaty resolved the matter. Emergency situations and good nutrition required a special deal with the law. The children would be bringing cooked scallops to her house daily now. Rules are made for people. Those nice noodles, they're so slippery, why not use a spoon, Ma?

Aunt Anna's husband, not a great success in life, had died years ago. Before he checked out, she was to be pitied, raising a numerous family with a husband who seemed like one of the children, only more boastful. During the Depression my parents carried baskets of food to them. The family didn't believe in Relief; the less contact with the state, the better. Aunt Anna's husband went out for a walk while the baskets were unloaded. Along with the baskets of food, filling the car each Sunday, came my brother and me. Sometimes we slept over at her house. She wouldn't let us play with matches. She wouldn't let us set the garage afire. She had, even then, thick glasses, thin hair, and a continual smile. I wondered what she was smiling about. I didn't resent too much not being allowed to burn things because her oatmeal cookies were refreshing after my mother's oatmeal cookies. I liked the dates she used instead of raisins. I decided the dates made her smile, and my liking her cookies more than my mother's made her smile more. They sometimes debated dates versus raisins, but it never came to a serious break between the sisters.

A few years earlier my grandfather had lived with Aunt Anna. He was white-bearded, said to be a rabbi, and spoke no English. He had never worked in America. I used the word *white* for his beard, but I knew he came from afar and it was snowfrost in his beard which made the whiteness. In America he played chess in the synagogue

with the other nonrabbis. Toward the end of his nonrabbinical career
he gave up chess for checkers. When we played, I liked the part where
I kinged him, also the jumping and skipping two jumps part. Although he smiled through the snowfrost during our checker contests,
he liked best, at this stage of his life, to pee outside in the yard. He
loved the dense green fields of the Ukraine and, very old now, began
to think that's where he was.

Nevertheless, he understood that I was four years old, needing
cookies along with the checkers, and he conspired with me to steal
them between meals, during the few hours when no eating was supposed to be going on while the world prepared for later eating.

After stolen cookies he took me into the backyard for a healthful
stroll in the Ukraine.

Aunt Anna came out to find us and bring us inside for our naps.
Since we had already eaten our cookies, we had no right to more; but
since they were good for us, especially the dates, as not everyone fully
understands, we were allowed another two or three with our warm
milk. She couldn't afford Ovaltine, due to hard times, but plain milk
could do the job. The milk should not boil. She touched it with her
wrist to make sure it was the right temperature—kids and old men
have wristlike throats.

Sometimes, if we didn't stay overnight while my parents took some
vacation from their two noisome sons, we drove back through Cleveland after the last Sunday meal and my brother and I fell asleep
watching the rhythmic patterns of streetlamps and telephone wires,
streetlamps, wires, until we were carried up to bed. My mother, Aunt
Anna's baby sister, listened respectfully to her advice about childbear-
ing. My brother and I fought her Ukrainian scientific theories about
enemas, feeding, and protective clothing, although we gradually gave
up lighting fires with kitchen matches. I'm not sure what convinced
us, maybe other things to play with. We formed a united front.

When Aunt Anna's children went off to Ohio State University to
prepare for their various professions, they kept close contact with
Cleveland, the fount of family. They sent the laundry home by mail.
In return they received, along with clean shirts and underwear, mason
jars of stewed prunes. A child can get constipated on that school food
far from home. Occasionally, unfortunately, the jar broke in transit,

although carefully wrapped in clean laundry, and sticky and tensely straining mornings were the result. Aunt Anna was not discouraged by the malice and stupidity of postal employees, and the proof of her wisdom is that almost everyone turned out to have an active career and a healthy stomach, if you don't count a few ulcers, acid conditions, cases of colitis, chronic constipation, diverticulitis, and generalized gas problems which are the inevitable reward of mind-stretching professional work.

When her father the nonrabbi died, it was a little like the future death of her husband. More room in the house for the children, more time for them, more cookies, dates, prunes, and space for mending the socks and taking out hems. Aunt Anna cared for men without requiring them.

As I grew older, I still watched the rhythm of the streetlamps but didn't sleep on the long drive from the East Side to the West Side. I noticed her children becoming successful, heavier, married, and the family expanding mightily, exponentially, as the children begat children. I left Cleveland long ago. On visits I saw Aunt Anna unchanging while her children and grandchildren grew older. She already had bald grandsons. She still lived alone, cooked, baked, darned, and talked on the telephone.

One of her sons gave her a tape recorder and asked her to dictate the story of her life for an oral history project. She talked for hours and hours about the past—poverty, migrations, triumphs—but she found greater pleasure in telephoning my mother to discuss the events of the day, not the past. Someone was eating good. Someone was not. Someone had a good job. Someone was getting a better one. Someone was pregnant. When would someone else wake up and stop doing whatever he or she was doing?

When she pointed out that my brother and I had left Cleveland, but her children could always be reached in a matter of minutes, she was only naming the facts. She wasn't gloating. She wasn't accusing my mother of total failure. She pitied boys whose ancestors came all the way from Kamenets-Podolski to a wonderful place like Cleveland and still something drove them on to San Diego, San Francisco, what kinds of names are those?

My mother, of course, argued her side of the story and received the counsel of her big sister. Family was all. Life is clear, painful, confused, and busy. Some things are better left out of the discussion, but neither of them could think of what these things might be.

My mother loved talking with her on the telephone. A little nagging, a little nudging, a little bragging, a little complaint—a nice contact to start the morning. She always had the time, no matter how busy she was with her own cooking and sewing and taking care. Aunt Anna was decisive and clear, and fun, unlike other people my mother could and frequently did name. Aunt Anna sat alone in her house, good riddance to the helpers she fired, peering through the lens chunks of her glasses, talking on the telephone with the amplifier attached, occasionally eating a nice hot noodle or two if someone had dropped some by in an unmarked container, talking with her children, her sister, her nieces, her nephews, her grandchildren. The days were too short for all she had to do and all the advice she had to communicate. If someone tried to push her into ninety-six when she knew for a positive fact she was only ninety-five or maybe ninety-four, she grew irritated, but it didn't last. The kids always gave in. She couldn't hold grudges. Grudges tend to age a person fast, and at her time in life she didn't want to age unnecessarily.

Even my own children, whom she almost never saw, took a place in her system. She transmitted orders to my mother to pass on to me so that I could act on them; immediately would be best. I usually reported back with the advice to leave this stuff alone, she didn't know enough about my life, and my mother translated this into language Aunt Anna could understand: They are fine, delightful, regular in habits, good in school, and send all their love.

Is he doing what I say? she would ask anxiously. I can't be responsible, Frieda, unless he listens to me. Your Herbert was never such a good listener.

I was on my way to France when I last saw her. What you need to go to the Old Country? she asked. We got out okay, didn't we? Why you need to go back?

France isn't the Old Country, Aunt Anna.

It's over that way, isn't it? Over there? I remember the Cossacks, plus no fresh vegetables in the winter. Isn't it winter now? Are you crazy wasting your time in the Old Country with the Cossacks and the potatoes is all you'll get?

Well, I'll let you know, Aunt Anna.

Have a good time. It's nice to travel if you're a young man. I bet nothing looks like it used to anymore. And one good thing about traveling, five is enough already these days, you can't have kids while you're traveling. Do you have a wife?

Not now.

So maybe you'll find a nice one in the Old Country.

That's not what I'm going for, Aunt Anna.

Here, put your face close to me so I can see if you deserve a new wife. Let me look. Where'd you get all the hair? You need money for a haircut? Okay, I guess you better try to find one in the Old Country.

A haircut?

A wife, dummy. But not one of those just wants a free ticket to Cleveland. They take advantage of nice young American boys in the Old Country. All they dream about is Cleveland. You better send me her picture first, also something about the family, a few details.

I'm going to France, Aunt Anna—

And get yourself a haircut or she'll think you're a bum. Which would show she's got a good head on her shoulders, if your mother asks me.

She was smiling at something she was not saying and I was not answering. There was a secret life beyond her advice-giving. What passages opened in her head when the house was quiet, the telephone at rest, her children not poking about, breathing up her air and bothering her thoughts?

The ancient past in muddy Russia. The grit, mystery, noise, and hope of America. Where was she now? Children getting old. Babies whose names it was not necessary to remember. A husband with a head that shook—long dead. Another day. Another night. All this is not so bad unless you think about it.

I know little of my own secret thoughts below the line of rumination and desire. How should I know hers?

A few weeks after I last saw her, Aunt Anna was moving through her house, perhaps to the kitchen, more likely to the telephone, and fell against the piano bench. Fell; broke her hip; thought she would die. I don't know how long she lay there until someone found her. She was still clear in her mind and annoyed. I don't know why a broken hip should be the final disaster for so many old people. Her son, the retired doctor, explained about calcium loss due to lack of exercise and nutrition and something normal in the aging process. The immobilized injured old person tends to die. Before Aunt Anna followed this normal pattern, she said good-bye, still alert and smiling and complaining about her difficulties in hearing and understanding, to her children and her surviving sister, my mother. She said she would die. She knew it was time now, no matter whether she was ninety-five or ninety-six, or even only ninety-four, as she preferred. She waited to make sure she had forgotten nobody. And then she died.

On the telephone to San Francisco my mother said: I was her little sister and she called me every day. She called me her little sister. I feel bad about fooling her with those scallop noodles, but she had to eat and keep her calcium up. She was really ninety-six.

My mother is eighty-two. She says she's only eighty-one.

I've lost my big sister, she said. I talked to her every day. I miss her.

Even your father, she said, and you know he never goes out anymore, he wanted to go to her funeral. Even your father. Even your father. But he can't know anymore how much I miss my big sister.

ANNIQUE

What a peculiar time to arrive in Paris. On Bastille Day the Revolution is sort of remembered, the descendants of those who tore down the Bastille are dancing in the streets until dawn, for any good reason at all, and Dan Shaper of Cleveland, Ohio, joined them despite his jet lag. Then he went to bed.

But at four in the morning, time zones bumping against each other in his head, still hearing the music in the streets, he got up to walk among the lovers, the drunks, and those like him who could not sleep in the midsummer heat and didn't want to. A few blocks from his hotel, on the Île St.-Louis, in front of the Alsatian restaurant near the footbridge leading to the looming shadow of Notre-Dame, the Communist rock band was still hard at work, pumping out knockoffs of old Rolling Stone hits. There was a wooden platform strung with colored lights. A giant ideological girl danced with a contribution box for *Humanité*, the Party newspaper, but most people danced with other human beings. Shaper stood to the side, weary, alert, not unpleasantly confused, and believed he saw the first pink streaks of daylight in the sky above the cathedral. Street vendors were selling off their last sandwiches, sweets, and drinks at bargain prices. He noticed a fair young woman, blond, her skin very pale under the garish red and purple bulbs strung over the dancers; like him, she was just watching things. Their eyes met.

He had no right to meet a stranger's eyes at 4:30 A.M., of course, so he looked away. It was only that he happened to be interested in the fact that she was wearing what looked like a boy's shirt, buttoned to the neck, and white American-style jeans, and her fair hair was pinned back, and that she was lovely. He had not meant to meet her eyes.

A moment later, to his astonishment, she was standing flat out in front of him and saying something which he couldn't understand, owing to the fury of the French Communist version of "Leddy Jen," Sweet Lady Jane. She repeated: "Aren't you the Moroccan film director—"

"No," he said in his pretty good French, "I'm an American journalist who just arrived in Paris today."

"Then you're not Moustapha, are you?"

Laughing, he said, "Oh, but I wish I were!"

And very quickly she was remarking how well he spoke French and he was confessing that everybody in Cleveland, Ohio, also confused him with Moustapha Ahmed Ben-Moussa, it was a real problem, but actually he worked on a paper called the Cleveland *Plain Dealer*—

"*Le Plen Diller? La Terre de Clèves?*"

And they were both giggling and enjoying teasing together and he was saying that Paris is really a northern city (acute crack reporter observation), so at midsummer the dawn comes early, doesn't it? when her *friend* got tired of this and came up to join the conversation.

The friend was a young architect, also blond, with a little wisp of blond mustache, and he worked for the Paris municipal art restoration licensing department; and although he had a motorcycle parked nearby, on which they had ridden to this street dance, he seemed to Shaper to be a total wimp. And the girl's color, equally fair, did not seem wimpy at all. That's how it is; they should have found opposites, opposite colors, shouldn't they?

"Where are you staying in Paris?" she asked Shaper.

"She's leaving on her vacation tomorrow," the wimp told him.

"At the Hôtel du Vieux-Marais," Shaper said.

And the wimp said, "If you don't get some rest, Annique, you'll be tired."

"Evidently," she said, climbing onto the jump seat of the motorcycle, shrugging her narrow shoulders, lifting the mesh of hair out of the collar of the funny shirt, unbuttoning the top button now to show a clavicle, a collarbone, to the breeze and to Shaper, lifting her eyebrows in a shrug which echoed the shrug of the shoulders, making a little pout concerning her lover-the-wimp's jealousy, and moving her lips in a way which confirmed a hope growing in Shaper's jet-lagged heart. What the lips were silently repeating, like a good student making sure she remembered the correct answer: *Hôtel du Vieux-Marais.*

As they roared off, wheels spinning carnival debris, the street dance was over for Shaper. He felt very light heading back to the hotel. He felt like having a good bath and then a good sleep.

When the telephone by his bed woke him up, the morning sun was pouring through a gap in the curtains at his window. "There is a lady for you downstairs. . . ."

"Please ask her to come up."

He rushed about, pulling curtains, flinging the doorlike windows wide open, taking care of matters in the bathroom, but he didn't have to hurry so. She took a few minutes getting there because she was arranging for the Portuguese woman in the kitchen to accompany her with a tray which included the following pastimes and occupations for getting over embarrassment while getting better acquainted: a pitcher of coffee, a pitcher of hot milk, two glasses of orange juice, a little plate of croissants and buttered bread, a little pot of jam, and a larger pot of something he had never before seen at breakfast in France—raspberries with honey. There was a clutter of dishes to take care of all this, including an extra small pitcher of cream for the berries.

The Portuguese woman, kindly and thoughtful and heavily mustached, left Shaper's visitor to set breakfast out as she liked. Shaper was in pajamas and the lady was in clothes very different from her sweaty Cub Scout shirt of last night. She was wearing a linen skirt with a kind of crumpled linen jacket over a silken tee shirt, but she removed the jacket and put it on his suitcase, not wanting to get raspberries on it.

Soon she also removed the silken tee shirt and the linen skirt, not needing coffee or raspberry stains on these holiday clothes. What remained on her body was nothing much worth mentioning.

Her hand slipped under the drawstring of the pajamas of the journalist from the *Plain Dealer* and he felt a number of nearly overwhelming physical reflexes, one of them being to shut his eyes and the other being the opposite, to keep his eyes open so that none of this could ever be forgotten or turned into vagueness. She was very precise.

Then for a while they just chatted. Did he really look like a Moroccan film director? Well, sort of. She had worked on a film in North Africa; no, she was nothing glamorous, not an actress or a model; she was a *standardiste* for French television—a kind of receptionist. "Because you're beautiful?" he asked.

She shrugged negligently. "Because I'm lazy."

Last night, with her shirt and jeans and the jump seat of the motorcycle, the gleam of the dance on her forehead and nose, she looked too young and probably she was. But now, when she told him she had received the *bachot*—high school graduation—seven years ago and worked in this job for five years, he was relieved to decide she was sort of a grown-up. She certainly was. They finished the raspberries but not the coffee, planning to have cold coffee later. He loved the way she tipped up her bottom, another raspberry, when she carefully put the breakfast tray out of the way on the floor by the bed.

The ridges of her mouth, her palate, her teeth gave up none of her secrets although he searched them diligently. Her tongue was smooth, yielding, unyielding. She was entertained by his impertinence, and when he finished, she sighed. That sigh—relief, pleasure, regret—was as close to a secret as she seemed ready to tell him. If he liked, he could find a suspicion of distant sadness in that sigh.

Perhaps there was another time in her life allotted to the sharing of secrets; or more likely, none. No time, no need, no one. Or perhaps he had her all wrong in thinking this way while she gave him her body all right. She was the most secretive person he had ever met.

But then he had never met anyone like her, either, so how should he expect to know anything?

That sigh again. He loved her breath whispering out with whatever part of her soul it carried. She was singing softly, as if to herself.

"*Qui parle de l'amour a des yeux tristes—*"

"I understand that."

"Do you?"

"Who speaks of love has sad eyes," he said in English.

"It's a song in French," she said, "and it comes from a poem from the heart. It's only a little song."

"I told you I understand," he said with a touch of irritability.

The afternoon heat radiating from the July walls outside was baffled by flapping curtains, by the good luck of catching breezes down the Seine, by their bathing, by their not caring about the heat. In Cleveland, even in the *Plain Dealer*'s little world—smaller now that the Cleveland *Press* had stopped publishing—people were concerned about avoiding sweat except on the racquetball court. Paris was, as most people noticed early on, different from Cleveland. In Cleveland no one danced the night through on either the fourth or the fourteenth of July, or if people did, they had a backyard barbecue the next day. This Bastille Day breakfast picnic seldom occurred in Shaper's experience of Parma, Lakewood, Cleveland Heights, or even the luxury highrises of the Gold Coast. And the breeze off Lake Erie seemed, oh, mottled after this breeze off the Seine near the Île St.-Louis.

"*C'est autre,*" he said, and she nodded, understanding his inaccurate French, which meant to whisper: *This is something else.*

He told her he had long ago, in college, read a story called "French Girls Are Vicious."

"Some might be," she said, nodding sagely, her hair soft against her shoulder.

He told her people used to think all French girls were called Fifi.

"None are anymore," she said. She propped herself up on one elbow. "How old are you?"

"Then may I ask you a whole lot of questions?"

"Of course," she said, falling back. "But I won't answer them."

"Forty-three," he said.

She did a rapid calculation. "Not quite old enough to be my father, even if you hurried," she said.

"That answers one of my questions, too."

"Twenty-six," she said. "Because you didn't ask."

"Last night," he said, "with that holiday sparkle and how late it was, you looked like a little girl—"

"And now," she said, impatient with discussion just before her vacation in Bruges, across the border in Belgium, where the canals were filled with solemn and boring swans and swanlets and her cousins sat nearby and didn't feed them, "and now, this. Let me do this, please."

Mostly silence.

At the end of the afternoon, after the sun had made a long arc across the sky and they had finished bathing together again, lying crumpled together again, telling the Portuguese lady they did not require that she enter to make the bed, and they were finishing the last of the cold coffee and a few stubs of bread and butter, he said, "Don't go!"

He didn't mean just now, she had no intention of leaving just now; she understood what he meant. "It's my vacation time," she said. "In French bureaucracy, all this is scheduled in advance. Isn't it that way in America?"

"Yes," he said, "but then let me come with you."

She laughed and touched him with a tolerant soothing on the back of his neck and said, "Oh, you didn't dry yourself, you count too much on evaporation." And then she explained that she wasn't leaving quite yet, not for an hour or so. And that he could not go with her because it was not arranged in that way.

"What a loss!" he said.

And again that light flight of laughter, "You've missed the point. If I weren't going away, I wouldn't be here."

"What's your full name?"

"Annique Valérie."

"Is that your real name?"

"Again!" she cried. "Again you miss the point."

He realized he had better stop all lines of stupid questioning and imploring if he wanted her to stay with him for another hour, crumpled like this on the sheets, sunk and lively as birds in their nest. He had better miss no more points.

Her mother was Flemish, which accounted for the fair skin, the light hair, the milky body. Her father was, as it happened, a film maker who had deserted the family when she was small, probably accounting for various things which Shaper was not presently in the business of analyzing, except that he did wonder why her first greeting to him had been to ask if he was a movie director. "Is your father French?" he asked.

"Not Moroccan!" she said, laughing and sticking out her tongue at him. And pulling his nose. And scratching his chest with light strokes of her fingernails. And then lying still, waiting for new moves or new funny remarks by the gentleman from Cleveland, Ohio (if they weren't funny to him, at least they were occasions for fun in Annique Valérie).

"Annique Valérie, Annique Valérie," he said.

"If that's my real name," she said.

"You're wonderful," he said.

"That's missing the point, too," she said. "But I'm being nice because you're so nice, that's all."

One more bath in the high small tub, fitting together so cozily with practice, like on a motorcycle, but closer, lukewarm water, no soap this time, and then she was fresh in her linen skirt, her silken blouse, her short linen jacket, her high-heeled sling shoes, and smiling, and saying good-bye to him. Wishing him a good trip to Paris, a happy Bastille Day, many happy ones in the future.

"Adieu."

No one had ever said that to him before. It is said on deathbeds. It seems to mean good-bye forever.

Men find it difficult to keep their great adventures a secret and Dan Shaper was no exception. Upon his return to Cleveland and the *Plain Dealer*, he told his friend and editor Jack Ashbury, as they drank coffee in front of a blinking blue word processing terminal, feet on Jack's Formica-topped desk, both of them busily not smoking anymore, as much as he could remember about Annique. "She was so beautiful. She was so sweet. She seemed so happy with me."

"You know what this is, laddie? It's a Shaggy Frenchgirl story you've told me. I don't get it."

"What's so hard to get?"

"You were happy with her."

That was it, of course, rephrased for the better, much more accu-

rately, a task which a good editor should always be ready to perform.
"Yes," he said.

"Then why didn't you put the heat on—?"

"What?"

"I mean, bring her back here, man! Bring her home with you!"

Shaper started to laugh. Here he thought Jack had been listening,
and yet he hadn't understood the meaning of the incident. "You've
missed the point!" he said. "Jack, tell me something. Do I have sad
eyes?"

"Always, laddie. I've been meaning to tell you for years, but it never
came up."

After a few months, something like this was what he had left of her
—a memory in Cleveland of Annique laughing, informing, and cor-
recting him in Paris about the foolishness of those who worry about
love. Her laughter. A taste of raspberries on her breath.

THE
SMALLEST PART

Their marriage was tender, practical, playful, and finally its body was obscured to both of them by the birth of their child and the convulsions of the time. People need freedom, at least I do, she said. Neither of them had expected this. Their divorce was amicable and mysterious.

She had a vision of herself as a Single Parent, fulfilling her destiny perhaps tragically, in the company of other women harassed by history and fate. (But now one could choose.) He had a vision of himself as abandoned by the woman who was once his delight. Suffering little hemorrhages, the day would suddenly be bloodied by loneliness for his wife, for his child.

He kept his daughter with him on Sunday, a claustrophobic, sticky, steamy long day of nonrest. He missed her just as much Monday morning when she went to school. He visited her on Tuesday and Thursday at dinnertime.

Since it was amicable, which doesn't mean friendly, he took her out of her mother's apartment; or if the weather was bad, the child tired, homework to do, mother permitted that they huddle together in the child's bedroom. He told stories. Father and daughter giggled. They used pens, paper, books, records. He liked this mini-game of house with his daughter better than their wandering Sabbaths.

Sometimes his wife—he had trouble saying ex-wife or former wife —was irritated by the noises they made and would ask him please, please, why don't you just go out someplace? Ordinarily she liked to "deemphasize" sweets, but in her desperation she even recommended going out for an ice cream cone. This, he supposed, meant that Single Parent was preoccupied with the reactionary dilemmas of a lover or a nonlover. She became fretful at such times, sometimes waiting at the telephone, sometimes not liking the telephone when it rang. Men were a burden to her now, and she alternated between jeans and boots and defiant, old-fashioned feminine drag, even to doing her nails and wearing a long skirt. This English country loveliness gave him a pang when she greeted him in it, hair brushed, skin glowing, long arms and legs moving with a grace subtly responsive to the consciousness of good clothes.

He did not understand her. He could not trace the meaning of jeans (rump awkwardly bound by studded pockets), boots, hair awry, against her occasional extravagance of décor. Her behind wobbled when she hustled up the stairs; then the next week she glided ahead of him, elegant and proud. She moved too fast. It was not his business to understand her anymore, especially since he had done such a poor job of it when it was his business.

He felt a loss of his independence of being as he slipped and struggled, failed to sleep and failed to wake, passed white nights and gray days in misery. This misery came of love, and he hated it. To kill himself—how to do such a thing? with a child he cherished every day? —was impossible. Yet he found himself wishing for an accident, so that he could not blame himself. Ah, this was foolish. And so he struggled with himself; it replaced the struggle with his wife. He fought against love, he fought against grief, he even fought against anger. They were all linked. He reminded himself when touched, moved, overwhelmed by the sight and smell of her, or a sight and smell which recalled her, or passing their old house or eating their foods or walking on their streets: Don't do this, don't feel. First he succeeded in removing her from the struggle; he translated it within, to himself, between himself; then he began to succeed in winning it. He lost love. He lost anger. She became a limited idea, like a newspaper death notice. He did not lose sorrow entirely, but he chipped away at it: Don't, don't, don't, he would remind himself in the middle of the night; don't feel; and then dreamlessly he could sleep. Perhaps he dreamt, but he did not remember the dreams.

When he was with another woman, he was only with that woman. He forgot their names, but he remembered to exist only in what happened then and there. The struggle was still within himself. There was no question of love in the pleasure he often felt, a pleasure like dreamless sleep.

He defended himself against the invasions of love and anger. He paid a price.

It was not neat, and that was okay, too. Probably it shouldn't be neat. That would be too dangerous. And so he allowed himself to feel sorrow at the loss of grief. He named it regret, but it was still sorrow. He took a chance in allowing this, but it was a necessary risk. He could no longer be loving, and he had to pay the price of loss. But he could not entirely give up sorrow in order to survive. That would be too much of a price, even in this cause.

And so, with all these penalties and losses, abandoning the goods of hope and joy, risks of love, risks of anger, thickening memories day by day and year after year, he believed life was now once more worth living. There was the air of early morning. There were certain tastes. He climbed into the newspaper with a certain satisfaction: other lives out there, a nervous large world. He treasured his hours with his daughter. It was interesting, he thought, very interesting indeed, that these things could be enough for a man. In the past he would never have believed it. He had expected something different. This, like the newspaper, constituted very interesting, distracting, objective information.

He read the regret which lay beneath as he read the obituaries in the newspaper. It was not grief, and yet it was still grief. It was merely regret for the disappearing past, rapidly diminishing into itself without his participation.

The chief rule for rescue of himself was not to think about her.

That was essential. He began to succeed in this enterprise—not remembering, not imagining, not conjecturing, not taking an imaginary place in her life. He began to succeed. As compensation for this withdrawal from her, he could think more about himself. What might have been a boring vanity seemed to become—an interesting vanity. For example, when he thought about himself, he was surprised at the success with women obtained by a melancholic, bedraggled, preoccupied, recently divorced, gray-flecked man. They liked him! (Some did.) They wanted to help. There is often something agreeable about a disaster. However, he didn't care about the women with whom he had this success. And this was probably the reason for it.

Or maybe these women just liked to gather round the disaster for the fun of it—watching the building crumble and entranced by how the embers flare up.

Sometimes, when all the conjunctions were right, his wife invited him to sit at the kitchen table, to have dinner with her and their daughter. He had no pride. When she asked him, he did, although afterward he often felt a new sharp sadness within the melancholia he carried almost by habit these days. It would be seasoned for a time by fresh regret. Nevertheless, he had to eat, didn't he? Even at the butcher block table they had chosen together one Saturday afternoon in May—didn't he?

Then one day, after such a supper—a Single Parent dinner of hamburgers and tomatoes and fruit and warmed-over coffee—she asked if he would like to put their daughter to bed. He would. He stayed. He wondered if she merely wanted a burden lifted, the one of good-nights, glasses of water, important First Grade gossip, but no, he smelled fresh coffee, he heard the grinder, she was making coffee.

She didn't offer him any yet. When he came back from their daughter's bedroom after the last, final kiss, and the one after that, and said good night, thanks for the dinner, she asked: Would you like a glass of wine?

Yes.

She wrestled with the bottle. Would you uncork it?

Yes.

He sank into the deep grandfatherly chair which used to be his. She sat on the couch and crossed her legs and uncrossed them and smiled. He thought how long it had been since he had seen her lips and teeth slightly stained by wine, and how nice it used to be when they would sit looking at each other, thinking they understood each other without words, not understanding each other even with words, smiling, loving each other and drinking wine.

She patted the pillow beside her on the couch. Come here.

Obediently, good dog, he came to sit beside her. He asked a question about their daughter's school. She shook her head stubbornly, that was not it at all, and her eyes were also smiling at him, as she said: Your lips and teeth are pink.

They kissed very lightly. He tasted the wine on her mouth. If it was pink on his mouth, it was red on hers.

During the first months of their separation, almost until their divorce was final, they occasionally made love. At first he would think this a reconciliation and she would fall into a rage about his presumption. Then he would take it only for what it was, as she said he had to take it, but he would grieve and weep when he went home to his own bed afterward, which was where she wanted him to go. A few times, when he was distraught and weak with sorrow, with regret for the lost dream of true love, she would watch him with narrow eyes, how boyish of him, and offer him a sympathy sexing. He accepted this several times. Then, although she never reproached him for it, he learned it was better not to accept it.

Now time had passed, he was familiar with sleeping alone, he was familiar with sleeping with many different women, either was okay, he was used to his life. He could say little more than that he was used to the second half of his life.

So when she, on this autumn evening more than two years after their divorce, in a way he dreamily recalled from the time of separation, decided they should now make love, his thoughts were: Not to be depressed tomorrow. Not to make anything of this. Not to care.

With these negatives in mind, too much freight for fun, he felt somewhat dulled and lacking in energy. But it was easy and comfortable to hold her in his arms, to rock her, to stroke and knead her with his hands, with his fingers, while her arch twisted and her slipper fell off, to kiss her not very much but to breathe on her and let his mouth follow the pleasant paths of her body. Suddenly she jumped up. He waited. Ah. Something she surely had to do with other callers: Make sure the child was asleep.

Then she went to the bathroom. When she returned, she was wearing only a robe. You're still dressed? she asked. Come.

He said: No, come here.

He didn't want to go to their bed.

She let him play with her. What he did was not so much make love; he was thinking of other things, even of other women, although with other women he often thought of her; it was not love he was doing with her. He was too dreamy and distant. He was overweighted with negatives. He simply engaged in diddling.

Surely she felt his abstraction.

He thought about the fatigue of driving home after lovemaking, the definition of the bachelor—he comes home from a different direction every morning—and he was in no hurry to leave off the repetitious, gentle, professional gestures he was performing. He could have been a masseur or a doctor. Nevertheless, he remembered her body, and he knew where to go. But he didn't go there. He simply played, in and out, round and about, treading byways, marking out the slim-fleshed skeleton.

He smelled the wine.

He smelled the coffee from the kitchen.

He smelled rich, thick, female smells of pleasure coming from her body. He didn't care. He smelled arousal on himself. He didn't care. Where did you learn that? Where did you learn that? Oh, it's good, she said.

He didn't care to answer, but he climbed into the rhythm of what he was doing, let the metronome tick, and he did it and did it, now thinking not about others but about her. But not thinking very much about her. She was just there. He was just there. And they were just making love.

And then it happened. She began to scream and toss and heave her body—thinking of other things, he had moved himself to press against the place which always relieved her toward sleep—and her eyes were open, her mouth was open, her tongue was longer than he had known, now her eyes were squeezed shut and the scream seemed to come from an absence. . . . Shush, he said, you don't want to wake—

Oh, oh, oh.

And then she subsided. When she seemed nearly asleep, he guided her to the bed, her head resting on his shoulder, drowsy, like a little girl too long in the bath, and he tucked her in and said good night. No, he said, he would not stay. She smiled. He went to the kitchen and took a swallow of the cold coffee from the Pyrex pitcher. He left.

Driving home, he took to his old bad habit: ruminating. Figuring it out. He called it thinking, but it was more like an obsessive daydream, the foolish, unquenchable child in the gray-flecked man. She had smiled in relief because he was not staying, because he was not making the mistake of making anything of this. Well, he knew. He might be stupid, but he could be educated.

This time perhaps he really had been thinking.

And so they formed a habit.

Not on every visit ("visitation"), but perhaps once a week, or maybe twice, when it seemed convenient, he would make love to her, he would make a love drill, a love exercise with her, when it seemed convenient, if she had nothing else for the evening, if he had nothing else for the evening. They never discussed it. She seemed deeply grateful at first, not for the lovemaking, of course, which was her due, but for his making nothing more of it than what it was. She was confident in her climaxes—not the little whimpers of their marriage, but howls and thrashings and bitings. She was probably sure he wouldn't do this again and again unless he also wanted to. And of course, he did want to, although he was not sure why.

Her slim, lank body began to feel like beef under his fingers, his tongue, his body. He was far from all this, but nevertheless, he understood that something new was happening to him, to this person who was far from what was happening to him. He was glad. He was careful not to show too much pleasure. He had liked to laugh and chatter and roar when they made love. Now he said nothing, he tended to business, and at his own climax, he stifled his moans and only his rasping breath could have been recorded. He did not feel it would be polite to give her words of love; not polite to her, not polite to himself.

It was supremely okay. His melancholia was lifting. He enjoyed his girlfriends, and would laugh, chatter, and roar with them when the occasion arose.

He began to feel well at last. In a way, he had a family. The long Sundays with his daughter were filled with adventures—junk food, children's theater, picnics—and he enjoyed them, and enjoyed dropping her back at her mother's house. Once he even took a shower before he made love to his former wife; never, however, would he stay the night afterward.

For that whole autumn she seemed bemused and at rest, and waited with no impatience, not entering into the games, when father and daughter played. When he heard the grinder and smelled fresh coffee, he knew this was one of their evenings. He put the child to bed (good night, good night, sweet thing). He went in to his wife. He liked the smell of the coffee, but if they didn't drink it first, he usually didn't warm it up later.

He was very patient with his wife. He fell into a state of abstraction. He would notice almost with surprise that he was aroused, and that he was very aroused, and that suddenly this was an extreme of pleasure. Sometimes she scratched and clawed at him. Once she lay there shuddering, pulling the blanket up to her chin, and asked if he would like to spend the night, they could cuddle and just sleep—

I'm not tired, he said. I don't think I could sleep. I would disturb you.

That's all right.

It would be confusing for *her* to wake up in the morning and find us. . . .

You're right.

When winter came, he began to wonder if this would go on forever. It did not interfere with his affairs with other women; at least, he thought it didn't, yet he felt nothing much but laughter or pleasure with the other women. However, that had been the case before, too. And the depression seemed to have lifted. Or at least he thought it had.

Sometimes he wondered what this must be doing to his wife's search. Was she free? Was she free of love and marriage? Was she free to be herself alone? Perhaps she was.

And then one night, eyes flashing, she asked him, as if it were a great joke: Why don't you ever at least take me to the movies?

And he, also joking, said to her: Because I think our marriage is in trouble.

Acknowledging their divorce, they went on making love. He was not sure she meant the joke in the same way he did. Of course, since they never had understood each other, this was in their tradition. And now that he had stopped trying, he too took pleasure, relish, even excitement, in making love to this stranger who, he used to think, was the closest person to him on earth.

Now, of course, their daughter was the dearest person, and as to the closest, there was no one.

One cold late night, as he drove homeward through deserted streets, damp glistening on the streetlights, he found himself uttering a thankful prayer: Not by might nor by power, O Lord, nor by love, does the spirit turn; but by indifference.

And this was the only time during those months when the old sadness returned. This prayer of gratitude brought back all the misery of loss. For the next two weeks he left as soon as he said good night to their daughter.

Why are you so busy these days? Are you in love? she asked him.

No, just busy, he said.

But then they began again. It was like lovers returning to one another after a vacation. And he did not begin on her on the couch and then go to the bedroom. He led her to the bedroom, or she simply walked to the bedroom, dropping her clothes, and he followed, dropping his own clothes in a careless pile near the bed, near the dresser which used to contain his socks, shirts, underwear, and which she now used for all the new things she had bought during her periods of more elaborate décor. He returned naked to that pile of clothes in the dark, dressing rapidly as she slept, slipping down the stairs and out into the cool nighttime street, and then breathing deeply, his face to the sky, before opening his car door.

Let me pursue where love leads me, he thought, so long as it is not love. And this is not a prayer, he thought, it is an observation. He did not want to suffer another episode of sullen grief, when he used to pray for his death, only asking that he not have the responsibility of it. Now he would take the responsibility for following out whatever finally might emerge.

And then he felt the grief. Because there seemed to be no way he could bury it, drown it, stifle it. Why? Why now? Why this time? Because he had loved his wife with the passion of his life. And now he indifferently stroked and played at her body, and waited for her to claw and shudder against him; and then, out of politeness, and also so that he might sleep afterward, he allowed himself the modest shudder of pleasure.

One night, after they had finished, both finished, finished both of them together (this was rare), she did not sink into that famished sleep of hers. She lay awake, her arm askew so that one hand rested on his shoulder, cupping it, and she asked if he was hungry. No. Sleepy? No. Would you like something to eat? Thank you, no. Would you like to stay the night—and her hand tightened on his shoulder to keep him from answering too fast—and have breakfast with both of us?

I don't think that would be a good idea.

His wife fell silent. They had agreed that to raise the hopes of their child would be frivolous. They were serious parents.

She was breathing shallowly, with a catch at the end of each breath, as she started to say something and stopped. Finally she said it. What is all this about?

Nothing, I suppose.

Why are you doing this?

He almost felt angry. That is, he remembered how anger used to feel, the rising flush and turmoil, but of course, he did not allow himself to feel this. Why are we doing this? he asked. Because we want to.

Because you want to and I do, too, she said.

Okay, if you like.

Is that all? she asked.

He did not like this conversation. It had the pattern of the repetitious explanations of early separation. I admit I want to, he said. We can stipulate that.

But why is that all? Why has it been so good?

Here in the dark, hardly seeing each other's faces, hardly speaking until tonight, trembling and convulsing and sleeping and fleeing, it had been as she said.

Why? she said.

And he answered: Because I don't like you very much, my darling.

But that, of course, was only the smallest part of the truth.

COHORTS

My father has grown old. He sits and waits in Cleveland. He sleeps and eats and sometimes trudges in the hall, past my brother's room, past my mother's room, past the laundry room, and then back to his room, or he can walk around the block if someone takes him. He used to be entertained by his troubles. Now they give him no pleasure.

Dad! I yell across the long-distance connection. How are you!

What? What? Are you here?

I'm trying to poke through the shriveled nerves of his ears. No, no, Dad, I'm in California, but I'm coming to see you soon.

Are you far away?

I'm coming to see you soon!

You're far away.

And so I fly back to visit him and he touches me, he reaches for my hand, he is nearly blind, he touches my face, he asks, Are you here, son?

Of course I'm here, Dad.

No, son, you're far away. I'm far away.

I smell the old man, the staleness, the medicines on his breath; I see the clothes which haven't changed in years—no need for new clothes. He used to be a natty dresser. A few years ago one of my sons sat on his lap and pulled the button off this shirt; my mother sewed a different button on it. Dad, I say, let's go for a walk.

This topcoat. This hat with the jaunty feather. A few years ago he took my sons for bus rides on his knees; before that he bounced me in the same way, Hup, hup, hup!

We take tiny steps on the sidewalk outside his apartment building and he says, I don't want to go to a home. Sometimes I think I better go to a home. I can't take care of myself.

You're still you, Dad.

I don't think I'm going to get any better. Mother keeps asking me if I'm going to get any better. I don't know what the doctors tell her. I don't think so.

Are they treating you okay around here?

What? What?

Are they treating you okay, Dad?

It would be better if you was here. I feel better when you're here. They don't dare get mean to me when you're around, son.

Dad, they're not mean to you.

Silence. Cars whooshing up the slope toward Shaker Square. A lawn mower. I'm watching the cracks in the sidewalk and his small feet in black slip-on shoes with elastic tops. It's hard for me to walk so slowly. He stops and turns with his hand on my arm. He says: I can't stick up for myself so good anymore. I used to be able to yell. I didn't need to hit since the Depression, that business was rough, but people knew I could hit. I can't see, I can't hear, I can't taste. . . .

You were very strong, Dad. I remember how you carried a hammer in your pocket and nobody bothered you.

I'm tired, let's go home, I'm dizzy, I need to lay down.

Back so soon? my mother asks. It's a nice day outside. Get some exercise, you'll eat better, Sam. I made pot roast today and I don't want you wasting.

I tuck him into his bed. Help me turn over, he says. He can turn himself over, but he likes to be touched, he can feel the hands.

Five minutes later he appears in his shorts and undershirt and says,
You're still here.

Of course, Dad.

Let's just walk down the hall. I can't sleep. Are you hungry?

No, Dad. Are you?

Well, if you're hungry, I'll eat a little Jell-O with you. Can you heat
the milk?

I can do that, Dad.

I think he is smiling. He says: You're learning. I wish you didn't
go far away, son.

Well, I'm here, I say. Let's not think about far away.

Nobody eats now! my mother says. I made a good dinner.

What time is it? my father asks. In a few days you'll be gone again.
And then who knows when I'll see you?

My father is tired of growing old. He wishes me to fix this for him.
He used to fix things for me. He helped me grow up. Why can't I help
him now?

Sometimes he makes a mess. I did it, he says. I did it.

Accidents happen, Dad. Anyone can make a mistake.

I did it, son. I didn't used to do that. Don't tell me anyone can do
it. I did it.

It's all right, Dad.

It's not all right. I don't want to do that. I shouldn't do that. How
come I let myself do that, son?

We sit in the room with his special chair, with his lamp with the
magnifying lens that he doesn't use for reading because he can't read
anymore, nothing seems to magnify print large enough, bright enough;
he can't work the machine, the arm and swivel over the neckrest, it's
too complicated; he rests his head, white face, white eyes, white hair,
against the black vinyl; he asks: Are you still here, son?

Of course I'm here, Dad.

You want to go out someplace? You want to have fun?

I'm all right, Dad. I'm staying with you.

You should go out, son. Don't leave me.

My mother has a meeting. It's good for her. How else can she
survive? The girls—that's what she calls them—have projects, the
hospital, the welfare federation, the bond drive, but tonight there is

a little game. My brother and I are supposed to make dinner for our
father. My brother squints at me and says, Dad likes delicatessen.

Dad? I ask. You want to go out for dinner?

Mother doesn't like me to go out. She left food in the box. She
said there's food in the oven.

Dad, it'll keep. Why don't we go to Sharpie's?

Sharpie's? He grins. Is that good for me?

I wouldn't worry about that, I say.

You can eat good things, mushroom barley soup, a sandwich,
pastrami, my brother says. I'll cut the fat off.

I can't worry about that, he says.

We help him dress. He asks: Where's my hat?

It's warm out, Dad.

Where's my hat?

My brother drives and tells him what we are seeing, where we are
going. Our father answers that he knows where we are going, and he
names the streets, he seems to see the houses. He knows what is out
there. He sees shadows, lights and darks, he knows. He says: Now turn
into this parking lot, it's a shortcut, now you're at Sharpie's.

That's right, Dad, my brother says. I can see that my brother is
happy. He too wants to eat out, mushroom barley soup, baskets of
good bread, wet coleslaw, spicy meats, cheesecake.

The delicatessen is crowded. They have expanded it since I was last
on the premises. In honor of the Cleveland Indians there are Indian
clubs on the walls. The framed mirrors make the place look even
larger and people can watch themselves eat if they are so inclined. The
extra floor space makes room for the many non-Jews who also have
developed cravings for corned beef. Jewish soul food, I say.

What? asks my dad.

My brother is shaking his head. Impossible to get through with an
explanation now. In the dead of night, when he wakes and calls to
be turned over, or wanders the hallway in search of a snack, he can
sometimes hear and follow whole sentences, he likes to ask questions
or tell stories, he can talk and listen. But now we have to talk like
Indians—minimal communication, stone faces.

I am not an Indian, nor is my father. I say: It's good for lots of
people, Dad. Everyone seems to eat here now. The goyim have picked
up on corned beef, pastrami, bagels and lox.

It's bigger, he says. It's noisy. Was it always so noisy?

His hearing aid is shrieking. He fiddles anxiously with the dial. It must hurt the dead nerves which are not quite dead. He snaps something; perhaps he is turning it off entirely. My brother says: He can't hear when it's noisy like this.

Plates are clattering. Children are yelling. The waiters are running. It's Sunday night. People are shouting at friends. It's a family night. In Cleveland they don't eat out so often, but on Sunday night they eat out at Sharpie's. The loudspeaker is calling names. Table for two for Bernstein. Party of four, Malinsky. Dr. Epstein, will you kindly call your service?

When can we sit down? my father asks. I usually eat at six.

You can wait, Dad, I say. It won't hurt you.

I have to take my medicine at six-thirty, after dinner. When can we sit down?

My brother says: Here's the lady, she'll show us our table.

It's Mrs. Sharpie and she says: Sam, Sam! How are you?

Fine, fine, fine, fine, he answers.

He can't hear, I tell her.

I heard! he says. What means this I can't hear?

That's wonderful to see you again, Sam.

Fine, fine, fine, fine. Everything been going fine, he says.

This a nice table, Sam? she asks.

Fine, fine, fine, you too, he says. And the husband, the kids. I hope the same for them.

The codgers who used to lag behind him, poorer, dumber, less renowned and respected, even less healthy, now they are ahead of him. They have the jump on him at last. They are scarfing down delicatessen—yelling, laughing, greeting, gossiping, judging the textures and perfume of smoked fish, chomping pickles, enjoying the chaotic eating all around them, digesting or doing their best. The codgers run up to grab my father's hand and say: Sam! Sam! Where you been? You look great, Sam!

Over here, Sam! Look over here! It's Jake, Jacob!

Hullo, he says, fine, good to see you, fine, fine, fine, fine.

They haven't seen him in a while, my brother says to me. They thought maybe he was dead. The ones who were jealous of him hoped he was senile. He knows. He's glad to be out.

We sit and he spreads the menu in front of him and studies it through the milky blue-white eyes. After he finishes running down the menu with his fingers, touching the glaze, feeling the tassel, pretending to read, he turns toward me and says: You order, son. You know what I like.

Dad! calls my brother. The mushroom barley soup?

You order for me, boys, he says. I feel kind of hungry today. I feel kind of good. Is this Sunday?

Of course, Dad. Everybody's at Sharpie's.

I knew, he says with satisfaction. Where are the breadsticks? The salty ones, please. Give me some butter, too. I can do it. Give me the knife, please, son.

My brother tucks the napkin under his collar. I say: No, don't do that, let him spill it if he wants to; and my brother says: I live here, you don't, he doesn't need to spill the soup on his shirt.

My brother is right.

While he eats, the codgers keep running up to the table, shaking his hand, crying out their identifications, Jake! Morris! Murray and Danny, Al the Printer's sons! Nice to see you, Sam! Good you're out again! Thought you was sick, Sam, but you look great! You gonna start doing the deli again Sundays, Sam?

Fine, fine, fine, fine, he says.

When we leave, threading ourselves like a holy procession through the eaters and celebrants, my father bows graciously in the direction of the praise and obeisance aimed at him, smiling, the milky eyes squeezed in smiles, seeing and hearing the praise somehow, his cheeks less gray, pink showing under the flat white bristles, blushing as he turns his head this way and that.

In the car, when the noise is gone, he switches his hearing aid up again.

You seemed to hear them without your machine, I say.

Yes, yep, seemed like that, he says. So much noise. I hear too much. It hurts the ears.

Dad, is it okay now?

Sure I can. Always can. Fine, son.

Dad, who were all those men?

What?

Who were all those people in Sharpie's, Dad?

He grins and looks at me. He looks in my direction, he looks hilariously into my eyes and seems to see me. He is laughing and laughing and holding my hand on the back seat of the car while my brother drives. It's a marvelous joke to him. You think I remember? he asks. You think I know?

The next day I have to catch a flight to San Francisco. I have work to do. I miss my children.

You'll come back soon? You'll call? But I can't talk on the phone so good. When will you come back? Next week? Soon? Tomorrow?

Fine, fine, fine, fine, I say.

No, he says. Not good.

He sits in his chair under the magnifying glass and the intense light he no longer uses for reading, enjoying the heat perhaps, and looks stiff and stony, unblinking in the light, like a statue.

He seems to know something.

Neither he nor I understand what it is. Just now, how should I know? But someday we'll both find out.

STAGES

They met; he let the crowd move him near her. She said no, no dice, absolutely not, to whatever joke he was making (it was a party); "I don't play those games"; but she licked her lips when he gazed at her. Laser eyes across buzzing space. He heard her no and was sad—he saw her no like the NO! in a balloon from a cartoon mouth—but his shrewd, aggressive, calculating eye also saw her tongue flicking across the shining membrane.

Although an engineer, and calculating, he was given to spending his time on love.

Although he looked for a yes like the YES! in a balloon, he was a bit of a scientist.

He tried her again with conversation. Down a step, modest and easy: "Washington is getting out of hand. All the charm of the North and the efficiency of the South—"

"John F. Kennedy said that first."

"I didn't even say it second."

Her tongue flicked. Yes, she didn't know what she did with tongue and lip. Yes, she intended to send her message.

At the movies their knees touched. The warmth sheltered them together. She shifted back in her seat. He sighed. He gripped her knee in his hand and waited and then pushed her knee back against his. A swarm of flesh and gesture. He felt strangely shy. He felt like a boy at the movies. Neither of them could remember the movie they saw, something about skiing, or maybe Eskimos, there was snow in there someplace, although the warmth of their touching may have been even more fleeting than the shadows on the screen.

He knew enough to go slow with this one, a shy and pride-haunted item. He went so slowly that she began to wonder about him. Was he masculine? Was he really a man? But then she would remember his first pressing kisses that she had denied, and his jokes about her mouth closed firmly with a thin white line of no, and his determination to be—okay, if that's how it is—friends. So he had been discouraged? She was worried.

He was pleased to worry her. She was a modern woman. He gave her space. To worry in. Let her take care of her own pride and shyness.

Making love, like packing the nostrils of a corpse, to make sure it doesn't run with awful slime . . .

He had a therapeutic woman whom he saw more frequently now that he was in love with a woman who was not an item. He lost weight. He slept little and dreamed too much. He howled upon his therapeutic woman. An impatient man, he knew his only chance was to find ways to pretend patience.

She decided to worry (touch of matured feminism) that she had never invited him to dinner. Sometimes she bought tickets for something. But perhaps he needed to be really encouraged after all. She had thought he needed to be discouraged. But like many men, most men, all men—her plan rolled downhill gathering speed—he needed confidence. And only she could give it to him.

"I'd like to make a light supper Sunday night," she said.

"Before a movie?"

"No," she said firmly, "a literary evening. We'll read the paper. I have to get up early. I have some sewing. Catch-up time. I'll make a light supper—oh, I said that already—and you can read and I'll sew and we'll talk."

"Well, it's true I get tired of restaurants."

She smiled, that thin smile of no sex as he knew it. "You're so gracious," she said.

And let him think about it from Tuesday till Sunday. She planned on Sunday to sleep late in the morning, and do a really good job on her shampoo, and spend more time on herself than on the food. A little supper, she had promised. A light supper it would be. A light white wine. Nothing to interfere with the heaviness of her plan.

She hoped, now that she had made up her mind, he would not dwindle on her. This was that part of the twentieth century. She knew, alas, all about the dwindlers.

He dwindled on her.

They had been at peace and at rest after a light supper. He was reading the New York *Times Book Review,* the New York *Times Magazine,* the New York *Times* "News of the Week in Review," the . . . and her needle was going in and out, in and out, and she moved to get nearer to the light, his light, their light, and her head rested on his shoulder. She was still sewing. He watched her needle darting in and out of the "Buttonholes of the Week in Review." He read. Her head felt warm on his shoulder, though it was just clean hair and skull and brain. Smell of blond shampoo and a body he liked.

She put the needle down, sighed, sucked her finger where she had pricked it, turned her head up, kissed him (let him kiss her, seemed to insist he kiss her).

He had put all this behind them. Everything felt cozy. But now he remembered he had judged her sleek freckled healthy arms and shoulders to be exactly how arms and shoulders should be. And now these arms were around his neck, reaching and twisting on the couch. The heavy newspaper slid off the coffee table. Sometimes toes hit it. She was smiling. She was unbuttoning. She was letting him watch her up to a certain point. She was pouting. She was unbuttoning him.

Ah, he was so scared. She would have to be helpful. She understood. It was not for nothing that she was born in the last half of the
century, with all the wisdom of the times absorbed in her bones,
marrow, sinew, and tennis-playing blond flesh through movies, song,
therapy, and a careful education. She smiled. She liked him pretty
much, she had decided. She would be helpful. Actually badminton
was her game. She helped and helped, with great confidence and skill.

And goddamn fuck him if he didn't dwindle on her.

"It's all right," she said.

"It is not," he said.

"It's really all right."

"It's really really really not."

She was too smart to try to win this argument. But she had a
marvelous idea. Perhaps it was original with her. She jumped up, as
if nothing really did matter, and went to the bathroom and left the
door carelessly open as she sat on the toilet. She knew he could see.
She peed. He looked on dejectedly. Then she turned her back to wash
a bit. Somehow, as he looked on, he looked less dejected. He was
grinning. Ted the Spy. Some people tend to make too much of things.
A toilet is definitely not a pedestal. She came back and sighed and
tucked her head into his shoulder on the mussed pillows and deep
rug where they snuggled.

Oh-oh.

But she didn't laugh aloud. Peeing at the proper moment, with the
door ajar, will never be listed among her inspirations. But it belonged
on her real-life list.

This time he didn't dwindle on her.

"Oh it was really good," she said.

He didn't reply.

"Really really really good."

She was proud of herself.

The next day—actually they skipped a day—she felt slightly dis-
pleased when he appeared at her door with flowers, such a macho
gesture, and the expectation that she would make a "light supper"
—her stiff, teasing, old-fashioned phrase haunted her—as before. But
he was in a terrible hurry. She was making sandwiches, she opened
a can of date-nut bread, she found some cream cheese, and he was

all over her. He devoured her. Her body felt slimy, with a fresh rain sleek smell. God knew what it smelled like to him. He seemed to like it. He was drinking and licking her body. Where were they? Were they back where they started? This eager, confident, dangerous kid? Wasn't this what she wanted to avoid, just a playground of sucking and licking and sticking and sexing?

Ah, but she decided to ride with it now. If his voice was too loud when he groaned over her, well, perhaps she wasn't perfect, either.

Maybe this is love, she thought. You don't have to give up judgment. You just have to be engrossed.

She found suddenly she could think of nothing but him, of his body on hers, over and under hers, in hers, and something must come soon to interrupt such an unwanted way of life or she would have to reorganize everything.

"Are we going together now?" she asked.

"I think so," he said.

"Then we can stop to eat the sandwiches."

"Oh, I'm hungry."

"I noticed before you did," she said.

Her tinkling laughter sounded artificial to him. It did the same to her. She was ill at ease for weeks. His abrupt recovery, her abrupt cure of him had gone according to plan, and yet nothing that was happening to her seemed like the plan. She was addicted. She grieved in his absence. She was too shy with him, as shy as if she had lost him when, in fact, she had only won him. She wanted to please him utterly.

She was forgetting about herself. For this, the insincerity of her laugh. She was most pleased when he pleased himself. Her body yearned for his pleasure. "Avis tries harder," she said. It was only his pleasure which mattered to her.

And then, because the weather changed, the month changed, or her period came—oh, she didn't know why—her pleasure changed. It was present in her own body. "Oh, God," she whispered. "Oh, God God God." A squeezing convulsion, so like his, squeezed him. And the water broke over her body, the sweat broke on her thighs like the breaking of the waters of childbirth.

She lay there gasping. She could say nothing. All that she wanted to say she preheard in her head and they were words worn thin by ridicule: *It's never been like this before. I died. I adore you.*

So she said nothing, but he knew. And, miracle, he loved her anyway.

"That was a doozer," she said.

She tried to talk about it because she thought he wanted to hear her, but in fact, he said less and less about it. This may have been a sign. She didn't notice. She wished to tell how she felt. As feeling grew deeper, her words grew more old-fashioned. This one must have gone back to her parents.

"You're wonderful," she said.

"Doozy is the word, I think," he said. "And wonnerful is what Lawrence Welk says. A-one, a-two."

"Ted. Don't you love me?"

"I just get sad sometimes."

"Why?"

"I think it's physical. I confuse tired with sad. Maybe I'm only tired."

"Ted, that was a doozy, but I'd like to do it again, I really would, so let me help like this—"

She helped.

He smiled. He wasn't so tired after all. She was learning. Even an adversary stance—he was often an engineer for the offense in public-interest land-use cases—could get some good results. It wasn't that he was paying her back for those months (weeks, actually) of giving him a hard time. It was just that he knew and she knew and both of them knew it was really important in love, if in nothing else in this life, to express and tell and communicate how you really feel. This was California, wasn't it? San Francisco? Her bed?

"The sweet spot," he said once, groaning in her arms.

"That's a tennis term," she said, "meaning the part of the racket where the twang is solid."

He looked at her, terrified and appalled, but then she was laughing and tickling him.

"Won't you allow me to make fun of you?" she asked.

She looked rather pensive one night. That is, hair lank, eyes chevroned with fatigue, voice small. "What's the matter?" he asked.

"I don't know."

"Never at a loss for words, are you?" he asked.

The light came on in her eyes. Anger. "Okay. I have the impression you're keeping a watch on me. I have the impression you're keeping score."

"Well, you're tired, I guess."

"And you?"

"I'm a little tired."

"Then stop keeping score. It isn't necessary. I'll remember you. I do my best to know you. I'm doing my best to let you know me. So don't."

The quarrel was mended in a traditional fashion. They decided to go further than they had gone before, and there was no place further in their bodies to go. They decided to take a risk they had never taken, and they took the one left to advanced thinkers who have thought all the advanced thoughts—a daring advance backward into the tradition.

With double rings they visited a justice of the peace in Nevada, laughing all the way. How silly. These days.

Dust all over the hood of the car and crushed insects on the glass and a fan belt that needed changing in Elko, although perhaps the gas station attendant was lying. Elko is famous for supplying unnecessary fan belts. They spent the money gladly. They were gladly rooked. They were happily married.

Sometimes the long rain of years seemed to drip-drip-drip on their happy marriage, a parade without music, a celebration with housework.

But then sometimes she winked at him as she undressed for bed and said, "Now's your chance," and jumped into the clean sheets before he could see more than the flapping of her buttocks. Her legs were slim. Her eyes were clear. Her hair was golden. But she showed him those buttocks and hips, as if to say, Let's be practical. Cool it.

Nevertheless, she still said it was his chance and hers. And he thought that later, maybe months or a year later, she would remember what it was for them. Love. Love. Love.

"That was nice," she said. "Enough. Now I have to get up early and so do you. Now sleep."

She turned over. She wiggled her behind into his lap. He lay curled to her configuration. He lay against the track of her spine. Why couldn't he sleep?

He talked to her; he gave words; he sought to be a husband; he rubbed her back and massaged her scalp; it was not too much of an effort for him. They did the business of marriage together. They made love in the dark. He remembered when they made love with lights blazing.

She lolled in the dreamy prosperity of marriage, pregnancy, child, another child, children. She was as busy as a farm woman with chores. She lay back smiling, efficient, wifely. It was like this, and then almost imperceptibly it changed. She grew pale and tired. They used to have fun.

His gloom? He loved it. He kept his mystery intact. Hers? He clung to her at night, in the dark, when she let him, howling with desire to penetrate mysteries, join flesh, be released of mysteries. She still liked him to rub her back, massage her scalp.

Joy of children. But did she need him now? She had something to think about, and she thought it over and over, until the question began to propose its own answer. *Do I need him now? Why do I need him now? What good is he now?* She meditated this one big question during the long afternoons between car pools and shopping, before he came home—"Hi honey, hi honeys, I'll just shower and be with you"—and then tried to put it out of her mind. And then took to thinking about it in the evenings, also.

She imagined a white knight (horse, golden hair), a black knight (intense unstable eyes), a rock-and-roll ravisher. He imagined her. As she hid from him, and closed off the lease on her body—first the breasts (sore after nursing), then the hips, the buttocks. "I guess this happens to women after childbirth," she murmured. "But you can do it to me."

He loved her. Patience. Wait. Love will come back; is there any reason why it shouldn't? In the meantime, he would survive in his own privacy and in the routines—outings, dinners, chores, birthdays, holidays, in-laws—of a normal marriage. Children.

We'll come out okay, he swore. There was grit and will in this.

All this is wrong about love and what I want; she thought about his silent vows, his grit, his will.

He thought of making love to his familiar wife with Rastafarian dreadlocks on his head. But what would she wear or do? He thought of her making love to him with black stockings, mouth full of wine, Medusa hair. But who would he be?

Ah, we're husband and wife, that's all. People can have fantasies, but we're parents, we're responsible people, we can't play silly games.

And yet he wanted to enjoy the wild in him. *Enjoy* and *wild* are separate worlds. Enjoy is ease and pleasure; wild is risk and excess. He swore life owed him both. But he could not will a depth of love from her, though he could conceive of it.

"Do you love me?" he asked

She gave it some thought. "Sometimes."

"I mean, do you really love me?"

"Are you asking me?"

He looked behind him. Nobody there. Yes, then he was the one who asked if she loved him.

"Okay, it's hard to say. I'll be honest. You're a good man. You're fun. You're a good father. You're . . . I wouldn't say you're handsome, but that's not a man's thing anyway, and you're fit. Will that do?"

"You sure do get off on the truth, darling."

"Well, what about me?"

Hoarsely he answered, "For some reason you are magic for me."

She shrugged. If he couldn't explain it, how could he expect her to know what it was? All she knew was that magic was someplace, someone, somewhere else. It could be no place and nowhere. She wasn't going to pretend.

Fun

The title of this episode is "Fun." Marriage can be fun, the conservative marriage counselor said. He was perhaps the last marriage counselor in California who counseled marriage. The rest counseled personal fulfillment, making your own space, taking responsibility for your own actions, and dumping that asshole who gets in your way. The counselor's wife was sweet, Irish, Catholic, and had given them three children despite the infantile paralysis which caused her lower limbs to grow increasingly immobile. Her braces clanked, but Dr. Feinberg had fun with his Irish wife. "Marriage is beer against cham-